Charley Chambers

RACHEL KENNEDY

Charley Chambers
Rachel Kennedy
© Rachel Kennedy 2016
The author asserts the moral right to be identified
as the author of the work in accordance with the
Copyright, Designs and Patents Act, 1988

Cover illustration: Rachel Kennedy/Graeme Clarke

Published by:
Fledgling Press Ltd,

www.fledglingpress.co.uk

Printed and bound by:
MBM Print SCS Ltd, Glasgow

ISBN 9781905916177

MIX
Paper from
responsible sources
FSC® C117931
FSC
www.fsc.org

For my late grandmother Illeene MacLeod,
my inspiration when I was young,
and for my daughter Sian,
my inspiration always.

*Those who don't believe in magic will never
find it*
- Roald Dahl

ACKNOWLEDGEMENTS

Thank you to Clare Cain and all at Fledgling for bringing Charley to life.

To my mum for her endless support and encouragement. To my stepfather Denzil for putting up with my frequent writing-related meltdowns and pointing me in the right direction. And to my dad for his sound advice and help along the way.

To Kimberley and Megan, thanks for the wine and boosting my confidence when it was low.

To Mhairi, I'm so glad you're coming home.

To John, my friend and aspiring writer, thank you for your faith in me.

And to Sian, my daughter and my best friend. I love you.

FIFTEEN YEARS EARLIER

Two strong legs stood rigid on the soft mattress, bouncing softly as a pair of beady eyes stared through the wooden bars of the cot. Her small, chubby hands gripped on tightly as a stream of saliva flowed from her mouth, causing the neck of her babygro to dampen instantly. She'd woken from her nap early as usual. Her mother was downstairs and completely unaware, as the infant was yet to make a sound.

She scanned the room, big baby eyes taking in all the sights before her: the music box that Mama played every night before bed; the giant teddy which was too large to sleep with but great for daytime cuddles; the reindeer snow globe Gran had given her for Christmas. The same things she looked at every day after naptime. She smiled.

As she peered out from the enclosure, she noticed her pink rattle slowly making its way across the floor. She let out a giggle. It had never done that before. It rolled over to the teddy bear and stopped when it hit its foot. The teddy fell over. Another giggle.

She could hear the sound of Mum's footsteps below, leaving the kitchen and heading for the stairs. Without warning, there was a loud crash as the picture that hung above her dresser came tumbling down, clattering off the floor and sending shards of glass all over the place. The snow globe fell next, shattering as it hit the hard surface, water exploding from its centre. Her music box did the same, slamming off the floor and breaking in two. The ballerina that turned ever so elegantly inside was twisted and bent.

No giggles.

The tiny one-year-old let out an ear-splitting shriek as she looked upon the mess in front of her.

'Sweetheart, what's wrong?' The voice was muffled as her mother dashed for the stairs, heading quickly to her daughter's bedroom. 'Hey, honey, what's the ma–?'

She stopped still as she surveyed the broken glass, the puddle of water, the battered music box. 'Oh my word, what on earth happened, darling?' Not expecting an answer, she scooped the child into her arms and took her downstairs, looking back, bewildered, at the disarray behind her.

ONE

The school bell gave off its piercing ring and a flurry of bodies hurried towards the entrance, some eager to return to class, most looking forward to sheltering from the rain that had been falling steadily for the past ten minutes.

Charley shrugged her shoulders and let out a sigh, forcing herself to walk slowly towards the doors. Her favourite time of the school day was over, the time where she could be alone, the time where she could just be Charley.

Charley Chambers wasn't an ordinary teenager, she was magic. Rather, she had magical powers – of sorts. The only problem was, Charley didn't know how to use them. Well, that wasn't entirely true. She was perfectly capable of releasing her powers, she just had no idea how to control them, which could occasionally get her into a bit of bother.

Okay, a lot of bother.

Like the time she set Mr Jenson's trousers on fire, and the whole school had to wait outside for an hour until the fire brigade were sure it was safe. Or the time she knocked coffee into Shirley O'Donoghue's lap from twenty yards away. Luckily the coffee was only lukewarm, but Charley – and the rest of her class – had had the great privilege of hearing Shirley whine about her ruined Gucci sweater for a month after.

The thing is, no one actually knew it was Charley doing all these things: causing accidents, spilling drinks, prompting Fred Anderson to walk in front of a bus – yes, that actually happened. He was all right, thankfully, but he had to spend a month at home encased in several different plaster casts while his bones fused themselves back together.

Might sound great, having magic, being able to make amazing things happen, being more powerful than everyone else at school. Well, everyone else, full stop. But for Charley, it was more like a nightmare. Every day she lived with the fear that someone would discover the truth, find out she was a freak. But even worse, she was terrified someone would get hurt again. Really hurt. And there was nothing she could do to stop it.

'Chambers? Gonna move from my seat?' The harsh voice jolted Charley from her trance, causing the group of boys in front of her to fall about laughing. All but one.

'Aiden . . .' Charley stammered, collecting her things in a panic. 'Sorry, I just . . . I didn't even realise I was at the wrong desk. I'm sorry . . .' More laughter erupted as she stuttered her apologies, fumbling over her books.

'Shut up,' Aiden snapped at the boys, causing the room to fall silent. 'Stop whimpering and just move, yeah?' He shot her a sarcastic smile as she manoeuvred herself from his chair.

'Ignore them,' Abbie snapped, her voice raised.

'They're just a bunch of lowlifes with nothing better to do.'

Abbie Gibbons was Charley's best friend. Actually, she was more like Charley's only friend. But she was a good one, and there for Charley no matter what.

'You okay?' she asked, swinging back on her chair so that it was balanced on just two legs. Her long, auburn hair was knotted tightly in a thick plait and hung casually over her left shoulder.

'Why wouldn't I be?' Charley smiled, trying her best to brush off the embarrassment of what had just happened.

'Just checking. Why were you sitting in Aiden's seat anyway?'

'I dunno. I was too tired to think about it. I just sat at the first desk I came to.'

'You not been sleeping again?' Abbie questioned, blowing a sticky, pink bubble with the gum she'd been ferociously chomping on.

'Not well,' she admitted. 'I'm knackered all day, then as soon as my head hits the pillow, I'm wide awake.'

'Sod's law.'

'Tell me about it.'

'Is it still happening, you know . . . at night?'

'It happens all the time, Abbs. I'm exhausted.'

Abbie had known about Charley's magic for a while, ever since the time Charley had accidently turned her lemonade to ice just by touching the glass. She'd tried to make up some excuse about the fridge temperature being too low, but when the glass exploded in her hand, she knew she had some explaining to do. She'd been petrified, finally admitting her secret to someone. Turns

3

out it was a good move; Abbie had never been anything but supportive towards her.

'What happened?'

'Nothing good, let's put it that way.' Abbie raised her eyebrows, obviously not satisfied with the vague reply. 'I burst all the light bulbs. Mum thought we had a power cut, until she stood on the glass and sliced her foot open.'

'Ouch.'

'Yeah. And today they're calling an electrician out to check all the wiring, which is costing them way more than it should, especially since there's nothing wrong with it.'

'You still don't want to tell them?'

'No way. Although I don't know how much longer I can hide it. They already think the house is haunted.'

'Really?' Abbie snorted.

'Well, not really. But they constantly talk about all the weird stuff that happens. This morning I made my breakfast disappear. Mum looked completely baffled, then told me I'd make myself sick if I ate too fast.'

'You can actually make things disappear?' Abbie raised her eyebrows.

'Apparently so.'

'How'd you do it?'

'Not a clue.'

'You didn't do anything different or unusual?'

'Like what?'

'I dunno. Click your fingers, or . . . chant some magic words or something.'

Charley frowned. 'Nope, pretty sure I didn't snap my fingers together or cast a magic spell. I was picking up my spoon, for God's sake.'

'Picking a spoon up isn't exactly out of the ordinary.'

'I wouldn't say so, no.'

'Do something now,' Abbie squeaked excitedly. She knew fine well Charley couldn't, yet she asked almost every day.

'You know I can't.'

'How do you know if you don't try?'

'Abbie . . .'

'Come on. Just focus on something.' She looked around, searching the classroom for the perfect object. 'Cam's water, see if you can knock it down.' Cameron McCreery was one of the boys who had been mocking Charley just five minutes before.

'I'm not spilling his water.'

'Go on. You know you want to.'

'No, I really don't. And I can't. Can we talk about something else, something normal?'

'Spoilsport.' Charley glared at her and Abbie held her hands up, backing down.

'All right, you win. I'll stop bugging you.'

There was a loud bang as the door slammed shut, Mrs Beattie strutting in quickly, her small heels clacking against the ground.

'Quiet, please. Take out your reading books and continue from where you left off on Tuesday. I want silence for the next half hour.'

Mrs Beattie was their English teacher, tall, thin and incredibly pretty. She was also impatient, rude and terribly strict. 'Charley, swap seats with Jonathan please.'

'But Mrs . . .'

'No buts. After the constant chatter between yourself

and Abbie last class, I want you two separated. Now move.'

Charley turned to see Jonathan collecting his belongings, not happy at all about the switch. He and Abbie hated each other. They couldn't stand being in the same room, never mind sitting in neighbouring chairs. Even worse, his current seat was next to Aiden, who looked just as unhappy as she felt about the whole situation.

'Can't stay away, can you?' Aiden smirked as she took her seat.

'Oh no, you're just far too dreamy,' she said sarcastically, and he laughed as if he hadn't been expecting an answer back.

'Well, I can't argue with you there.'

'Are we interrupting something?' Mrs Beattie snapped, annoyed at being disturbed in her classroom.

'No, sorry,' Charley said quietly.

'If you can't stop talking, Miss Chambers, you'll be working outside from now on. Book open, now.' She did as she was told, feeling foolish yet again.

She took out her book and opened it, flicking through to find where they'd left off.

'Uh oh,' she said to herself as she stared down at the blank pages. Something told her she'd had something to do with it, how she'd done it though was a mystery. Every page in the book was bare, the front and back cover still intact. She couldn't show Mrs Beattie, how would she explain what had happened?

'Excuse me, Mrs Beattie. I can't find my book,' she said as she slipped it back into her bag. Aiden frowned as he watched her hide it, wondering what she was up to.

'For goodness sake, Charley, are you going to be anything but a hassle today? Go along to the library and ask for a copy, and when you come back, continue to work outside. You're giving me a headache.'

TWO

The rest of English was pretty uneventful. Charley had managed to collect her book and return to class – well, outside the class – without anything disastrous happening. She'd knocked over a stack of magazines, but there was no magic involved, just her lack of coordination and unsteady hands. She was now sitting in her last class, impatiently watching the clock and willing the bell to ring.

'Charley, would you like to read now, please?' She looked up, pulled from her daydream by the stout, grey-haired woman who stood before her.

Mrs Macarthur was her history teacher, a lovely but very ditsy lady who'd been showing her age for quite some time.

'Sorry, I was just . . . where are we?'

'Charley, you must pay attention. Page forty-four, half way down. "On his return to Scotland . . ."'

'I will, sorry.' She began reading. Although the words came out clearly from her mouth, her mind wandered away someplace else. Somewhere without books or teachers or students giving her funny looks.

'Oh my God!'

'What's happening?' Shouts and screams came from all over the room, bringing Charley back to reality. She looked up, and to her horror she saw dust and plaster falling from above her, the ceiling caving in before her eyes.

She started shaking her head. 'This can't be happening. Is this . . . no, I can't be doing this.'

'Charley! Hurry up,' Lucy Wheeler called from the door. Everyone was making for the exit, including a shaken Mrs Macarthur. She was waving her arms about, wailing as she scrambled towards the door.

'Charley, dear, get a move on.' But Charley stood rigid. She felt as though she was glued to the spot, watching the interior collapse around her.

'Charley!' Lucy called again. 'Charley, come on!'

'I have to stop this, I have to do something.' Her head was spinning. Was it all her fault?

'Honey, let's go.' Lucy was now at her side, clutching her hand. 'We need to go.' And with that, she pulled Charley forcibly towards the door, giving her no choice but to stumble out of the crumbling classroom.

'Thank goodness,' Mrs Macarthur gasped as the girls tumbled into the corridor. 'Everyone, make your way downstairs in a quick but orderly fashion. Stay together once you're outside.' She was trying to keep calm, but the waver in Mrs Macarthur's voice gave away how worried she was.

Teachers from the neighbouring classes had come out to see what all the commotion was about, and after seeing the destruction they were now ushering their own pupils outside in single file. It wasn't long before the entire school had been evacuated and the students were huddled together in the pick-up zone, squashed against each other like sardines in a can.

'Bit much drama for one bloody classroom,' Abbie barked, pushing her way through the crowd and stopping just behind Charley.

'Charles, what's eating you?' It was a nickname that had grown on Charley since Abbie had first started using it. Somehow, it seemed completely normal now.

'You didn't see it, Abbie, it was awful.'

'Hey, what's up? You look terrible.'

'I think it was my fault.'

'Don't be stupid, no way could you have done that.'

'Why not? We don't know what I'm capable of.'

She glanced at Charley and the look she saw on her face sent shivers up Abbie's spine. 'Come on,' she said, pulling at Charley's arm.

'Where are we going?'

'Away from here.'

The two girls walked along the street, not in any particular direction.

'So you gonna tell me what that was about?' Abbie asked eventually. 'You totally freaked out.'

'What if that was me, Abbie? What if I did that?'

'Come on, you don't know anything so don't go blaming yourself.'

'But if it was? I could've killed someone.'

'But you didn't. You gotta stop beating yourself up when something like this happens. That school is a shambles, it's like a million years old. It probably had nothing to do with you.' Her words were kind, but they fell upon deaf ears. All Charley could think about was the fact that it might have been her fault, and despite what Abbie said, probably was.

'You're right,' Charley whispered unconvincingly, 'I'll stop blaming myself.'

'No, you won't. But I'm glad you're at least trying to lie to me.' The girls smiled at one another and Charley linked her arm through Abbie's, grateful she had someone so understanding to turn to. But things had to change. How could she be around other people when there was a risk of them getting hurt?

'I need to do something.'

'Something as in . . .?' Abbie pressed, having no idea what Charley was talking about.

'I need to work out what powers I have. I've got to find out how to use them.'

'Charles, you've said this before, many times. And every time you've tried you've failed miserably.'

'And then I just give up.'

'You don't give up, you just . . . run out of leads. Look, I know I joke with you, but how is this time gonna be any different?'

Charley sighed. 'It just will. It has to be.'

'I still say it was the school's fault, dude.'

Charley barely said a word at dinner as she sat pushing her lasagne around the plate. Her sister, Jessica, was sitting next to her, occasionally – and deliberately – kicking her beneath the table. Charley didn't notice.

'Honey, are you all right?' her mum asked, offering her the garlic bread. Charley shook her head to refuse and continued to play with her food.

'I'm fine.'

'You haven't said a word since you came home, and you clearly aren't hungry.'

'I had a massive lunch,' she said blankly, hardly hearing her mother's words.

'Why don't you leave it in the oven then? You can have it later.'

'Okay. May I leave the table?'

'Of course, pet. But you would tell me if something was bothering you?'

'Sure, Mum. I'm fine, honestly. Anyway, I have loads of homework.'

'All right, on you go.'

'Can I leave the table?' Jess pouted, the half-eaten lasagne sitting in front of her.

'Finish your tea.'

'But how come Charley gets to leave?'

'Because I said so. Now eat your food.' Although she didn't know about Charley's magic, Linda Chambers knew her daughter was different. And she worried about her constantly.

When Charley was safely inside her bedroom, she sank to the floor and sighed. The day had been too much for her and she felt utterly exhausted. Abbie was always brilliant, but she could never understand completely how helpless Charley felt. Having powers was meant to be a gift. To Charley, they seemed more like a curse.

She sat with her head buried in her hands for the next hour or so, her legs pulled in close so that her chocolate-brown hair spilled over her knees. Eventually, she climbed up from the floor and took out her laptop, settling herself on the bed as it started up. Once it was ready, she opened up the internet browser and began typing the usual things she searched for: moving objects, breaking things without touching them, mind control.

The same links came up as always: telekinesis, psychokinesis, you'reafreak.com. Okay, that one didn't really pop up, but it was how she felt.

Closing down the page in defeat, she picked up the phone and dialled.

'Hello,' came the familiar voice at the other end of the line.

'Gran? It's me . . . I really need to talk to you.'

Dorcas Blightly lived in a small cottage with her two cats, Mosley and Bap. Charley adored them; she'd always loved animals but had never been allowed a pet of her own.

'Get a black cat,' Abbie had always joked, as if she were some sort of witch – though the idea wasn't beyond the realms of possibility.

Dorcas watched out the window as her eldest granddaughter raced up the path. Before she could heave herself from the chair, there were three loud raps at the door.

'Come in, darling,' she said once she eventually reached the door, ushering the young girl inside.

'I'm sorry to just appear like this. I just need–'

'Charley, don't be so silly. You can always talk to me.'

'I don't know what to do, Gran. It's getting out of control.'

'All right. Start from the beginning.'

13

Charley spoke for what felt like a lifetime, telling her gran everything there was to tell. She knew she was taking a huge risk, confessing her secret to someone so close, but she felt she had no choice.

'Charley, have you ever heard of telekinesis?'

'I've read about it, but I don't really understand it all,' she replied honestly.

Dorcas hesitated. 'Well, my mother, your great-grandmother, she was what you would call telekinetic.'

'Wasn't she the crazy one?' Charley asked, immediately feeling bad. Dorcas laughed, feeling a sudden rush of sympathy for her mother.

'Not my words,' she said gently. 'She wasn't crazy. She was like you, always making things happen without any explanation as to how.'

'What did she do?' Charley asked, her interest piqued. 'Did she manage to stop them – her powers?'

'No, she couldn't make them go away. But she learned how to manage them.'

'How?'

'Charlotte, I'm afraid there is no easy cure. She simply had to teach herself. It took a great deal of time and effort, but eventually she began to understand her abilities.'

Charley's heart sank. 'You mean I have to learn on my own? How can I do that when I don't know why it happens? What if I end up hurting someone, Gran? I've done it before. What if it's worse this time?'

'I can't give you all the answers, dear. I can only tell you what I know. But one thing's for sure, you'll find a way. Trust me, I know my granddaughter.'

'And if I don't?'

'You will.' There was no point in arguing. The trip had

been about as useful as a chocolate teapot. Maybe she would get a black cat after all.

THREE

Charley stayed off school the following day, telling her parents she had a migraine. Her mum told her to go back to bed, though dubious of her daughter's sudden strange behaviour.

'Honey, I've brought you some tea and biscuits,' Linda called at just after ten.

No answer.

She pushed open the door to find Charley in bed, the covers pulled tightly over her head. 'Sweetheart, I've made you a drink.'

'Thanks,' came a muffled reply from under the quilts.

'Head still sore?'

'Yeah.'

'Have you taken any painkillers?'

'Uh huh.'

'Charley, are you sure nothing else is bothering you? Is it what happened at school yesterday?' Despite the ceiling caving in, the school was still open as normal, the history department out of bounds while it was being repaired.

'What? How do you know about that?' Charley gasped, suddenly jumping out from under the sheets.

'Why wouldn't I know?'

'Have you spoken to Gran?'

'Charley, what's got into you? The ceiling of your history class collapsed, all the parents were informed.'

'Oh,' she whispered, realising she'd got the wrong end of the stick. Her secret was still safe.

'Is that what's wrong? Maybe you have a concussion. Are you sure you didn't hit your head?'

'No, Mum.'

'It could be post-traumatic stress. Maybe we should go see a doctor.'

'Mum, I'm not a baby. I didn't hit my head and I'm not traumatised. I have a migraine.' Charley didn't want to lie to her mum, and she definitely didn't want to hurt her feelings, but what else could she do? 'I'm sorry, okay? I just feel really lousy today. Would you mind if I went back to sleep?'

Linda gave up, realising she wasn't going to get anywhere. 'Of course, darling. Just give me a shout if you want anything.'

'I will.'

Abbie sat in her usual seat, preparing herself for another one of Mrs Beattie's horrendous classes.

'Hey, where's your loser pal today?' called a voice from the back of the class. It was Gary Bishop, a complete jerk and friend of Aiden Cunningham.

'Get lost, asshole,' she snapped, as a load of hissing came from the back.

'No need to be rude. Just wondered where your

freaky friend was, that's all.' A couple of them joined in, laughing as they made jokes at Charley's expense.

'Enough,' Aiden barked. He was sitting in his chair, doodling something on a piece of paper. He looked just as moody as he always did.

'We're only having a laugh,' Gary smirked. 'What, do you fancy her or something?' The boys just about wet themselves laughing at the very thought.

'I said, enough,' Aiden replied through gritted teeth, getting up and heading for the door just as Mrs Beattie arrived.

'Where do you think you're going?'

'I'm leaving.'

'You most certainly are not!' she exclaimed as he marched out of the classroom.

'I think he most certainly is,' Cam laughed, causing giggles to erupt from across the room. Mrs Beattie's anger was evident, her hands clenched into fists at her sides. Abbie decided it would be fitting if steam were to start surging from her ears.

'Open your books and start reading. NOW!'

Aiden stormed down the hallway and out the double-doors that led to the staff car park. His friends could really get to him sometimes, and this time they'd pushed him over the edge.

With a surge of anger, he swept his hand through the air in front of him. He watched the little blue Nissan Micra rock from side to side, the windows shattering instantly. He walked up to the wreck and this time, with no magic involved, began to kick the car repeatedly with his steel toe-cap boot. Once he was finished, he gave it a last jolt, causing the registration plate that read B34TT1E to break in two. As he stalked off, he turned back and glanced at the security camera which was camouflaged on top of a lamppost. It exploded, and he smiled as he continued on his journey away from the school grounds.

At three o'clock, Charley pushed back the covers and stared up at the ceiling, hoping that this one wouldn't come down on top of her. She was done sulking. It wasn't doing anyone any good and it certainly wasn't making her feel any better.

She sat up, scanning the room for something she could use. Her eyes settled on the wooden photo frame that held a picture of herself, Jess and her parents. Concentrating, she fixed her gaze on the frame, pouring all her energy into what she was trying to do. After what felt like a lifetime, she gave in, letting out a huge sigh of disappointment and flopping back on the bed. Why couldn't she do it? Surely if she had the ability to make things move, it couldn't be that hard to do it as and when she wanted to? Apparently it was.

She manoeuvred herself out of bed and raced down the stairs.

'Mum, I'm going out,' she called, flinging her coat and shoes on.

'Charley, you've been off sick. I really think it would be a good idea for you to stay indoors.'

'I'm not sick, I had a headache. It's gone now.'

'I'm afraid my answer's still no.'

'Mum, I need to . . .'

'Charley, I don't know what has got into you today, or

last night for that matter, but my word is final. You're not to go out. Now let's drop it, please.'

'Fine, all right. I won't go out.' Linda looked at her for a second, wary of her daughter's sudden surrender, but when Charley began to take her coat off and kick her shoes away, Linda smiled, happy that she was finally doing as she was asked.

'Thank you,' she breathed, relieved that there hadn't been more of a fight. Charley smiled sweetly and wandered through the living room and into the hall.

'Charley, don't you dare,' Linda yelled, suddenly realising what she had planned. As she looked out from the front door, she could see Charley racing down the street, almost out of view, in just her T-shirt, jeans and bare feet.

By the time Charley reached the end of the road, her feet were bleeding from repeatedly pounding the pavement's hard, uneven surface. She used the cobblestone wall next to her to balance as she picked what seemed to be a sharp piece of glass from one of her toes.

'Looks sore,' said a familiar voice.

'Aiden . . . what are you doing here?'

'Walking. You?'

'Erm . . . running, I guess.' She straightened herself, aware of how ridiculous she must have looked.

'Who you running from?' he asked sceptically.

'My mum. She wouldn't let me out. I was off sick.'

'I noticed.' There was an awkward pause as they both tried not to look at one another. 'You have no shoes on.'

'Nope,' she answered, not sure what else to say.

'Dare I ask why?'

'I wouldn't . . . I mean . . . it's not important. Why are you talking to me anyway?'

'What?'

'Why are you talking to me? It's bad for your reputation to be seen talking to a freak, you know.'

'Who said you were a freak?'

'Your friends . . .' She looked down at her bare feet. 'I'm probably not helping my case, running about the streets with no shoes on.'

He was quiet for a moment, before saying, 'We all have our reasons. Listen, I have to go just now.'

'Oh, okay. Well . . . bye.'

'See ya, Chambers.'

'Bye,' she said again.

And then he was gone.

'He actually said, "See ya."? Like, he used your name?'

'Well, he used my last name. But he was . . . different.'

'You mean he wasn't an asshole?'

'No, he was . . . nice.'

'Don't think I've ever heard Aiden described as nice before.'

'Amazing, isn't it?'

She'd arrived at Abbie's shortly after her encounter with Aiden. After cleaning up her foot and making tea for the two of them, Abbie had ushered Charley through to the living room to hear all about the meeting with – in her words – Newford's 'number one wanker'.

'So what else happened?'

'That was about it,' Charley replied, shrugging her shoulders as she took a large gulp of tea. 'We spoke for about two minutes, then he said he had to go.'

'That's a bit dull.'

'What did you want to hear?'

'I dunno. That you zapped him with your superhuman powers or something. Now that would've livened things up a bit.'

'Superhuman powers I don't know how to use. Helpful.'

'You'll figure it out one day,' Abbie replied nonchalantly, helping herself to a chocolate biscuit from the tin she'd brought through.

'I thought you said I was never going to work it out?'

Abbie laughed, choking on her biscuit. 'Honestly, Charles, I lose track.'

'Uch, I'm doomed,' Charley replied dramatically.

'Have faith, woman. If it happens, it happens. Now, enough magic talk. You have an essay for Mrs Beastly to do.'

'I do?'

'Yep. For tomorrow. I was told to "make sure you were aware of this". I did say you were sick, but she was having none of it.'

'Have you done yours?'

'Hell no. I plan to do it later using my good friend, Mr Google, and his two friends, Mr Copy and Mr Paste.'

'Ah, of course.' Charley giggled.

The girls spent the next two hours completing Charley's half-hearted attempt at an essay on contemporary playwrights. Abbie spent most of the time as she'd promised, copying and pasting large chunks of text to use later in her own assignment. Once Charley had what she said 'would do' down on paper, she gathered her things up and began preparing for the inevitable – facing her mother.

'Will she be mad?' Abbie asked as she flung a cardigan at Charley's head.

'Thanks. Eh, I dunno. She might be to start with, but you know what she's like. Nice as pie once you shed a tear or two.'

'You devious little bugger,' Abbie laughed, this time throwing a pair of trainers Charley's way. 'Borrow them, too. Can't have you walking back with no shoes on – people will start to think you're weird.'

'Bit late for that.'

'Weird is better than ordinary. Ordinary's boring.'

'Sometimes I don't think boring would be that bad.'

'Trust me, normal's overrated. You're special, Charles.'

'Well, thank you. Your words mean the world,' Charley replied sarcastically. 'I gotta go. See you tomorrow.'

'Yup. In the words of Aiden Cunningham, see ya, Chambers.'

As Charley turned the handle to the front door, she readied herself for a rollicking. Her mother was as soft as butter most of the time, but in circumstances like these, she could be quite scary. She pushed open the door and slowly stepped inside, scanning the empty room.

'Mum?'

'Yes?' The voice came from the kitchen.

'I'm back,' Charley said as she wandered through to where her mother was washing up dishes.

'Okay.' So it was the silent treatment she was getting.

'Mum, I know you're angry–'

'I'm not angry, I'm just disappointed.' Charley's face fell.

'Mum! Disappointed is so much worse than angry. Can't you just yell at me?' Charley petted her lip.

'No, I can't. Because I am disappointed. I'm disappointed that you disobeyed me and I'm hurt that you lied to me.'

'I'm sorry . . .'

'That's the thing, Charley. I don't think you are. I'm going for a bath before I start dinner. I would say stay indoors, but what would be the point in that?'

After two weeks of apologies, flowers and doing endless chores, Linda finally gave in and forgave Charley for disobeying her. She hadn't been mad that Charley had left the house when she'd been told to stay indoors – not really – and she wasn't even too bothered that her daughter had lied to her; she was a teenager, lying to their parents was what they were supposed to do. She was simply worried. She knew something was . . . unusual about Charley, and she would do anything in her power to protect her.

FOUR

'You coming to mine tonight?' Abbie asked as they made their way home from school. They'd taken the slightly longer route past Bryan's Bakery, something Abbie always insisted on doing.

'I dunno, I guess so.'

'Well that's enthusiasm for you,' Abbie replied sarcastically.

'Sorry, I just thought we could go out. I've been stuck in my house all week and it's driving me crazy.'

'Yes, but you won't be in your house, will you? You'll be in mine. And besides, my mum's going out, so we'll have the place to ourselves.'

'Oh, I see,' Charley grinned. 'We could raid her booze cupboard, help ourselves to a beer or two.' She was only joking, but the smile on Abbie's face implied she had other ideas.

'Charles, you rebel! Two whole beers? I mean, maybe one . . . but two? You might end up drunk.'

'Shut up,' Charley laughed, hitting her friend on the arm a little harder than intended. 'You know what my mum thinks about alcohol.'

'You can stay over, problem solved. Anyway, that's not even what I had planned. I was thinking we could maybe play about with your magic?'

'Abbie, no. I can't.'

'But you never try.'

'I have tried.'

'Like, once. Come on, I bet we can make it work. You always struggle on your own, but you'll have me there as your guide. We can do a Ouija board, or a séance!'

'Isn't that to summon spirits? I don't think that would help.'

'Well, we can Google it. I promise, we'll get it to work. Please, let's just try.' Abbie gave Charley her famous puppy-dog eyes, knowing full well it never failed to get her what she wanted.

'Argggh, fine. But if nothing happens this time, you stop badgering me, okay?'

'Absolutely, yes! Deal.' She excitedly held out her hand to shake on it and Charley reluctantly accepted, secretly cursing her persistent friend. She knew how the evening would go, but if it meant finally getting a bit of peace from Abbie, she would indulge her.

'Hello, darling,' Linda said cheerfully as Charley came bounding through the door, tripping over a pair of boots. 'Oh dear, are you all right?'

'I'm fine,' she replied, shoving her dad's large walking shoes to the side with her foot. 'How's your day been?'

'Oh, you know. Work was busy, one of the temps is off with flu, so it's been hectic. How was school?'

'Dull.'

Linda smiled. 'Surprise, surprise.'

'I'm going to stay with Abbie tonight.'

'All right, honey. Will Carol be in?'

'Yes, her mum will be there.' Charley rolled her eyes.

'I was only asking. Try to behave, okay?'

'Always do,' Charley beamed, kissing her mother on the cheek and dashing upstairs to pack a bag.

She walked into her room, surprised to find her sister perched on the end of her bed, raiding one of her jewellery boxes.

'Jess? What are you doing?'

'Looking for clasps. I lost all mine.' Her eyes were red and they looked sore, as if she might have been crying.

'Jess, what's wrong? You okay?'

'Fine. I just need a Kirby grip,' she snapped, her voice hoarse.

'All right, but there's none in there. Here.' Charley fished a new strip from her top drawer and handed them to Jess, who quickly snatched them from her hand. She picked herself up and scurried out the room without another word.

'You're welcome!'

Charley arrived at Abbie's house just after six, laden with bags.

'Christ, how long you staying for, a fortnight?' Abbie joked as she helped her friend inside.

'Very funny. I brought crisps and chocolate. Oh, and marshmallows. We can toast them on your fire.'

'Oooh, yeah! We could do that when we're having the séance.'

'We are not having a séance.'

'Uch, you're boring, Charles.'

'I'm here, aren't I? I'm letting you have your fun.'

'I guess. Come on, I've made something for us,' Abbie said as she pushed Charley into the kitchen. 'Cocktails!'

'Really, Abbs?'

'Oh, lighten up. There's hardly any booze in them. It's mostly fruit juice.' Charley guessed this probably wasn't true, but decided to have it anyway. One wouldn't hurt.

Abbie picked up one of the glasses and Charley did the same, toasting her friend before taking a large gulp.

'Shit!' Abbie yelled, causing Charley to nearly choke on her drink.

'Bloody hell!' Charley took in Abbie's wet clothes and studied the glass which was scattered across the floor. 'What happened?'

'My glass smashed!' Abbie grinned.

Charley frowned and said, 'Why are you smiling?'

'Because, you just used magic.'

'What, you're saying that was me?' Charley shook her head.

'Of course, it's not like you've never done that trick before.'

'Abbie . . .'

'These glasses are solid, there's no way I could've done that.' She took Charley's glass and began squeezing it, proving that there was no way to smash it using just her hands. 'See? It's way too thick.'

'Well if it was me, it wasn't intentional.'

'Yeah, I know. But it's a good start. Now we have something to work with.' Charley sighed. Maybe the evening wasn't going to go exactly as she'd thought.

FIVE

By nine o'clock, Abbie had managed to devour another four cocktails and was beginning to slur her words. Charley had indulged her by having another one, but had stuck to tea after that. They'd spent an hour experimenting, seeing if they could get Charley's magic to work again, but it was no use – the earlier incident seemed to have been a fluke. It didn't look as though any other magic was going to take place that night.

'This sucks,' Abbie muttered, shoving a marshmallow she'd been toasting into her mouth. 'Bloody hell, that's hot!'

'Let it cool down first.' Charley bit her tongue to stop herself laughing, but she couldn't help it. She let out a giggle, causing Abbie to look at her, unimpressed.

'Ith not funna,' Abbie spat, unable to speak properly with a mouth full of hot goo.

'It's hilarious. I'm sorry, I'll stop.' Charley sat, face straight, for all of ten seconds before she let out another snort of laughter.

'If you were any good at controlling your magic,

you could've cooled that down for me.' Abbie took a generous gulp of water, finally swallowing the scalding sweet.

'Well, we've definitely established that I'm not good at controlling it.'

'Come on, Charles. Let's make this happen. Think of all the things we could do.'

'We?' Charley gave her an inquisitive look.

'Oh, you know what I mean. You could be fabulous.'

'I'm already fabulous,' Charley grinned, flicking her hair back in as glamorous a manner as she could.

She finished the rest of her tea while Abbie sipped what she'd promised would be her final cocktail of the night. Just as Charley got to her feet to take her mug to the kitchen, the doorbell went, giving her such a fright she dropped it on to the soft, green carpet.

'Good thing that was empty,' Abbie smiled jokingly, looking round at the numerous stains that were scattered across the floor. Neither Abbie nor her mother were the most careful of people, always spilling drinks or knocking things over.

Charley made her way to the front door, unlatching the chain and pulling it open.

'That's weird,' she called, hanging out to get a better view, 'there's no one here.'

'It'll be the kids next door – they're always playing chappy, little buggers. Get lost, weasels!' Abbie yelled without budging from her spot.

'Weasels?'

'Their surname's Weisel,' she smiled, 'but I prefer weasel.'

'Oh, so it is. Lovely,' Charley giggled as she shut

the front door. Before she could stop it, it swung back, smacking her in the face and causing her to let out a yelp.

'What's wrong?' Abbie gasped, stumbling to her feet. 'Did I do that?'

'Did you do what? Jesus Christ, Charles, your nose is bleeding.' Charley put her hand to her nose, smiling as the blood began to retreat backwards, inside her nostrils.

'Is it working?' Charley asked, impatient for an answer.

'Bloody hell! Are you doing that?' her friend asked, staring open-mouthed as the last drop of blood disappeared.

'That was me, Abbie, I did that! And I actually meant for it to happen.'

The girls stood in silence, Abbie gaping awkwardly at Charley's now spotless face. Her nose was already beginning to bruise, proving that the incident had really happened and it wasn't all in their minds.

'I can't believe it,' Charley mumbled, 'I could feel it, the control, I knew exactly what I was doing.'

'This is insane,' Abbie choked, excitement beginning to build up inside her. 'Do it again.'

'I don't know if I can.'

'What do you mean? You finally managed to do it. This is a major breakthrough.'

'I know it is, but I'm still not sure.' She focused on the first thing that came into view: a picture of an Italian town, hanging alone on Abbie's wall. She tried to concentrate, to make something – anything – happen. But it didn't move. 'See.'

'What do you mean, see? Look!' Abbie pointed at

the picture, staring in amazement as the colour began to drain from it.

'Wow, I didn't . . . I mean I can't have. I didn't feel a thing.'

'Maybe you still need to work on it.'

'Ugh, let's face it,' Charley sighed, 'I'm screwed.'

Abbie nodded, folding her arms and said, 'Yeah you are, my mum loves that painting.'

'Charley, what a nice surprise. Do come in, pet.' Charley followed the hunched old lady into her small sitting room, taking a seat once she was inside. The television was on in the corner, volume blaring as usual. 'How are you?'

'I'm okay thanks, Gran. Actually, there's a reason I came. It's about the . . . my, eh, my powers.'

Dorcas looked sceptical. 'Yes?'

'The other night, I did something, something I've never done before.'

'Well go on then, dear. What was it?'

'I used my magic, but not by accident. I made something happen.' Dorcas continued to watch her, not seeming particularly startled by what she'd just heard.

'And what did you do?'

'Well, it's a bit odd.'

'You're talking about magic, Charley. Of course it seems odd.'

'I was at Abbie's. We were messing about, usual stuff. Anyway, I got hit in the face with a door.'

'Is that where the swollen nose came from?' Dorcas pointed an arthritic finger towards Charley's face.

'Yeah, it was a lot worse than this. But when it

actually happened, my nose started bleeding. I somehow managed to stop it – the blood started flowing back inside my nose.'

'And you were in control of this?'

'Yes, I knew exactly what I was doing, it was unreal. Then I drained a picture of its colour, but that wasn't on purpose.'

'Well, it will take time. But it's a good step forward.'

'You don't seem all that surprised.'

'Truthfully, Charley, I'm not. I had a feeling this would happen a lot sooner than you expected. You're a clever girl.'

'I thought you said it was just telekinesis?'

'Well, I did, but–'

'Gran, you talk about it as though it's all completely normal. I'm . . . strange.'

'You're not strange, dear, you're special,' Dorcas said sternly.

'That's just a nice way of saying strange. I'm weird, Gran, I'm a freak. I'm not normal!'

With her final outburst, they heard a loud explosion, followed by sparks and crackling. Charley dived at her gran, immediately wanting to protect her as smoke poured from the old television set.

'Oh my God, Gran, I'm so sorry.'

Dorcas spoke through heavy coughs. 'It's all right, I needed a new one anyway.'

Once again, weeks went by without any strange occurrences. Charley hadn't managed to use her powers again. In fact, nothing magical had happened recently, not even accidentally. She'd felt exhausted since the night at Abbie's and hadn't been up to doing much since; somehow the whole experience seemed to have left her feeling drained, physically and emotionally.

Aiden had gone back to his usual sullen self. They'd shared an awkward hello at one point, but that was as far as it had gone. Charley wasn't sure if she was glad or disappointed.

Abbie's mum had gone mad when she discovered her missing painting of the beaches of Ischia. The girls had had to get rid of it – they couldn't exactly explain how it had somehow gone from beautifully bright to completely colourless in the time that she'd been away.

They'd removed the picture and replaced it with something similar that they'd printed from Abbie's computer, but her mum didn't buy it. She told Abbie she would have to earn the money to pay for a new one, with Charley insisting that she would of course give every penny back.

On the Monday morning, Charley strolled unenthusiastically into her temporary history class.

'Settle down, settle down. Take your seats, please, rather . . . take whatever seat you can find.' Mrs Macarthur scurried about at the front of the class, preparing books and various worksheets for her lesson. Since the accident, they hadn't had a classroom as the ceiling was being repaired, so they were always shoved into whatever spare room was available. On this occasion, it was a pokey little room with no windows and too few chairs for her substantial amount of students. 'I know this isn't ideal, but it will have to do for now. Aiden, what are you doing?'

'Trying to find a seat,' he muttered as he walked into the class, late as usual.

'Well, just take whatever one you can find. You can squeeze in beside Charley.' His expression suddenly changed, eyes darting to where Charley was seated. He let out a sigh but made his way over, dropping his bag with a thump on the floor.

Mrs Macarthur began handing out worksheets, muttering to herself at the same time.

Aiden was deliberately avoiding Charley's gaze by staring in the opposite direction. She couldn't have felt more awkward if she'd tried. If this ceiling collapsed as well, it would be no bad thing, at least then she would have a reason to escape.

To distract herself from her unfriendly neighbour, she focused on a pot of pens at the front of the class, wondering if she could gain enough concentration – or command – to make it move, if even a little. To her surprise, the pot began to shake, rattling from side to side.

She thought back to the night at Abbie's: the glass, the door swinging back, the blood, the painting. All of a sudden the pot fell over, sending pens flying across the table.

'For goodness sake!' the teacher shrieked, getting the fright of her life. Aiden's head shot up – he looked puzzled for a second, then he looked at Charley accusingly.

'What?' she said, casually shrugging her shoulders.

'Nothing,' he replied, but she wasn't convinced. He looked flustered, shocked even. He hadn't been expecting that.

Why does he care? she thought to herself. She half-smiled and turned to look at the paper that had just been placed on her desk, just as Aiden's disappeared from his.

Again, he looked unsettled as he leaned down to pick it up. As he resurfaced, he let out a gasp as he looked down at his sheet, the words slowly fading away.

'What the . . .?' was all he could manage.

'What is it?' Charley asked, leaning over to see what he was so upset about.

'You.'

'Don't walk away from me, Chambers.' Aiden was chasing down the hallway after Charley, who was already quite a bit in front of him. Mrs Macarthur had demanded silence for the duration of the class, so he'd had no time to quiz his classmate about his suspicions regarding her recent behaviour.

'What do you want?' she demanded as he finally caught up with her.

'We need to talk.'

'So talk then. What is it?'

'Not here. Come with me.' He grabbed her wrist and pulled her away from the crowd, leaving Charley no choice but to follow.

'Are you going to tell me what this is about?' she asked Aiden once they were finally far enough away from the school grounds. She knew exactly what it was about, but she was having too much fun seeing him so flustered.

'Don't play dumb, Chambers. I know a magician when I see one.'

Charley just about choked. 'You what? A magician? Stop kidding . . .'

'This isn't a joke. Are you denying you did those things? The pens, my sheet . . . that was you, wasn't it?'

She looked at him, serious now. 'Yes, that was me. I

have these . . .' Charley faltered, 'I don't know. Some sort of weird powers. I know that sounds crazy–'

'It doesn't.'

'But a magician, really? You have to admit that sounds a bit barmy.'

'How long have you been able to do things like that?'

'All my life, I guess. But I've never been in control until now, and I'm not always. I do crazy things I don't want to and I don't know how to stop them from happening.'

'I'll need to teach you then.'

'Wait, you're . . . what? Like me?'

'Yes, Chambers, I'm like you. I'm a magician.' Just hearing the word made her want to laugh. It was like something from a fairy tale.

'How do I know you're not lying to me?' she asked, crossing her arms firmly over her chest.

What if he was tricking her? Trying to make her confess so that he could torment her from then on – everyone would find out.

But her concerns were soon put to rest as Aiden swiped his hand through the air, creating such a wind it knocked Charley off balance, sending her toppling to the ground.

'Ow!' she yelled as he offered her a hand up.

'Sorry.' He pulled her up with a little too much force, causing her to stumble straight into his arms. 'Sorry – again.'

'It's fine.' She pulled away quickly and began brushing away the gravel which was now stuck to her skirt. 'So what else can you do?'

'A lot.' He looked down at the chain wrapped around

37

her neck and within seconds it began levitating. 'I could snap it in two if I wanted.'

'I'd rather you didn't.'

Aiden didn't reply.

'So . . . how long have you known about, you know, your 'abilities'?' She waved her hands about in a spooky manner but Aiden only shot her a look of disapproval.

'It's not something to joke about. Your 'abilities' make you incredibly powerful – and dangerous. You aren't just a normal school kid anymore.'

'I've never been a normal school kid. And this isn't new to me – like I said, I've been like this for as long as I can remember.'

'But now you can start learning. Once you gain full control, you'll be less dangerous in that you won't hurt people unintentionally. But there will be a whole new range of possibilities – of temptations.'

'Wait a minute . . . what do you mean, temptations?'

'You'll see. For now, let's keep it simple.'

'Simple?'

'Yes, you have much to learn,' he said, trying to act serious, but his grin gave him away.

'Right, okay, Obi-Wan.'

Charley had agreed to meet Aiden after school. He'd said his house would be empty and had told her to come round as soon as she was ready – they had a lot to discuss apparently.

Charley was nervous. Her stomach had been doing somersaults since their earlier conversation. She couldn't believe she'd found someone else with powers like her own – especially Aiden of all people. Yes, he'd always been mysterious, very dark and brooding – but a magician? She'd thought he was just some troubled kid with anger issues.

She sat impatiently through her last class – Maths, of all things. Time went so slowly she could have sworn the clock was moving backwards. After what felt like an eternity, the bell rang, sending Charley leaping across the table and heading straight for the door.

'In a hurry to get home, Miss Chambers?' She came to a halt, turning to see her disapproving teacher eyeing her carefully over his glasses.

'Sorry, Mr Grayson, I just have some stuff to take care of.'

'Kids these days, always in such a rush. On you go,' he said, shooing her away. She ran out the door, bag swinging behind her, before he could change his mind.

She didn't bother going home, she was far too anxious about meeting Aiden. She knew full well that it wasn't a date – it was the opposite if anything. Yet she couldn't get rid of the butterflies in her tummy, her sweaty palms or her racing heart. Charley Chambers was terrified, and it was all because of a boy.

SIX

'Chambers,' he greeted her, as she stood patiently on his front step.

'Cunningham,' she mocked, 'you gonna invite me in, then?' His lips curled slightly and Charley was sure she saw the hint of a smile.

'After you.' He held the door open and she made her way past, stopping to stare as she took in her surroundings. 'Wow, your house is amazing.'

'It's all right, I guess.'

'All right? Aiden, it's huge.' The hallway seemed to go on forever, and above her was a crystal chandelier, hanging from the ornate ceiling that seemed a million miles away. Large, framed paintings hung along the length of the wall and at the end of the corridor – when they finally reached it – she noticed a beautifully carved, Indian sculpture placed beside the stairwell.

'There's more to life than having a pretty house, Chambers.' She glanced up at him, not sure what to say. 'Come on, my room's up here.' She followed him up the spiral staircase, a slight awkwardness now between them.

His room was nothing like the rest of the house; very simple and plain. It gave nothing away, only that he clearly wasn't sentimental and was a bit of a clean freak.

'You certainly don't like clutter, do you?'

He let out a quiet laugh. 'Before I learned how to use my powers, a lot of things got . . . broken. Including a TV that exploded in my face – still surprised it didn't blind me.'

'Hey, I did that,' Charley said excitedly.

'What?'

'Blew up a telly, at my gran's.'

Aiden didn't respond, instead he carried on with his story. 'Well, after that, I cleared out my room. That way, there was nothing to break. Guess I didn't think about putting all the stuff back again. Anyway, we're not here to talk about me, we're here for you.'

'So what you gonna teach me?' she chirped.

'Everything, in time. Let's start with the basics.'

Aiden sat on the floor, motioning for Charley to do the same. He pulled out a baseball from underneath his bed and placed it in front of him, his hands cupped round but not quite touching it. Charley wanted to laugh, casting her mind back to all Abbie's talk of séances. Slowly, he pulled his hands from it, the ball rising at the same time. He held it, mid-air, for about a minute, before letting it drop. Charley's hand shot out, catching the ball before it hit the floor.

'Your go.' She turned the ball over in her hand, studying the intricate detail sewn into its surface. She put it down and cupped her hands around it, just as Aiden had done. The ball flew into the air, hitting the ceiling before falling back down to the ground.

'I did it!' she shrieked, but Aiden only scowled.

'No, you didn't.'

'I made it move, didn't I?'

'That's not what I showed you. You were meant to make it rise and hold it there, not shoot off into the air like a bloody rocket.'

She rolled her eyes at his tone and for the second time, cupped her hands around the ball. The same thing happened again. 'Damn it, Chambers, be careful,' he yelled, as the ball narrowly missed his head.

'I'm sorry! Don't shout at me, you said yourself I'm still learning.' Aiden sighed, patience apparently not one of his best qualities.

'Try again. Wipe everything else from your mind. This time, focus. Hold the ball with your eyes.'

Once again, she stretched out her hands. She closed her eyes, trying not to think about anything but the ball; when she opened them, it was slowly beginning to rise.

'I'm doing it.'

'Shhh, concentrate.'

'I am . . .'

'No, you're talking,' he snapped. 'Stop it.' She stuck her tongue out, but did as he asked. The higher she lifted her hands, the more the ball rose. When she pulled her hands apart, it began to spin.

'Wow,' she gasped, mesmerised by the whirling ball.

'Aiden?' a voice came from downstairs, startling Charley and causing her to lose concentration.

'Shit,' Aiden muttered, quickly getting to his feet.

'What's wrong? Who is it?'

'Aiden?' The door flew open, revealing a woman, stick-thin and impeccably dressed. 'Who's this?' she asked, glaring at Charley.

'This is Charley, a friend from school. Chambers, this is my moth–'

'Get her out of here, Aiden. I have told you before.' She took off back down the hall, her heels clacking against the wooden floor.

'What was that about?' Charley asked. 'Did I do something wrong?'

'No, you didn't do anything. I didn't realise they'd be back. You need to go.'

'Oh, okay. I'll let myself out.'

'I'm sorry about this, Chambers. I didn't know–'

'It's fine. I'll see you.'

'He says you're what?' Abbie squawked as Charley flung herself on to the bed. She'd gone straight over there, wanting to fill her friend in on all the details of her visit.

'I know, it's insane, right?'

'It's pretty crazy, yeah. But I suppose it makes sense.'

'Makes sense? Abbie, he said I'm a magician.'

'Well, you're obviously something freaky, no offence.'

'None taken.'

Abbie cocked an eyebrow. 'And he's the same as you? He can make things move, disappear, blah, blah, blah?'

'Yeah, although he seems to be a bit of an expert.'

'So what did he show you?'

'Not much, really. He helped me make a ball float in thin air, but that's about it. His mum came home and chucked me out.'

'What? Why?' Abbie's disgusted expression was priceless.

'Not sure. She seemed really uptight, barely looked me in the eye. Aiden went all weird as well when he realised she was home. I dunno . . . she definitely doesn't like me though, that's for sure.'

'Learn how to use your powers and turn her into a worm or something.'

'A worm?' Charley laughed.

'Yeah. Who wants to be a worm?'

'You're such a freak.'

Abbie pulled a face. 'Well, from one freak to another, I'm hungry. Let's go out and grab dinner.'

The girls spent the rest of the evening eating chips and playing games on Abbie's computer. Although they didn't mention Aiden again, Charley couldn't help letting her mind wander back to him. She wanted to speak to him, to ask more questions, but she knew that wasn't really the way Aiden Cunningham worked. They would do things his way. Anyway, she didn't even have his number.

At just after nine, Charley said her goodbyes to Abbie and made her way home, once again mulling over her mysterious new companion. How had he managed to hide his secret so well? She'd managed – but it had been a mammoth struggle doing so. Aiden was popular, he had heaps of friends, and girls were always after him – although he never returned their affections. Despite being quiet and incredibly grumpy, he never seemed fazed by anything.

She trudged up the stairs and opened the front door, nearly banging into Jess as she stepped into the house.

'Watch it!' Jess snapped, scowling as her sister tried to apologise.

'Sorry, it was an accident.'

'Whatever.'

'Who rattled your cage?' Charley asked, kicking her shoes into the corner. Jess didn't answer, instead choosing to skulk back up to her room.

'Hello, darling. How was Abbie's?'

'Hey, Dad. It was fine. How was work?'

'Oh, you know how–'

'Charley, there's chicken casserole in the oven if you're hungry,' Linda interrupted from the kitchen.

'I already ate. Thanks anyway.'

'Okay. Nick, could you help me in here for a sec?'

'Sure. Sorry, honey, I'll be with you in a moment.' Charley started for the stairs, knowing fine that 'a moment' would turn into much longer.

'Oh, Charley, before I forget. A boy called for you. Aiden something . . .'

'What? When? What did he say?'

'He just asked if you were in, said he'd catch you another time.'

'Did he leave a number?'

'No, sorry, pet. Ow! Nick, that was my finger.'

'What time was–?'

'Nick!'

'For goodness sake, Linda, I'm trying.' Charley realised she would be better off talking to herself. She climbed the stairs to her bedroom, a smile spread across her face. He'd called.

SEVEN

Charley rushed into registration class the next day, nearly knocking over Mr Aitkens. She gave him a smile, apologised for being late, and took a seat beside Lucy Wheeler.

'Listen up, everyone,' Mr Aitkens called from the front, 'we have a new student joining us. His name is Marcus Gillespie,' he gestured to a boy sitting near the door, 'and he's just moved from Milton Academy up in Oakshore. Please make him feel welcome. Charley, can I ask you to show Marcus around, help him get his bearings?'

'Sure, no problem.' She glanced at the boy who was now looking at her over his shoulder. He had dark brown, messy hair, and chestnut eyes to match. Charley was about to give him a wave, not knowing what else to do, but he turned away.

'Charley? What's the matter?' Lucy frowned, studying Charley's expression. 'You look a little pale.'

'I do?'

'Here, borrow this,' she said, offering Charley a tub of bronzer.

'No thanks, I'm fine. I should go say hi.'

Lucy shook her head. 'Whatever.'

Charley pushed her chair back and headed towards Marcus, grateful for an excuse to leave.

'Charley Chambers, it's an honour.'

'Hey, how do you know my name?' Charley asked, giving her new classmate a quizzical look.

'Well, specky called you it a minute ago,' he said, nodding towards Mr Aitkens, 'you know, when he was asking you to be my babysitter. Plus he gave me a list of everyone in the class – you're the only Charley, so I put two and two together.'

'Right, of course.'

'Listen, you don't need to show me around. I'm sure I can find everything – besides, I don't wanna be a drag. You probably have your own stuff to do.'

'No, you wouldn't. I mean, yeah, you probably don't need my help . . . but if you want a little company, I'd be happy to . . .' Marcus smiled. 'Sorry, I'm babbling. I do that sometimes.'

'It's okay. If you're sure you don't mind then, yeah, I'd love someone to hang out with.'

'Cool, that's settled then.'

'Okay,' Marcus laughed, resting his hands behind his head. He was incredibly handsome. 'I have chemistry first period, Mrs Murrell I think?'

'Oh, unlucky. She's a bitch,' Charley whispered.

'Brilliant. Are you in that class?'

'Afraid not, I didn't take chemistry.'

'What a shame.' He grinned at Charley, and her legs suddenly felt like jelly.

'We could meet up for lunch? Only if you want . . . I mean you don't have to . . .'

'Lunch would be great, Charley.'

'Great.'

'Great . . .'

There was an awkward pause before Charley muttered, 'Okay. See you later,' and scuttled off.

The bell rang and Charley eagerly packed her books into her bag. She'd been looking forward to lunch all morning.

She made her way out the door and immediately walked into someone. 'I'm sorry,' she yelped, before looking up to see Aiden gazing at her.

'You really aren't very coordinated, are you?' he asked, his eyebrows coming together in a frown.

'You know me. I'm not exactly the most graceful.'

'You can say that again.' Charley felt her face flush. 'Listen, I thought we could get out of here for an hour. I have time to teach you a few basics . . .' Her heart sank as he continued talking. Suddenly Marcus seemed so insignificant – a burden, almost.

'I can't today. I told Mr Aitkens I'd look after the new kid.'

'What new kid?'

Right on time, Marcus strode up, his bag casually flung over one shoulder. 'Hey, Charley,' he smiled, his eyes crinkling at the corners, 'ready for lunch?'

'Sure, one sec . . .' She turned to Aiden. 'Sorry, can we catch up later?'

For a moment Aiden looked frustrated, disappointed even, but he quickly recovered and shot Marcus a disdainful look. 'Sure, Chambers, whatever. Another time.' Charley watched him as he walked in the other direction, quickly catching up with Gary and Cameron.

'Did I interrupt something?' Marcus asked, giving Charley an apologetic smile.

'No, nothing important. Come on, let's get lunch.'

They made their way down to the cafeteria, grabbed a slice of pizza each and took a seat near the window. Marcus scoffed his in no time, while Charley nibbled at her crust before giving up and setting it down. She wasn't hungry anymore.

'So, how was your morning?' Marcus asked. He gestured towards her uneaten pizza, 'Do you mind?'

'Hungry, are you?' Charley laughed, crossing her arms as he demolished what had been her lunch.

'Starving.' He licked his fingers and swallowed down the last bite. 'You have a beautiful smile, Charley.' She looked away from him, chewing on her thumbnail to distract herself. 'I hope that wasn't too forward?'

'Thank you. And no,' she beamed, 'it's fine.'

'I'm sorry if I barged in between you and your boyfriend earlier, I really didn't mean to.'

'Boyfriend? No, Aiden's not . . . we're just friends.'

'Oh, I see. You just seem a bit, I don't know, down.'

'I'm not down, I swear. I am being rude though. I'm really sorry, Marcus, I must make a terrible first impression.'

'Nonsense.'

'So, tell me about yourself.'

'Well . . .' He rubbed his chin as if considering what to say. 'I'm roguishly handsome,' – Charley blushed – 'I have an enormous appetite, as you saw for yourself. I'm terrible at Maths. I have a dog named Peewee . . .'

'Peewee?'

'Don't ask. My little sister named him, I didn't get

a say in the matter. She was always spoiled, being the youngest.'

'Tell me about it. My sister can be such a brat. What's your sister's name?'

Marcus looked down at the table, the atmosphere suddenly changing. 'Bud.'

'Bud?' said Charley. 'As in Buddy?'

'No, just Bud. Well, it's short for Boudicca, but I never liked that. I always called her Bud.'

Charley studied him, a bad feeling in the pit of her stomach. 'Called?'

Marcus sighed. 'Yeah. She . . . she died.'

'Oh my God. Marcus, I'm so sorry.'

'Thank you.'

'I don't know what to say.'

'It's fine, really. It was years ago.' His eyes grew cloudy, his whole demeanour changing.

'Even so, it must be–'

'It's okay. I don't talk about it much so could we maybe, I dunno, just forget I said anything?'

'Of course, I'm sorry.'

'You really don't need to apologise.'

They sat in silence for a moment, Marcus deep in thought and Charley awkwardly chewing on her nails. The mention of Bud's death left her unsure of what to say, and she couldn't stand the awkwardness between them. Still, a part of her was incredibly curious to know what had happened. It was really none of her business though, and if Marcus didn't want to talk about it, she wouldn't broach the subject again.

'Abbie!' she cried suddenly, spotting her friend across the cafeteria.

'Who?'

'Come on, you need to meet my friend. I'll introduce you.' Charley hurried Marcus over to where Abbie was standing, stuffing her face with greasy chips.

'Marcus, I would like you to meet my best friend, Abbie.'

'Heh, ice oo eet ou,' she spluttered, spraying Marcus with soggy potato as she shook his hand.

'Eh, yeah, you too.'

'Sorry about her, she can be so rude.' Charley glared at Abbie who returned her gaze with a 'What have I done now?' look.

'Yes, that's me. Rude, rude, rude. And to be even more rude . . . I have to go. I said I would meet Connor for lunch and I've kind of started without him. Nice meeting you, Marcus.'

'Abbie!' Charley yelled after her friend, who was already darting around the corner and out of sight.

'Just you and me then,' Marcus smiled, his eyes glinting as the light bounced off them.

'I guess so. Anything you wanna do?'

'I can think of one thing.'

'Yeah?'

'Come on, I'll show you.'

They'd been walking for ages, and Charley was pretty sure they weren't going to make it back to school for their next class. The sun was peeking out from behind a cloud but the air was still cool – crisp and refreshing, just the way Charley liked it.

'Em, Marcus. Maybe we should think about heading back.'

'Ah,' he scratched his head and gave her an innocent smile, 'I wasn't really planning on going back.'

'Oh.'

'Don't tell me you've never ditched school before?'

She shrugged impassively.

'Come on, Charley, live a little.'

'It might help if you actually told me what we were planning on doing.'

'You're in luck. We're here.' He gestured to the space in front of them and Charley looked on in astonishment. They were standing above the river, looking down at the still, blue water beneath them. Marcus climbed on to the bridge and hooked his legs through the gaps.

'What are you doing?' Charley gasped, taking in the distance between him and the water – it was quite a drop.

'What do you think? We're jumping.'

'We? Are you insane? I'm not jumping off a bridge.'

'It's fine. It's not as high as it looks and the water's deep enough. Trust me, it feels amazing.' She could feel herself shaking – she wasn't really going to do this, was she?

'You're serious, aren't you?'

'Deadly. At least come and sit next to me. If you don't wanna jump, I promise I won't make you.' She stood there for a moment, tempted to just say, 'What the hell!' and join him on the bridge. But her sensible side took over and she shook her head, backing away in the other direction.

'I can't.'

'The only reason you can't is because you keep telling yourself that. Why not say, you know what? I can do this. I can and I will.'

'Why are you so desperate for me to jump off a bridge?'

'Stop analysing everything, Charley. Don't think and just do.' She looked down at him hanging casually over the edge, his long legs swinging back and forth. He didn't seem fazed in the slightest.

'All right, why the hell not?'

'Really? I wasn't expecting that to work,' he laughed.

'Yes, really. Let's jump off a bridge.' She flung her bag to the ground and carefully made her way over to where Marcus was sitting, his hand already outstretched for her to grab on to.

'You sure about this?' he smiled, dimples forming in his cheeks.

'Nope,' she said, utterly petrified. 'On the count of three?'

'One . . .'

'Two . . .'

'Three!' they said together, and all of a sudden they were in mid-air, the wind slamming against their chests as they fell towards the water.

Everything seemed as though it was in slow motion. Charley could feel the air rushing through her fingers, her hair, against her cheeks. Her eyes were streaming and her lips felt dry. She wanted to scream, not out of terror, but from excitement. Marcus was right, it felt amazing. She could have sworn she was flying – at that moment, anything felt possible.

The next thing she knew, she was underwater, her body suddenly aching from hitting the river's hard surface. She was a perfectly good swimmer, but now her arms felt heavy, her legs like lead as she slowly sank. She wasn't worried though; she could feel the exhilaration pulsing through her, the rush from jumping still with her as she floated in the freezing water.

All of a sudden, two strong arms linked hers, hoisting her up towards the surface. Air filled her lungs as she gasped, flailing her arms as Marcus steadied her. How long had she been under? She didn't care. She felt incredible.

'That was unbelievable,' she yelled, sweeping the wet strands of hair from her face.

'It's a good feeling, isn't it?'

'Good? That's an understatement.'

'Let's get you out, it's pretty cold in here.' They swam side by side over to the verge, Marcus giving Charley a boost before pulling himself up on to dry land.

'Can we do it again?'

Marcus laughed, still out of breath from the swim back to shore. 'Take it easy, you. I think that's enough for one day.' His T-shirt was sticking to him, his body showing through the wet cloth. Charley blushed and he smiled back, moving closer as he pulled the shirt over his head.

She was sure he was about to kiss her – did he want to kiss her? Did she want him to kiss her? Her mind flashed to Aiden, and she immediately felt guilty. What was she doing?

'We should get going,' she said quickly, making her way back up to where her school bag was sitting. 'If we get caught–'

'Yeah, I get it. That's enough risks for one day.' He grinned, hiding his disappointment well. He knew exactly what was in the way – or rather, who.

EIGHT

Marcus could tell Charley felt uncomfortable on the walk back. They weren't heading for school; the wet hair and soaking clothes might prompt a few hard to answer questions. They reached the turn off for Beaton Road, where Marcus slowed to a halt.

'This is me.'

'Oh, you live here?' Charley looked along the street at the row of enormous, identical buildings, all complete with hanging baskets and driveways housing expensive cars. Did all the guys in her life have rich parents and live in mansions?

'Yep. Not exactly unique, are they?'

'They're lovely though.'

'I guess I can't complain. I'll see you at school tomorrow, yeah?'

'Yeah, see you then. And thanks, Marcus, I really did have fun.'

'Anytime. If you ever wanna take a risk, you know where to find me.' He gave her a wink before heading towards the house, his smile disappearing as soon as his back was turned.

Charley strolled along the street, in no hurry to get home. Her mum was bound to be finished work and she couldn't be bothered explaining why she was dripping wet.

Looks like I have some time to kill, she thought, pulling her sodden shirt away from her skin – it was starting to itch and she half-wished she hadn't jumped off the bridge. Okay, she didn't wish that at all, but she did at least hope the sun might come out and help her dry off a bit – not likely though.

'Where the hell have you been?' came a deep voice, making her jump.

'Aiden. What are you doing here? Why aren't you in school?'

'I should ask you the same thing. Why are you all wet?' He took in her damp hair that looked like rats' tails, and then became embarrassed as he glanced down at her almost see-through shirt. 'Well, I see you don't care too much about your dignity.'

'What?'

He raised his eyebrows, nodding down towards her chest.

'Shit, I didn't even realise.'

'So what were you doing?' Aiden frowned, his deep blue eyes boring into her.

'I . . . I was down at the river. I kind of . . . jumped off the bridge . . . with Marcus.' She attempted an innocent smile.

'You what? What the hell were you thinking? Do you know how dangerous that was?'

'It's fine, it wasn't that high, and I'm a good swimmer.'

'I don't care if you can swim or not, that's not what

I mean. That kind of thing is the perfect way to set off your powers. Do you want the world to find out what you really are?'

'What I am? No, of course not.'

'Jesus, Chambers, you need to be more careful. What were you doing with that new kid anyway? Why weren't you in school?'

'Oh my God, Aiden, what's with all the questions? It's not like you're my boyfriend.' She hadn't wanted to let it slip, but for some reason she couldn't help herself.

'No, I guess you're right, I'm not.' Was she really seeing this? Did Aiden Cunningham actually look . . . upset?

'I mean . . .' – what did she mean? – 'It's not like we're . . . you know. . .' She was babbling again. Why did she always prattle on when she was nervous?

Before she could continue rambling, Aiden pulled her close, his hand cupping the back of her neck. He placed his other hand on the small of her back, holding her body just inches from his. Then he kissed her. If she'd tried to imagine a better feeling, she'd have failed. It was perfect.

'Wow,' she said, pulling away to look up into his gleaming eyes. An orange tint ran around his pupils; she'd never noticed before. 'Aiden, that was . . . wow.'

'Shut up, Chambers,' he whispered, his lips once again finding hers. She didn't object – she'd never dreamt anything could feel so magical. And for someone with powers, that was saying something.

Marcus closed the door, sighing to himself as he kicked off his shoes. He took a seat at the large wooden desk and opened his journal – a small, brown, leather-bound book – and began scribbling on the first empty page.

He cursed. It had all been going so well, until . . .

Sunlight poured in through the window and he glanced up, dropping the pen as he set eyes on Charley, seconds from where he'd left her, locking lips with none other than Aiden Cunningham. His jealousy spiked and he could no longer contain it. He got to his feet and launched the stool he'd been sitting on across the room, laughing as it bounced off the wall and fell to pieces. He'd known this was coming, she'd made that much clear. But this soon? Had the afternoon they'd spent together really meant nothing?

'Game on, Aiden,' he muttered, looking at them a last time before stalking off, leaving his journal lying open on the desktop. His messy writing covered the two visible pages, but only one word was written. Over and over again: Charley.

Charley gripped Aiden's hand as they walked along beside each other. His jacket was wrapped around her shoulders, and even though she was just about dry, she wanted to keep it there.

'Charley,' Aiden said, gently pulling his hand away. She immediately felt embarrassed.

'What? Oh my God, you didn't . . . I'm sorry.'

'I just think we should take this slow, what with me teaching you as well.'

'Yeah, I get it. Sure.' She tried to shrug it off but she was mortified. Of course he didn't want a relationship. How could she have been so stupid?

'Don't be like that.'

'Like what? I'm not being like anything. You don't want anything serious. That's cool. Listen, Aiden, I really need to get going. Thanks for the jacket and . . . well, bye.'

She shoved the coat into his hands before he could argue and took off down the street, desperate to avoid yet more embarrassment. He stood, watching her go.

Tell her how you feel, a voice in his head screamed. If only it were that easy.

Charley unlocked the front door, relieved to find that no one was home. She didn't know where her mother was, but she didn't really care; she was just happy to be alone.

She still couldn't believe she'd been so naïve. To think Aiden would want to be with her, after only a kiss. Idiot, she thought to herself, climbing the stairs.

'Charley? Is that you?' The voice came from the room next to hers.

'Jess? What are you doing here?' The sound came, muffled. She was crying. 'Jess, are you all right?'

'I'm fine. Don't tell Mum, okay?'

'Can I come in?' Charley went for the handle, but as she turned it she heard the lock click.

'No! I'm sick. Just leave me alone.' Her tone was brusque but she didn't sound angry. Nor did she sound sick. Charley considered trying to use her powers to open it again, but decided against it. If Jess wanted to be alone, that was up to her. Besides, it probably wouldn't work anyway.

'All right, but if you need me, just shout.'

There was a loud bang from the other side of the door

before Jess called back, 'Go away. I don't need anyone's help.'

Charley gave up and went into her own room, pulling off her crumpled clothes, and got into the shower. She thought back to the days when she and her sister had got along, the time when they could spend more than five minutes with each other without getting into an argument. They used to be close – she couldn't remember when that had changed.

She'd only been in the shower for a couple of minutes before she started feeling light-headed. Her vision clouded and as she reached to steady herself, she knocked over the tray of toiletries that sat to her right.

I really shouldn't have skipped lunch, she thought to herself, blaming lack of food for her dizziness. Or jumped into the river.

But the dizziness was just the start. Moments later, she began to feel sharp pains all over her body; it felt like hundreds of tiny electric shocks all at once. She called out as they pricked her skin, an ache forming in her stomach. She climbed out of the shower and grabbed a hold of the sink with both hands. She was going to throw up. She was sure of it. She was going to be sick . . .

But as quick as it had come on, it disappeared again. The pins and needles eased off and the pain in her stomach vanished.

Strange, she thought, wrapping herself in a towel and making her way back through to the bedroom.

She stopped dead.

Her room was trashed. Books were scattered across the floor, clothes everywhere – all of her jewellery, photos and trinkets lay on the ground in a heap.

'What the . . . ?'

She opened the bedroom door and her jaw dropped – it wasn't just her room. The pictures that usually hung on the hall's pale, cream wall were now broken on the floor, plants knocked over, ornaments damaged.

Please say I didn't.

Who was she kidding? Of course it was her fault, how could it not be? But her powers had never been this strong before – they'd never caused her physical pain. She had to talk to Aiden. As much as she hated to admit it, she needed him.

'Chambers, hey,' Aiden said quietly, glancing over his shoulder and stepping outside before his parents could hear. 'What are you doing here?'

'I need your help. I don't even know if you can help, but I need someone to talk to.'

'All right, but not here. Let's go for a walk.'

He shut the door and followed her down the steps, looking back to see if he was being watched. His mother stood by the window, shaking her head as he continued walking. He would deal with her later.

'What's up?' he asked as they started down his street. 'Must be important, you only left me an hour ago.'

'It is, I think.'

'Go on.'

'Something strange happened when I got home. I was in the shower and I started feeling weird: dizzy, sick, just really odd. Then I felt all these shocks over my body. It was like pins and needles, only much worse.'

He gave her a look. She knew that look.

'Have you called a doctor?' He was mocking her.

'I'm not ill. When I got out the shower, it all went away. I felt fine again. I went through to my room and it was ruined.'

'What do you mean, ruined?'

'Trashed. The place was a mess. Then I went through to the hall and it was the same. I must have done it . . . somehow. But it's never been like that before. I've never felt pain with my powers.'

'And you shouldn't.'

'So what's going on?'

Aiden sighed and said, 'I don't know. But it doesn't sound right.'

'Will it happen again?' She desperately hoped it wouldn't.

'I have no idea. If it does, you need to call me straight away. Understood?'

'Understood,' she mimicked sarcastically, causing him to throw her a disapproving look.

'I mean it, Chambers. I've never heard of that happening before. I'll look into it, all right? For now, just . . . keep out of trouble. If you can.'

'What kind of trouble am I likely to get myself into?' she asked, crossing her arms.

'Oh, I don't know. Maybe try and stay away from rivers, bridges, guys like Marcus.'

'Are you jealous or something?' Charley smiled, secretly hoping that he was.

'No, I'm not jealous. I don't like the guy. And okay, yeah, I guess it kinda sucked knowing you decided to ditch school and have a laugh with someone else.'

He does have feelings for me!

'Why don't you like Marcus? You don't even know him.'

62

'I just don't trust him. Listen, I'm not telling you who you can and can't see. It's up to you. Just be careful, okay?'

'I will, I promise. And for the record, I'd rather spend time with you over Marcus any day.'

He smiled and took her hand in his, squeezing it gently.

'That's good to know, Chambers. Good to know.'

NINE

Charley woke with a start, cradling her head in her hands as she came to. She felt awful. She'd been feeling poorly for a few days, but this was the worst she'd felt by a long stretch. She laid her head back on the pillows and reached for her phone: two missed calls, one from Abbie and the other from Aiden.

She hadn't seen either of them for days, since even her mum had said she was too ill to go to school. She'd tried to protest, which only ended up confusing Linda even more. Charley hated school.

But, for once she didn't want to be cooped up inside. Staring at the same four walls was driving her mad. She wanted to speak to Abbie and she was also dying to see Aiden. Of course she wanted to find out if he'd discovered anything about her – condition – but she was more anxious just to see him, to hang out with someone who made her feel normal.

I miss him, she thought to herself, although she would never dare say the words out loud. That would make them seem too real.

'You feeling any better yet?' Jess asked enthusiastically as she burst into Charley's room. She was in the door for less than a minute before Charley retched into a bucket by her bedside.

'No,' – Charley heaved, shooing her sister away – 'I feel terrible.'

'You look it.'

'Thanks.'

'You're welcome,' Jess smiled.

'Why are you so annoyingly upbeat this morning?'

'Dunno, I guess you look so bad that it's making me feel better.'

'Funny. What do you want?' Charley's patience was wearing thin – she wasn't in the mood for games.

'There's a boy at the door for you. He's kinda cute.'

'What?' Charley sat up, pushing the sweat-soaked hair from her face. She really needed a shower.

'Not really my type, but still, he's not bad.'

'Why didn't you say?' She pushed herself from the bed and began shoving on clothes.

'You can't go out like that, you stink.'

'Thanks for the sisterly advice, Jess. Always appreciated.' She wrapped her hair in a tight bun and hurried down the stairs, ignoring her sister's unhelpful comments.

Tugging open the door, her smile faded a little faster than it should've done.

'Marcus . . .'

'Hey, Charley. I just wanted to see how you were doing.'

Charley forced a smile. 'I'm okay, thanks.' She paused for a second and then said, 'Actually, I'm not.

You can probably tell.' She tried her hardest to disguise the disappointment in her voice.

'I won't lie, you don't look too healthy. Take it you aren't going to school?'

'No, although I wish I was. This house is driving me insane.'

'Come for a walk with me then, I'm skipping first period anyway.' His eyes gleamed, making the muscles in Charley's tummy tighten. Once again, she noticed how good-looking he was.

'Skipping class again?' Charley grinned.

Marcus returned her smile. 'I like to live dangerously.'

'A walk does sound good.' She stood for another few seconds before shoving on her shoes and stepping out the door. 'Let's go.'

'You sure you don't need a coat or something?' he said, pointing to her rather baggy T-shirt and dark grey jogging bottoms. 'It's kinda cold.'

'Are you kidding? I'm melting. Trust me, cold is good.'

After about half an hour, Charley began to feel much better. Her headache had disappeared and she no longer felt queasy; a relief she couldn't describe. The hot flushes and constant sweats had stopped as well, and she was finally feeling cool.

'You're shivering,' Marcus said, noticing goose bumps on her arms.

'Maybe you were right,' she laughed, 'it's pretty cold.'

'Here, take this.' He wriggled out of his coat, draping it over her shoulders. It made her think of when Aiden had done the same.

'Thanks.'

'It's cool, I've got a jumper.'

'I don't just mean for the jacket. Thanks for coming to see if I was okay. For the walk and, well, the company. I guess I needed it.'

'Anytime. I like hanging out with you. You aren't like most of the other girls at school.'

'Is that a good thing?'

'You have no idea.'

Their eyes met for a moment and Charley, not looking where she was going, caught her foot on a loose tree root. She lost her balance and began falling forward, flinging her hands out to cushion the fall. But Marcus grabbed her before she hit the ground, one arm quickly wrapping around her waist, the other resting on her hip, turning her to face him.

'Careful where you walk,' he smiled, pulling her up.

'Thanks,' she giggled, 'again. I have a lot to thank you for today.'

'Nonsense. I'm happy to help.'

'Shouldn't you be thinking about getting to school? You'll miss second period if you wait much longer.'

'I'd skip all day if it meant spending time with you.' His smile faded and his face all of a sudden bore a serious expression. 'I really like you, Charley.'

Once again, she withdrew. 'I like you too, Marcus. I like hanging out with you. You're . . .' Charley faltered. She still wasn't sure how she felt about Marcus. Was that really all he was – a friend? Her mind flashed to Aiden. At least Marcus had bothered to check on her to see if she was all right.

'I'm drop dead gorgeous and fantastic company,' Marcus grinned smugly.

Charley giggled. 'Your company's not half bad. Hey, you wanna go to the bridge again?' she asked, suddenly getting excited.

'I don't think that's such a good idea. You're not well.'

'I feel so much better, really.' It was true – since leaving the house, she felt almost back to normal.

'No, I'd feel terrible if anything happened, if you got worse–'

'Marcus, I promise, I'm fine.'

'You don't give up, do you?'

'Nope.' For a moment, she thought he was going to give in.

'Sorry, Charley, we can't. You should really get back to bed, and I should get to school.' He started walking in the opposite direction. 'Besides, what would Aiden think?'

'What? I don't know, and I don't care.' She knew it was a lie, and so did Marcus.

'I'm sorry, Charley.' Before she knew it, he was just about out of sight.

'Bye then,' she mumbled.

The bell for second period rang just as Marcus walked through the front doors. There were already a few students bustling about the main hall, some at their lockers, others making their way to the next class. Marcus sighed as he climbed the steps to his own locker, opening it and at the same time reaching for his jacket pocket. But as his hand met his jumper's cotton fabric, he realised he'd left his jacket with Charley, his rushed departure causing him to forget all about it.

'No, no, no,' he said, cursing as he slammed the locker door shut.

'What's wrong with you?' He turned to see Aiden next to him, looking on with a perplexed expression.

'Nothing, doesn't matter.'

'All right. Sorry I asked.' Aiden turned to go, wondering why he'd bothered to speak to him in the first place.

'No, I'm sorry,' Marcus said, realising he had the perfect opportunity to make Aiden jealous. 'I left something with Charley, something I need. It's fine though, I can drop by and get it.'

Aiden's face fell as he muttered, 'You were with Charley?'

'Yeah, this morning. We went for a walk. Think she was glad of the company.'

'How was she?' Aiden hated that he had to ask Marcus, of all people, how Charley was doing. He hated himself more though, for not going to check on her.

'She looked terrible when I first showed up. Think the fresh air did her some good – she was trying to convince me to spend the day with her.'

'Right.' The sly grin which was plastered across Marcus's face riled Aiden. Who did he think he was?

'I'd better go,' Marcus smirked, 'I'll tell Charley you were asking for her, shall I?'

'You do that.' The boys exchanged a hostile look before heading in opposite directions.

Aiden hated Marcus with an absolute passion, but Marcus hated him more.

As Charley pushed open her front door, a wave of nausea washed over her. She immediately felt out of breath and her limbs began to ache.

'What's wrong with you?' Jess asked as she peered over the back of the sofa. 'You look worse than you did before.'

'I was fine a minute ago,' Charley stammered, clutching the door frame for support. 'Why aren't you at school?'

Jess shrugged. 'I have a sore stomach.'

'You didn't mention that earlier.'

'Sorry, Mum,' Jess said sarcastically, turning around to avoid Charley's stare.

'Speaking of Mum, did you tell her?'

'Tell her what?'

'That you weren't going to school.'

'Charley, quit bugging me. And don't tell her, okay? Or Dad. You know what they're like.'

'Jess, you can't ask me to lie to them.'

'Why not? You do, all the time.'

'I don't–'

'Leave it, Charley, please. I really don't feel like a lecture.'

'Fine. I'm going back to bed.'

She stood for another minute or so before leaving the room, glancing back at Jess who was now glued to the telly. Her sister really was changing, and fast.

She climbed the stairs, stopping halfway to catch her breath again. She felt horrendous. She reached for her pocket, wanting to call the doctor to try and arrange an appointment – as much as she hated doctors, she was going to have to go see one. All she wanted to do was feel better. But as she reached down, she noticed Marcus's coat, still wrapped around her shoulders. She hadn't even realised she was still wearing it. Shrugging it off, she made her way up the rest of the stairs and into her room, throwing the jacket down on her bed.

'Crap,' she muttered, as the contents of his pocket fell out across the duvet. Nothing exciting: a Snickers wrapper, some loose change and a photo, landing face down, writing scribbled across the back.

'Charley?' Jess called, her footsteps suddenly sounding on the stairs. 'She's in her room, second door on the left.'

'Thanks.' A second voice, deeper. Male.

Before he had time to knock, Charley pulled open the door.

'Marcus,' she smiled.

'Hey, Charley. Sorry to bother you again. I left my . . .' His voice tailed off as he saw his belongings scattered across the bed sheet.

'Jacket?' Charley said, finishing his sentence for him.

'Why were you going through my stuff?'

'Oh, I wasn't . . . I flung your coat and the stuff fell out. I was just going to . . .' She stopped talking as Marcus pushed past her, shoving his things back inside the pockets.

'Did you look at any of it?'

'What?'

'Did you look at it?' His tone was no longer kind and Charley found herself taking a step back.

'No.'

'Okay, good.' He pushed a hand through his hair and sighed. 'I'm sorry, Charley. I'm just big on privacy. I didn't mean to snap at you.'

'It's fine.'

'No,' Marcus shook his head, 'it's not. Let me make it up to you.'

'I'm tired, Marcus. I think you should go.' Now it was Charley's turn to be blunt.

'All right, some other time, yeah?'

'We'll see,' she replied, holding the door open.

'Charley–'

'Goodbye, Marcus.'

'Okay,' he murmured, 'I get it. I'm going.'

He walked from the room, turning back once he reached the stairs, but Charley didn't see – the door was already closed.

TEN

'Chambers, wait up.' She didn't need to turn round. She recognised him from his voice alone. That and the fact that no one else called her Chambers.

'Free to talk now, are we?' Charley huffed, pushing open the doors from the science department.

'Don't be like that. I'm sorry I didn't come see you.'

'It's fine, Aiden.'

'No, it's not. I know I should've swung by. I did call though – Abbie gave me your number.'

'You did, that's true. And I didn't even have the decency to phone you back.'

'I don't mind about that. I just don't want you being mad at me.'

'I'm not mad. Well, at least not anymore.' She slowed her pace and glanced up at him. He looked tired.

'That's a relief. What with Marcus taking the time to call round, I know I didn't win myself any brownie points.'

Charley stiffened at the mention of his name, which Aiden noticed immediately.

'He told me he was with you. Everything go okay?'

'I don't know. I'm not sure what to think of him to be honest. One minute he's really nice, the next he's storming into my room and grabbing his stuff, face like thunder.'

'He did what?'

'Accused me of rifling through his pockets, invading his privacy. I swear, the stuff fell out of his coat. I didn't even look at it.'

'I knew there was something off about him, the son of a–'

'I'm not saying he's a bad guy,' Charley quickly interrupted, 'he just took me by surprise. I didn't expect him to lose it like that.'

'Even so, Chambers, he had no right. In your own house of all places. You don't have to defend him.'

'I guess not. Can we talk about something else? I don't really want to spend all day thinking about Marcus.'

'Gladly,' Aiden scoffed as they walked through the main doors, out into the courtyard. It had been a long day and Charley was more than ready to get as far away from school as she could.

'Did you manage to find anything about, you know . . .'

'I've not had much of a chance so far. Sorry, I've been dealing with family . . . issues, shall we say.'

'Everything all right?'

'As all right as it ever is. Don't worry about it. How are you feeling now anyway?'

'Don't change the subject,' Charley grinned, batting him softly with the back of her hand. 'You sure everything's okay?'

'Everything's fine, I promise. How are you feeling?' he repeated.

She'd only been back at school a day but if she was honest, she felt better there than she did at home. Her constant headaches had finally subsided and she was no longer being sick.

'I'm good. Well, better at least.'

'It is a bit of a coincidence.'

'What? Me having some strange episode, wrecking the house, then throwing up for a week.'

'That's one way of putting it,' he laughed, finding her hand and squeezing it. Charley was sure she stopped breathing – just for a second.

'So where are you taking me?' she asked. 'I could do with a distraction, and you're my number one choice.'

'Oh, is that so? I don't know if I can match the bridge jumping scenario. Are you sure I'll suffice?'

'Hmm, I'm pretty sure you'll do.' She grinned at him cheekily and he gently wrestled her into his arms.

'Come on then, Chambers. Let's see if I can live up to your expectations.'

Charley let out a deep breath as they finally reached the top of the hill. They'd been climbing for ages, and she was exhausted.

Once she managed to catch her breath and finally straighten up, she saw why Aiden had suggested they come here. The view was spectacular. The sun was glistening, its rays pouring down across the fields and trees before them. She could vaguely see the houses she knew so well, but they were like toys now, tiny speckles scattered far below.

'Aiden, this is amazing.'

'Nice, eh?'

'It's beautiful.'

'You never climbed a hill before?' he joked, and then became serious as she slowly shook her head. 'Really?'

'Nope. At least, I don't think I have. Maybe my parents took me when I was younger, but–'

'If you can't remember, it doesn't count.' He wandered across to a large rock, waving Charley over and offering her a seat.

'Thanks,' she smiled, sitting down, hoping he would do the same. He did.

'No problem.' Their eyes met for a second and Charley thought he was about to . . .

'Look,' he said, gesturing into the distance.

Okay, maybe not.

'Look at wh–? Wow.'

Charley gaped at the huge rainbow which was now stretching across the sky. She'd never seen one like it, the colours so bright she could have sworn somebody had painted them against a pale blue background.

'It hasn't even been raining.'

'Who needs rain when you have magic?' he smiled.

'You did this? Aiden, it's–' He didn't let her finish.

'Shh.' His fingers stroked her cheek, finding a stray hair and brushing it away. His other hand moved gently down her arm, touching her elbow, her wrist, then down to the small of her back. They didn't move for a moment, the space between them larger than either wanted.

And then it was gone, the gap filled as he leaned forward and kissed her. A different kiss from the last time – more intense, more passionate. The first kiss they'd shared had been perfect, but it had felt almost – pretend, as if she'd imagined the whole thing. This kiss was heated, powerful, like neither of them had ever wanted anything as much before in their lives.

'So, am I a good enough distraction?' Aiden asked as Charley finally pulled away.

'The best.'

She moved forward so her forehead was resting on his. They were so close, she could feel his hot breath on her face, making her want to kiss him again. Kiss him and never stop.

Instead, he tilted her head and kissed her softly on the cheek, withdrawing slightly so he could look at her properly.

'You're pretty awesome, Chambers.'

'You aren't too shabby yourself, Cunningham.' He gave her a sarcastic smile before grabbing her hand and pulling her up.

'Well, since we're up here, I might as well teach you some tricks.'

'Tricks? What are we, circus performers?'

'Well, we are magicians,' he teased, leaning forward and pulling a coin out from behind her ear. 'See.'

'Funny. You know what I mean. Tricks are for magicians you see at holiday parks and kids' birthday parties. I thought we were proper magicians.' She knew mocking him would probably end badly, but instead of huffing he simply shook his head and smiled, tossing the coin back at her.

'Okay. Spells. Better?'

Charley laughed. 'I guess so, Merlin.'

'Can you stop being cheeky for one minute?'

'You don't make it easy,' she said, still giggling. Aiden crossed his arms, giving her a stern but playful look. 'All right, all right. I'll behave.'

'Thank you.'

'Teach me how to make a rainbow then.' Aiden grunted, causing Charley to frown. 'What's so funny?'

'Chambers, you're still a beginner. There's no way you can do something like that yet.'

'Why not? Are you saying I'm not good enough?' The doubt in his voice insulted her.

'Not at all. I'm saying it's a big spell and it uses a lot of energy. You have to build up to bigger spells.'

'Aiden, I turned my house upside down the other day. I'm sure I can handle big.'

'And look how sick it made you. Absolutely not.'

Charley sighed, but realising he wasn't going to relent, she gave up and agreed.

'Okay. What are you going to show me then?'

'How to get rid of the rainbow.'

'Why? I don't want to get rid of it, it's beautiful.'

'Yes, it is. But as you said, it hasn't been raining. People might wonder where it came from.'

'People being your parents?' Aiden clammed up at the mention of his mother and father.

'No–'

'Come on, Aiden. Normal people wouldn't usually go about scrutinising the sky. You don't want them to see, do you?'

Aiden let his head drop for a second, giving himself time to think. What should he tell her? How much should he give away?

'If they found out I'd been using magic so . . .

irresponsibly, as they would put it, let's just say all hell would break loose. And that's an understatement.'

'Wait . . . they know you're–'

'Yep.'

'Are they?'

He frowned. 'What?'

'Magicians.'

'You ask too many questions, Chambers.'

'Can you blame me?'

'No. But that doesn't mean I'm going to answer them all. Now, come and stand in front of me.'

Charley reluctantly did as he asked, her head now swimming with questions. Who were his parents? Did they have powers? What else were they hiding?

'Okay. Give me your hand.' Aiden placed her palm down on his, closing his fingers around it. 'Empty your head.'

'Easier said than done,' Charley scoffed.

'It won't work unless you concentrate. Focus.'

Charley closed her eyes and tried to think of nothing, which seemed just about impossible. She began picturing everything and everyone: Abbie, her parents, her school, Jess, Marcus . . .

She tried to forget them all, picture black, darkness – nothingness. She imagined a dark hole, so deep it was impossible to see the bottom. It seemed to go on forever, stretching further and further away. She visualised herself standing above it, hovering over the edge. She was balanced half on land, half off, her toes sticking out over the abyss. She wobbled, then somehow managed to steady herself.

Easy, Charley, she thought, inching round the rim of

the chasm. Looking up, she saw Aiden standing to her left, too far away to reach.

Aiden? What are you doing here? He didn't answer, instead nodding and pointing to the right. She turned to see Marcus, perched on her other side.

Marcus? He waved her towards him.

Charley, come here. Take my hand. He started moving, slowly getting closer.

No. I'm not meant to. Aiden? She turned to see Aiden, swaying over the pit. He lost his balance and fell, landing on a small ledge just a few feet below.

Aiden! Her first instinct was to dive on to the ledge after him, but she was momentarily distracted as she heard the other voice yell out.

Charley, help! Marcus had also fallen, and was now clinging on to a twisted branch, his life hanging in the balance. If he fell, he would most certainly die.

Charley, don't trust him. It was Aiden's voice this time, but something wasn't right.

You called me Charley . . . She was getting more confused by the second. Aiden called her Chambers. He always called her Chambers.

Charley, help me. This time, Marcus.

She didn't know what to do. She stood between the two feeling completely helpless.

Charley, don't be stubborn and help me. Marcus again, only not Marcus. Charley could tell: the way he looked at her, the way he spoke. She didn't know what was happening, but she knew one thing for sure, or at least, she thought she did. Marcus was Aiden, and Aiden was Marcus.

Before she could change her mind, she quickly made her way to where Marcus was hanging.

Take my hand. He did as she asked, scrambling with his feet as she pulled him to safety. He reached the top and fell to the ground, panting as Charley checked he was okay.

Aiden was still on the ledge, which was now beginning to crumble. He looked over at her, his eyes pleading. Brown eyes. Marcus's, not Aiden's. Then the ledge gave way.

Aiden began to fall. When he looked back up at her, slowly plunging into the darkness, all she saw in his eyes was fear. Big, deep, blue eyes.

Aiden?

Too late, Charley. She turned to see Marcus, grinning wickedly beside her. *He's gone, and it's your fault.*

You tricked me.

She turned back to the gaping hole, looking only at blackness. Marcus had played her and she'd fallen for it. How could she not have known?

Aiden . . .

A tear rolled down her cheek, her heart breaking as the reality set in. Aiden was dead, and she was to blame.

Soft rain drops began to fall, quickly turning into larger droplets. Before she knew it, she was standing in a hail storm, icy bullets bouncing off her skin.

'Chambers. Chambers!'

Charley opened her eyes to see the fields and houses she recognised, a dark grey cloud covering the sky.

'What just happened?' she asked, pulling her hood up over her head. It was pouring.

'Well, you got rid of the rainbow . . . and the blue sky. And any sign that it was a nice day. You did it though, well done.'

'Aiden, I don't remember doing any of it.'

ELEVEN

'What do you mean, you don't remember?' Aiden asked, his cheeks glistening as heavy raindrops ran down his face.

'I don't know how I did it, any of it. I felt like I was somewhere else.'

She didn't want to tell him about her vision, if you could call it that. Even the thought of it was so terrifying, she couldn't bring herself to say it aloud.

'I'm scared, Aiden. Can we get down?'

'Slow down, Chambers. You're okay. Talk to me.'

'I want to get down. It's raining, I'm soaking and,' – she was starting to panic – 'I just want to get down, okay?'

Aiden lifted his hand and, as he began to lower it, the rain slowed to a light drizzle. The grey clouds began to part and the sun poked through, spreading a little light back over the town.

'Rain's off. Now tell me what happened.'

Charley took a deep breath, trying to figure out what she was going to say. She pieced the words together in her head, but none of them seemed acceptable: I went into some weird daydream where there was a never-ending black hole; you were there; Marcus was there; you were him and he was you; he tricked me . . . I let you die.

None seemed appropriate, so being Charley, she said them anyway.

'I drifted off into some sort of dream. I don't know how, I was just trying to concentrate, clear my mind. I was alone at first, but then you were there, so was Marcus. I was in the middle and you both fell and I had to save you. You, Aiden, I was trying to save you. But I think Marcus was in your body, and you were in his. I'm not sure, but he tricked me and I saved him and I let you die.'

Aiden stared at her blankly, before smiling and running his hand down her arm.

'It wasn't real, Chambers.'

'But it felt real. And I was awake. How do you–?'

'You were probably just trying too hard. Honestly, don't worry about it.'

But she was worried. Even his gentle touch and the calmness of his voice couldn't stop that. It wasn't until now that Charley realised how much she cared for Aiden. Despite his bossy manner and quick temper, his mysteriousness and his secretive side, she couldn't imagine him not being there. She never wanted him not to be there.

Marcus sat at the desk in his room, frantically scribbling in his journal. Every few minutes he would curse, score out what he'd written and start again. There was a large pile of crumpled paper sitting next to his chair, quickly growing as he discarded yet another scrunched-up page.

'You wanting supper, Marcus?' his father called from outside the door.

'No thanks, I'm busy.'

'You're always busy. You still need to eat.'

'Later. I have to finish this.'

He heard a sigh, and then a mumbled 'All right, son,' before his dad stalked off down the hall.

'Later. I have to . . .' Before he'd finished the sentence, his hands were at his face, muffling the screams that came from his aching throat. Screams that his parents were more than used to.

Charley knocked the door several times before turning back down the path. She wanted to see Abbie so much, but she had no idea where she could be.

'Charley, hey.' She turned to see Abbie and her mother making their way down the street, stacks of bags in hand.

'Hey, you need some help?'

Charley rushed up and took a bag from each of them, trying desperately to avoid the disapproving look she was getting from Carol. She hadn't spoken to Abbie's mum since the incident with the painting.

'You coming in?' Abbie asked as her mum, with difficulty, unlocked the front door.

'If you don't mind.' Charley discreetly nodded towards Carol; she didn't want to cause any problems.

'Not at all. Right, Mum?'

'Of course, Charley. Just make sure the pair of you leave the artwork alone.' Charley's cheeks quickly turned scarlet, but Abbie just laughed, ushering her friend inside.

'How you doing, Charles? You look beat,' Abbie said once they were safely inside her bedroom.

'That's your way of saying I look like crap.'

'No it isn't. You just look . . . peaky.'

'Peaky?' Charley frowned.

'Yeah, peaky. You know–'

'I know what peaky means. I'm not peaky. I'm—'

'Beat?' Charley sighed and chucked a pillow at Abbie.

'All right, I'm beat. I have so much to tell you, I don't really know where to start.'

'At the beginning?' Abbie said, ripping open a packet of Jelly Babies and throwing a handful at Charley, who – despite being incredibly clumsy – somehow managed to catch them all.

'I'm not sure where the beginning is anymore,' Charley replied. With a sigh, she told her friend everything that had been happening.

'Jesus,' Abbie murmured, shoving the last of the Jelly Babies into her mouth. 'Your life is like something you'd see in a movie.'

Charley went on to tell her about the visit from Marcus, his strange behaviour and her confusion about how she felt towards him.

'I think you like him,' Abbie grinned.

'Marcus? No way. I mean I did, well I thought I did. When we jumped off the bridge–'

'Wait a minute. You did what?'

'Oh, right. I never told you about that, did I?'

Abbie raised her eyebrows, picking a gummy piece of sweet from her teeth. 'Must have slipped your mind.'

Charley quickly filled Abbie in on all the details, convincing her friend more and more that she had feelings for Marcus.

'I swear, I don't,' Charley said, 'there's something about him.'

'Yeah, something you like. Face it, Charles, you can't lie to me.'

'Yes I can. And I'm not. Anyway, it's not Marcus I like.'

'Of course. How are things with the wonderful Aiden Cunningham?'

Charley spent the next half hour rambling on about Aiden. She told Abbie about the hill walk, the rainbow, her vision. She explained how calm Aiden had been when she'd told him about it, and how as much as she wanted to, she couldn't shake the feeling that something bad was going to happen.

'I'm sure he's right. You're probably just reading too much into things.'

'Ugh, you're as bad as him,' Charley sighed, letting her head fall back on the bed.

They sat for a while, talking more about Charley's chaotic life – and Abbie's uneventful one – before Charley pushed herself up and started collecting her things.

'I better head home. Thanks for the chat, Abbs, I needed it.'

'Anytime. I'll chew your ear off sometime, you can return the favour.'

'It's a deal.'

'My life will have to get a tad more exciting first. No one wants to talk about school and homework, let alone hear about it.'

'You'd be surprised,' Charley smiled, 'I wouldn't say no to a bit of normality right now.'

'You'll figure things out. You always do.'

'I hope so. See you tomorrow.'

Charley closed the door and made her way outside. When Abbie was quite sure she was gone, she picked up her mobile and dialled a number, pressing the phone to her ear.

'Hey, it's me. You told me to call you when she left.'

Aiden walked down the long corridor, stopping at the sitting room door. His mother was resting in a large, olive-green armchair, a copy of *Jane Eyre* in hand. She didn't acknowledge him, but he didn't expect her to.

'You're reading that again?' he asked, crossing his arms and leaning against the door frame.

She didn't answer.

He stood for a moment, waiting, and then finally turned to leave. She couldn't say he hadn't tried.

'What do you think you're playing at?' Her tone was soft but cold. Even as a child, her voice alone had always been enough to send shivers down his spine.

'I was coming to talk to you. Am I not allowed to speak to my own mother?'

'You know very well what I'm talking about.'

'And what's that?'

Her eyes were fixed on him, her face severe. Tabitha Cunningham did not like games.

'I know what you're doing with that girl, Aiden.'

'Who, Charley? I like her, Mum–'

'I don't care if you like her. I told you before, it needs to end. Now.' She held his gaze for a second before looking back down to her book. 'And don't think I don't know it was you who was messing about with the elements today. Another reason you need to stay away from Charlotte Chambers.'

'It's Charley,' he snapped. 'And it wasn't her idea, it was mine. I was trying to help–'

'Well, you can stop trying to help her. I will not keep telling you. Keep your distance and stop being so careless. Do I make myself clear?'

Her mouth stretched into a thin line, her expression so fiery that no ordinary person would dare argue. But Aiden wasn't your average teenager. Even without magic, he was stubborn, opinionated and difficult, and above all else, he was Tabitha Cunningham's son, and that meant it was in his blood to react.

His arms tensed, the veins protruding as he clenched his fists. Aiden was almost always in control, but right now even he felt vulnerable.

Is this how Chambers feels all the time? he wondered.

'Yes,' he breathed, feeling a little more confident that he could contain his powers.

'Good,' she said sternly, just as the front door opened. 'Your father's home. Stay and say hello.'

'I'll pass. I've had enough pleasant conversation to last me the night.' His sarcasm irritated her, but before she could reply, he was gone, the sound of his distant footsteps the only indication that he'd been there at all.

'Darling?' came a deep voice from the doorway.

'Hello, Fergus.'

'How are you, dear?'

Tabitha sighed. 'Spectacular.'

Fergus frowned and simply said, 'Aiden?'

'Gone to his room.'

'I'll go–'

'He doesn't want to talk.' She closed her book and placed it on a small wooden table beside her.

'When does he ever want to talk?'

'This 'Charley' problem isn't going away.'

'We'll make it go away, Tabby. It'll be all right.'

'Well, you can think of something then. I have a headache, I'm going to bed.'

She got up from the chair and walked past her husband into the hall, stopping a few feet from the door. She glanced back at him and tried to smile. He could see it was forced.

Aiden was the spitting image of him, although blonder and slightly taller. Apart from the similar hair colour, her son didn't resemble her at all.

'Do something, Fergus.'

'I will.'

She nodded and then made her way down the hall.

'I'll try,' Fergus breathed once she was gone.

TWELVE

'Where are you taking me?' Charley asked as they made their way down the crowded street.

Aiden had insisted he was taking her out, mainly to distract her and stop her thinking about the recent hallucination. She'd barely slept for days, the image of Aiden falling into a never-ending pit haunting her every time she closed her eyes. He could tell her it meant nothing until the cows came home – she knew there was more to it. There had to be.

'So where do you want to go?' Aiden asked, gesturing to a row of cafés and restaurants. 'There's plenty, so take your pick.'

'I really don't mind. You can choose.'

'If you insist,' he said, linking his fingers through hers. Her dainty hand fitted perfectly inside his, like the last piece of a jigsaw puzzle. Like it was meant for his hand and his hand alone. She never wanted to let go. 'We'll grab something to eat, then go some place quiet. I want to show you some more–'

Before he finished speaking, Charley was already shaking her head frantically.

'No. No way, I can't.'

'Chambers, come on. You need to get past this. It was only a vision, it wasn't real.'

'Aiden–'

'I promise I won't let anything happen to you.'

'It's not me I'm concerned about,' she said in a low voice.

'You worry too much, Chambers. If you don't do this now, you're gonna get a complex about it.'

She knew he was right. She was already developing a phobia about using her powers. She had to get past it, deal with it somehow.

'All right,' she said reluctantly. 'I'll try, but I'm not promising anything. Dinner first though?'

'Of course.'

Eventually, they came to a halt outside a small Chinese restaurant. Aiden held the door open for her, but just as she was about to step inside, her phone rang.

'I better take this, it's Abbie.'

'Cool. I'll get a table.' Aiden let the door close behind him as he went to find a waiter. Charley pressed the accept button on her mobile, but just as she put the phone to her ear it rung off.

'Dammit,' she said, tossing it into her bag. She didn't have any credit to call back, so she pushed open the restaurant door instead, deciding she would ask Aiden if she could borrow his.

Before she could go in though, she heard a voice saying, 'Charley?'

A voice she knew far too well. She froze at the familiarity of it.

'Marcus,' she said, glancing back at him over her shoulder.

'It's good to see you,' he replied stiffly. 'Listen, I'd really like it if we could talk.'

'It's not good to see you, Marcus, and I don't want to talk.'

'I know I was completely out of line, Charley. I can't apologise enough. Please, at least let me try to explain.' She let her eyes wander to his face – his impeccable features, his big brown eyes. She immediately turned away, wishing she hadn't looked in the first place.

'I don't have time for this. I have–'

'I get it, you're busy. You want any excuse not to speak to me. I understand that. But if you change your mind, I'd really like to talk.'

With that, he was off, suddenly lost in the bustle of people who were rushing through the crowded street, shouldering one another out of the way.

Charley stood for a moment, mulling over what he'd said. Should she give him another chance? A voice in her head quickly interrupted her thoughts.

Are you for real? Do you remember your vision, the one where Marcus tricked you?

But–

The one where he tricked you so that Aiden would die?

Aiden said it was a load of nonsense. What was she meant to believe?

It's your funeral–

'Shut up,' Charley said aloud, causing a few passersby to look in her direction.

Great, she thought, now I'm talking to myself.

She shoved open the door and walked in, deciding to put Marcus out of her mind completely – for the time being anyway.

'Chambers,' she heard Aiden call, 'over here.'

She took a deep breath and smiled, walking over to where he was sitting.

'Everything okay?' he asked, passing her a menu.

'Of course, why wouldn't it be?'

'I dunno . . .' He gave her a puzzled look. 'How's Abbie?'

Right, she was meant to be speaking to Abbie. 'Yeah, she's fine. Just wanted to ask my advice on . . . washing machines.'

Washing machines? That's the best you could come up with?

'Why?' Aiden snorted, closing his menu and nodding to a nearby waiter. Charley watched him intently; he looked a lot older than sixteen.

'What?' she said, momentarily distracted. 'Oh, right. Yeah, her machine broke. They need a new one.'

'And you were the best person to ask?' He raised an eyebrow and looked at her doubtfully.

'Apparently so. The waiter's coming, can we just order, please?'

The waiter took Aiden's order, then turned to Charley who quietly mumbled, 'I'll have the same.'

'You all right, Chambers? You're awfully quiet.'

'I'm okay. I'm just . . . you're right. I need to get over whatever issues I have. I need to try and use my powers again.'

'You've changed your tune.'

'I can't let the fear of what was probably nothing, stop me from exploring something so wonderful. I have this amazing gift, it would be foolish not to take advantage of it.'

'That a girl,' he said, giving her a knowing smile.

After they'd eaten, Aiden paid the bill, refusing to take any money from Charley. Once they were outside, he took her hand and led her away from the restaurant. There was a path behind the buildings that led down to the boathouse, and it was normally deserted.

'So what will I try?' she asked timidly, immediately feeling anxious.

'Whatever you like,' Aiden said, taking a seat on the edge of the dock. 'There's no one around, and I think it might be better if you judge this one for yourself. I don't want to interfere.'

'You won't be interfering. I don't know if I can do it on my own. What if–?'

'I'm right here, Chambers. If anything happens . . .' He paused as she looked at him, her bright eyes pleading. He could see how scared she was. 'I'm right here,' he repeated, and she gave him a slight nod.

Ready, Charley.

She turned away from him and began breathing deeply, finding it somewhat soothing. Her concerns began to slowly seep away, and she let her mind wander – only a little though. She was still terrified of falling too deep into her own imagination.

Raising her hands, she pictured the sea; a far cry from the dirty lake that stretched out in front of her, but more pleasant to visualise.

'You doing okay?' she heard Aiden murmur, cautiously though, as he didn't want to disturb her.

'So far.'

He watched her for a while, still unsure of what she was trying to do. He thought about stepping in, telling her to take a break, but decided to leave it, at least for a moment or so more.

Just as he was finally about to intervene, he noticed the water beginning to ripple. He took a step back and watched as it began to pucker, small waves forming at the edge of the pier.

She's doing it, he thought.

As the waves got bigger, forming a pattern over the water's shiny surface, a small whirlpool developed in the middle, directly in front of where Charley was standing. She raised her hands higher and the vortex got wider, deeper, white foam frothing at the edges.

Where's she going with this? Aiden frowned, beginning to worry that she was pushing herself too far. A few small waves were one thing – a whirlpool was something else entirely.

'Chambers,' he said, taking a step towards her.

'I'm all right.'

He walked over so he was standing next to her; her eyes were open and the smile on her face was infectious. She looked euphoric.

'I'm doing it, Aiden. Look.'

She lifted her hand and swept it to the right. A wave crashed down in front of them, sending water up over the dock and soaking their shoes.

'And this . . .' She moved her arms apart and the whirlpool got wider again. She then brought them closer, and when she touched her hands together, the whirlpool was gone, the bubbling foam the only evidence that it had ever been there at all.

'I had every faith in you,' Aiden smiled.

'Don't lie. Part of you thought I was gonna crash and burn again.'

Aiden looked at the ground before glancing back at her and smiling, just ever so slightly.

'All right, a little,' he said, 'but that doesn't mean I didn't believe in you. I've been where you are. I know how difficult it can be.'

'What if it was just a one-off?' she said, suddenly beginning to worry.

She turned to face the tall trees that stood to one side of the water, stretching up towards the beautiful steel-blue sky.

Charley looked at the trees, and they immediately began to sway gently in the wind. The longer she gazed, the more they shook, crisp leaves falling and landing in the lake.

'I think you've got it down to a tee,' Aiden smiled, taking her hand and pulling her close. She smelled like peppermint.

'I hope so.'

'How d'you do it anyway?' Aiden asked. 'The water?'

'I just thought of a mini hurricane,' Charley giggled, twisting a lock of hair around her index finger.

God, she's cute, Aiden thought to himself.

'How do you do it?' she asked him. 'You seem to have it all mastered.'

'Do what? Magic? It's all kind of second nature now. I used to . . . nah, never mind. It's dumb.'

'Tell me,' Charley said, nudging his arm. 'Please.'

'It's stupid, Chambers. Forget it.'

'It won't be stupid to me. Please, I really want to know.' She clasped her hands, smiling, and Aiden sighed and gave in to her pleas.

'All right, but if you laugh, we're done.'

'Deal.'

'When I was learning, like you are now, I used to struggle–'

'I know the feeling,' Charley interrupted.

'Way worse than you. I was . . . pretty out of control, put it that way.'

'How do you mean?'

'Let's just say, bad things happened when I was around. I couldn't grasp it, any of it.'

'So what did you do?'

Charley gazed at him. He was tall and slim, but muscular too. He looked as though he could squeeze every last breath out of her if he tried. She looked into his eyes; kind eyes, possibly the kindest she'd ever seen. So deep . . .

Full of secrets, probably.

'I used to pretend I was a puppet.'

'A puppet?' Charley gave him a quizzical look.

'Yeah. Told you it sounds daft. But it really helped me. Think about it. A puppet's stuck, tied down with strings. They can't move the way they want, they can't control their actions. They can't think for themselves.'

'Puppets don't think, full stop,' Charley said in jest.

'Shut up, Chambers.'

'Sorry.'

'That's how I felt. I couldn't control the things happening around me. I couldn't control myself. It was like someone, or something, had taken over my mind. They were pulling the strings, deciding what was going to happen.

'It wasn't until I really thought about it, really thought it through, that I discovered ways to deal with it. I had to cut the ties to regain the power. My power.'

'I never knew you were so cryptic.'

Aiden smiled, but it wasn't his usual smile – it seemed false, somehow.

'Thank you for telling me,' she said. 'And just for the record, I don't think you're stupid.

'Well I appreciate that. You wanna head back?'

'Sure thing, Pinocchio,' Charley giggled.

'Pinocchio?'

'Yeah. Puppet, no strings . . .' She shot him a mischievous smile and began running up the grassy bank, Aiden in close pursuit.

THIRTEEN

Marcus woke with a start, panting desperately as he wiped the sweat from his damp forehead.

He'd had another nightmare, the same one he always had. She was back – Bud – she was alive, and she was standing right in front of him. He'd reached out, the way he always did, but as his hand got closer, she got further away. He'd started running, determined not to lose her again. Not this time. But it was no use; the closer he got, the faster he ran, it was never enough. When he was finally too tired to run any further, she would stop. Her eyes were open wide, full of pain, full of disappointment.

'Help me, Marcus,' she would say.

'I can't reach you, Bud.'

'Marcus, help me. I'm scared. Don't let it hurt me.'

'I'm trying . . . I can't get to you!'

This time when he'd tried to run, his legs had buckled beneath him. It didn't matter what he did, the dream was always the same.

'Goodbye, Marcus.'

Those two words broke his heart every time he heard

them. And hearing them every night was tearing him apart.

'Oh, Bud,' he murmured, sitting up in his bed and wiping away a stray tear as it ran down his cheek.

He pushed his hair back and made for the door, heading towards the bathroom at the end of the hall.

'Morning, son,' came the cheery voice, just as he was about to close the bathroom door. 'How are you?'

'I'm fine. Going for a shower.' With that, he shut the door and climbed into the cubicle, turning the dial as far as it would go. He wanted a hot shower. The hottest. It always made him forget.

'Nice to talk to you, too,' he heard his father say before carrying on down the hall.

Marcus gasped as the scalding water began to pour from the showerhead above him. He should be used to it by now – it was becoming a daily ritual – but still, the shock of the boiling water on his skin reinvigorated his senses.

When he finally emerged from the shower, he had completely lost track of time. He'd spent so long baking himself that his skin was now a deep shade of scarlet and he was starting to feel disorientated.

He fumbled for his toothbrush and, without much success, tried to squirt a dollop of toothpaste on to the end of it.

'Marcus, there's a visitor coming to the door,' he heard his mum call from outside. 'I think it's for you.'

'What . . . who?' He spun around but, no longer having the sink to steady himself with, collapsed on to the hard, marble floor.

'What are you doing in there?'

'Nothing,' he called, his voice hoarse, 'I'll be out in a minute.' He heard her footsteps making their way back towards the kitchen.

Get a grip, he told himself, before struggling to his feet with the aid of the towel rail. He splashed a handful of cold water on his face and quickly grabbed a towel from the rack, wrapping it round his waist and heading towards the front door.

'Charley?' he frowned when he saw her. 'What are you doing here?'

Her eyes ran over his body and her cheeks immediately turned pink.

'Hey,' she mumbled, 'I was just passing. I, eh . . .'

She looked down at the ground. Why did he have to be practically naked?

'I wanted to . . . to chat. See if we could, I don't know, work things out? We didn't leave things in the best way.'

'No, that's true.'

Marcus held on to the door frame, wheezing slightly. He felt better than before – probably due to the fresh air – but he was still a bit light-headed.

'You okay?' Charley asked, noticing him flag.

'Yeah, I'm fine. Spent a bit too long in the shower, that's all. Why, am I not looking too hot?' He raised an eyebrow playfully; he couldn't resist joking with her.

'Actually, that's exactly how you look.'

'Ooh, Charley, buy me dinner first, eh?' He managed a smile, and she couldn't help but return it, gently punching his arm in fun.

'Marcus, you're roasting.' This time she put her palm flat on his shoulder. She could only keep it there for a few seconds, it was that hot.

'Told you,' he said, 'too long in the shower.'

'Your skin's on fire . . .'

He looked down into her eyes. They were magnificent. He thought of Bud's eyes, how they'd pleaded with him in his dream. Charley's were just as glorious, similar but at the same time very different. There was something enchanting about Charley's eyes, whereas Bud's had been innocent – full of hope, wonder . . . disappointment.

He wanted to stand there all day and gaze into them, but he knew if he didn't sit down, he'd have more to worry about than just his temperature.

'I've got a few things to do before school, Charley. Can we meet up for lunch or something?'

'Sure, I'll see you in registration.' She turned to go, pausing on the bottom step. 'I hope you feel better.'

'Thanks,' he said. He watched her go. His eyes followed her until she was finally out of sight, and then he closed the door.

'Charles, you big scrubber. Two guys at one time? I would never have taken you for a man-eater.'

Charley glared at Abbie across the table as they both sat in the cafeteria, shoving chocolate biscuits into their mouths.

'Shut up, it's not like that. Aiden's helping me with . . . you know. And Marcus is, well, Marcus. I know he was a prat, but I don't think he meant to be.'

'And is that all Aiden is? Someone to help you with your powers?'

'Shush, keep it down,' Charley said, spinning around to see if anyone had heard.

'Charles, calm down. No one's here. Now, stop changing the subject.'

Charley looked down at the table, but she could feel Abbie's eyes on her. She was her best friend, after all. She'd always been able to read her like a book.

'I like Aiden. I like him a lot. But I don't want things to get complicated. I'm just gonna take things . . . slow.'

Abbie raised her eyebrows. 'Oh yeah, sounds like you've been taking it real slow.'

Just as Charley was about to cram another Jaffa Cake into her mouth, Aiden appeared at the end of the table. His tie was hanging messily round his neck, and his hair looked as though it hadn't been brushed. Somehow, though, he looked perfect.

'Hey, lover boy,' Abbie smiled, winking cheekily at Aiden. Charley kicked her under the table.

'Abbie,' Aiden said, nodding in her direction but keeping his eyes firmly on Charley. 'Chambers.'

'Aiden,' Charley said sarcastically, pursing her lips at him.

Abbie looked like she might throw up. 'Get a room, you two. Or at least give me a bucket.'

'Someone's cheery this morning,' Aiden grunted.

'Well I was until you came along and ruined our conversation,' Abbie said in jest.

'What were you talking about that was so important then?' he asked.

'As a matter of fact, you. Now go away so Charley can finish talking about you behind your back.'

Aiden gave Charley a look, smiling as she began to blush.

'Okay, I'm going. I have to get to registration early anyway. Chambers, I'll catch up with you at lunch.'

'Actually, I . . .'

But it was too late. Before she could tell him who she was planning on meeting, he was gone.

'I'm glad I'm not you right now,' Abbie said, picking up another biscuit. Charley sighed. It was going to be a long day.

When the lunch bell finally rang, Charley packed her books away and headed to the canteen, searching the place for any sign of Aiden. She knew he wouldn't be happy she was meeting Marcus – far from it – but at least if she got a chance to explain things first, he might see it from her point of view.

Probably not. But she could try.

She wandered over to the vending machines and bought herself a can of Sprite, opening it and slurping the foam which was spilling from the top.

'Thirsty?' said a voice behind her.

She turned to see Marcus, leaning casually over the railing between them.

'Hey, how you feeling?' she replied with a smile.

His eyes seemed brighter than usual, and for a moment she couldn't remember why she'd been mad at him.

'Much better, thanks. Told you it was nothing to worry about.'

Charley smiled again, then glanced over her shoulder to have a last look for Aiden.

'Are you ready?' Marcus asked. 'Or were you wanting to wait for someone?'

She couldn't see him anywhere, and she couldn't wait all day. She spotted Abbie in one of the queues, filling her tray up with various cakes and pastries. They made eye contact and Charley mouthed, 'Do you never get full?' to her. Abbie shrugged her shoulders and helped herself to a plate of chips, grinning at Charley as she sprinkled a handful of cheese over them.

'I'm a growing girl,' she shouted, pointing to her non-existent hips.

'I'll be two seconds,' Charley said to Marcus, 'I just need to ask Abbie something before we go.'

She hurried over to her friend, who was already half way through her plate of chips.

'Aiden's not here yet,' she said, her eyes still searching the cafeteria.

'So? Just go, it'll be fine.'

'But I haven't had a chance to speak to him.'

Abbie glanced over at Marcus, who was waiting patiently where Charley had left him. 'Aiden will understand – eventually. Now go.'

Charley nodded, hugged her friend and walked back over to where Marcus was standing.

'Ready?' he asked.

'Yeah, let's go.'

Abbie watched them leave, still cramming food into her mouth as if she hadn't eaten for weeks. She was about to pay when she felt a hand on her shoulder.

'Hey, you seen Chambers?'

'Really, Aiden, you have impeccable timing,' she sighed, handing a pile of change to the grumpy dinner lady.

'What's that meant to mean?'

'She just left. I'll tell her you were looking for her.' She tried to step by him, but he moved in front of her, blocking the path.

'Where'd she go?'

'Out.'

'Who with?'

'Aiden, you know perfectly well who she's with. Now if you don't mind, I would really like to eat my lunch.'

Charley walked along beside Marcus, anxiously fidgeting with her fingers. She'd been so concerned about talking to Aiden that she hadn't even thought about what it would be like with Marcus. She was nervous. Very nervous.

'So, how's your day going?' Marcus asked, scratching the back of his head. Charley wasn't the only one on edge.

'It's been fine. Long, dull, you know.'

'Yeah, mine's been pretty much the same. Although I think Lucy may have been flirting with me in gym class earlier.'

'Wheeler?' Charley asked, raising an eyebrow.

'Yeah. She was in these tiny shorts and she kept . . .' Marcus looked at Charley who was now pulling a rather strange face. 'And you really don't wanna hear about that.'

'It's fine,' she laughed, 'I don't mind. Lucy's . . . fun.'

'Yeah, not really my type.'

Charley glanced up to see him gazing at her intently. She quickly turned away, unsure of what to say next.

She still couldn't work him out. She got this vibe from him telling her she could trust him – that she should trust him – but something was holding her back. At the same time, he somehow screamed danger.

'Charley, about the other day. I'm so sorry. I was completely out of line.'

'It's fine, really. Let's put it behind us. Just try and make sure it doesn't happen again.'

'It won't, I promise.'

They smiled, both glad the problem had been resolved.

'So . . . fancy another dip in the river?' Marcus joked.

'I think Aiden might freak,' Charley said without thinking.

Marcus's face immediately fell, but he kept quiet. She tried to work out what he was thinking, what he was feeling. Was he mad? Jealous? Intimidated, worried . . . ? She couldn't tell. She wanted to drop the matter, but she couldn't help herself.

'You don't like him, do you?' she asked, stopping just before the road. They hadn't even left the school grounds.

'Charley . . .' – he stuttered, his cheeks reddening – '. . . you know I like you.'

She stared at him for a few seconds, her mouth ever so slightly open. 'Oh,' was all she could manage, even though he'd told her before.

'I know you're with Aiden. But that doesn't stop me being insanely jealous. The guy doesn't know how lucky he is.'

The pair of them stood in awkward silence for a few minutes. This time, it was Marcus who was trying to read Charley.

'Where does this leave us?' she asked. 'Can we still be–?'

'Friends? Yes, I'm sure I can manage that. You can't blame me though, if I admire you from afar.'

Charley cocked her head to the side, a disapproving look on her face.

'Kidding,' Marcus smiled, holding his hands up. 'I'll behave.'

Just as they were about to carry on walking, Charley heard a voice that made her stomach tighten. The voice she'd been waiting for.

'Chambers!'

She let out a sigh. 'You're gonna have to give me a minute.'

Marcus stood patiently, waiting for Charley and Aiden to finish up their lovers' tiff, which didn't look like it was coming to a close any time soon. He was leaning against a wall, arms crossed and head down, trying not to eavesdrop. Or rather, trying to look as though he wasn't eavesdropping. Really, he wanted to hear every word.

Abbie appeared behind him clutching a giant bar of chocolate.

'Want a bit?' she offered, holding it out for him.

'Cheers,' he said, breaking a piece off and tossing it into the air, catching it in his mouth as it came back down.

'Show off,' Abbie grinned.

Meanwhile, Aiden and Charley were still arguing, Aiden failing to see things from Charley's perspective.

'I just wanted to put it all behind us,' she said, fidgeting nervously with the cuffs of her jacket.

'Why? He's bad news, you said so yourself.'

'It's my decision, Aiden. Please just accept it and–'

'Accept that you want to hang around with someone like him?'

'What is that suppose to mean?' Charley demanded.

'Nothing. Never mind. You do what you want,

Charley.' That was the first time she'd ever heard him call her by her first name.

He must be mad.

'No, go on. Tell me what you mean.'

She was so angry. She could feel the tension building up in her stomach, as though it were eating away at her insides. She couldn't stop.

'Don't walk away from me, Aiden,' she yelled. He ignored her and carried on. 'I said, don't walk away from me!'

She felt as though her eyes were going to explode from their sockets. Her pulse was racing and she wanted to scream. Suddenly, there was a smash from above, then a second, and a third. Charley looked up to see glass falling from the street lamp beside her, shattering into tiny pieces as it hit the ground. The same thing happened with the lamp only a few feet away, and the one after that. Another smash, making an almost popping sound. Another one gone. Every lamp in the street blew, sending shards of glass everywhere.

Aiden was already on his way back, pulling Charley into his chest to protect her from the sharp splinters as they landed on the ground around them.

'It's okay, baby,' he whispered as he held her close.

Despite the chaos, Charley couldn't help but smile.

Marcus watched in astonishment, his mouth wide as he took in the scene which was unfolding before him.

'Jeez,' Abbie gasped, 'must be a bunch of dodgy fuses.'

Marcus smiled to himself. 'That was more than just a faulty circuit.'

শ্ল

'Lie back and pop your head on the pillow, pet. Now, I'll be back in a sec, you make yourself comfortable.'

Gina Lawson, the school nurse, turned to leave, but was momentarily blocked by Aiden, Marcus and Abbie, who were standing together in the doorway.

'Try to give her some space,' she said to them, in turn receiving a couple of grunts and a nod of the head.

'Thank you, Mrs Lawson,' Charley called as Gina left. Aiden moved to Charley's side, crouching down next to her, a concerned expression etched across his face.

'How are you feeling?' he asked.

'I'm okay,' Charley said, pushing herself up with her elbows. 'Could you go get me a can of juice? I think I need some sugar.'

'I'll come with you,' Abbie joined in, 'I need the toilet.'

'No way. I'm not leaving you.'

'What's going to happen to me, Aiden? I just want something sweet . . . for the shock. Honestly, I'm fine.'

'Not happening,' he said again, this time glancing over his shoulder.

'What do you think I'm going to do to her, Aiden?' Marcus sneered.

Aiden got to his feet and within seconds, had Marcus by the collar of his shirt. 'You ever touch her and I'll–'

'You'll do what?' Marcus said, pushing him off. 'You think I'd hurt her? What have I ever done to give you that impression?'

Charley couldn't stand it anymore. The arguing, the snide remarks. She got to her feet and pushed past them towards the door. 'I'll get my own bloody drink,' she snapped, storming out and letting the door fall shut behind her.

'Nice work, guys,' Abbie said, giving them the thumbs up. 'No, really, that was the perfect way to woo the girl you're both head over heels for.'

Aiden frowned, turning towards Marcus who was trying his best to suppress a smile.

'I'll go,' was all he said, walking out and leaving Abbie and Marcus alone.

Abbie stood for a moment before taking a seat on a nearby stool. 'God, boys are dumb,' she muttered, and Marcus laughed, nodding in agreement.

FOURTEEN

Charley reached the vending machine and slammed a coin into the slot. She thumped one of the buttons without looking and turned around to lean against it, sighing as she saw him coming out the corner of her eye.

'Don't start, Aiden, please.'

She heard a crash as her drink fell.

'Listen, I'm sorry. I was just concerned.'

She bent down to pick up her drink. Dr Pepper. She hadn't meant to press that. She hated Dr Pepper.

'Concerned about what? I am capable of taking care of myself. I get that you were worried, but–'

Aiden stepped forward and, looking around first, put a finger to her lips. 'It's not only about that, Chambers. I don't trust Marcus,' – Charley sighed – 'I know, old news. But what just happened, what he saw, yeah I'm worried.'

'But it could have been anything,' Charley said, 'lights go out all the time. Things break, blow up, smash; it's not that unusual.'

'Not like that, and you know it.'

Charley looked to the floor, thinking about everything that had occurred.

'I saw the look on his face. He knew it wasn't as simple as an electrical fault. I don't know how much he knows, but he's on to us. We have to be incredibly careful now.'

She tried to process the information, turn it all over in her head. Had it really been that obvious? She hadn't thought so. Maybe Aiden was right, maybe she was underestimating Marcus.

'Let's get out of here,' Charley said, already on her way towards the door.

'What, where?'

'Anywhere.'

Aiden ran to catch up with her. 'Your drink,' he said, pointing back towards the vending machine.

'Leave it. I can't stand Dr Pepper.'

Jess lay on her bed, flicking through the channels on her portable television. She'd always been bitter about the fact that Charley had been given a new flat screen T.V., while she was stuck with this piece of old junk.

'I bought you new trainers last week,' her mum had said, 'and a CD player the week before. You've had your share for a while.'

It still didn't seem fair though. The CD player was a tiny thing her mum had bought secondhand from a woman down the street. And the trainers . . . well, okay. Jess had to give her that one, the trainers hadn't been cheap. Even so, she still felt hard done by.

She continued channel flicking, unimpressed by the poor selection of programmes daytime television had to offer. She checked her watch. Nearly half two, which meant her mum would be home soon. Great, she thought to herself, switching off the T.V. and grabbing her coat. If she didn't want to be caught skipping school, she would have to make herself scarce.

She grabbed her bag and, not bothering to fasten it, hung her tie around her neck. She was about to head out when all of a sudden she stopped, letting her bag fall to the floor. All she could hear was a sharp, piercing sound, screeching in one ear and out the other. She dug the heels of her hands into her temples, screwing her face up at the high-pitched noise. Her vision began to blur as tears streamed down her face, creating a burning sensation on her cheeks. The noise got louder. The pain got sharper. And then she began to scream.

Charley sat beside Aiden, swinging her legs gently in time with his. He looked serious – still incredibly handsome – but he was definitely in a pensive mood. His breathing was laboured and she couldn't tell what he was thinking.

'Is he dangerous?' she asked quietly.

'I don't know. I can't be sure . . . It was just the look on his face – his eyes. They lit up in a way I've never seen before.' Charley wasn't sure what he meant. 'And besides, that kind of thing doesn't happen every day. You get angry, start yelling, and suddenly things begin to blow up.'

'You couldn't make it up,' Charley smiled weakly. Aiden caught on to the gloom in her voice; he could tell she was scared.

'I'm not going to let him hurt you, Chambers. Whatever happens, trust me, I'll keep you safe.'

'I know,' she whispered, and he pulled her close, stroking her cheek as she let her head rest on his shoulder.

'So, now are you going to keep your distance?' Aiden said, squeezing her arm. She was quiet for a moment.

'Maybe that's not the best idea.'

'What?' He tilted her chin up so they were face to face. He looked mad.

'Well, if he does know, or does suspect something, wouldn't it be better to carry on as normal? He'll know something's wrong if I suddenly start ignoring him.'

'He already knows something's wrong,' Aiden said sharply.

'And besides, this way I could find out what he knows – find out more about him. Let's face it, we don't have the first clue about the guy. This could work to our advantage.'

Although he hated to admit it, she did have a point.

'I don't like it, Chambers.'

'I know you don't.'

'I don't want to put you at risk.'

'You won't. I can look after myself.' Aiden raised his eyebrows. 'Anyway, I'm sure you'll never be far away,' she added with a smile.

He sighed. 'Okay, you win. I guess you're right. What is it they say? Keep your friends close, and your enemies closer.'

Charley didn't like thinking of Marcus as the enemy. It didn't feel right. But she knew things couldn't go back to the way they were before.

'Everything's happening so fast,' she said. 'I only just found out about all this . . . magician stuff,' – Aiden snorted – 'and now I'm about to go all double agent on the new kid because he may or may not know what I really am.'

'I wouldn't go as far as double agent,' Aiden laughed, 'more of a second-rate spy.'

'Excuse me? I'd make an excellent spy.'

'You'd make a terrible spy.'

She tried to keep a straight face, but it was almost impossible. Instead, she put a hand on his cheek and turned his face towards hers.

'Kiss me,' she whispered.

'As you wish,' he smiled.

They sat for a while – kissing, talking, holding each other – completely unaware of the eyes that were watching them from behind an oak tree in the distance.

A figure stood, hand resting on the soft bark of the tree trunk, observing the two teenagers closely. She stayed there for a while, her long hair blowing in the wind's soft breeze, until finally she gave up and began to walk back towards the road. Her boots made footprints in the soft mud and she bent down to wipe them clean with the cuff of her sleeve.

'Did you hear something?' Charley asked, as Aiden played with a strand of her tangled hair.

'Nope,' he murmured, 'was I supposed to?'

'No. I just thought I heard, I don't know . . . humming?'

'What?' he laughed, tugging a knot from the lock he'd been playing with.

'Must be my imagination.'

'Indeed,' he said. She snuggled into the crook of his arm. 'Don't get too comfy.'

'Why?' She sat up again, wondering what he was up to.

'We're jumping. You ready?'

Charley looked up, her eyebrows coming together as she frowned unintentionally at him. 'I thought you said jumping from here was stupid?'

'It was when you were with Marcus.'

'Aiden–'

'Come on, you don't think I'm going to let him have all the fun, do you?'

She thought about it for a second. It was the first time all day that he wasn't mollycoddling her. He was telling her to do something daring – something dangerous.

'On the count of three?' she said excitedly. Aiden nodded and she began to count. 'One, tw–'

And then they were away, falling from the edge, hand in hand. As they hit the water, a huge clap of thunder sounded in the sky, and then it began to pour.

'Look to the left. Good girl, now the right, please. Excellent, now follow the torch. Again. Smashing, I think that will just about do.'

'So what's your verdict?' Linda asked the doctor as Jess sat quietly on the end of her bed.

Linda had come home to find her daughter unconscious on the floor, pulse racing and eyes shut, though she could see the frantic movement underneath. When Linda had tried to wake her, Jess had begun to shake, as if having some sort of fit.

'To be honest, I can't say. Everything seems normal.'

'She was burning up,' Linda said, shaking her head at his lack of concern. 'She was having a seizure, I watched it myself. You must be able to give her something.'

'How can I prescribe her medication, Mrs Chambers,

if there is nothing to be cured? She seems perfectly healthy. If you have any further questions though, please don't hesitate to call me.'

Linda sighed as she let him out, cursing as she shut the front door.

'I'm fine, Mum,' Jess said from the top of the stairs. 'Please don't worry.'

'Jessica . . .' Linda stopped, wondering what it was she had intended to say. 'Go lie down and I'll make you some soup.'

'Are you mad?'

'I'm tired, Jess.' Without another word, she made her way to the kitchen, grabbing a can of chicken soup from the cupboard and filling the kettle with water. Just as she was about to spoon some coffee into a mug, Charley bounded through the door, soaked to the skin, strands of wet hair stuck to her rosy cheeks.

'Hello, Mother dearest,' she chirped happily, grabbing a biscuit from the tin.

Linda did not return the greeting. Instead, she made her coffee, handed Charley the tin opener and said, 'Heat your sister some soup up, will you? I need some air.'

She slipped her shoes on and wandered out the back door, coffee in hand, leaving Charley standing, bewildered.

'What was that about?' she said to herself, pulling a face and putting the soup into the microwave. Once it was ready, she carried it up the stairs, cursing herself for not bringing a towel as the scorching bowl began to burn her fingers.

'Ow, ow, ow. Jess, open the door!'

'Leave me alone,' Jess called from inside.

Charley wasn't waiting; her hands felt like they were on fire. She managed to turn the handle using her elbow and shoved the door open, hurrying into the room to put the soup down.

'What did I just say?' Jess asked, scowling at her from the bed.

'Don't choose now to be stubborn. I just got blisters helping you.'

'I never asked for soup.'

'Well, I got asked to make it, so the least you could do is say thank you.'

Charley sighed. Why did her sister always have to be so difficult? They'd been so close once, years ago, when they were both small and carefree. Jess had always looked up to Charley, idolised her in a way no one else ever had. There was only two years between them, although it used to feel like more. Now it was starting to feel like much less.

Charley couldn't remember when they'd grown apart, or why. It had just sort of happened with no real warning. They'd gone from being sisters, best friends, to two people who lived in the same house yet barely spoke. And when they did, well, it was usually to insult one another.

'Fine, eat it, don't eat it. See if I care.'

Charley tossed the spoon on to the floor and stormed towards the door, stopping for a second when she heard a sob.

Brilliant. Turn on the waterworks.

'What's wrong, Jess?' she asked sternly. 'You treat everyone like crap, yet you want to be treated like a bloody saint.'

'You aren't exactly an angel yourself,' Jess retorted.

'At least I'm not an ungrateful little cow.' Charley wanted to take the words back. She knew she couldn't, but she wanted to. Yet she said nothing. Neither of them spoke for a moment.

Eventually Jess whispered, 'It's not like that, Charley.'

'What is it like then? Tell me. Give me some idea of what it is you're going through. Because I'm dealing with a few stresses of my own, Jess, and I don't give you grief every time I set eyes on you.'

Charley's head was beginning to hurt. She didn't know why – the arguing, perhaps? She felt dizzy, and for a moment she was sure she was going to be sick. The nausea passed quite quickly, but it still left her feeling unsteady. She moved closer to Jess and took a seat on the end of the bed. She was still soaking, and for a moment she thought Jess was going to chide her for getting the duvet wet. She didn't.

'Talk to me,' Charley said, gently this time. 'What's wrong?'

'Nothing,' Jess murmured. 'Everything. Something's happening to me, and I don't know what.' Charley was listening more intently now – could Jess be . . . ? Surely she would have realised?

'Something, as in . . . ? I need a little more than that, Jess.'

'I don't know, weird things. I keep blacking out, having hot flushes, that sort of thing. I have no energy, my whole body aches, and the screaming . . . the screaming's the worst part.'

'Screaming? What do you mean, screaming?'

'Never mind.'

'Jess?'

'I want you to leave now, Charley. I need some sleep.'

'Jess, what are you talking about? You're scaring me now.'

'Go away, Charley. Thank you for the soup.'

'Jess . . .'

But Jess had already turned over, humming quietly to herself. Charley walked out of the room and closed the door.

FIFTEEN

The wind was strong and Charley struggled to keep the hair from her face, continuously tucking a long, persistent strand behind her ear which was determined not to stay there.

She'd phoned Aiden after leaving Jess, but when he didn't pick up, she'd gone for a shower instead, immediately relaxing as the hot water made contact with her ice-cold body. Why she kept insisting on jumping into water so painfully cold, she didn't know. Yet she didn't regret it for a second.

She scuffed her trainers on the edge of the kerb as she walked, pulling her large khaki parka tightly around her middle. It seemed to be taking forever to get to his house.

Eventually, she turned the corner to see Aiden's – or rather, his parents' – familiar mansion, standing looking like something from an Edwardian period drama. Charley climbed the steps to his front door and rapped the knocker several times, a heavy brass ring that probably cost more than the door itself. There was no answer, so she tried again. Still nothing.

She took out her phone and called him, putting it to her ear as she nosily peeked through his sitting room window.

Stop it, Charley, she thought, imagining his mother's face if she ever caught her snooping. The thought made Charley giggle. And then she thought better of it.

'Chambers?' His voice caught her off guard, even though she'd been the one to call him, and she just about toppled over the metal railing beside his door.

'Aiden! Hi,' she said, sounding flustered.

'What's up?'

'Where are you? I came round to see you but you aren't here. Well, obviously you know you aren't here, because you're, well, wherever you are. Where . . . are you?' She was aware of how stupid she sounded, but sometimes she was just incapable of forming a coherent sentence around him.

'I'm busy at the moment, can it wait? I'll call you when I get back.'

'It's pretty important. I guess it can wait though.'

'Okay, I'll call you.'

'All right, bye–' Before she could finish, the phone went dead. 'Nice talking to you too,' she said, making her way back down the steps and up the street, leaving the Cunningham residence behind.

'Hello, dear,' Mrs Gibbons said, 'looking for Abbie?'

Charley smiled sweetly and nodded. 'Yes, please. Is she home?'

'I'm afraid not. She left about an hour ago.'

'Did she say where she was going?'

Carol laughed. 'Abbie? Tell me where she's going?

That'll be the day. I'd give her a ring if I were you, that girl could be anywhere.'

'Okay, thanks, Carol. See you later.'

'Goodbye, pet.'

Charley didn't know where to go next. The two people who she could confide in, tell anything to, were both away doing . . . well, she didn't know what.

Could they be . . . together? Charley thought, but quickly dismissed the idea. Of course they weren't together.

She did as Carol had suggested and called Abbie's mobile. She answered after a few rings, speaking in a hushed voice.

'Hello?'

'Hey, it's me. Where are you?'

Abbie coughed into the phone. 'I'm just . . . out. With . . . Connor. You?'

'I came by to see you.'

'Sorry, Charles, we'll catch up tomorrow, yeah?'

'Yeah, all right.'

But even as she said it, Charley knew something was wrong. She didn't know why, or what prompted her uncertainty, but she was sure that Abbie was lying.

'Put Aiden on the phone.'

'What? What are you talking about?' Abbie squeaked. She'd never been able to react well under pressure.

'Don't give me that, Abbie, I know he's there. Put him on the phone.' The line went silent, and for a moment, Charley thought Abbie had hung up. Eventually though, she heard his voice.

'Chambers.'

'You lied to me,' she said, her voice wavering.

'I never lied–'

'You might as well have.'

'Chambers, it's not like that. It's not what you think.'

'I told you I needed someone to talk to, I told you it was important. And you're with Abbie. My best friend.'

'And I have a good reason for being with Abbie. I asked her to help me.'

'Whatever, Aiden, I'm not interested. Enjoy your night.' She cancelled the call and, resisting the urge to launch the phone at a nearby wall, stormed off in the direction of Beaton Road.

'Well, hello, firecracker,' Marcus said as he opened the door.

'Can I come in?' He noticed how upset she looked and quickly became concerned.

'Sure, what's wrong?' he said, ushering her inside.

'I don't want to talk about it. Well, I do. But I don't.'

'That's okay, we don't have to. You want something to eat?'

'Not really.'

'Not even chocolate? Charley, I'm disappointed in you.'

Charley let her lips curl into a tiny smile. 'How could I possibly refuse chocolate?'

They hurried past the kitchen where his parents were sitting, drinking red wine and discussing English literature.

'Shouldn't I say hi?' Charley asked, as he took her hand and pulled her up the stairs.

'Nah, they'll just assume you're my new girlfriend and ask you a million questions. I'll never hear the end of it.'

Charley giggled sweetly, causing Marcus to go weak at the knees. Everything about her really was perfect.

He showed her to his room and shut the door, quickly trying to grab the clothes that were strewn across his floor.

'Sorry, I wasn't expecting company.'

'It's fine, I don't judge.'

'So what you wanna do?' Marcus asked, handing Charley a Twix and a can of Coke from the mini-fridge by his bed. She turned the can over in her hand and he said, 'Or would you prefer beer?'

'What? Oh, God no. This is great, thanks.'

She put the can down along with the uneaten chocolate bar and began biting her nails, glancing up at him every so often. 'I can't do this,' she muttered.

'Can't do what?'

'This. All of it. The lies, the apprehension. I can't do it anymore. It's the not knowing . . .'

'Charley, what are you talking about?'

'What did you see today? Tell me. Because I know you know something.'

'Charley–'

'Don't lie to me, please. I've had enough. I know he said it could put me in danger but I don't even care. I need to know–'

'Charley, calm down. Who said what would put you in danger?'

Charley tried to take deep breaths. In, out she told herself. In, out.

'Tell me what you saw,' she asked again.

'I saw a bunch of street lights blow up.'

'And?'

'That was it.'

'Marcus–'

'You did it.'

'What?'

It was what she'd been expecting to hear. She'd been goading him, begging him to say it, but it still took her by surprise.

'You blew them up. You got angry and they smashed.'

There was silence for a minute, and then Charley said, 'Oh no.'

'It's okay. You don't need to be frightened, Charley.'

'I should never have said anything. I should go–'

'Wait, don't leave. Don't you want to know how I could tell? I knew you'd done it because,' – Marcus unscrewed the light bulb from his bedside lamp and tossed it into mid-air – 'I can do it, too.'

The light bulb stopped about an inch from his palm and hovered there, the same way Aiden had manipulated the baseball. It began to shimmer, the filament inside sparking as energy travelled along its length.

He let it fall so that it landed gently in his hand, the orb slowly beginning to fill with a black mist.

'You're . . . you're a magician,' Charley stuttered, 'like me?'

'Sure am.'

Charley looked at the light bulb and she could no longer see inside it. Its centre was completely black, the smoke taking over its small shape. Slowly, it began to swell, and then with a loud crack, it burst, the smoke slithering away like a snake, through the air and out the window, into the cool night.

'What was that?' she asked, rushing to the window

to see the thing that had just escaped. She was too late though, it was gone.

'Nothing,' he shrugged, 'just smoke.'

'That was amazing,' she said, turning back to look out the window. 'I've never seen Aiden do anything like that bef . . .' She managed to stop herself, but it was too late. 'I mean . . . I've never seen, eh, he's not. Oh, God.'

'It's all right, Charley, I already know about Aiden.'

'Wh . . . what?' she stuttered.

'I can tell. Besides, he's so protective. I kind of guessed that whatever it was involved both of you.'

'So, you already knew?' she asked, bewildered. 'How long . . . I mean, when did you–?'

'I had an idea, although you confirmed it for me today.'

'Does Aiden know you're a magician?'

'Not as far as I'm aware.'

At that moment, Marcus wanted to ask Charley not to mention it to Aiden – any of it. But he knew he couldn't ask her to hide it from him. It would look too suspicious.

'So what happened?' Marcus asked, changing the subject.

'I really don't want to talk about it.'

'I know. Doesn't mean I'm not gonna ask.'

Charley sighed. 'He lied to me.' Marcus didn't need to ask to whom she was referring. 'So did Abbie. They were together, in fact they're with each other as we speak, and they both lied about it.'

'Maybe there's a reasonable explanation,' Marcus said, shrugging his shoulders.

Charley raised her eyebrows.

'Or, maybe not.'

'I don't know, maybe nothing's going on. But why

could they not just tell me they were together? Why'd they have to go sneaking around behind my back? And then there's all this stuff with my sister, Jess. I really just wanted someone to talk to.'

Marcus suddenly seemed very interested.

'Your sister, what's going on there?'

'Oh, I don't know. She's been acting so strange recently. And now she keeps blacking out and having fits. And half the time, when I'm near her, I feel like I'm going to throw up. Or I do throw up. It's all a bit crazy at the moment.'

'Yes, it definitely sounds it,' Marcus said, scratching his cheek with his pinkie. 'Listen, Charley, I hate to do this, but I have something I forgot to do. Think we can finish this another time?'

'Oh, okay. I guess so.' She tried, but she didn't hide her disappointment well. Did nobody want to spend time with her? 'I'll see myself out.'

'Don't be silly, I'll walk you to the–'

'Honestly,' she said, cutting him off, 'it's fine. Go do your thing. We'll catch up later.'

She hurried down the hallway, blinking frantically to keep the tears at bay. She didn't want to cry, but at the same time she did. She wanted to cry, and shout and scream.

She walked out the front door and closed it behind her, a lot harder than she meant to. At the same time, as Marcus sat where she'd left him, the junk on his desk began to shake. The books in his bookcase came loose and several fell to the floor.

Marcus sat, chin resting on his closed fist, and smiled. 'Gotcha,' he said.

आ

Dorcas Blightly sat at her kitchen table, a lukewarm cup of coffee in one hand, a black marker pen in the other. In front of her was a large photo album, crammed full of pictures of her two grandchildren, going right back to when they were toddlers. As she turned the pages, she sighed – a deep, heavy sigh. Dorcas had known the time would come sooner or later, but now – why so soon?

She picked up a small, white handkerchief and coughed into it, closing her eyes as a searing pain made its way across her chest. She placed the handkerchief back down on the table; it was now crimson, splattered with deep, red blood.

She turned yet another page to find a more recent picture of Charley and Jess, sitting side by side on a park bench. It couldn't have been more than six months old. Dorcas stared at the picture for a while, frightened to look away. How was it possible that she was only just seeing this now?

'So, this is when it started,' she breathed.

She took the lid from the marker and began to blacken out one of the girls' faces. Once she was finished, she put her head in her hands and did something she hadn't done for a long time. She wept – she wept for one grandchild's safety, and for the other grandchild's fate.

SIXTEEN

Charley walked towards her registration class, anxious at the thought of seeing Abbie. They'd been best friends for so long, and this was the first time Abbie had ever lied to her. Changing her mind, she turned back, hurrying down to the nearest toilet and locking herself in a cubicle once she'd made sure she was alone. There was graffiti scrawled across the toilet door: doodles, hearts with initials penned inside, the odd obscenity here and there.

She let out a half laugh, half sigh when she spotted Aiden's name at the bottom of the cubicle wall.

LUCY AND AIDEN FOREVER

'Take him,' Charley grunted, not that she really meant it.

'Excuse me?'

Charley stopped at the sound of the woman's voice. It was deep, sultry – not the voice you'd expect to hear coming from a teenager. But where had it come from?

She'd checked all the stalls and she hadn't heard anyone else come in.

'Hello?' she said, but no one answered this time. She unlocked the door and pulled it towards her, peeking out to see the main door to the toilets closing. 'Wait . . .'

Charley ran towards the exit and heaved the door open, running out into the corridor.

'Where did you go?' she said breathlessly, turning around in circles but still not seeing anyone. She did see something on the floor though, only a few feet away. She walked over to where it lay and bent down to pick it up, the light reflecting off its shiny surface as she turned it over in her hand.

It was a tiny silver locket on a chain so thin, Charley was scared she might break it. She looked closer. There was something engraved on the surface – a letter, perhaps? A symbol? But it was so faded and scratched that she couldn't make it out. All that was visible was a border of roses around the rim of the locket. She tried to open it, but as hard as she tried to prise the two sides apart, it stuck tight.

She was in two minds whether or not to take it to lost property and tell them where she'd found it, or to simply slip it into her pocket and try herself to find its mysterious owner.

'Chambers . . .'

She shut her eyes tightly when she heard the voice, cursing herself for leaving the toilet. She'd gone in there to be alone. She could've had that . . . but now she was going to have to face him.

'What do you want?' she said without turning around.

'You.'

'Tough.'

'Talk to me, please. Stop shutting me out.'

'Me . . . shut you out?' Charley's jaw nearly dropped. 'That's rich.'

'You haven't given me a chance to explain. I'm not fooling around behind your back. Do you really think that's who I am?'

'It doesn't matter, Aiden. You don't have to be fooling around behind my back, with my best friend of all people. The fact that you were out with her, the fact that you lied to me about it – you both did. That's enough.'

'I was lying to you for your own good. I wasn't trying to hurt you. That's exactly what I was trying to avoid.'

A tear rolled down Charley's cheek and she quickly wiped it away. She wasn't sure if Aiden had noticed or not, but if he did he said nothing. He took a step forward, then stopped when he saw her flinch.

'I'll go if you want. I'm not trying to cause a fight and the last thing I want to do is upset you. But you need to talk to me at some point.'

He gave her a smile, though she could tell it wasn't genuine. This one was weak and sad.

At least it's a smile, right?

Wrong.

Charley would have rather seen no smile at all than that one. She wanted him to shout, to get angry and tell her she was being stupid. She wanted him to pull her close, hold her and give her no choice but to kiss him.

But this . . . this was the worst thing in the world. She couldn't bear seeing him sad.

'Aiden, wait. Don't go.'

He didn't move.

'I'll talk to you. I'll let you explain. But you need to tell me everything.'

'I will.'

'And you won't leave anything out?'

'I won't.'

'Okay.'

The bell for first period had already gone and the corridors were once again empty, giving Aiden and Charley the privacy they needed.

They sat under one of the stairwells, backs to the wall in case anyone did decide to walk by, not that it was likely.

'What's with the locket?' Aiden asked when he noticed Charley playing with the dainty chain.

'I found it,' she said blankly, shoving the trinket into her pocket. 'We're here to talk about you.'

'I know.'

'So . . . talk.'

Aiden didn't say anything for a moment. He looked at her and then looked away, unsure how to begin.

'Your gran's sick.'

Straight to the point, then.

'What do you mean she's sick?' Charley asked impatiently.

'I think she's dying, Chambers.'

Charley cleared her throat and after a few seconds said, in a voice too calm for what she'd just been told, 'Wait a minute, how do you know this?'

'I heard my parents talking about it.'

'And how do they know?'

'I don't know.'

Charley stared into space for a moment, unsure of what to say.

'Why were your parents discussing my family? My gran? Why would they–'

'I don't know, Chambers.'

'Do you know anything?' she spat harshly, regretting it a few seconds later. Her vision went cloudy, her eyes filling with tears, and she turned away so he wouldn't see her cry.

Aiden wanted to do nothing more than comfort her, but he knew better. Charley was fiercely independent, and he had to let her deal with things in her own way.

'I know this is hard,' he said, 'but it's not all bad.'

'You just told me my gran may be dying. What's good about that?'

'Well, I don't think it's from ill health or old age, put it that way,' he said, causing Charley to turn her head ever so slightly so she could see him. Her eyes were red and bloodshot and there were several strands of hair stuck to her damp cheeks.

'What are you talking about?' she sniffed.

'Magic.'

'What?'

'Is your gran . . . does she have powers? Have you ever seen her do anything that–'

'No, never,' Charley interrupted. 'She isn't a magician, Aiden.'

'That you know of.'

'I'd be able to tell.'

'Of course you would. Just like you could tell with me?'

Just like you could tell with Marcus?

135

'Stop it,' she said, unintentionally out loud.

'Stop what?'

'Nothing, never mind. You're right. Maybe she is and she just hasn't told me.'

'I'm not saying she is or she isn't. I don't necessarily mean that she has powers. But I do think magic's involved somehow.'

'Why? What makes you think that? And is this why you were with Abbie last night?'

'Yes.'

'What were you doing that you needed her help with? What is she, the sorcerer's apprentice?'

Aiden couldn't help but laugh, stopping quickly when he noticed Charley didn't share his amusement.

'I wanted her help finding out about Dorcas. Where she grew up, who she was friends with, where she'd worked. I needed to see her medical records, her–'

'Her medical records – how did you manage that?'

'Abbie and I went to the surgery last night.'

'You broke into the medical centre?'

'No, I let myself in.'

Charley frowned and said, 'Why do you have a key for the surgery?'

'I don't need a key, Chambers. Perks of being a magician. Anyway, that doesn't matter. What's important is that I was right. There's nothing in her records that shows her to have ill health.'

'Maybe she's just not been to see them. She doesn't like doctors.'

'She was there a week ago for a check-up.'

'And?'

'Fit as a fiddle.'

'So why do you think she's sick then?' Charley pressed, bemused.

'Because my parents said so, I told you.'

'And that automatically makes it true?'

'They're rarely wrong.'

Charley's head was beginning to spin. When she'd woken up that morning, the worst thing on her mind was that her boyfriend had lied to her and was sneaking about with her best friend. Now, said boyfriend was telling her that her only remaining grandparent might be dying due to some sort of unknown wizardry.

'So how is it not all bad?' Charley asked sadly.

'Well, if I'm right and it does come down to magic, then it can most likely be stopped.'

'What do you mean? We can save her?'

'Yes, I would say so. If she's sick because of magic then there's almost definitely a way to cure her.'

'Does my family know?'

'I don't think so, no. You'll need to ask your gran yourself, although be prepared not to hear the truth. People involved with magic tend to lie a lot.'

'I'm beginning to realise that.'

'You should speak to Abbie as well. She's been up worrying all night.'

'How do you know?' Charley asked accusingly.

Aiden grinned. 'Because she sent me a message saying–' He took out his phone and held it in front of Charley. 'How is she? I haven't slept, I've been up all night worrying.'

'Oh . . . right.' Charley looked away sheepishly. She'd always had a suspicious nature, but deep down she knew she could trust Aiden. Maybe part of her just didn't want to.

'What you thinking, Chambers?'

'Why didn't you ask me? Why did you go to Abbie?'

'I didn't want to hurt you. I thought she'd be able to help . . . I knew this wouldn't be easy for you to take in.'

Charley sighed and got to her feet. 'It would have hurt less if you'd told me in the first place,' she said, before walking towards reception and out the door.

Aiden didn't follow her. Instead, he picked up his bag and slid out from under the stairs. Heaving himself up off the ground, he climbed the two flights of stairs to the chemistry department and walked towards his class. All the pupils were outside, working on the computers. Marcus was there, standing at the end of the table, unzipping his coat and laughing with a pretty redhead called Bethan Pugh.

Mrs Murrell, their chemistry teacher, came out and crossed her arms, frowning as she watched the two teenagers teasing one another.

'Marcus, you stroll into my class late and then refuse to do as you're told. If you're not in a seat with a computer on in the next two minutes, you can come by at lunch instead.' She walked back into the classroom without spotting Aiden, and Marcus began to laugh, sending rude gestures in the teacher's direction.

Aiden walked as casually as he could towards the table.

'There's my boy,' Cameron shouted from his chair in the corner. 'Where you been, mate?'

'All right, Ai–' Marcus tried to say politely, but Aiden cut him short with a swift punch to the face.

'What the hell . . .?'

'Did you see that?'

'He punched his lights out!'

Everyone went wild. Kids were climbing out of their seats, punching the air as they all began to shout, 'Fight, fight, fight,' over and over again.

Aiden bent down and pulled Marcus up by the collar. 'Stay away from her,' he said, quietly yet in such a sinister manner that anyone but Marcus would have at least been a little bit intimidated.

Marcus laughed, running his tongue along his bottom lip. He could taste blood.

'I'm serious,' Aiden snarled, pulling the collar harder.

'When are you anything else?' Marcus smiled slyly. 'It's hard to keep away from her though, when she keeps coming round to see me.'

Aiden wasn't sure what Marcus meant, but he didn't react.

'She didn't tell you, did she? Of course, you were too busy with her friend, weren't you? No wonder she ended up back at mine.'

Aiden punched him again, just as Mrs Murrell came rushing out of the classroom.

'What on earth is going on? Aiden, get off him this instant!'

Marcus turned his head to the side and spat, his saliva now tinted red as his mouth began to fill with blood.

'You'll never guess what she told me,' Marcus continued, searching Aiden's eyes for any hint of emotion. He might have been on top of him, beating the crap out of him, but despite that, Aiden's face was deadpan. 'Imagine my surprise when Charley finally admitted what she was. It was only a matter of time, of course, but for her to come to me – now that did catch me off guard.'

'You're lying,' Aiden said through gritted teeth.

'Ask her yourself. I'm sure she'll tell you all about it.'

Aiden let go of Marcus and pushed him to the floor, knowing full well that if he didn't walk away, he'd kill him.

'Oh, the most interesting part of our conversation,' Marcus yelled, when Aiden was nearly at the bottom of the hall, 'was when we got on to talking about you. I must say, your girlfriend isn't the best at keeping secrets.'

Aiden didn't turn around. If he had, Marcus would've known all about it.

SEVENTEEN

The cool breeze blew crisp, orange leaves along the path, and Charley made sure to step on them; the crunching noise beneath her feet being one of her all-time favourite sounds.

She was nearing the car park behind Aldune Estate, which was normally filled with skateboarders and Emo kids, smoking cigarettes and showing off in front of their mates.

Charley and Abbie often hung out there. They liked to sit and watch, either from the rusty swing set next to the duck pond or from the roof of the old library building. They would gossip about which guys they thought were cute and laugh at the ones who fell off their skateboards after a few too many drinks from the hipflasks they kept stashed down their jeans.

She turned the corner and her heart sank as she saw the swings, unoccupied, swaying in the gentle wind. She'd thought – hoped – that Abbie would be there.

With all the punks and scene kids still in school, the car park was empty, apart from a stray dog that had decided to take up residence in an abandoned trolley.

What's the point in having a car park when there are never any cars in it? Charley thought, heading towards the library. She went round to the back of the building and began to climb, using the lattice to help her scale the wall.

When she reached the top, she let out a sigh of relief as she saw Abbie lying flat on her back, staring up at the cloudy sky. Charley walked over and sat down next to her friend.

'That one looks like a bunny rabbit,' Charley said, pointing to a cloud that didn't really resemble a rabbit at all.

'What kind of creepy looking bunnies have you seen lately?' Abbie asked, the words coming out in a croak. She coughed, trying to clear her throat. She looked exhausted.

'I get them in my garden all the time. Three eyes, two tails, big teeth. I think they might be killer bunnies.'

Abbie snorted, but she didn't laugh. Charley had never been very good at jokes; she wasn't really a funny person. That was more Abbie's forte.

'Aiden told me about my gran.'

Abbie used an elbow to push herself up and said, 'I never meant to lie to you, Charles. He asked for my help and I didn't know what to do. I knew you'd be devastated about it and I thought if, maybe I could help somehow–'

'I know,' Charley nodded. 'I understand why you didn't tell me. Both of you. I guess I just felt shut out – my best friend and my boyfriend in cahoots together.'

'You know it's not like that.'

'Yeah, I know.'

Abbie was quiet for a moment, and then she grinned

and said, 'You do realise you just referred to Aiden as your boyfriend?'

'I did? And . . .'

'And, you haven't done that before.'

'I guess not,' Charley said, smiling.

'You really like him, don't you?'

'I do, yeah.'

For a moment neither of them said anything, the wind and the noise of passing cars the only audible sounds. Abbie began to twist a lock of Charley's hair around her finger, weaving several strands together into what was meant to be a plait, but looked more like a knot.

'I'm sorry about your gran.'

'Thanks.'

'Aiden said you might be able to help her . . . is that true?'

'I think so. I'm not sure to be honest. I didn't speak to him for very long.' Charley paused, a solemn expression on her face. 'It was a lot to take in.'

'Of course,' Abbie said, putting an arm around her.

They stayed on the rooftop for ages, neither one of them wanting to return to the dramas of everyday life. Abbie began to shiver as a few drops of rain fell, and she pulled her mauve poncho around her tightly. Summer was definitely gone.

Without thinking, Charley gave a quick nod towards the sky and the rain stopped immediately.

'Was that you?' Abbie asked.

'What? Oh, right. Yeah, I guess it was.' Charley put her hand out in front of her and raised it ever so slightly, the bitter edge to the air disappearing as she lifted it higher.

Abbie, feeling warmer than she had done for weeks, let the poncho fall from her shoulders and said, 'You're getting good.'

'I'm getting better,' Charley said modestly. 'Although I don't think I'm meant to mess with the weather.'

'Why?' Abbie giggled.

'I dunno. Something Aiden said. Maybe it was personal.'

'I don't wanna know,' Abbie laughed. 'The pair of you are way too complicated for me.'

Right on cue, as if his ears had been burning, Aiden stalked into the car park below. Charley could tell from the way he was holding himself, the way he was walking and from the scowl on his face that he wasn't happy.

What is it this time? she wondered.

'Chambers!' she heard him yell, and not in the most pleasant tone she'd ever heard either. She pushed herself to her knees and let out a groan.

'I think I have to go deal with this,' she said to Abbie.

'Deal with what?' Charley nodded towards the angry looking teenager, storming across the car park. 'Oh dear, what have you done?'

'Beats me,' Charley muttered.

'Chambers, I need to talk to you!' His voice was getting louder and she could tell he was losing his patience.

Charley made her way back to the edge of the roof and began climbing down the lattice, the same way she'd come up.

'Can't you just fly or something?' Abbie said mockingly, although she did genuinely wonder if it was something Charley could do.

'Don't know, never tried. I highly doubt it.'

'You'll never know if you don't try,' Abbie said, mimicking her mother's favourite phrase.

'Yeah, try and then end up breaking my neck. I'll stick to climbing for now.'

She climbed down until she was almost at the bottom and then jumped, wincing in pain as her feet hit the ground. She hobbled round to the car park, preparing herself for whatever Aiden was about to say.

'I'm here,' she yelled, and he turned immediately and began marching towards her.

'What the hell have you done, Chambers?'

'Excuse me? What are you talking about?' she asked, startled.

'After everything I've said about him, after what you've seen for yourself, you go to Marcus of all people and tell him what you,' – he lowered his voice – 'what you are.'

'Yes, but you don't understand–'

'You're damn right I don't understand! Are you insane? Not only do you go and spill your own secret, you told him about me as well.'

'That was a mistake, I never meant to–'

'It's done now,' Aiden spat, his voice harsh.

'Aiden, I'm sorry. I needed someone to talk to.'

'So you thought blabbing this of all things was a good idea? How could you be so stupid?'

Charley was lost for words for a moment. That one had hurt.

'It's not what you think. If you would just listen. Marcus is like us.'

Aiden frowned and said, 'He's what?'

'He's like us. He's a magician. He showed me . . . he

145

had this light bulb and . . .' Charley teetered off as she saw Aiden's expression change from one of anger and frustration to one of complete horror. 'What's wrong?'

'There is one thing that Marcus Gillespie is not, and that's a magician.'

He didn't say another word to her. He looked at the ground, as if deep in thought, and then he turned and began running the other way. Across the car park, round the corner. Then he was gone.

'Not go so well then?' Abbie called, hanging over the edge of the rooftop.

'Does it look like it went well?' Charley yelled back. 'Not sure how I'm going to fix this one.'

'He's crazy about you, he'll get over it.'

'I don't think it's that simple. He's really mad.' She sighed. 'I've messed up.'

'You always mess up, Charles. One more time won't hurt.'

'Gee, thanks. Some friend you are.' She didn't mean it though. Abbie was the best friend she could ask for. She wouldn't have traded her for the world.

Just as Charley was contemplating whether or not to go after Aiden, she heard a sudden shriek from above her and turned to see Abbie toppling off the library roof.

'Abbie!' Charley screamed, running over.

Abbie was lying, face down on the ground, her body still. Charley put a hand on Abbie's neck and she heard a soft groan coming from somewhere in the mess of auburn hair.

'Abbie? Abbie! Oh, God, be all right. Please be all right. I'm gonna phone for help, honey. Don't move, I promise it will all be okay.'

Charley got out her phone and called for an ambulance, then for Aiden. He didn't pick up so she tried again. And again. And again . . .

As she pointlessly redialled his number, stroking Abbie's arm at the same time, someone stood above her, looking down at the tragedy unfolding beneath them.

The figure smiled; an unpleasant smile. 'You should watch who you're messing with, little girl.' As the shadow slowly disappeared, the words were lost on the air.

EIGHTEEN

Newford Royal Infirmary was bustling with activity and Charley felt invisible as she sat on a chair in the corner of the waiting room, desperately hoping that someone would soon be able to tell her something – anything – about Abbie's condition.

She'd been up and down to reception umpteen times to ask if they could give her some information, but the woman behind the desk had been no help at all. Now, every time Charley looked in the receptionist's direction, she was greeted with a glower. She didn't care; she got to her feet once again and marched over to the desk, clearing her throat to alert the receptionist, who was ignoring her on purpose.

'Excuse me?' Charley said, as the woman stuffed half a cheese sandwich into her mouth. 'Have you heard anything yet?'

'Look, kid,' the woman groaned, wiping pickle from her chin, 'if I'd heard anything I would have told you. I know about as much as you do.'

'I doubt that.'

'What?'

Charley ignored her. 'Could you possibly ask someone for me? A nurse, a doctor . . .? I've been waiting for ages now and no one's told me anything.'

'Listen, the doctor will call you when he knows something. Now, take a seat.'

'No, you listen,' Charley said, raising her voice, 'I've asked nicely, I've been patient and you've done nothing at all to help me. If you don't get me a doctor now, I swear to God I'll–'

'Chambers, calm down.' She turned just in time to see Aiden approaching her side, his hair messy from the rain outside and his breathing laboured, as if he'd been running.

'What are you doing here?' she demanded, but he could hear the relief in her voice and pulled her into his chest.

'I'm sorry I missed your calls. I wasn't ignoring you, I promise.'

'It's fine. I didn't know what to do. She just fell, Aiden, I didn't even see what happened. I saw her falling, but by then it was too late.'

'How is she now?'

'I've no idea. She won't tell me anything.' The receptionist glared at Charley, and Aiden raised his eyebrows at her unpleasant expression.

'Look,' – he glanced down at her nametag – 'Doris, I'd appreciate it if you could find out what's going on. Or at least let us talk to someone who can help.'

'I've already told your friend, you will just have to wait for–'

'Waiting isn't an option. Either you get me someone I can speak to or I'll go find them myself.'

Doris thought about it for a moment and then, huffing, pushed herself out of the chair.

'I'll be right back.'

'How do you do that?' Charley asked, wrapping her arms around his waist. For a moment, she was almost able to forget their fallout. But when he lifted her arms from his body and walked across to the other side of the room, she knew he hadn't forgotten.

'Experience,' he said quietly, and he took a seat.

Charley joined him, sitting herself on the chair's arm. 'I'm so sorry, Aiden.'

'I know.'

'I still don't see how it's terrible news. I told you, Marcus showed me what he can do. He's just like us.'

'No, he's nothing like us, Chambers. You need to remember that. I don't know what he is, but he's no magician.'

'How do you know that? If you'd seen him do what I saw, then–'

'And what exactly did you see? What did he show you?'

'Well . . .' – she thought about it for a moment – 'he threw a light bulb into the air and made it float, just like you did with the baseball. Then it filled up with this black, smoky stuff and exploded, and the smoke turned into this sort of snake-like thing, as if it was slithering out the window and–'

'Wow, slow down. Snake-like thing?'

'Yeah, why? Is that important?'

'Maybe.' He paused for a moment. 'Chambers, do you mind if I run home? I need to check something. I won't be long.'

'No, I don't mind. What is it? You know something, don't you? What was that thing?'

Aiden looked around and lowered his voice. 'I think it might have been a nost.'

'A nost? What's that?'

'Trust me, you don't wanna know.'

'Aiden . . .'

'I'll explain it all later. You sure you're okay with me going?'

'Yeah, it's cool. Just hurry back.'

'I will.' He put his hands on either side of her head, tilting it upwards so he could kiss her. 'Try to stay out of trouble until I get back.'

'I'll do my best.'

And then his hands were gone, the warmth from them leaving with him as he made his way out the door. She was alone again. Not even the snotty-nosed receptionist was there to give her the evil eye.

'Excuse me? Are you here with Abbie Gibbons?'

Charley turned to see a doctor, standing next to dismal Doris whose expression was now stonier than ever.

'Yes. Is she all right?'

'I'm Dr Pomeroy,' he said, holding a hand out for her to shake. 'Are Abbie's parents here?'

'No. I've tried calling her mum but she's not answering her phone. I've left a bunch of messages.'

'All right,' the doctor said, looking down at his clipboard.

'Is everything okay?' Charley asked impatiently. Why was everyone so reluctant to tell her anything?

'She's conscious now. She's fractured her clavicle and there's a cha–'

'Clavicle?' Charley interrupted, making a mental note that she had to brush up on her knowledge of anatomy.

'Collarbone,' he said. Doris smirked, but Charley didn't notice.

'Can I see her?'

'Yes, of course. Now, we're going to have to wait forty-eight hours to rule out the possibility of paralysis, but in that event–'

'Wait, what? Paralysis . . . are you saying she might not walk again?'

Dr Pomeroy pushed up his glasses. 'Right now, she has no feeling from the waist down. We think she's suffering from spinal shock syndrome. Now, it could just be impact from the fall, but we won't know for certain until she either regains feeling in her legs or . . .' The doctor tailed off.

'Or she doesn't,' Charley said, finishing his sentence for him.

'Yes, that's correct. Because of the trauma and inflammation, it's hard to make much of the scans or x-rays, not that there appears to be anything wrong, but you can never tell until things calm down. Don't worry, we'll keep a very close eye on her. I just feel it necessary to make you aware of this, so as not to panic Abbie. People find the word paralysis rather frightening, but at this stage, it's just a precaution. If you come this way, I'll show you to her room. Doris, try to get the girl's parents on the phone. I want to speak with them immediately.'

'Yes, Dr Pomeroy,' Doris said, shuffling back to her seat behind the desk.

Charley followed the doctor along the corridors until they came to a room marked '26', and underneath, on an A4 sheet of paper, someone had scribbled 'Abbie Gibbons'.

'She's right inside,' Dr Pomeroy said, offering Charley a kind smile. 'She's still quite groggy, so take it easy.' Charley nodded and pushed the door open, rushing over to the bed as soon as she laid eyes on Abbie.

'Oh my God, look at you! You really don't do things by halves, do you?'

'Charles,' she said, her voice hoarse, 'you have no idea how good it is to see you.'

Charley took Abbie's hand in hers and said, 'How are you feeling?'

'Like I've gone ten rounds with Mike Tyson.'

'What happened?'

'I don't know. The whole thing's pretty hazy. One moment I was on the roof, talking to you, the next I wake up in here feeling like I've been hit by a bus.'

'Did you lose your balance?'

'That's the thing, I don't think so. I wasn't that close to the edge. Honestly, Charles, I don't know how it happened.'

'Well at least you're all right, that's the main thing.'

Abbie looked down, twiddling her fingers. 'You think?'

'What do you mean? Of course you are.'

'I'm not going to walk again, am I?'

'Listen to me, Abbs. There's no way in hell one little fall is going to keep you off your feet. You'll be up and out of here in no time.'

'I know what they're saying, Charley. They might try and sound optimistic when they're talking to me face to face, but you can tell by their expressions . . . they're not holding out much hope.'

'That's rubbish,' Charley said as convincingly as she could. 'Once you've had time to recover, you're going to walk out that door, good as new. I promise.'

Abbie forced a smile, and the pair of them sat quietly for a few minutes. 'You don't need to stay, Charles,' Abbie said eventually, 'I know you have stuff to sort out with Aiden.'

'Don't be ridiculous, I'm not going anywhere. Things with Aiden will be fine.'

'You sure?' Abbie asked, rubbing her eyes. 'I really don't mind if you want to go find him.'

'He was here a moment ago. He's away to ... well, I'm not sure actually. He said he had to go check something.'

'Oh,' Abbie said in surprise.

'I'm all yours,' Charley replied, wandering over to the corner of the room where a stack of board games were piled. She picked up the top one – Monopoly – and turned back to Abbie, smiling. 'I'm gonna thrash you at this.'

Aiden marched into his house and closed the front door, louder than he'd meant to, but at least it made a statement. Or so he'd thought ...

'Mum?' he called, checking the living room first but finding it empty. 'Mum!'

'Kitchen,' she said tersely, and he walked in to find her baking her famous cherry and almond turnovers. 'Please don't storm into the house slamming doors, Aiden. You know how I feel about your moods.'

'I have good reason for my mood swings, Mother, and you know it.'

Tabitha said nothing. She carried on twisting pastry as if he hadn't spoken.

'Is it still possible to conjure up a nost?' he asked matter-of-factly.

'Why?' He had her attention now. 'Why would you ask me about nosts?'

'Because I need to know if it's still possible to create one.'

She thought about it for a second, refusing to look away from the task before her. He could tell she was upset – she hated discussing magic with him.

'Of course it is, but only if the correct magic was used. We would never have the right sort of powers to produce one.'

'A demon would though, right?'

'Aiden, why are you asking me these questions?'

'Will you just answer me?' he snapped, slamming his fist on the counter.

Tabitha cleared her throat and placed the rolling-pin down in front of her.

'A demon could generate enough power to create a nost, yes, but they would have to have good reason to do so.'

'Good? How could a nost be used for good?' Aiden asked, confused.

'It wouldn't be good for anyone but them. They would use a nost to their own advantage. A demon in charge of such dark magic would have no good intentions, let me assure you. But in their eyes, they must be certain that conjuring up a nost is the only option left to help them fulfil their mission, if you will.'

'Demons don't have missions,' Aiden scoffed. 'They don't have hearts. They destroy everything they touch, everything that ever gets in their way. They're monsters.'

'You don't really know enough about them to say that,' Tabitha said, flattening the pastry again, this time with her fingers.

'Are you sticking up for them?'

'No, I'm not. I'm saying you don't know a lot about demons, or what they can do. Hence why you're here now, talking to me because you don't have the answers yourself.'

'I know they can't be trusted.'

'In most cases, that's correct, and you'd be wise to keep your guard up around them – if you were ever to meet one that is.'

Tabitha stopped kneading for a moment and glanced up at her son, who was standing stock-still in the doorway. The pair of them shared a look – a look of confusion, intrigue. Neither one was quite sure what the other was thinking.

Does she know I've met a demon already? Aiden thought.

Has he figured this out yet? Should I be worried? Tabby's mind ran wild.

Aiden broke the silence, saying, 'Yeah, well, thanks. I'll see you later.'

'Be careful, Aiden. I don't know what you're up to and I know there's little point in asking, but don't get yourself involved with magic as depraved as this.'

He didn't say another word, simply turning and walking out the door.

'Don't say I didn't warn you.'

NINETEEN

There was a quiet knock on Abbie's door, and she let out a sigh of relief as Charley walked in, carrying a beautiful bunch of carnations and a punnet of grapes. She'd hardly slept, and she couldn't bear the thought of yet another doctor or nurse coming to pester her.

'Morning, sunshine,' Charley chirruped, 'where's your mum?'

'Away home just now, bringing me in fresh towels. I told her I have no need for fresh towels, but would she listen? To be honest, I'm glad she left. Glad to get half an hour without her prattling away in my ear.'

'Be grateful for small mercies, eh?' Charley said, and actually managed to get a smile from Abbie.

'I guess so, Charles, I guess so.' She paused for a few seconds, deep in thought, and then said, 'So how's Aiden? Have you two worked things out yet?'

'I think we're okay. I haven't seen him since . . . since the day you fell.'

'Seriously?' Abbie asked, raising an eyebrow as Charley shook her head. 'That's poor, Charles. On his part of course, not yours.'

'To give him his due, I have been with you most of the time. He phoned me from his house, the day of the accident. Said he was happy to come back if I needed him, but he had some things he wanted to look into. I said it was fine. He's trying to find out about something called a nost.'

'A nost?' Abbie frowned.

'I don't know much about them, only that they're incredibly dangerous.'

'Oh, superb.'

'Tell me about it. I'm meeting him later, so hopefully he'll fill me in. I hate being left in the dark.'

'Don't we all?'

Charley got up and walked towards the door, but instead of leaving, she pulled the little brown table over to Abbie's bedside.

'No, Charles!' Abbie cried, 'I'm really not in the mood for board games, especially not Monopoly. That game the other day lasted for bleeding hours.'

Charley smiled as she lifted the lid from the game and emptied the contents on to the table. 'Which piece do you want to be?' she asked.

'None.'

'Abbie . . .'

'Seriously, none.'

'Fine, I'll pick for you. You can be the boot, because you're acting like one.'

Abbie snorted. 'Gee, thanks. All right, fine, you can be the dog then, seeing as you're acting like such a bi–'

'Is that any way to talk to your best friend?' Charley interrupted, tossing the playing piece at Abbie and setting up the board.

'You're the one who called me a boot,' Abbie laughed. 'Besides, you are known for your . . .' Abbie stopped mid-sentence and gripped on to the bed's handrail.

'What's wrong?' Charley asked. 'Abbs, you okay? Are you in pain?'

Abbie didn't reply.

'Babe, answer me. What's happening?'

'My feet,' Abbie said weakly.

'What about them? Do they hurt? I'll get a doctor.' Charley got up and made a dash for the door, stumbling over her bag on the way.

'No, they aren't sore. I can feel them!'

'What?'

'They're tingling . . . like pins and needles. Charley, I can actually feel them!'

Charley stood by the door for a minute, gaping at Abbie. She couldn't believe what her friend was saying. It's not that she wasn't happy to hear the news – on the contrary. It's just that Charley had been beginning to think she was never going to hear those words. She thought she was never going to see Abbie's face light up the way it just had.

My feet. I can feel them.

Simple words, yet they meant so much.

'Abbie, that's wonderful!' Charley flung her arms around Abbie's neck, just about choking her friend as she held on, just a little too tightly.

'Shoulder!' Abbie yelled, and Charley leapt back.

'Sorry, your clavicle. I forgot.'

'Clavicle? Aren't we posh,' Abbie said, rubbing her shoulder gently as the pain began to ease. 'God, that was sore. Only you could manage that, Charles.'

159

'Sorry,' Charley said in a low voice.

'Don't be. I still love you.'

'I should call someone. A doctor, I'll get a doctor.'

She jumped off the bed and ran back to the door, managing to avoid her bag this time as she hurtled from the room. She sprinted down the corridor, nearly knocking an elderly man with a walking frame over as she rushed past.

'Sorry,' she called over her shoulder, still running towards reception.

Much to her delight, Doris was nowhere to be seen. This time behind the desk sat a woman – early thirties? – with long, brown hair, pulled back into a ponytail.

'Can I help you?' the woman asked politely, smiling at Charley.

'I hope so. I really need to speak to a doctor. My friend, Abbie Gibbons, has just regained feeling in her feet for the first time in about,' – Charley checked her watch – 'nearly forty-seven hours. She was in an accident, fell from a rooftop.'

'All right, I'll get a doctor along to see her,' the receptionist said.

She hurried away and Charley stayed where she was, letting her weight rest on the desk in front of her.

Just then, the main doors opened and Abbie's mum wandered in, carrying a pile of neatly folded towels, a box of sandwiches and various bags, probably filled with things Abbie would neither want nor use.

'Carol,' Charley said, waving and walking over to help her.

'Hello, dear, how are you? How's Abbie doing? Is she still awfully down?'

'She's much better. She managed to move her feet.'

Carol stood in awe for a moment, as if Charley's words hadn't registered.

'She . . . she did what?'

'Yeah, I know. Well, I'm not sure if she actually moved them, but she got pins and needles. She said she could feel them again.'

Carol began to cry, her eyes crinkling at the corners.

'Are you all right?'

'I've never been more all right. Oh, sweetheart, thank you,' she said, pulling Charley in for a hug.

'You don't need to thank me, I really didn't do anything.'

'You're here, pet. You've kept my daughter in good spirits and I couldn't have asked for more. Thank you, Charlotte. You have no idea how much I appreciate it.' Carol beamed at Charley once more and then took off towards Abbie's room.

Charley smiled, fetching her phone from her pocket when she heard the familiar message tone.

It was a text from Aiden, asking her to meet him. She typed a quick reply and then started for Abbie's room.

She saw him as soon as she turned the corner, sitting on the swing and holding something large on his knee – a box? She couldn't tell.

She wandered over, her hands stuffed in her pockets to protect them from the cold. It was only October, but Charley was already finding the abrupt change in weather a little unseasonable.

'Hi,' she said, and he looked up from what she now realised was a book, resting on his lap.

'Hi,' he replied, and she took a seat on the swing beside him. 'How's Abbie?'

At the mention of her name, Charley turned to look at the library. The roof seemed higher now than it usually did; it was a miracle Abbie had even survived.

'She's a lot better. The numbness is easing off.'

'She'll walk again?' Aiden asked, and Charley nodded. 'That's good.'

'It's fantastic,' Charley corrected him.

'Yeah, sorry. It's brilliant.'

Aiden glanced down at the book again, and Charley noticed this time how distant he was. His mind seemed to be somewhere else, somewhere far away. Somewhere unfamiliar.

'You okay? You don't seem yourself.'

'I'm fine,' he said unconvincingly, and Charley reached over to take his hand.

'Did you find out more about these nosts?'

'I did . . . I asked my mother who was as helpful as ever.'

'What did she say?'

Charley knew she had to tread carefully when talking to Aiden about his parents. She still didn't know if they were like him – magicians – or if they only knew what he was.

'She didn't say much. Just that nosts are dangerous and I should keep well away from anyone who has anything to do with them.'

'Has she ever conjured up a nost?' Charley asked cautiously, and he shook his head.

'Magicians can't summon nosts. We don't have that kind of magic.'

'So your parents are magicians.'

Aiden immediately looked defeated, and Charley couldn't help feeling somewhat triumphant as he glanced up at her, his eyebrows raised.

'Well played, Chambers. I didn't realise how devious you could be.'

'I learn from the best.'

He let go of her hand and flicked through the book again, the pages turning so fast that it was impossible to read.

'Yes, my parents are magicians. This is my mother's book. I took it when I realised she wasn't going to give me any answers.'

'Did you find anything in it? About nosts or . . .' Charley wasn't sure what else there was to find out about, but the book was so big, she was intrigued to know what else was in it; what other secrets it held.

'Take a look at this,' Aiden said, flipping the pages until he came to the right one. On the left hand side, there was a drawing: a thick, black, wavy creature, just like the one she'd seen that night with Marcus. 'Is this what you saw?'

'Yes, that's it.'

'It was definitely a nost then,' Aiden said, his voice wavering slightly. 'According to this, a demon can create a nost to–'

'Wow, wait a minute. A demon?'

'Yes, a demon.'

'You're saying that Marcus is a demon?'

Charley wanted to laugh. She wanted to tell him how foolish that sounded, that Marcus couldn't possibly be a demon. She didn't know why the idea seemed so ridiculous though. After all, it wasn't long ago that Aiden had first told her she was a magician, something that seemed so absurd at the time.

'That's exactly what I'm saying. Apparently, the only creature that can create a nost is a demon.'

'Creature?'

'Well he's hardly human, is he?'

Charley couldn't think of anything to say that would contradict his argument. 'So what does a nost actually do?' she asked instead, not entirely sure if she wanted to hear the answer or not.

'As far as I'm aware, they can be used for a number of things. But the main reason for conjuring one is to lock it on to somebody. Once it's attached itself, it's almost impossible to remove it. Only the demon who created it can separate the nost from its victim.'

'Can they choose who it latches on to?' Charley asked, imagining the snake-like varmint wrapping itself around a person's body, their soul, worming its way in until it had consumed them, leaving nothing but an empty shell.

'Yes, that's kind of the point. Before it's been summoned, the demon chooses who the nost is to pursue. Once it has materialised, it will find that person, link itself to them, and slowly kill them.'

'What?' Charley gasped.

'They'll get sicker and sicker but show no indications of ill health. Well, there might be signs, but no doctor or scientist will be able to help them. They'll simply deteriorate, their body shutting down as the nost lives off their vitality.'

'My gran . . .'

'I know.'

'Is that what's wrong with her?'

'Certainly sounds a lot like it.'

'But why would Marcus want to hurt my gran? He doesn't even know her.'

'I'm not sure, Chambers, but I plan on finding out. I know this doesn't seem good, but at least we know what's wrong with her now. We have a better chance of helping her.'

'But we'd need to get Marcus to remove it. Why would he do that if he created it in the first place?'

'Well that's what we're going to find out.'

TWENTY

The two teenagers walked through the school courtyard, Charley clutching on to Aiden's hand as the cool wind brushed past her nose. His skin was warm, familiar, and Charley felt content as she held on, her fingers entwined with his.

'You okay?' he asked, pulling her closer as she shivered, either from the cold or from the trepidation of what they were about to do. Who they were about to see.

'Yeah,' Charley answered meekly. 'Are you sure this is a good idea?'

'He won't do anything here, not when there are so many people around. To be honest, this is probably our best opportunity to confront him.

'But what if he doesn't like being confronted? What if we make him mad and he sets nosts on us?'

Aiden laughed, pulling Charley towards him. 'You're adorable, you know that?'

'I'm only being careful.'

'Yes, painstakingly. Don't worry about Marcus. If he tries anything, I'll be there to stop him.' He raised his eyebrows slightly. 'You're gonna be there too, you know.'

'So?' She wasn't sure what he was getting at.

'So . . . if anything happens, it's two against one. I know you aren't that confident yet, but you have more control of your powers than you think.'

'Aiden . . .'

'I'm just saying, don't discard them completely. You're talented, Charley Chambers.'

'Full name? Are you feeling all right?'

He nudged her gently with his elbow and she grabbed on to it, linking her arm through his. They picked up their pace and walked towards the main entrance, both of them growing more anxious as they reached the double doors.

'Ladies first,' Aiden said, half-smiling as he held the door open.

'No, you go,' Charley said, hanging back slightly.

Aiden shrugged his shoulders and walked in through the door, letting it shut as Charley followed close behind.

They walked along the busy corridor, squeezing through hordes of hungry students, all of them desperate to get to the cafeteria.

Lunchtime – the time when school turned into a mad house, with children fighting their way to the front of the line, determined to grab a pudding cup or that last slice of pizza.

'Remind me why we chose lunchtime to do this?' Charley asked, flinching as someone stood on her toe.

'Because none of the teachers will notice that we've been gone half the day. Or days, for that matter.'

Neither of them had been back to school since Abbie's

accident and Aiden's unfortunate incident with Marcus in the science department, and neither of them had any real desire to return.

'He's over there.'

Charley looked to where Aiden was pointing and sure enough, there he was, sitting at a table with Cameron McCreery and Gary Bishop. Aiden felt a twinge of jealousy; not only had Marcus tried to steal his girlfriend, he was now trying to nick his friends as well.

They walked towards the table, Charley becoming increasingly anxious by the second. One of the ceiling lights burst, and Aiden looked towards Charley to check she was all right.

'I'm fine,' she said, as if reading his mind.

'Up to your usual tricks?' He nodded towards the ceiling.

Right on cue, the light next to it blew, this time attracting Marcus's attention. His eyes scanned the room, stopping when they found Aiden and Charley amongst a mass of students. His lips turned up into a smile and he leaned back in his chair, resting his hands behind his head.

'No time like the present,' Aiden sighed, stalking off towards Marcus, Charley's hand still gripped firmly in his. 'Can we have a word?' he asked as they approached the table, unintentionally glaring at his two trusty sidekicks.

'Aiden, where've you been?' Cameron asked.

Aiden turned away, replying without even looking at him. 'Not now, Cam, I need to speak to Marcus. Alone.'

'All right,' Marcus said, slowly getting up from his chair. 'Just can't keep away from me, can you?' He winked at Aiden, grimacing as pain shot through his left temple. The skin around his eye was a mixture of purples, greens and blues, and Aiden took pleasure in knowing that he'd caused Marcus that discomfort.

The three of them walked over to the side entrance and carried on out into the courtyard.

'What's this about then?' Marcus asked, biting down on his bottom lip to stop himself from laughing.

'Is this amusing to you?' Aiden asked, and Marcus shrugged.

'I guess. Can think of better things to do.'

'We know what you are.' Charley's tiny voice came from behind Aiden, and Marcus cocked his head slightly to see her better.

'At last, she speaks. You're awfully quiet there, Charley. It isn't like you.'

'Answer the question,' Charley said through gritted teeth.

'You didn't ask me a question. But in response to your – comment – of course you know what I am. I already told you–'

'A pack of lies,' Aiden spat. 'You aren't a magician.'

'Sure I am.'

'And magicians can now harness the power to summon nosts?'

Marcus went to speak, but instead raised his eyebrows, smiling to himself. 'Someone's been doing their homework.'

'You really think I'd have believed for a second you were like me?' Aiden barked, his voice harsh. 'Like us?'

'She's more like me than you know,' Marcus smirked,

but neither of them replied. 'I knew it wouldn't be long until you figured it out.'

'So what do you want? Why lie to Charley? If you involve her in anything, I swear–'

'I don't want to hurt Charley,' Marcus sighed, tired of repeating himself.

'What about my gran then? What's she ever done to you?'

'What are you talking about?'

'You set a nost on my gran. She's dying now, all because of your vindictive–'

'Charley, slow down,' Marcus said, talking to her as if they were still friends. He took a step closer and Aiden's hand flew up, sending Marcus toppling to the ground.

'Thanks for that,' he said sarcastically, getting to his feet.

Marcus looked at Charley, her eyes pleading with him for answers. He wanted nothing more than to pull her close, hold her and never let go . . .

'I never cursed your gran, Charley. I don't even know her.'

'But she's sick.'

'And that's my fault because . . . ?'

'Because she's sick with no explanation and all the signs are screaming out nost. They're all pointing towards you,' Aiden snarled.

'Well, it wasn't me. I wouldn't know Charley's gran if I passed her in the street. If there's a nost after her, it wasn't my doing.'

'Stop lying,' Aiden yelled, but Charley began frantically tapping his shoulder.

'He's telling the truth.'

'What? How do you know?'

'Because the nost he conjured up when I was with him, that was after my gran got sick. That was the night you and Abbie went to the medical centre. Whoever that nost was for, it wasn't my gran.'

Aiden turned slowly back towards Marcus. 'So who was that one for then?'

Marcus laughed. 'Why do you care?'

'Because you've just given someone a death sentence.' Aiden spat the words out like venom, motioning for Charley to stay well behind him.

Charley tilted her head ever so slightly, trying as best as she could to concentrate despite the situation, and a gust of wind rushed towards Marcus, enfolding itself around him like a tiny hurricane.

'Nice try, little witch,' Marcus smiled, throwing his arms up and shattering the hurricane like glass. 'You'll need to do better than that though.'

'I am not a witch,' she said angrily, and he stumbled, his back slamming into the large metal bins that sat at the edge of the courtyard. He let his hands rest on his knees for a second and then straightened, looking directly at Charley.

'My apologies,' he said sarcastically, bowing in a mocking fashion. 'It's just that Aiden seems to use the term 'magician' very lightly. From what I've heard, you have the capability to be one of the most powerful sorceresses there is.'

'And where have you heard that?'

Marcus shrugged. 'Around.'

'This is useless,' Aiden said, just as a group of kids appeared around the corner. 'He isn't going to tell us anything.'

Charley sighed, realising he was right. She felt defeated. A part of her had hoped that Marcus was responsible for the nost that had attached itself to her gran; at least that way she might have been able to reason with him, somehow convince him to undo the spell.

'I guess we're done then,' Charley said sadly.

'I guess we are,' Marcus agreed, moving into a crouching position to ease the pain in his back.

'You really aren't going to tell us?' Charley asked. 'Who the nost was for?'

'What's the point? You've already made up your mind about me.'

'You're right, I have.' She turned and began walking away, back towards the school. Aiden didn't follow, instead choosing to walk the other way towards where Marcus sat, hunched over on the ground.

'Do we really need to do this again?' Marcus asked, easing himself up and stretching his arms out to the sides. 'Go on then, have another pop. Really, I like being punched in the face, it's exhilarating.'

'Did she really hurt you that badly?'

'What?'

Aiden nodded towards the bins. 'Chambers.'

'She's stronger than you think,' Marcus said quietly, conscious of the stares that were coming their way.

'I know how strong she is,' Aiden said defensively.

'See, that's where you're wrong. You have no idea. Charley might be a good little witch, Aiden, convincing herself that she's all lily-white, but she has a dark side. She might not have found it yet, but it's in there.'

'And why should I believe a word you say?'

'You don't have to believe me, I couldn't care less. But

I'm not lying; Charley Chambers is a lot more powerful – and dangerous – than you know.'

'And how do you know?'

'Know what?'

'How powerful Chambers is? How come you're suddenly so clued up on her?'

'A magician never gives away his secrets,' Marcus jeered. Aiden scowled, the thought of knocking Marcus's teeth out seeming more appealing by the second. 'Oh, sorry, that's you. A demon quite often gives away secrets.'

'Stop with the games, Marcus.'

'I still think the term demon seems a little . . . barbaric, doesn't it? Makes me sound like an ugly brute, when really–'

Aiden gave up trying to be nice. He swung his right fist out and hit Marcus's jaw, sending him once again into the bins.

'Seems more than appropriate,' Aiden said, and turned to follow in Charley's footsteps, past the gawking students at the bench.

Marcus closed his eyes and leaned back against one of the bins, clutching his forehead as it began to throb, the pulses in his temples vibrating furiously.

He sighed just as the heavens opened, large droplets of rain pelting down from the sky, soaking everything in sight.

The kids at the bench darted for the doors, jackets pulled over their heads to protect them from the sudden downpour.

'Really, Aiden, a monsoon? That's the best you could do?'

173

Marcus stumbled to his feet – soaked to the skin and less than impressed – and trudged towards the doors just as the bell rang. He gripped one of the handles and tugged, cursing when the door didn't budge.

'Oh, come on!' he yelled. 'Really?' He punched the glass, the impact turning his knuckles red, and spun around, letting his back slide down the length of the door. He looked up at the sky, rain still cascading from it, and began laughing manically.

Dorcas took the kettle from the stove, her hand shaking as she carried it across to where her teacup sat. She poured the boiling water out slowly, using her other hand to guard her mouth as she began coughing, her palm becoming wet as warm blood made contact with her skin. She pulled her hand away and gasped, her fingers coated with sticky, black blood. She dropped the kettle carelessly on the table and hurried to the sink, turning the taps on and shrieking as the water began to run, thick and red from the taps. She spun around and once again gasped as she looked upon the liquid spilling from the kettle's spout: blood. Dark blood spilling across her yellow cotton tablecloth. Dorcas ran from the kitchen, struggling for breath as she slammed the door, edging back from it slowly.

She heard a floorboard creak behind her and cautiously looked over her shoulder, crying out as she saw the familiar figure standing there.

'Hello, Dorcas.'

TWENTY-ONE

The wind was picking up as Charley rounded the corner, her gran's house now only a few yards away.

She'd had enough – enough games, enough waiting, enough Marcus. Something had to be done.

She knew Aiden meant well, but she wasn't going to let him fight all of her battles for her. He couldn't protect her from everything . . . from everyone.

She knocked on the door several times before trying the handle, but it was locked; unusual for Dorcas, she just about never locked her door.

'Gran? Are you there?' she called, moving towards the window and peering inside, using her hand to shield her eyes from the sun's harsh glare. 'Oh my God, Gran!'

Dorcas was lying on the floor, unconscious from what Charley could see, next to the kitchen door. Charley ran round the back, panicking when she found that door locked as well.

'Hold on, Gran, I'm coming.'

She grabbed one of Dorcas's terracotta flowerpots and, struggling, managed to launch it through the kitchen window. She swept away the excess glass and climbed in. Running quickly to the door, she eased her way through the small gap, crouching down to see if Dorcas was all right.

'Gran? Can you hear me?'

Dorcas groaned, and Charley pulled her up, cradling her head. 'Charley?'

'I'm here.'

'Oh, Charley.'

'What happened?'

'I . . .' Dorcas faltered. 'I can't remember.'

'Did you fall?'

'I don't think so. I was . . . the last thing I was doing was . . . oh, gosh.'

'Slow down,' Charley said, 'take your time.'

Dorcas tried to push herself up and, with Charley's help, found her way to the couch.

'I was making some tea. Yes, that's right. I was making myself a drink and then . . . I don't know. Everything's a blank after that.'

'Did you feel dizzy? Maybe you blacked out . . .'

'I don't remember leaving the kitchen,' Dorcas said, her voice wavering.

'I'm phoning an ambulance.'

'No! No, sweetheart, that's really not necessary.'

'But, Gran–'

'Charlotte, I'm fine. I just got a bit of a fright, that's all.'

'Very well. Stay here,' Charley said, squeezing her gran's hand. 'I'll go get you that tea.'

Charley made her way to the kitchen, grimacing when she saw the shattered glass and shards of broken flower pot strewn across the floor. Her gran was going to freak.

She picked up a few pieces of broken glass and began tidying the mess that had already been there before she arrived. The kettle was upside down on the floor, a puddle of water surrounding it. The table cloth was also drenched, the damp material still warm.

The taps were running, splashing the thin net curtains that hung from the curtain rail above the shattered window. One curtain was ripped from when Charley had leapt in, grabbing a hold of it to help pull herself inside.

'Your kitchen might need a bit of a clean,' Charley said gingerly, filling the kettle and placing it on the stove to heat. 'Or remodelled . . . the window's kind of . . . not there any more.'

'It's all right,' Dorcas replied, laughing slightly. 'I'd expect nothing less from you, dear.'

Charley let out a long sigh. She was relieved. Hearing her gran laugh after seeing her so helpless only moments before was somewhat comforting.

'You want a cake or something?' Charley asked, opening the biscuit tin and finding a large selection of biscuits, bars and some tiny blueberry muffins – she could always count on her gran to have a stack of sweet things tucked away in the cupboard.

'No thanks, darling.'

'You sure? Sugar might help with the shock.'

'What shock?' Charley's head whipped up at the sound of a second voice; a very familiar voice.

'Hello, poppet,' Dorcas said softly.

'Jess? What are you doing here?' Charley asked, walking through from the kitchen and raising an eyebrow as she laid eyes on her sister. 'And what are you wearing?'

Jess was dressed from head to toe in leather, her lips scarlet and her nails black. She had her hair tied up in a high ponytail, making her normally pretty features appear harsh and severe. Her eyelids were nearly as dark as her nails; a combination of liquid eyeliner and charcoal eye shadow.

'Clothes,' Jess replied bluntly.

'I can see that. But why those ones? You look like a punk with 'I hate the world' issues.'

'Thanks for your opinion, Charley. Not that anyone asked for it.'

'And when did the panda look become fashionable again?' Charley said, swirling her finger towards Jess's made-up eyes. 'I thought that went out in the seventies.'

'Screw you, Charley.'

'Excuse me?'

'You heard me. Drop dead.'

'Stop being a brat. I was only joking. What's wrong with you today?'

'Go to hell.'

'Jessica, that's enough,' Dorcas scolded her, but Jess just smiled.

'What are you doing here, Jess?' Charley asked again.

'Came to see my gran. Is that not allowed? Are you the only one who's entitled to visit poor old granny?'

'I suggest you leave, before I do something I regret.'

'Oh, and what would that be? Enlighten me.'

Jess smirked as Charley stood stock still, everything around her beginning to shake. Old magazines and papers flew from the table, as if there was some sort of gale picking up, although none of them could feel a spot of wind. Charley didn't move from her space on the floor, her eyes never leaving Jess.

'Is this meant to impress me, Charley?' Jess yelled over the dull, buzzing sound which was getting louder by the second.

The furniture began violently rocking, a lamp flying into the back of Jess's head. She winced, although for some reason it didn't hurt.

'Come on, Charley. Show me what you've got. Show me you aren't as pathetic as everyone at school says. Prove that you can actually—'

Charley lifted her hand and twisted it in a snapping motion, as if she were quickly turning a door handle. Jess's neck bent to one side – in a way that did not look natural – and she collapsed to the ground, everything else in the room falling to the floor.

Dorcas gasped. 'Charlotte, what have you done?'

'She's fine, Gran. Don't worry,' Charley sighed, gathering all the rubbish from the living room floor.

'What do you mean, don't worry? You just snapped your sister's neck.'

'I didn't snap her neck. I put her to sleep – temporarily. She'll wake up in a foul mood in no time at all.'

'And how did you know how to do that?' Dorcas asked. 'Did someone teach you?'

Charley was silent for a moment. 'No . . . I guess it was instinct. I just knew how to do it.'

Dorcas put a hand to her forehead and said nothing, thinking about the events that had occurred only moments before. She'd had no idea how strong Charley's powers were – how dangerous, if used incorrectly. She wasn't sure what to do next. She wasn't sure how much time she had left to help . . .

There was a loud knock on the front door, pulling Dorcas from her worried thoughts and sending Charley hurtling towards the hallway. She wasn't particularly in the mood for any more surprise guests.

'Aiden,' she said as she opened the door, startled to see him standing there. 'What are you–?'

'I came to see if you were okay.'

'How did you know I was here?' she asked, standing aside and gesturing for him to come in.

'Lucky guess,' he grinned, but the smile quickly disappeared when he saw Jess on the floor, lying in an incredibly awkward position. 'Do I want to know?'

'Probably not. Aiden, this is my gran. Gran, this is Aiden – my boyfriend.'

Dorcas raised her eyebrows. 'Nice to meet you, Aiden.'

'Likewise.'

'You look awfully familiar,' Dorcas said, frowning slightly. 'Have we met before?'

'I don't think so.'

'Hmm, oh well,' she said, brushing it off, just as a moan came from the crumpled heap of limbs on the floor.

'Oh, goody,' Charley groaned. 'Sleeping Beauty's waking up.'

Jess opened her eyes and squinted at the three figures looking down at her. She felt like she'd been hit on the head with a mallet.

'You in a better mood yet?' Charley asked, giving her a hand up.

'What happened?'

'Em, you–'

'Wait a minute, I know what happened. You did something with your freaky powers and knocked me out. You did that to me, you, you–'

'Wait,' Charley asked, eyes wide, 'how did you–?'

'Oh, come on. Don't think I've grown up in the same house as you and not noticed. I'm not an idiot.'

'Jess, I did it for your own good.'

'My own good? Yeah, right.'

'I did. If you hadn't–'

'You know what, Charley. You aren't the be-all and end-all. You're not that bloody special. Just because you can do some fancy party tricks doesn't make you better than everyone else.'

Charley went to speak but no words would come out. Aiden could see the hurt in her eyes.

'Jess,' he said calmly, 'your sister's only trying to help you. Give her a break.'

Jess turned her head towards him, her red lips forming a smile. 'Well hello, Mr Cunningham. Don't you look fine today?'

'Oh, for God's sake,' Charley sighed.

'Cunningham? I knew I recognised you,' Dorcas said suddenly, something finally clicking. 'Fergus and Tabitha's son?'

'Yeah, you know them?' Aiden asked, sounding worried. He didn't like talking about his parents. He especially didn't want to talk about them with Charley's grandmother.

Dorcas shrugged. 'Vaguely.' There was a long pause. 'You look like him, your father.'

'People say that a lot.'

'You look like her, too. Your mother I mean.'

Aiden shook his head. 'Not really.'

'Maybe not now,' Dorcas said, 'but when she was younger.'

The four of them stood, awkwardly, neither one quite sure what to say. Jess smirked at her sister and then began batting her eyelids furiously at Aiden, who didn't seem to notice anyone or anything but Charley. Charley stood with her arms crossed, glaring at Jess. She wanted to knock her out again, this time with her fists. Dorcas looked at the three of them in turn: Charley, her sensible granddaughter, or so she'd thought; Jess, her young, naïve, mischievous granddaughter, and Aiden, the son of a woman who had changed Dorcas's life completely.

'Charley,' Dorcas said, smiling, 'take Jess home. I'm terribly worn out now. I'd like to go for a lie down.'

'But, Gran, the house . . . the kitchen. I'll stay and clean up, make you something to eat . . .'

'There's really no need, darling.'

'I insist. You've had a rough–'

'Charlotte,' she said softly, 'I'd really rather be alone. I can take care of myself.'

'But–'

'I promise, I'll be just fine. You're right, it's been a rough day. I just need some peace and quiet.'

'Take the hint, Charley,' Jess scoffed, 'she doesn't want you here.'

'You watch your tongue, young lady,' Dorcas said harshly. 'I've had quite enough of your cheek. Go home and at least try to behave yourself.'

Jess rolled her eyes and stormed towards the door, embarrassed at being told off in front of Aiden.

'Are you sure you'll be okay, Gran? I hate leaving you like this.'

'I'll be just fine, Charley. Now, scram. Aiden, it was lovely to meet you. Look after her. God knows, she needs it.'

Jess trudged along the street, her face like thunder as she pulled her hair from its bands. She reached the public bathrooms and went inside, immediately catching her reflection in one of the oblong mirrors that sat above the sinks.

Who is that?

She went to one of the sinks and turned on the tap, cupping her hands underneath it and splashing handfuls of cold water on to her face. She grabbed some tissue paper and started to scrub: her cheeks, her eyes, her lips, until the makeup was gone, leaving her pale skin red and sore. Tears began to roll down her cheeks, stinging as they made contact with the broken skin.

Who am I?

The salty tears mixed with the cold tap water as Jess continued to soak her face, the coolness refreshing yet painful.

Everything hurt. She didn't know what was happening to her. She wasn't sure who she was anymore.

She knew the things she was doing were wrong and she hated the way she was acting, the way she was treating the people she cared about. But she couldn't help it. She couldn't control her actions any more than Charley could control her powers.

'Help,' she murmured as she sank down to the floor. 'Someone help me, please.'

ॐ

'So talk me through this,' Aiden said as he heaved himself on to the roof.

'Talk you through what?'

'What you're about to do here.'

Aiden crossed his arms while Charley let hers relax, dropping them to her sides and closing her eyes. She inhaled the air around her; crisp, fresh, yet musky, as though it wasn't pure. As if it wasn't completely clean.

She opened her eyes and looked down at the car park, rubbish and debris scattered across the length of it. She took a breath and the rubbish rose – cans, crisp packets, old cardboard boxes – hovering a few inches from the ground. The swings that they'd been on only a few hours before began to sway, back and forth.

Aiden could feel the wind altering around him, as if it was changing direction somehow. The harsh breeze picked up, making him stumble backwards.

Charley took another deep breath as the swings swung faster, the rubbish rose higher and the wind got stronger. The leaves that lay underneath the bare trees blew towards her, circling her as they reached the rooftop.

Aiden couldn't believe what he was seeing. She looked magnificent, engulfed in autumn leaves, her hands now outstretched towards the sky. The wind whistled and Aiden could have sworn that he could see colours. All around Charley were shades of blue, pink, orange and green, like tiny lights emanating from inside of her.

She's . . . glowing, he thought to himself. And she was.

She pushed her weight on to her toes, feeling as though she could float away.

But all of a sudden, the peace was shattered as Charley let out an ear-splitting shriek. She pressed her palms to her temples as she fell to the ground, as did everything else she'd been controlling. She started to shake, her legs flailing as her body convulsed in uncontrollable spasms.

'Chambers!' Aiden yelled, and he was at her side in seconds.

'Make it stop!' Charley screamed, searing pain coursing through her body.

'I . . . I can't. Chambers, you need to tell me what's wrong.'

'A woman. She's . . . oh, God. Aiden it hurts!'

Aiden began to panic as he tried to stop her from thrashing around. How was he supposed to help her when he didn't know what was wrong?

But just as quickly as it had come on, it stopped, and Charley's body went limp in his arms.

'Chambers?' he said gently, cradling her head. 'Chambers!'

'Hmm?' she moaned, opening her eyes, and he let out a sigh of relief.

'What happened?'

'Abbie . . .'

He frowned and said, 'What about her?'

'I saw her. Here . . . Aiden, Abbie didn't fall. I saw it all. She was pushed.'

'What do you mean?'

'I saw what happened . . .'

'Like a vision?'

'I guess so, yeah. It was like I was standing there watching it. Abbie was sitting, alone, and then suddenly there was someone behind her. A woman . . . she pushed her.'

'Who was it? Did you see her face?'

'No, I couldn't make it out. It was just a blur.'

'So who has it in for Abbie then?'

'Maybe this wasn't about Abbie,' Charley said, getting to her feet with Aiden's help.

'You think this was aimed at you?'

'I don't know. But with everything that's happened . . .' Charley sighed. 'Maybe I'm being stupid.'

'You're not being stupid, Chambers.'

'What do we do now?' Charley asked quietly.

'We need to find out who this woman is, and fast, before she targets anyone else.'

TWENTY-TWO

Marcus lay in bed, his left arm twitching every few minutes, stirring him slightly from his doze. Beads of sweat ran down his forehead and his eyebrows crinkled as he let out a distressed whimper. It wasn't even dark yet, but the blinding headache Marcus had developed over the course of the day had left him wanting to do nothing but curl up in bed, hide himself away and forget about everything . . . everyone.

Everyone except her.

His eyelids fluttered and he mumbled something, the dream he was having drawing him in, further and further, until there was nothing else. Just him, just Bud. And blackness.

'Where did you come from?' Marcus asked, as he looked at her standing only a few feet away.

'Same place I always come from,' she said sombrely.

'No, it doesn't normally start like this.'

Bud laughed, but nothing was funny. She stopped laughing and her childish expression disappeared almost instantly; her soft features became hard, her mouth a thin line and her eyes dark.

'You have to stop this, Marcus.'

'Stop what?'

'You know what.'

'This isn't right,' Marcus breathed, 'this isn't how it's supposed to be.'

'You're forgetting me,' Bud whispered.

'No, never. I could never forget you.'

'Then you should know this isn't right. You should remember what kind of person I am,' – she hesitated – 'what kind of person I was.'

Bud started twisting her fingers, and Marcus could hear each one of them snapping consecutively.

'Don't do that, Bud.'

'You need to stop this before it's too late.'

'I don't like this!' Marcus yelled. 'This isn't how it's supposed to be.'

He reached out towards her, and when his hand touched her arm, her smooth, warm skin, he gasped.

'No . . .'

'What's wrong?'

'I'm not meant to be able to touch you. I can never reach you. That's how it always is.'

'Poor Marcus, he isn't well today,' Bud said, and she giggled.

'Where am I?'

'You know where you are.'

'I don't. I don't know anything right now. Everything is wrong.'

'It's not too late, Marcus. You can fix what you've done. You don't have to go through with it . . .'

'Please try to understand,' Marcus panted, sinking down to his knees. 'It's for you, all of it is.'

'No.' She shook her head. 'Please make things better.'

'I'm trying, squirt.'

'No, you're not. I have to go now.'

'Where are you going? I'm not finished yet–'

'Do the right thing.' She began backing away, her bare feet skimming along the nothingness beneath her. 'And Marcus . . .'

'Yes?'

'Stop her.'

'Stop who?'

'She's doing very bad things. You need to make her stop.'

'But I don't know what you're . . .'

He never got time to finish. All of a sudden, his eyes were open and he was sitting upright in his bed, the light outside finally beginning to dim.

He looked at the clock, then at his watch and frowned. Both said 11:47. It wasn't quite dark outside and there was no way it was nearly midnight.

His memory stirred, a pain driving into his chest.

He flung the watch to the floor and pulled the covers up to his chin, willing the throbbing in his head to disappear.

'Are you sure this is a good idea?' Charley asked as Aiden gripped her hand and pulled her up the front steps. 'Your mum really didn't seem to like me the last time we met. In fact, she seemed to dislike me. A lot. I'm tempted to use the word hate.'

'Cool it, Chambers. I'll deal with my mother. You just focus on being your usual . . . chipper self.'

Charley frowned. 'You hesitated. Why did you hesitate?'

Aiden laughed and let his hands rest on her shoulders. 'Calm down. You don't need to worry about her, she's just very . . . old-fashioned. And family orientated. She doesn't like what she doesn't know. Or understand . . .'

'Understand?'

'Trust me, it's nothing to worry about. All the women in my family are a little unhinged.'

'That's comforting,' Charley murmured as he opened the door, standing aside to let her in. He followed her and kicked off his shoes, Charley doing the same out of politeness.

'I don't think they're home,' Aiden said, turning on the lights in the hall.

'What a shame.'

'Mum, Dad? Hello?' he called. 'Nope, it's your lucky day.'

Aiden pulled Charley towards him, tilting her head and kissing her softly.

This never gets old, Charley thought, wrapping her fingers around his neck, but she was pulled from her bliss by a noise from the sitting room: a faint giggle followed by the clink of glass on glass.

'I thought no one was home,' Charley whispered.

'So did I.' Aiden started towards the sitting room, which was in darkness, and picked up a large metal poker from the umbrella stand by the sideboard.

'Why is that in your hall?' Charley asked, raising an eyebrow at the sizeable weapon.

'For situations like this.' He took another step closer so that he was nearly at the door. 'Who's there?'

'Why do you need a weapon anyway? Can't you just zap them to death? Or poof them into a cloud of smoke or something.'

'Chambers, please.'

Charley sighed and held her finger to her lips, her way of promising to be quiet.

Aiden reached round the corner and found the light, switching it on as he just about jumped into the room.

'Right, get the hell out my . . .' Aiden stopped, spotting a pretty blonde girl sitting cross-legged in his mother's hideous chair. 'Quinn?'

'Hey, little cuz, long time no see.' The girl leapt from the chair and flung herself into Aiden's arms, her furry grey sweater nearly smothering him.

'What are you doing here?' he smiled, relieved he didn't have to beat anyone up with a poker and chuffed to pieces to see his big cousin.

'Just passing through, thought I'd drop by. It's been far too long.' Quinn picked up a champagne flute from the table and took a large drink, draining the glass.

'That it has,' Aiden said, nodding in agreement. 'How have you been? And how's Dru?'

Druanna was Quinn's twin sister, identical in almost every way bar their hair. Neither one of them had ever dyed it, yet Quinn's was silvery-blonde and almost down to her bottom, while Dru had fiery red hair which she wore in a messy bob.

'Wouldn't know,' Quinn shrugged, topping her glass up with the bottle of Moët that sat at her feet. 'Haven't seen her for months. Honestly, I thought I might find her here.'

'Is that my mother's?' Aiden asked, gesturing towards the bottle. Quinn nodded. 'You're brave.'

'Oh, stop,' she said, waving a hand. 'Aunt Tabby won't mind.'

'You haven't talked to Aunt Tabby for a while,' Aiden scoffed, 'she doesn't do much smiling or sharing nowadays. Especially not champagne with her seventeen-year-old niece.'

'You worry too much. Sit down, catch me up. What's new? And when are you going to introduce me to the little mouse hiding behind the door?'

Charley gulped, taking a step into the room.

'Quinn, this is my girlfriend, Charley. Chambers, I'm sure you've gathered this is Quinn.'

'Nice to meet you, kitten.'

'Same to you,' Charley said shyly.

'So are you both gonna hover by the door all night or are you gonna sit yourselves down and entertain me? I didn't come all this way to sit in the dark and drink alone, you know.'

Aiden pulled out one of the dining chairs for Charley but didn't sit down himself, his mind switching between the arrival of his cousin and his parents returning home.

'What's up, shorty?' Quinn asked, winking at a confused Charley.

'Shorty?' Charley said.

'She's called me that for years. She always hated being small, so I used to tease her rotten about it when we were kids. She decided that if she had to be short, so did I. Well, metaphorically speaking.'

Charley gave a half smile but didn't reply, giving Quinn the opportunity to push Aiden further.

'So what's wrong?' she pressed. 'You don't seem yourself.'

'I'm fine,' he mumbled.

'You're a terrible liar.'

'So you always say.'

'What about you, little mouse? What's your story?'

Charley looked startled. 'Me? Eh . . .'

'She's a magician,' Aiden said, jumping in for her.

'Just like us then? Thought as much,' Quinn smiled. 'You couldn't not come from a magical family with a name like Chambers.'

'Oh, I'm not . . . I mean, it's just me. My family are all normal. At least I think they are. Some of them I'm . . . I'm not so sure about but . . .'

'Does she always babble like this?'

'Quinn,' Aiden snapped, closing the curtains and walking towards her, snatching the champagne bottle before she could reach it. He took a large gulp. 'Don't speak to her like that.'

'Aiden, it's okay,' Charley said, trying to calm the situation.

Quinn got up, her seven-inch stilettos making her appear much taller and to Charley, much more intimidating than she really was.

'It's not okay, little mouse. I'm sorry. As Aiden will tell you, I can be a little bit rude sometimes. Runs in the family.'

Charley faked a smile. She was feeling more and more awkward by the second. 'I'd better go,' she said quietly. 'I told my mum I'd be home for dinner.'

'Chambers . . .'

'It's fine, Aiden. I'll call you later. Quinn, it was really nice meeting you.' Charley bolted for the door before Aiden had time to change her mind.

'You too, cupcake,' Quinn called, helping herself to one of her uncle's chocolates that sat in a fancy box on top of the piano.

'What the hell is wrong with you?' Aiden yelled, slamming the lid back on the chocolate box.'

'Wrong with me? Nothing at all,' Quinn shrugged, but Aiden only sighed. 'It's good to be back, shorty. Good to be back.'

TWENTY-THREE

Charley woke up, her head splitting, and reached for the glass of water on her bedside table. Half asleep, she knocked the glass with the back of her hand, sending it tumbling towards the floor. Before it could reach the carpet, Charley grunted 'stay', flicked her hand towards the ceiling and turned to look at the floor. The glass was frozen in mid-air, the water still swirling around inside.

'Nice one,' she smiled as she took hold of the glass, removing it from its spot in the air and drinking the water, immediately wishing there'd been more.

Her dreams had kept her tossing and turning all night and her body was sore. She grabbed on to her shoulder and winced as she clicked it into place.

What the hell was I doing in my sleep?

Trying not to think too much about the pain, she got out of bed and went to her dresser, picking up a comb in an attempt to brush the tugs from her tangled hair.

'What the . . .' Charley's eyes widened as she looked in the mirror, her pale face draining of its little colour.

There were large, ugly bruises right the way up her left

arm. Her right arm was bruised too, although it wasn't as bad. It did, however, have a large gash on it, starting just above her elbow and stretching to her shoulder. It was deep and raised like a knife wound and Charley was pretty sure it looked infected.

'This is bizarre,' she said aloud, prodding the wound with her index finger to check it was real. 'Ouch!' It was.

She'd expected not to sleep well, to dream odd dreams. After meeting Quinn, there was no way she was going to have a good night's sleep. Not that Quinn wasn't nice – she was just . . . different. Unforeseen. Sudden. There was already so much going on in their lives what with Abbie, Marcus, Jess . . . she just wasn't sure if they needed another distraction, another complication.

Complication?

Charley immediately felt bad for thinking it. Quinn was Aiden's cousin after all, his family, and he obviously didn't get the chance to see her very often.

'Who am I to wish she wasn't here?' Charley said to herself. 'I'm sure she's lovely.'

She pulled on a sweater, cursing as the fabric rubbed against her cut, irritating it, and made her way downstairs.

'Mum? Jess?' There was no sign of anyone. Her dad was always away early for work, so she never expected to see him, but it was unusual for her mum to be gone, or Jess for that matter, especially without saying anything.

'Guess it's just me then,' Charley said, pulling a box of cereal from the shelf and filling a bowl. 'A goodbye would've been nice.'

'Goodbye? I just got here.'

Charley jumped, the cereal box flying out of her hand

and falling towards the floor, sending tiny sugar loops everywhere.

'Bloody hell,' Charley breathed, holding her hand to her chest. 'What are you doing here?'

'Just popped by to say hello.'

'You don't sneak up on people like that, Quinn. You nearly gave me a heart attack.'

'Only nearly? Shame.' Quinn took an apple from the fruit bowl and bit into it, her red nails almost matching its vibrant colour.

'What?' Charley scowled.

'Nothing. You got anything decent to eat? I'm not really a fruit and cereal type of gal.'

'I don't think so. Quinn, what are you really doing here? And how did you get in?'

Quinn sighed and put down her apple. 'How's your arm?'

'What?'

'Does it hurt?'

'How do you know about my arm?'

'Actually, arms. Plural. That one's sore, too,' she said casually, pointing at Charley's left arm. 'Oh, and your shoulder. Ouch.' Quinn's mouth twisted into a wicked smile.

'How do you know that?'

'Because, it was me who did it to you.'

Charley took a step back, spying the block of kitchen knives next to the sink. 'What are you talking about?'

'Don't play dumb, Charley, it doesn't suit you. Anyway, I just came to finish the job.'

'Get out, Quinn.'

'Come on, I just got here.'

'Get out of my house.' Charley lunged towards the sink, grabbing a knife and holding it out in front of her. Quinn got up and walked towards her, a sly grin still on her face.

'Or what? Are you going to stab me? Plunge that knife into my gut and twist it until I bleed to death on your floor. Now that would make a mess, wouldn't it?'

'I'll do what I have to.'

'Only because you know you can't use magic to beat me.'

'Why are you doing this?'

'Because, Charley. It's a message.'

'What?'

Quinn got closer and closer until they were face to face. They both looked down at the knife Charley was holding, the knife which was now embedded in Quinn's chest. Quinn's face went white and she fell to the floor, her body disappearing as she hit the ground. Everything disappeared. Everything went black.

Charley woke with a start. She reached for her glass of water and let it fall, just as it had done already that morning. This seemed all too familiar.

'Stay,' she murmured and flicked her hand, but the glass hit the floor, water spilling over the carpet. 'Oh, thank God,' she gasped. 'It wasn't real . . .'

She got up and went to the mirror, her head spinning as she tried to make sense of the nightmare she'd just had. A nightmare, that's all it was. Just a bad dream.

'What? No . . .'

Charley stopped dead as she looked in the mirror. Her skin was still purple and the cut was still there.

She didn't know what was a dream and what wasn't.

আ

Charley's phone rang at quarter to ten, just as her eyes were beginning to close for the umpteenth time since she'd left the house. She was so tried, so drained, that all she wanted to do was sleep. Sleep . . . not dream.

'Hello?' she answered groggily, her throat dry.

'Where are you, Chambers?'

'I'm just trying to get some rest. You?'

'At school, where you're supposed to be. What's up?'

'I had a bad night. I don't think I can cope with school today.'

'Okay, tell me where you are and I'll come find you.'

'No, it's all right. I'd rather be alone.'

'Is this about Quinn?' he asked, and she started shaking her head before realising he couldn't see her.

'No, of course not. Why would you say that?'

'Well, you seemed a little off last night. I know it was a bit unexpected, her showing up.'

'It has nothing to do with Quinn!'

'All right, calm down. What's up then?'

'Nothing, I . . . I just need some time to myself. I'll call you later.'

'Wait,' Aiden cried, 'don't hang up yet.'

'Why? What is it?' Charley stayed on the line for a few moments but Aiden said nothing. Finally, he broke the silence.

'Okay. Speak to you in a bit.' The line went dead and Charley took the phone from her ear, giving it an odd look.

'That was weird,' she mumbled, putting the phone away and pulling her knees up to her chest.

She was huddled in the tiny playhouse at the park, not far from the school. She didn't want to speak to anyone, especially not Aiden. What was she supposed to say to him?

By the way, your cousin who I only just met beat me up in my dream last night and was planning on killing me, but I got in there first. But now I'm not really sure if it was a dream because I woke up with all these strange bruises and an eight inch cut that seriously resembles a knife wound.

Yes, because that's what any normal person would say. Charley wasn't normal though, and she was well aware of that. In fact, she was getting a little too aware.

'So why are you hiding in a play park?'

Charley let her head fall forward, banging it off her knees.

'How did you find me?' she asked.

'I held you on the line so I could do a seeking spell.'

'I told you I wanted to be alone.'

'And I told you I would come see you. Something's up, Chambers, and I'm not leaving until you tell me what it is.'

Charley looked at him and sighed. She knew he meant well and she loved that he cared, but she didn't particularly want to be around him. She knew he could read her like a book and she didn't want to have to explain.

'Nothing's up,' she said, hauling herself from the playhouse and walking away. 'I just need some space, okay?'

'No, Chambers, not okay. I'm not leaving until you—' Aiden grabbed Charley's shoulder to make her stop, not hard, yet the pain she experienced was excruciating.

'Let go!' Charley screamed, clutching her shoulder, which felt like it had just been ripped from its socket.

'Wow, Chambers, what happened?' Charley didn't answer. 'Why is your shoulder so sore?'

'It's nothing. I . . . I fell.'

Aiden's face hardened. 'What happened?'

Charley thought about what to say, how to put the words, structure them so that they made sense, if even a little.

'I had a dream,' she said meekly, 'about Quinn. I was covered in cuts and bruises, my shoulder was out of place. She was in my house, acting . . . I don't know, strange. She told me she'd done it to me, said she was going to finish me off.'

'All right . . .'

'I stabbed her, in my dream, only because she was going to kill me. That's when I woke up. I thought it had all just been a nightmare, but then I saw these . . .'

With difficulty, Charley pulled the jumper over her head to reveal the angry bruises, the deep cut and a rather misshapen shoulder.

'Holy shit,' Aiden whispered, unable to take his eyes off his girlfriend's battered frame. Her pale skin was barely visible through the mass of black marks, and the wound was without a doubt infected.

Charley winced as she moved her shoulder, pain searing through it.

'It's dislocated,' Aiden said softly.

'What?'

'Your shoulder, it's dislocated. We need to get you to a doctor.'

'I'm not going to a doctor.'

'Someone needs to put your shoulder back in place, and that needs to be seen to,' he said, pointing at her arm. 'You need antibiotics–'

'Aiden, listen to me. I'm not going to a doctor. You can click my shoulder back–'

'It's more than a click,' he said, screwing his face up at the thought. He'd had to reconnect his own shoulder on several occasions and it wasn't something he had fond memories of.

'Whatever, you can fix it. And I'll wrap a bandage round my arm or something . . .'

'Chambers . . .'

'It's not medical, Aiden, it's magical. Antibiotics aren't going to do anything. Honestly, I don't know what will.'

She was right and he knew it; believing it was where he was having trouble. If it was down to magic, which was the most likely scenario, then something – or someone – was deliberately trying to hurt Charley, and they were doing a pretty good job. And the worst part of it was, there was nothing Aiden could do to stop them. Not without knowing who was behind it or what magic they were using. He was completely in the dark.

'What else happened?' he asked. 'Was anyone else in your dream?'

'No, just Quinn.'

'Did she say anything, mention anyone? Anyone who might want to hurt you?'

'Not that I remember. She said something about a message.'

'What message?'

'The dream . . .' Charley tried to think back, the dream

slipping further from her memory as the day went on. 'She said it was a message.'

'We need to find Quinn,' Aiden said, taking his jacket off and draping it over Charley's good shoulder, then carefully over the other.

'Ouch,' she cried, screwing her eyes shut as she tried to hold back the tears.

'Sorry. I'm not trying to hurt you.'

'I know . . .'

'Come on. We'll get you back to mine and fix your shoulder. Then we better talk to Quinn.'

'Do you know where she is?' Charley asked as they made their way from the park.

'Unfortunately, yes.'

'Is that not a good thing?'

'Not really, no.'

'Why? Where is she?'

Aiden raised his eyebrows. 'She's with my mother.'

TWENTY-FOUR

The two women sat in the corner of the café, blethering to one another and sipping their drinks. To look at, they were both breathtaking, although in completely different ways.

Quinn's beauty was hard to miss, from her long shiny hair to her soft pale cheeks, she appeared almost perfect. She had an exceptional figure too, although she certainly didn't get it from excess gym sessions or low-carb diets; Quinn liked food almost as much as she loathed exercise.

Tabitha's good looks, however, were more subtle. She was older than Quinn, obviously, but with age had come style for Tabby – an elegance that most women fail to pull off, even after hours of primping and preening. At thirty-nine, Tabitha was often mistaken for someone in their late twenties, a misconception she was happy to perpetuate.

Although both were attractive in their own unique way, it was clear that they weren't related by blood. Neither Quinn nor Dru looked particularly like either of their parents, but they bore a huge resemblance to their Uncle Fergus.

'So what brings you back to Newford?' Tabitha asked when Quinn was finally finished speaking.

'I told you, I wanted to see you all. Spend some quality time with the family, have a catch up, you know.'

Tabitha took a sip of her latte and shook her head. 'Really, Quinn, the real reason?'

'I don't know what you're talking about,' Quinn protested, but Tabitha only raised her eyebrows.

'You're about as good at lying as Aiden is. And you may remember, Quinn dear, that my son does not lie well.'

'Tell me something I don't know.' Quinn gulped down her cappuccino and helped herself to another slice of carrot cake, shoving the whole thing in her mouth to buy some time.

'You're stalling, dear.'

'I'm not,' Quinn choked, 'I swear.'

'All right, I'll stop pushing. But I'm on to you, young lady.'

'I wouldn't have it any other way.'

Tabitha smiled at her niece and waved the waiter over, asking him rather brusquely to fetch them their bill.

Tabitha Cunningham rarely smiled anymore, but she admired Quinn's positive outlook on life. She'd always had a soft spot for the girl, and even though she barely saw her now, it was still there.

'How's Druanna?' she said, and her tone changed dramatically. The way Tabitha felt about Quinn did not stretch to her sister.

'Oh, you know Dru. Kinda hard to keep track of.'

'I see,' Tabitha said, almost whispering the words.

'I'm sure she's just the same old Dru–'

'She's not here, Quinn.'

'What?'

'Druanna. She isn't here. I haven't seen nor heard from your sister in a long time.'

'I know. I didn't think she was . . . well, maybe I thought she could have been but–'

'What are you doing here, Quinn?'

The room was eerily silent, apart from the sound of Aiden's footsteps pacing up and down, making Charley more and more nervous by the second.

'Are you ready?' he asked as Charley sat down looking petrified.

'Not really.'

'You sure you don't want to go see a doctor?'

'Positive. Just do it.'

Aiden nodded and gently took a hold of Charley's shoulder, her face contorting as he touched it.

'Sorry,' he mumbled, wishing there was some way to fix it without having to hurt her.

He knew there wasn't.

Magic wouldn't help, not if the injury had been caused by something supernatural in the first place. Something which was most likely a lot stronger than he was. Besides, it was a known fact that magicians weren't allowed to heal people.

He knew he had to do it the old-fashioned way.

'I'm going to count to three, okay? Then I'll . . .'

There was a loud crack and Charley's screams filled the room, the last bit of colour draining from her face as she tensed her body, trying to ease the pain.

'You said you were going to count to three!' she cried, a burning sensation emerging inside her.

'I know.'

'You lied!'

'I know.'

'Oh, God, that was excruciating.'

'I know.'

'Stop saying that! I can't believe you tricked me—'

'I'm sorry, Chambers. That really wasn't fun for me.'

'But it was a walk in the park for me?' Charley barked, but she wasn't really angry. In fact, although she was still in severe pain, she felt a huge sense of relief. At least it was done.

'At least it's over,' Aiden said, mimicking her thoughts, and he pushed her hair back, kissing her gently on the forehead. 'You were very brave.'

'Well, now it's your turn to be brave.'

Aiden rolled his eyes. 'Yep, I guess so. Let's go find mother dearest.'

Quinn's hands started to shake and her mouth immediately dried up. She was about to start panicking when the café door swung open, Aiden striding in with Charley not far behind him.

'Aiden, over here!' Quinn yelled. 'Your timing is impeccable.'

'Isn't it just?' Tabitha muttered under her breath.

They made their way over to the table, Charley faltering slightly as she made eye contact with Quinn.

'Hey, kitten, how are you?' Quinn asked in a cheerful voice. 'You don't look too good.'

'That's because I just had to pop her shoulder back into place.'

'What? Oh my God, what happened?'

'Someone dislocated it,' Aiden said, pulling a chair out for Charley who shook her head, saying it was more comfortable to stand.

'Someone dislocated your shoulder? You poor thing, that's awful. Who was it?'

Aiden glanced at Charley who just shrugged in return. 'Apparently, it was you.'

Quinn frowned at them and then giggled. 'I'm sorry, what?'

'It's a long story, one I'd rather not get into here. You think you could meet us back at the house when you're done?'

'We're done,' Tabitha said, interrupting Quinn who was just about to speak.

Tabitha collected her belongings and got up from the table so that she stood face to face with her son. She glanced at Charley, giving her a frosty look, and then let her eyes find their way back to Aiden's. He held her gaze, both of them silent until she said, 'I told you this would happen.'

Aiden scowled, his fists clenched at his sides. 'Excuse me?'

'I don't know what trouble you're in now and frankly I don't want to. No doubt I'll find out though, when I'm clearing up your mess.'

'You're unbelievable, you know that?'

'No, Aiden, you are unbelievable. I told you to stay away from her, and with good reason, too. Not that I ever expected you to listen. Hear me now though, this will not end well. Finish it, before it's too late.'

She tried to walk around him, leave after having the last word, but Aiden side-stepped, blocking her path.

'Get out of my way, Aiden.'

'There are a few things I'll be putting a stop to, but my relationship with Charley isn't one of them. Hear me when I say this, Mother: Charley isn't going anywhere, so you better get used to her. And if you don't want whatever it is you're talking about to end in disaster, then you can stop being so bloody cryptic all the time and work with me for a change, instead of always making things so difficult.'

A few heads around the café turned to see what was happening, but no one moved apart from Quinn who jumped up from her seat, shouting enthusiastically that everything was all right. Charley began fidgeting nervously, wishing she was somewhere else. She still felt lightheaded and a little sick from earlier, and hearing Aiden's mother stand there and criticise her was not an ideal start to the afternoon.

'Well that's me told then, isn't it?' Tabitha whispered.

Her voice was cold, ominous, and Aiden could tell there was hurt buried in there somewhere, albeit hidden well. He understood. It stung that he'd gone against her once again, picked Charley over her, his own flesh and blood. She felt betrayed.

Aiden understood how she felt, he just didn't care.

'It sure is,' he said through gritted teeth, his eyes never leaving hers. Tabitha nodded in return, her forehead crinkling as her eyebrows came together, forming a scowl. This time she succeeded in walking past her son and out the door, leaving the three of them – and the rest of the customers – unsure of what to do next.

Quinn shuddered involuntarily. 'What the hell was that?' she asked, looking at Aiden for answers as she brushed a stray hair from her face. In the café's fluorescent lights, it looked almost white, a milky colour to match her chalky complexion.

'That was good old Aunt Tabby,' Aiden replied, raising his eyebrows at Quinn in an 'I told you so' way.

'So what do we do now?' she asked.

'We go home and figure out what the hell's going on.'

TWENTY-FIVE

Charley jumped up when she heard the kettle whistling and rushed to the kitchen to make them all some tea, despite Quinn and Aiden both saying they didn't want any.

Well, what Quinn actually said was, 'I'll have a brandy instead,' but changed her mind at the frosty look her cousin gave her.

Charley made her way into the kitchen and raked around until she found three mugs, dropped a tea bag in each and filled them with water.

She was well aware no one wanted to sit around and drink tea. She wasn't particularly thirsty herself, but at that moment she needed normality.

Unfortunately, as she was quickly learning, magicians didn't seem to have that luxury.

Once she was finished making the drinks, she carried them through with one hand, the other still giving her grief whenever she used it too much.

'Here you are,' she said, setting them down on the table and taking a seat beside Aiden, who wasn't paying attention to anything but the book in front of him.

'Thanks, chicken,' said Quinn, smiling as she pulled a mini bottle of bourbon from her jeans pocket and tipped it into her tea; the sobriety hadn't lasted long.

'Aren't you supposed to do that with coffee?' Charley asked.

'Tea, coffee, juice. They're all much the same to Quinn.'

'Hey, don't take it out on me, just because you're no fun. I remember the days when you would've done anything for a laugh.'

'Hardly, Quinn. I was a kid.'

'Even so. You're so serious now.'

'That's because I need to be,' Aiden barked. 'You should try it sometime. Life is just one big joke to you.'

Quinn's playful smile disappeared. 'You know that's not true.'

'Do I? If there isn't fun involved, you aren't interested.'

'You think I'm here to have fun?'

'I've no idea why you're here because you haven't told me. How am I meant to know if you keep me in the dark?'

'You're one to talk, telling me to stop messing around even though you haven't shed a bit of light on what's going on with Charley, how I'm supposed to have done that to her.' Quinn gestured to Charley's arm. 'You're such a hypocrite.'

'I'm not . . .' Aiden meant to go on but the words wouldn't come. He knew he wasn't being fair. 'All right, I guess I am.'

'You guess?'

'I'm sorry, Quinn. I didn't mean to snap. You just appeared out of the blue with no word of why you're here. Don't get me wrong, I'm happy to see you. But I know you came for more than a family catch up.'

'I didn't–'

'You don't need to tell me. Just don't treat me like an idiot, okay?' Quinn looked at her feet and then nodded in agreement, some of the tension lifting as Aiden smiled in return.

'So, what happened?'

As Aiden began to fill Quinn in on the day's extraordinary events, her body turned cold. The more she listened, the more anxious she became, pacing the room in a fearful way.

'No, no,' she murmured, 'this isn't good.'

'No, it's definitely not good,' said Aiden, 'but if we can figure out what–'

'It's Dru,' Quinn said, biting her lip until it started bleeding. 'It has to be.'

'Dru's doing this?'

'No . . .'

'Quinn, what's going on?'

Charley stood in the background watching the pair of them, pretty sure that if she left they wouldn't notice, at least not for a while. She'd barely spoken two words since they'd arrived back at Aiden's, and she felt slightly out of the loop – an outsider, almost. It was probably silly, but she couldn't help feeling somewhat . . . unnecessary.

'Aunt Tabby was right . . .'

'What?'

'You want to know why I came here? I came for Dru . . . I knew she probably wouldn't be here, a part of me just hoped . . . God, I hoped she might have come back. It was stupid . . .'

'So how is this connected to Dru? Has something happened? She's not . . . you know?'

There was an awkward glance between the two of them and Charley realised they must be talking about something she wasn't aware of. Something else she wasn't clued up on.

'Don't mind me,' Charley said whilst pacing back and forth, adrenaline building up as she got more and more annoyed. 'It's not like I'm the one that had the dream, that got battered and woke up as if it was all real. Don't feel like you need to include me in your conversation.'

'Chambers, what's wrong with you?'

Charley dug her knuckles into her temples, grimacing in response as a sharp pain stabbed at her shoulder. 'Quinn, Quinn, it's always Quinn!'

'What's wrong with her?' Quinn asked, pulling a face as Charley fell to her knees.

'I don't know,' Aiden murmured. 'Chambers?'

'What's . . . what's happening?' Charley cried, unable to control the visions that were flashing before her eyes.

'Chambers . . .'

'It's always Quinn, always has been. Little ray of sunshine, never does anything wrong. What am I meant to do? I can't even . . . it has to stop. All of it. But it can't . . . I can't. I . . . I need to go on living this, this torment–'

'Chambers!' Aiden grabbed her shoulders and began to shake her, desperately trying to bring her back from the trance she'd fallen into.

'I just . . . I . . . I want everything to be quiet,' Charley stuttered incoherently, 'nothing's quiet anymore.'

'It's Dru . . .' said Quinn, bending down by Charley's

side as her head began to loll, her inconsistent ramblings lessening slightly.

'Everything's bloody Dru today,' Aiden snapped brusquely, but then feeling bad he said, 'What's Dru done this time?'

'She's somehow connected to Charley, or rather, Charley's connected to her. I don't know who's done what, but that isn't Charley talking, it's Dru.'

'Are you insane?'

'Listen to her, Aiden. Little ray of sunshine, it has to stop, nothing's quiet . . . who does that sound like?'

Aiden thought about it for a moment. 'Chambers wouldn't know any of that stuff.'

'Exactly. How could she? Dru must be in there somewhere; she must be using Charley to get to me, to speak to me.'

'Why would she say that? Quinn, are you sure? None of this seems very plausible.'

'You got a better theory?'

Aiden sighed. 'I got nothing.'

After an hour of dabbing Charley's head with an ice-cold flannel and listening to Quinn prattle on about her twin sister's selfish and erratic behaviour, Aiden had had enough.

'I'm taking her to the hospital,' he said, scooping Charley into his arms.

'They won't be able to do anything for her.'

'They'll do more than I can. This is useless, Quinn, you said she'd be better by now. Look at her.'

'Shorty, calm down. She just needs time to recharge, she'll be good as new in . . . there you are, see.'

Aiden looked down as Charley started to come to, her eyes flickering open and slowly focusing on his face.

'Aiden?'

'I'm here,' he said, setting her down on the couch. 'How are you feeling?'

'Confused . . .' She looked at Quinn. 'I'm guessing the dysfunctional redhead is the other half of you.'

'That's one way to put it,' Quinn shrugged.

'She seems . . . nice.'

'Where is she?' Quinn asked frantically. 'What did she say? We could hear bits of your conversation but–'

'I wasn't talking to her. It was like I was . . . watching her past, her memories. I could feel what she was feeling . . . it was unbearable.'

Quinn looked disappointed. 'So you don't know where she is?'

Charley shook her head and then turned to Aiden. 'I'm sorry. Was I meant to–?'

'You weren't meant to do anything,' he said, quietening her. 'You need to rest, get your strength back.'

'I'm fine.'

'No, you're–'

'Aiden, I'm fine. Tell me about Dru.'

'What about her?' said Quinn, almost slightly amused. 'Where do you want me to start?'

'Why is she in so much pain?'

The atmosphere in the room grew colder as Charley asked that question. Quinn sank back into her chair, her face deadpan, and Aiden cleared his throat, fetched the brandy bottle from the liquor cabinet and handed it to Quinn. Charley frowned, confused at his sudden tolerance of Quinn's drinking habits.

'She's allowed,' he said, giving Quinn a pitying look. 'Trust me, for this one she needs it.'

Quinn unscrewed the cap and poured a generous measure into her empty teacup, draining it and then pouring another. She grimaced at the spirit's pungent taste, yet it didn't stop her drinking the next.

'Dru and I have always been quite . . . different,' she began. 'I was always very outgoing, confident. A people's person, you know? I liked to be surrounded by friends, have fun. Dru's more of a private person, keeps herself to herself whenever she can. She's never liked people interfering in her life, even when they're just trying to help.'

She spoke the last few words with resentment, as if she had first-hand experience in that department.

'It's not that she wasn't confident. She's a sarcastic bugger most of the time.' Quinn looked thoughtful for a moment, took a large gulp of brandy and continued. 'Dru's pretty good at taking care of herself, trust me. She just never seemed content. I don't know if it was how we started out that first caused it. I think she's always felt trapped in this world.'

'How you started out?' Charley questioned.

'Our birth wasn't exactly straightforward. There was . . . a complication.'

Aiden got up and walked to where Quinn was sitting. As if reading his mind, she held out the brandy bottle which he took without hesitation.

'It's called TTTS: Twin to Twin Transfusion Syndrome. It's basically when the placenta isn't shared equally and one baby isn't getting the nutrients they need to survive.

'Dru was what they called the donor twin, meaning

there was a blood transfusion within the uterus from her to me. Although she was born a lot smaller, she was okay, despite the lesser blood volume. I, on the other hand . . .'

She stopped for a second, the memories bringing back so much heartache; years and years of guilt and unhappiness, all brought to the surface after such a long time.

'I wasn't going to survive. They told my parents before either of us were born. I'd become overloaded with blood and my heart was failing – they said that labour would have put too much of a strain on it, I wasn't strong enough.'

Charley didn't say anything. She wasn't really sure what to say. She knew Quinn wasn't finished though; she was here, after all, alive and well.

'My parents were distraught. They couldn't face losing either of us, so they made the decision to do a linking spell.'

'What does that do?'

'The spell linked Dru and me together, meaning that Dru's essence was enough to keep us both alive, on one condition: we weren't just linked for the birth – we were linked forever. If one of us dies–'

'The other dies too . . .' Charley whispered.

'That's right. My sister's chance of dying doubled from the second she was born. Imagine having to deal with that, live with the knowledge that your parents did that to you, gave you that curse. Only that isn't what bothers her. Dru's problem is not being able to die.'

'What?' Charley said softly.

'She's never been happy here, not really. I do think I'm to blame – the magic did something to her, I'm sure of it.

She wouldn't have been like this if they'd just let me–' Quinn paused, the word too painful to say. 'Anyway, of course she can't do anything about it, otherwise she takes me too. Dru isn't cursed to die, Charley, she's cursed to live.'

TWENTY-SIX

Marcus slammed the door as he came in from school that day, his mood dampening as he laid eyes on his mother standing at the bottom of the stairs.

Her hair was pulled back into a perfect French braid, secured in place with a number of Kirby grips. She was wearing a black pencil skirt, high heels, and a red chiffon blouse with scarlet lips to match.

'Where are you going?' Marcus grunted, dumping his school bag on the floor.

Judith raised her eyebrows. 'Nowhere.'

'Cool, whatever.' He walked on past her and up the stairs, stopping halfway when he heard her speak.

'A word, please, Marcus. Whenever you're ready.' She wandered off towards the kitchen, stopping just before she was out of sight. 'And please pick up your bag. You know I don't like clutter.'

Marcus waited until she was gone and then muttered something rude under his breath.

Deciding to get whatever conversation she wanted to have out of the way, he trudged back down the stairs, thundering into the kitchen and plonking himself down on a stool.

'What is it?'

'Well, aren't you testy today?'

'I'm tired,' he groaned.

'I'm not surprised. You were up half the night screaming.'

'What's your point?' said Marcus irritably, not at all in the mood to discuss his unusual sleeping patterns.

'It's getting out of hand, Marcus. You're giving yourself away.'

'How am I? It was a nightmare, a dream, nothing more.'

'You were saying her name again, crying out for her. Your father doesn't know what to do. He wants to get help for you.'

'So tell him it's nothing. He listens to everything you say.'

'Marcus, when I told you about this, I–'

'You said you would deal with him, Mum. I can't make the dreams go away, you know that.'

'And you know that I can. If you'd only let me–'

'No! I told you already, I don't want them to stop. I need them . . .'

'They're destroying you, Marcus.'

'I'm fine.'

'You're far from fine.'

'Listen, I can handle them, okay? You said last night that it won't be much longer. I need these dreams, whether or not they're tearing me apart. I need to see her.'

Judith nodded, recognising her son's reliance on his

disturbing nightmares. She wasn't really sure if he would cope without them. However harrowing they might be, it was the only time he got with her.

'You're sure you can keep it together?' she asked dubiously.

'I'm sure.'

'I still don't know what to do about your father. He's getting more and more suspicious–'

'I'm sure you'll think of something,' Marcus said, cutting her off. 'Are we done?'

Judith didn't say anything, but from the look she gave, Marcus knew it was safe for him to leave. He slid off the stool and grabbed an apple from the fruit bowl before walking towards the door.

'Marcus?'

'What?'

'Is she going to be a problem?'

'Who?'

'Who do you think? Charley.'

Marcus felt apprehensive as soon as he heard her name. 'No, she won't be.'

'All right, then. Dinner's at six. Try and make an appearance tonight, for your father's benefit if nothing else. It's too late for slip-ups now.'

'Fine, I'll be down for dinner. Happy?'

Judith smiled. 'Ecstatic.'

Charley stared up at the ceiling, squinting at the giant chandelier that hung above her head. This one was made of brass and looked much more old-fashioned than the one in the hall.

This one was ugly.

She tilted her head back further so she was looking at Aiden.

'Do you have chandeliers in all your rooms?' she asked, a hint of sarcasm to her voice.

'My room doesn't have one.'

'Your room doesn't even have a telly,' she laughed.

'True.'

'When you two are done canoodling, can we get back to this, please?' said Quinn as she flicked through Tabitha's book.

'Oh, how the tables have turned,' Charley smiled. 'Aiden, what have you done to her?'

'Beats me. This is the first time I've seen her with a book in front of her in . . . well, ever.'

'That is not true,' Quinn giggled. 'I read. Sometimes.'

'Yeah, the drinks menu at the bar.'

'I'm too young to drink in bars,' Quinn winked.

'Like that would stop you,' Aiden snorted.

So far, they hadn't learned anything about Charley's dream or her vision of Dru. Quinn was convinced the two were linked, she just didn't know how. She'd searched through every book in the house that had anything to do with magic or sorcery and was now back to the first one: the one that belonged to Tabitha.

'Will Aunt Tabby mind us looking through this?'

'You kidding? She'd have a fit.'

'Should we put it back? I don't want to–'

'Who cares?' Aiden grunted. 'She won't help me when I ask so what am I meant to do?'

'I dunno. She just seemed pretty mad earlier.'

'I couldn't care less. Things are happening here, Quinn, bad things, and if she isn't willing to help put a stop to them then we're going to have to do it ourselves.'

'So where do we go from here?'

Aiden looked down at Charley. 'Maybe I should pay Marcus another visit.'

Charley sat up quickly. 'What? No. Why?'

'Because we're running out of options. We haven't found anything out yet and he's really the only thing we've got to go on.'

'You think he has something to do with the dream?'

'No, not really, but I think he has a lot to do with everything else. Marcus is hiding something and I want to know what it is.'

'You aren't going alone.'

'Chambers . . .'

'No. If you're going then I'm coming too,' she insisted, folding her arms.

Aiden shook his head. 'Fine, if you must. But if I get even the slightest inkling that you're in danger then you get out, okay?'

'I'm sure it'll be–'

'Okay?' he said more sternly.

'Yes, okay.'

He got up and headed for the door, grabbing his coat on the way.

'I'm coming too,' Quinn yelped, running after him with the magic book tucked under her arm.

'I thought as much,' said Aiden testily. 'Put that back then and let's go.'

They arrived outside Marcus's house just as a black Mercedes was pulling into the driveway. A tall, good-looking man got out, clutching a briefcase and a pair of leather gloves – Garth Gillespie.

Charley thought he was very handsome, for an older man – dark hair, square jaw – and she clearly wasn't the only one who thought so.

'Oh, my!' Quinn spluttered, her own jaw just about hitting the ground.

'Seriously?' Aiden frowned.

'What? A girl's not allowed to look?'

'Put your eyes back in your head,' he said, and Quinn stuck her tongue out at him behind his back.

'Excuse me!' Charley shouted over to Garth, her knees going weak when he looked up, his brown eyes glinting. They were just like Marcus's . . .

'Hi there,' he smiled, showing off his shiny white teeth.

'Hi, I'm looking for Marcus. Is he home? We're . . . friends of his, from school.'

Garth's face lit up. 'Well, isn't this delightful. You know, I've yet to meet any of Marcus's friends here, he doesn't like to talk about them much.'

'He doesn't?'

'Not really, no. Keeps an awful lot to himself, that boy. It's a pleasure to meet you . . .'

'Charley. This is Aiden and his cousin, Quinn.'

'Wonderful,' Garth said cheerfully. 'Do come in. I'm sure he's probably inside, sulking in his room no doubt.'

The three of them followed Garth into the house, all feeling slightly apprehensive as Quinn closed the door behind them. They weren't really sure what they were doing there, or what they were going to ask Marcus when they saw him. Would he cause a scene, out them and tell his father that they weren't his friends at all?

Only one way to find out . . .

'Marcus!' Garth shouted from the hall, taking off his long trench coat and hanging it on one of the hooks by the door. 'Visitors.'

'You have a lovely home,' Quinn gushed, admiring a large glass vase filled with beautiful pink lilies. She leaned over to smell them, just as a woman came strutting down the hallway.

'Hello,' she said, surprised to see more than just Garth standing there. 'And you are?'

'These are friends of Marcus,' Garth smiled, bending down to kiss his wife on the cheek.

'Really? Well, this is a nice surprise. I'm sure he'll be just thrilled.'

She grimaced at the three of them, secretly cursing her husband for letting a bunch of bothersome teenagers into her house, especially so near dinner time. She was just contemplating how to get rid of them when her eyes settled on Charley, recognising her straight away.

'Well, well. Hello, Miss Chambers.'

Charley gave her a blank look. 'I'm sorry, have we met?'

Judith lifted her chin, studying the young girl in front of her. 'No, I don't believe we have.'

'Can I get you kids something to drink?' Garth interrupted, motioning for them to go through to the kitchen.

'I'm sure they're fine, darling,' said Judith. 'They probably just want to get up and see Marcus. Am I right?'

'Yeah, let's get this over with,' Aiden sighed, then realised he was getting a rather odd look from Marcus's parents.

'What Aiden means is . . . well, we have a lot of homework to do tonight. Can't stay too long.'

Judith looked unconvinced. 'I see. And you are?'

'Quinn. I'm Aiden's cousin.'

'Yes, you do look familiar.'

'I do?' Quinn was pretty sure she'd never met the woman before in her life.

'Straight up the stairs and down the corridor,' Judith said, ignoring Quinn. 'Just follow the stench of dirty laundry and you'll find Marcus no problem.'

She didn't say any more, but simply turned and walked back towards the kitchen, her hips swaying in an exaggerated fashion.

'Please excuse my wife,' Garth murmured under his breath. 'She isn't intentionally rude.'

'No, not at all,' said Charley. 'We probably should have called first.'

'Don't be silly, it's nice to meet his friends. Can you find the room on your own? I better go and see to things through there,' he gestured towards the kitchen.

'Of course.' Charley smiled. 'I've been here before.'

'Brilliant, make yourselves at home.'

As Garth took off down the hall, Aiden's frown grew deeper.

The thought of Charley being in Marcus's room, the two of them alone together, troubled him more than he'd ever let on, especially now that he knew who Marcus was – what Marcus was.

While thoughts of ripping Marcus in two drifted through Aiden's unsettled mind, Charley was having a more sympathetic approach to the situation.

She was feeling guilty. She actually felt bad for Marcus.

She knew what he was, what he was capable of, yet she felt terrible for lying; pretending to be his friend to gather information from him. It wasn't something she felt comfortable doing.

'That woman's awfully peculiar,' Quinn murmured as they climbed the stairs. 'Why does she recognise me? I swear I've never met her before . . .'

'Neither have I,' Charley replied, wondering the same thing herself.

'You've been here before, haven't you?' Quinn asked. 'You sure you didn't meet her then?'

'No. They were here, but I never spoke to them. Marcus took me straight upstairs.'

'She probably recognises you from all the photos Marcus has pinned up on his wall,' Aiden snorted.

'Why would he have photos of me?' Charley didn't understand what Aiden was implying.

'Crazy stalkers tend to do things like that.'

'Shut up, he isn't my stalker. He doesn't even like me.'

Aiden laughed this time, raising his eyebrows. 'Are you serious?'

'What's so funny?' she retorted.

'Marcus likes you nearly as much as Quinn likes vodka. Probably more, in fact, and that's saying something.'

'Hey, that's not . . .' Quinn started, but then shrugging her shoulders said, 'Okay, fair enough.'

'No, he doesn't, and especially not like that. We were only friends before . . .' Charley tailed off as she thought about everything that had happened since the first time she and Marcus had met.

'Yeah, and I'm just an insig,' Aiden grunted sarcastically.

'Insig?' Charley frowned. 'What does that mean?'

'Insignificants,' Quinn said. 'It's what we call non-magical people.'

'Charming.'

Once they reached the end of the hallway, Charley gently knocked on the door, her heartbeat drumming in her ears.

'Marcus?' she called, pushing the door open.

'Let yourself in, why don't you?' came a muffled voice from inside.

Charley walked into the room, Aiden stepping in after, followed by Quinn. It was dark inside, the lights all off and the curtains drawn. Charley searched the wall for a light switch and turned it on once she finally found where it was.

The room was a mess, making it difficult to find a clear spot to stand in.

'What do you want?' Marcus asked without looking up. He was lying face down on the bed, his head buried in a pillow, wearing just a pair of black jogging-bottoms.

'We came to talk to you,' Aiden said, and Marcus stirred at the sound of his nemesis' voice.

'Oh, goody. You brought your boyfriend. What a treat.'

He rolled on to his back, squinting as the bright light caught his eyes, momentarily blinding him.

'Bloody hell, turn that off, will you?'

'And do what?' Aiden said sharply. 'Stand and talk to you in the dark?'

Marcus stretched over to his bedside table and flicked a switch on the lamp that sat there. 'Satisfied?'

Aiden swore under his breath and turned off the overhead light.

'Well, well,' Marcus smiled once his eyes finally began to focus. 'Who's your friend?'

Aiden looked at Quinn protectively, as if he didn't really want to introduce her to Marcus. She might have been older than him, but he still felt responsible for her.

He knew fine well though that this was not the first demon Quinn had come into contact with. She was perfectly capable of handling herself.

'My cousin, Quinn.'

'Hello, darling,' Marcus winked, 'how you doing?'

Quinn rolled her eyes dismissively. 'In your dreams. I like my men, well . . . manly.'

'Trust me, sweetheart, I can show you all kinds of manly.'

'Oh, dear Lord,' Charley sighed.

'What's wrong, beautiful? You jealous?'

'As if.'

'God, you lot are no fun,' Marcus said, heaving himself out of bed and wandering over to where Quinn was. He stood in front of her, his brown eyes searching her steel-grey ones.

'What are you staring at?' she scoffed.

Marcus cleared his throat. 'I need a top. The drawers . . . you're in the way.'

Quinn felt her cheeks grow hot, and for once there was a flush of colour to them.

'Could have just said so,' she snapped, stepping out the way.

'I thought I just did.'

Marcus fished about in his drawer for a T-shirt while the other three stood awkwardly waiting for him. Well, Charley and Aiden stood awkwardly; Quinn began prancing around the room, taking a peek at anything interesting he had lying about.

'You looking for something?' Marcus asked, watching Quinn with interest as she examined his curtains.

'Just looking for clues,' she shrugged.

'Clues?'

'Quinn, shut up, will you?' Aiden grunted.

'Well, if you look behind them, you'll find a big, shiny see-through thing called a window,' Marcus mocked her. 'What do you guys want?'

'Answers,' said Charley. 'We want answers.'

'Haven't we done this already?'

'Yeah, but we're doing it again.'

'Gosh, it's my lucky day,' Marcus said, exasperated.

'Did you have anything to do with Abbie's accident?'

'What? No, of course not.'

'And why should I trust you?' Charley asked, folding her arms. 'Why should I believe a word you say?'

'I'm not asking you to believe me. I'm saying I wasn't involved. I didn't know anything about it until I heard at school . . .'

'What about Chambers?' Aiden asked, his jaw-line hardening. 'You been messing with her?'

'She hasn't given me the chance to mess with her,' Marcus grinned.

'This is serious. I'm dreaming about people trying to kill me, Marcus. Beating me to a pulp, threatening me in my sleep.'

'We all have wacky dreams sometimes, gorgeous. Doesn't mean I'm screwing with you. Although I wouldn't say no . . .' Marcus winked in an attempt to charm her, but she merely choked at his proposal.

'Well, someone is, seeing as I woke up black and blue with a dislocated shoulder.'

'You're hurt?' Marcus suddenly seemed concerned.

Aiden glowered at him. 'Why would you care?'

'I'm not a monster, Aiden, despite what you might tell her. I do care, you know.'

'Save it,' Charley said firmly. 'Did you have anything to do with it or not?'

'Not guilty, love.'

'And the nost? Are you going to tell me who it was for yet?'

He sat down on the chair next to his desk and said, 'No one you need to concern yourself with.'

'Quinn, take Chambers home,' Aiden said, the tone of his voice matching his stony expression, 'I wanna have a chat with Marcus . . . alone.'

'It's pointless,' Charley shook her head. 'We've heard all we're going to hear.'

'We have, yeah. I plan on getting a little more out of him when you–'

'He isn't going to tell you anything,' Charley said, turning on him. 'If he was going to talk, he'd be more likely to talk to me than you.'

'She's right you know,' Marcus smirked, putting his feet up on the desk. 'I'd rather have a heated conversation with her over you any day. No offence, mate, you're just not my type.'

'Chambers, he'll just–'

'Let's go, Aiden.'

Aiden stood for a moment, his own frustration building, not just at Marcus, but at Charley as well.

'Fine,' he snarled, before storming out, Quinn in close pursuit.

'I'll get you outside,' she shouted from the hallway, not wanting to let Aiden get too far ahead. She knew what her cousin was like; she knew his character, she knew his nature. Describing Aiden as hot-headed would be putting it mildly.

Charley waited a few seconds before turning to go as well, but Marcus jumped up when he saw her leaving, grabbing her arm as she reached the door.

'Charley, wait . . . I know you think I'm a lowlife but that's not how it is. That's not me. I just talk big . . . I'm not really that guy.'

Charley looked into his eyes, searching for the kindness she'd seen the first time she looked into them.

'No, Marcus, you're right. You're not that guy. You're not a guy at all. You're a demon. A filthy, disgusting, murderous demon. A complete waste of time and space.'

'Chambers . . .'

'Don't you dare call me that.'

His eyes crinkled at the corners, the glint slowly fading away. The cocky, arrogant boy from a few minutes before was replaced by someone confused and insecure – someone in pain.

Charley pulled her arm from his grasp and walked out the door.

TWENTY-SEVEN

Charley sat at the breakfast table, her mother on one side and Jess on the other. Her father was sitting at the end of the table, pouring himself some coffee.

No one had said anything for almost seven minutes, Charley had been counting. All she could hear was the loud crunching noise of Jess eating her Coco Pops, which was driving her insane.

'Is anyone going to tell us what's going on?' Charley eventually said. Linda put her spoon down and looked towards Nick. 'Come on, Mum. Something's obviously wrong. Dad hasn't had breakfast with us on a school day for years.'

Nick's face fell at his daughter's words, and he realised that what she'd said was true. He knew he wasn't around as much as he should be, but he always managed to somehow push it to the back of his mind.

'It's your gran,' Linda said softly, and Charley's eyes widened.

'What about her? Is she all right?'

She'd meant to go back and check on Dorcas, or at least tell her mother what had happened, but with the dream and the vision, it had completely slipped her mind.

'I don't want you girls to panic, but she's been taken into hospital. She's okay, but–'

'Hospital?' Charley cried. 'Why?'

'A couple of days ago her house was broken into. She said she didn't want to bother us, so she kept it to herself. Daft woman . . .'

'A break-in?' said Charley, puzzled. 'How do you know? I mean . . . was she there at the time?'

'Apparently so, yes. She said the doors were both locked, but they smashed the kitchen window, ransacked the place, and then left her there, traumatised. There are some sick people around, girls, let me tell you.'

Charley and Jess looked at each other. 'So you're saying it was the burglars who smashed the window? That's what gran said?'

'Yes, Charley. Why?'

'Just asking.'

Nick cleared his throat. 'I know this must be a shock for you both, but your gran's going to be fine. It's the best place for her. They can get her back on her feet and she'll be home in no time.'

Shows what you know, Charley thought.

'I need to see her.'

'I'll take you after school, dear,' Linda smiled, although her eyes seemed tired. She looked stressed and her skin was grey.

'No, I want to go now. Mum, I have to.'

'Charley–'

'Let her go,' Nick said calmly, squeezing his wife's

hand. 'In fact, I'll take you myself, darling. How does that sound?'

'Really?' Charley frowned. 'You don't have anywhere more important to be?'

'No, sweetheart, I don't.'

Charley nodded. 'Yeah, okay then.'

'You can go as well, Jess. Your dad will drop you both off at school once you've been to the hospital.'

Jess shrugged her shoulders. 'Nah, I'm good.'

'I'm sorry?' Linda said.

'I said I'm good. As in, no thanks, I don't want to go.'

'Jessica . . .'

'Leave her, Linda. It's a lot for the girls to take in. Maybe Jess needs some time–'

'I don't need time. I don't need anything. I just don't want to go and see Gran.' She got up from the table and swung her bag over her shoulder. 'I'm going to school.' With that, she walked out the front door.

Dorcas lay in the hospital bed, her back aching every time she moved. Her chest felt tight and she was finding it hard to catch her breath, although whenever the doctors did their rounds they said she was doing just fine.

She hadn't wanted to go into the hospital; she knew it wouldn't do any good. But she also knew she didn't have a choice. Linda was going to start realising soon that her mother's health was deteriorating quickly.

Not that being in the hospital helped her much, as the doctors were still saying that apart from the injuries caused by the fall, there were no underlying problems. There was no reasonable explanation for the pain she was experiencing. How would she explain all of this without involving her daughter in a world she'd tried so hard to protect her from?

Maybe it was better she knew – after all, with Charley being what she was, Linda was going to have her hands full, unless Charley decided to keep the truth from her altogether.

Dorcas didn't know what was best anymore. She was too tired.

'You want me to give you a minute?' Nick asked Charley when they arrived outside Dorcas's room.

'Is that all right?'

'Of course, darling, take as long as you need. I'll go in and see her when you visit Abbie.'

'Okay,' Charley whispered, kissing Nick on the cheek. 'Thanks, Dad.'

'You're welcome, sweetheart.'

As Charley went to grip the door knob, she let out a shriek as her hand made contact with the steel handle. It was red hot, her skin sticking to it as she tried to loosen her grip.

'What's wrong?' Nick yelled, rushing to his daughter's side.

'The handle!' Charley screamed. 'It's burning me and I can't let go.'

Nick grabbed his daughter's arm and pulled her away from the door, both of them tumbling on to the ground. Charley looked at her hand, blisters already beginning to form all over her palm.

Nick rushed back over to the door and, using his foot, he kicked it down. Charley raced over as well, dashing into the room before her father could stop her.

'Charley, wait!' he cried, but it was too late. Charley ran in to find Dorcas thrashing about in her bed, deep purple veins bulging from her forehead. Machines were beeping all over the place and Dorcas was ripping the needles from her hands, screaming as her skin started burning her from the inside out.

'Gran!' Charley shrieked. 'We need help in here, something's wrong!'

A doctor came into the room, followed by a student nurse. He tried to usher a frantic Charley out of the way, but with no success. It was Nick who finally managed to get Charley to stand back, her knees going weak as he held her up.

Another doctor raced in, followed by another, and another. Soon, the room was packed full, with Charley and her dad in the corner, almost invisible.

A tear rolled down Charley's cheek.

Eventually the machines stopped beeping. Dorcas stopped screaming. Everybody stopped rushing and everything began moving in slow motion.

'She's gone,' the first doctor said. 'Calling it . . . time of death, nine twenty-two.'

Charley went numb.

'I'm afraid there was nothing we could do,' he said to Nick. 'I'm very sorry.'

'What . . . what happened?' Nick stammered.

'We're not sure.'

'The door . . .'

'Probably just a dodgy hinge.' The doctor glanced over his shoulder. 'Could I ask you to take a seat in one of our family rooms for a moment? I'll have someone bring you some tea and we can–'

'Tea . . .' Charley whispered. 'Gran wanted some tea.' She started walking towards the door, her eyes wide.

'Charley? Honey, we need to–'

'Later, Dad. Gran wants me to make her some tea.'

'Charley?'

Nick followed her out into the waiting area and gently put his hand on her shoulder.

'Honey, I am so sorry you had to see that. I need to call your mother. Let's take a seat for a moment and then we'll . . . well, we'll deal with this.'

'Don't worry, Dad. I won't be long.'

'Charley, where are you going?'

'I told you. I'm going to make Gran some tea.'

'Princess, stop saying that. We need to stay here for a while so we can–'

'She needs to see me, Dad. I have to go.'

'Charley . . .'

'You don't understand. She needs to talk to me.'

'Who does?' Nick said, louder than intended. He didn't mean to shout, but Charley wasn't making any sense.

'Gran . . .'

'Charley, your gran is . . . she's gone.'

'She's waiting for me. I won't be long.' Charley began meandering down the corridor again, Nick watching in confusion.

Marcus sat hunched over his desk, a pencil gripped firmly in hand. He was sketching a young woman with beautiful, deep eyes that he'd portrayed perfectly. Her lips were pursed and her hair was swept back, a single strand left loose. He knew the sketch didn't do her justice, it never could, yet he felt a sense of achievement when he looked at it, some success at capturing her beauty on a single page.

There was a knock at his door and he quickly covered the drawing.

'Hello, dear,' his mother said as he let her into his room. 'You aren't dressed for school.'

'Bad night,' he muttered.

'So I heard.'

Judith sat on the end of his bed, waiting for him to speak. He didn't.

'We need to talk,' she said calmly.

'About?'

'I'm not sure about things anymore, Marcus.'

'What do you mean?'

Judith sighed. 'I think you're becoming a liability.'

'What? No, I'm not.'

'You're obsessed.'

Marcus glared at her, his eyes dark. 'We all need a little bit of obsession in our lives.'

'Darling, I'm afraid you may end up being more of a hindrance than a help.'

'Oh, come on!' he yelled. 'It was only a dream, they're all just dreams. They don't mean anything . . .'

'Marcus–'

'She was my sister, Mum. You can't expect me not to think about her.'

'I wasn't talking about your sister.'

Judith got up and walked over to the writing desk, shifting the papers aside to reveal the drawing. She held it up with two bony fingers and raised her eyebrows at him.

'You said she wasn't going to be a problem.'

'She isn't. She won't be.'

'Marcus, what has this girl got over you? You know how important it is that we do everything right from here on out. If you're having doubts then you need to tell me now.'

'Doubts?' he snarled. 'How can you ask that? You know how much this means to me. Trust me, Charley Chambers won't be a problem. I'll take her out myself if I have to.'

Judith smiled and casually dropped the sketch into the waste-paper basket by her feet.

'Good boy.' She walked towards him and bent down, kissing him gently on the cheek.

'Oh, and Marcus . . .' she said as she was leaving.

'What?'

'The dog wants out. If you aren't going to school then you can take her for a walk.'

'Why do I have to–?'

'Because she's yours,' Judith said sternly.

'Actually, she's Bud's.'

'Was Bud's. And until things return to normal, she's your responsibility.'

'Fine,' he muttered testily, wishing she would hurry up and go away.

'Thank you.'

Marcus wandered over to the bin and took the drawing back out. He looked at it for a second, then carefully folded it in half, placing it in a drawer with several others, all different, yet still incredibly similar. All of them drawings of Charley.

ঝ

Charley ambled up the path, stopping once she reached the door. She'd walked from the hospital to her gran's house without a jacket and her hands were red-raw from the bitter wind. She could barely feel them though. She couldn't feel anything apart from a dull throb in her head, making it hard to concentrate.

'Tea,' she murmured before turning the handle – it was unlocked. Shouldn't it have been locked . . .?

She made her way inside, stopping once she was in the centre of the living room.

'I came to make you tea, Gran. That's what you wanted, isn't it?'

The room was colder than the air outside, and Charley's hair began to blow, as if there was some sort of wind.

'Cha . . .'

She could hear something, but it was too far away to make out.

'Can you hear . . . ?'

'Hello?' Charley said. 'Is someone there?'

'Charley . . .'

'Gran, is that you?'

'Yes, Cha . . . I'm here. Can . . . hear me?'

The voice was broken and Charley could only make out the odd word.

'Gran? I don't know what you're saying. Where are you?'

'Danger, Charley. You need to . . . help . . .'

'Help who? What danger?'

'Can't help . . . you . . . anymore. Know . . . your strengths, Char . . . I lo . . . you . . .'

Then the voice was gone. The wind stopped and Charley collapsed.

TWENTY-EIGHT

Charley opened her eyes, her head thumping as she took in her surroundings. It took her a moment to figure out what had happened, where she was . . . and then it all came flooding back.

'No . . . no, no, no . . .' She let out a long wail, hugging her knees as she wept uncontrollably. She was gone. Her gran was really gone.

Charley didn't remember leaving the hospital, but she had a faint memory of arriving, standing in Dorcas's living room – hearing her voice.

Gran brought me here. She was trying to tell me something . . .

But Charley had barely been able to work out a word of what Dorcas was saying. It had been like a bad telephone connection; she knew her gran was there, at the other end of the line, she just couldn't communicate with her.

Charley stayed like that for a while, huddled on the floor, not sure what else to do. The house looked exactly the same as it had the last time she'd been there. A tear rolled down her cheek.

'Chambers?'

She lifted her head when she heard his voice, her eyes red and swollen from crying.

'She's gone,' Charley whispered.

Aiden stood in the doorway for a moment, watching Charley as she began to cry again, and then he went to her. He knelt down and pulled her close to his chest.

'I'm so sorry, Chambers.'

She looked up at him. Her eyes were bloodshot, her face blotchy, and her nose was running. To Aiden though, she was still the most beautiful girl in the world.

'Take me somewhere,' she said softly.

'Where do you want to go?'

'Somewhere quiet.'

'Okay.'

He helped her up and the two of them walked to the door, Charley's legs still trembling as she clutched Aiden's arm.

He took her back to the boathouse, knowing that they'd probably be alone; no one really went there anymore, most of the abandoned boats deteriorating, the wood rotting away from underneath.

Charley didn't need much convincing this time. In fact, she didn't need convincing at all. She walked to the end of the pier and flung her hands in the air.

She was ready.

'Rise,' she said, and the water began to gently splash, a few waves rolling along the surface. She wasn't impressed. 'I said, rise!' she bellowed, and the lake split in two, the water climbing through the air until it was nearly as high as the tree tops.

'Now, let's have a little breeze,' she muttered, swirling her finger in the air, the wind picking up all around her.

She smiled to herself, but it wasn't enough. She was bored of messing around with the elements. She needed more, something stronger, more powerful.

She pointed over to one of the boats and it shattered, sending bits of wood up into the destructive wind. 'Again,' she cried, and one by one, the boats exploded, the pieces almost instantly disappearing.

'You want me to cry?' she yelled. 'You want tears? I'll give you tears . . .'

Rain began to pour from above and it suddenly turned dark, as if night had just fallen. There was a blast of thunder and then a huge bolt of lightning shot across the sky, hitting one of the trees and setting it alight.

'Chambers!' Aiden yelled, rushing towards her. 'You need to stop!'

But it was no use. Charley had no intention of stopping. She lifted her hand and swept it through the air, and Aiden was thrown backwards, landing in a heap a few feet away.

The fire was spreading and the lake was still separated, leaving a hollow space in front of her. She climbed down from the pier and walked into the centre of the lakebed, feeling tiny against the huge walls of water on either side of her.

She clicked her fingers and the wind calmed, the fragments of wood slowly changing colour, changing shape, morphing into something else completely: butterflies, thousands of them. Charley giggled and for a moment she felt at ease. She was carried back to her childhood, when her gran used to take her down to the field on the outskirts of town where they would have picnics and chase butterflies for hours.

She pictured her gran's face and the contentment ebbed away. The golden field turned to a dull, dank waste ground and the butterflies all died, falling to the ground as if the plague had just struck. Dorcas's nose began to bleed, her eyes sliding down her cheeks. Her features were all blending together, like wax dripping from a burning candle.

Charley didn't want butterflies anymore.

'You want darkness?' she whispered gravely. 'Fine, I can do that.'

The butterflies were just a huge blur of colour now, consuming Charley as she watched the devastation unfolding. She didn't want colour, not anymore. She wanted blackness.

The bright shades of orange and yellow and blue began to fade, all blending together like paint. The colours faded and they were left with just a black mass, the creatures flying so fast that Aiden couldn't make out what they were.

'Chambers, what is that?' he shouted over the noise of flapping wings. He could barely see her through the black haze, whatever it was shifting at such a pace that it now looked still, as if it wasn't moving at all.

Charley turned to him, a look on her face he'd never seen before. A look that sent shivers down his spine and put a knot in his stomach.

'Bats,' she said.

The swarm of bats flew up into the air, high above Charley's head. Black smoke was beginning to flow from her fingertips, followed by tiny sparks of electricity.

Aiden got up and ran towards her, leaping from the end of the pier on to the hollow ground.

'Chambers, make it stop,' he called, but a flash of light shot from her finger, hitting him in the chest, causing him to double over in pain.

'I'm not done yet!'

The water rose even higher, far above the bright orange flames that were travelling further and further afield. The bats had slowed and were now drifting in and out of the water barricades, a rhythmic pattern forming as they soared through the air.

Charley clasped her hands and one by one, the bats burst, turning into a dim, grey powder that floated slowly down to the ground.

Aiden whispered something and waved towards the sky. Something shot upwards, some kind of energy, letting the water fall slowly towards the ground and putting the fire out as it drenched the smouldering trees.

He struggled through the water towards Charley, grabbing her roughly by the shoulders.

'Stop!' he yelled. 'You need to stop, Chambers. Now!'

He looked into her eyes but there wasn't anything there. Anyone there. They were empty, dark pools of nothingness. She let out a long, deep moan before going limp in his arms, leaving him to support her in the middle of the freezing lake.

Tabitha shrieked as she heard the front door crash open, knocking a hot cup of tea from the arm of her chair.

Aiden burst into the living room with Charley in his arms. He was dripping wet, soaking the carpet and covering it with mud from his dirty boots. Before Tabby could object, he laid Charley gently down on the table.

'Aiden . . .' Tabby said in bewilderment.

'Don't, Mum, I mean it. Something's wrong.'

Tabitha sighed, looking at Charley lying motionless on the table. She was only a girl after all, just an innocent child caught up in things more dangerous than she could possibly know. Tabby could relate to that.

'What happened?' she asked, rushing to Charley's side.

'She was out of control. I've never seen her like that. She was so powerful, but it was dark. Really dark.'

'What set her off?'

'Dorcas,' Aiden said quietly. 'She's dead.'

'What?' Tabitha sounded genuinely shocked. 'How?'

Aiden gave her a knowing look.

'Is that why you were asking about nosts?'

'Yes. I thought we had time to help her, but it happened so fast.'

'Tell me exactly what happened,' Tabitha said, putting a hand to Charley's head, an orange glow shining brightly beneath her palm.

'What are you doing?' Aiden asked.

'Keeping her warm. Come on, you need to tell me what happened.'

'I found her at her gran's house. She was alone. She asked me if we could go somewhere quiet, so I took her to the boathouse. She just let loose. Everything was cold, dark. There was fire and floods and . . . and bats, thousands of them. I couldn't stop her, she was too strong.'

'Did you try? To stop her . . .'

'Of course I did. She hit me with something though, something big. I couldn't fight her.'

'You shouldn't have intervened.'

'Mum, she was out of control. She set fire to the trees, blew the bats to smithereens. If I didn't try–'

'Stopping her was incredibly dangerous. That 'something' that hit you was probably powerful enough to kill you. It's amazing you're not hurt.'

'Chambers wouldn't kill me,' he muttered, still able to feel the pounding in his chest where the bolt of light had struck.

'She didn't know what she was doing. She probably wasn't even aware it was you.' Tabitha could see her son trying to get his head around it all, and she softened a little. 'What was it like . . . to watch?'

'I don't even know how to describe it. I've never seen anyone with that much power before, except . . .'

Just as he was about to say her name, Quinn walked through the door.

'You,' he said, pointing in her direction.

'Me? What about me? Why is Charley sleeping on the table?'

'Quinn and Dru,' Aiden said to his mother. 'That's the only time I've seen a magician as powerful.'

'As powerful as what?' Quinn frowned. 'And we're not that powerful,' she replied modestly.

'You are when you're together. I've never seen anything like it.'

'He's right, Quinn,' said Tabitha. 'When the two of you combine your powers, it's quite spectacular.'

Quinn shrugged her shoulders. 'Yeah, well, it's just me now, isn't it? Little old average me.'

'You're far from average,' Aiden scoffed.

'So what happened?' Quinn nodded in Charley's direction. 'I'm guessing all this power must have come from her.'

'Her gran's death has unleashed a darkness in her,' Tabitha sighed. 'I take it she was aware of the nost?'

'Yeah.'

'And do you have any idea who's responsible for it?'

'No. We thought it might be this kid called Marcus–'

'The Gillespie boy?' Tabby asked.

'Yes, how did you–'

'I know who he is, Aiden.'

Of course she does, she knows everything.

'How do you know it wasn't?' she asked.

'Timing was all wrong. Charley saw him summon a nost, but her gran was already sick by then.'

'So there's another one loose?'

'I think so, yeah.'

Tabitha put her hand to her head. 'Someone else is going to die then, Aiden.'

'Well, we need to stop it before that can happen.'

'Like you did with Dorcas?' she said cruelly. She knew her words were uncalled for, but she was only trying to get through to her son, make him aware of the dangers they could be facing.

'We didn't know how to stop that one because we didn't know who conjured it up – we still don't know. But we have more to go on this time. If we can convince Marcus to–'

'To do what, call it off? You think if you ask nicely, he's just going to undo it all?'

'No, I don't. We've tried asking nicely and that got us nowhere. I think it's time for a different approach.'

As Aiden, Tabitha and Quinn stood looking at one another, deciding what to do next, Charley began to stir. She pushed herself up, groaning as her head started pounding mercilessly.

'What's going on?' she croaked, her voice hoarse. 'Aiden?'

'I'm here,' he said, rushing to her side. 'How are you feeling?'

'Like I've been hit by a truck.'

'Well, it serves you right for getting ahead of yourself,' said Tabby. 'Stupid girl, you don't know your own strength.'

Aiden shook his head at his mother's tactless outburst; she really did choose her moments.

Tabby knew she was being harsh on Charley, but she also knew it was important to scold her for her rash decisions; it could have turned out so much worse.

'Are you all right?' Tabby said, fetching Charley a glass of water. 'That must have been quite an ordeal.'

Charley looked at Aiden. 'Why is she being nice to me?'

'Because she knows I'll lose the rag if she's not.'

Tabitha frowned. 'Charley, I know I've been hard on you. I suppose it's not really fair.'

'No, it's not,' Aiden said sharply.

Tabitha groaned. 'Aiden, be quiet.'

'Why should I? It's true.'

Tabby sighed and walked away without saying anything else, trying her hardest to avoid an argument.

'Are you not even going to apologise?' he called. 'I think she deserves that at least.'

'No, Aiden, I'm not. Your girlfriend just spent a good chunk of the afternoon tearing the sky apart. She put you in danger. That shock should have killed you. I'm sorry about Dorcas, really I am, but you are my concern. You are my son and I love you, and losing you doesn't bear thinking about. So, no, I will not apologise.' She turned and left the room, scared she would lose her temper if she stayed for another moment.

Aiden turned back towards Charley, wiping Tabitha from his mind.

'I almost killed you?' she whispered, her eyes filling with tears.

'No, Chambers, I'm fine. I'm tougher than I look. Not as tough as you apparently, but hey, we can't all be superheroes.'

Charley's face crumpled. 'I'm not a superhero. Your mum's right, Aiden. I'm dangerous.'

'Chamb . . .' He stopped to think, something in his brain suddenly clicking. 'Wait a minute. Maybe that's not a bad thing.'

'How can it possibly be good?'

'I'm with sparky,' said Quinn promptly. 'I'd rather not be zapped with bolts of killer lightening. I've got a dodgy ticker, remember.' Quinn winked and Aiden hit her gently on the arm.

'I'm serious. No one ever got far by playing it safe. They want a war, we'll give them one.'

Quinn cleared her throat to get Aiden's attention. 'And, eh, who exactly are we fighting, apart from a daft demon kid and a killer we can't identify? Don't you think it's a bit early to be calling it war?'

Aiden gave her a bewildered look. 'No, I don't. I think it's the perfect time to do it. Dorcas is dead and Abbie's in hospital after being shoved from a rooftop. You're trying to slice Chambers open in her dreams and we have a demon on our hands who seems quite adept at conjuring up nosts. More people are going to die if we don't do something.'

'Aiden,' Charley said quietly, 'if Marcus is a demon, does that mean his parents are, too?'

'Not necessarily. I mean look at you, your parents are insigs.'

'I guess there's only one way to find out,' Quinn smiled.

'Oh, yeah? And what would that be?' Aiden said dubiously.

'I should seduce Garth; after I'm finished with him, he'll tell me everything I need to know.'

Aiden's disgusted expression amused Quinn no end, and she burst out laughing.

'I'm joking, you idiot. Well, sort of.'

'God, Quinn, you really don't have any boundaries.'

'Of course I do. You just don't have a sense of humour.'

'Yeah, I lost it when you started telling me about your seedy desires for older men.'

As the pair of them bickered, Charley drifted away into a daze. She still couldn't accept that her gran was gone. Some part of her had really believed they would manage to save her, that they would find the culprit in time and convince them to stop before it was too late. It had all just been wishful thinking.

Charley didn't know what was coming, she didn't know what to expect. But she was certain of one thing: when she found the person who murdered her gran, she was going to kill them.

Jess wandered along the street, her eyes streaming as the cold wind irritated them. She knew that her dad would be mad at her for leaving her mum by herself, but she just had to get out of there. She couldn't stand sitting there listening to her mother's constant whining for another second.

They'd gone straight to the hospital when Nick had phoned, and almost as soon as they'd arrived, he'd dashed off to look for Charley, asking Jess to stay with her mother.

She didn't mean to be so selfish and she didn't know why such horrible thoughts were cropping up in her mind. She didn't want to think them, but that didn't matter. They were there, screaming from inside her head.

She could feel her fingers tingling and, glancing down at them, she noticed the tips were turning black, the skin peeling off them like glue.

'What the . . .?'

Jess panicked, quickly shoving them into her pockets. She knew something was wrong – very wrong – she just didn't want to deal with it. She hurried over the road and, not looking where she was going, bumped straight into someone.

'Sorry,' she mumbled, keeping her head down and walking away.

'Hey, wait a minute,' the voice called, and Jess slowly turned around. 'You're Charley's little sister, aren't you?'

'Jess,' she nodded.

'Marcus,' he gestured to himself. 'We met once when I came round to see Charley.'

'I remember.'

'What are you doing? Shouldn't you be at school?'

Jess shrugged. 'Shouldn't you?'

'I guess so, yeah. Not really a massive fan of it though.'

'I hear you,' Jess murmured.

'So what's your excuse?' Marcus asked casually. 'You don't look like you're having much fun.'

255

'My gran just died.'

His expression changed and Marcus took a step towards Jess. 'Oh, God, I'm sorry.'

'It's okay.'

'You must be–'

'No, really. It's okay. I don't care. I know I should be heartbroken, crying my eyes out and blubbering to anyone who'll listen, but I don't feel a thing. I'm not sad, it doesn't hurt. There's nothing there.'

Marcus didn't say anything.

'And now I'm ranting to a total stranger about how much of a selfish cow I am. The day gets better and better.'

'You're not selfish,' Marcus said kindly. 'People deal with grief in different ways.'

'What grief? I'm not grieving. I don't even miss her. I'm not sorry that she's dead. What kind of a person does that make me?'

'You're just confused, Jess. Don't be so hard on yourself.'

'I'm not the one who's confused. Apparently Charley strolled out of the hospital saying she was going for a cup of tea with Gran.'

Marcus cocked his head to one side. 'Really?'

'Yeah. Dad said she went into some sort of trance-like state, wasn't making a bit of sense. I swear, she'll do anything to get attention.'

'That explains the storm then.'

'What?'

'Hmm . . . oh, nothing. Is she all right?'

'Charley? Who knows? Who cares,' Jess groaned.

As the breeze got stronger, she tucked a strand of hair

behind her ear, a pointless move really, seeing as the wind blew it straight back out again.

Marcus frowned. 'What's wrong with your hand?'

'Oh, nothing. I, eh, burnt it. I have to go.' Jess took off down the street and turning the corner, bumped right into Marcus again.

'Jess–'

'How did you do that?' she interrupted, looking over her shoulder.

'Tell me what happened,' he said, his voice gentle but firm.

'It's nothing.'

'Doesn't look like nothing.'

'I'm . . . I'm not sure. I only noticed it a few minutes ago. The other one's the same.'

She put her hands out in front of her and gasped at what she saw. Both were now black, the flesh rotting away like something from a horror film.

'Holy shit,' Marcus whispered.

'What's happening to me?'

Marcus took her hands in his and told her not to panic. He held on to them, his eyes not leaving hers, and when he let go, Jess frowned in confusion, holding her hands up and studying them closely.

'How did you . . . ?'

They were back to normal, the skin pink and perfect with no signs of decay.

'Parlour trick, precious, nothing to it.'

'Marcus,' she said, crossing her arms.

'It was nothing.'

'God, is there anyone around here that doesn't treat me like a kid?'

Marcus smiled at her petty outburst. 'You are a kid, Jess. Heck, I'm still a kid.'

'You know what I mean,' she said sadly.

'Listen, trouble. I'm not trying to be condescending. Let's just say, your sister isn't the only one who can pull off fancy pranks.'

'They aren't pranks, the things Charley does. I've seen it for myself.'

Marcus nodded. 'Yep, she's powerful, that one.'

'She's a freak, that's what she is.'

Marcus cocked an eyebrow. 'Says the girl whose hands were just wasting away.'

'Says the guy who just magically healed them,' she retorted.

'Fair enough,' he laughed. 'You hungry?'

'Not really.'

'Could you eat?'

'Probably not,' she said honestly.

'Cool. Wanna come watch me eat? I'm starving.'

Jess giggled. 'Sure, why not?'

She felt more relaxed than she had done all day. In fact, she couldn't remember the last time she'd felt so content. Marcus was a breath of fresh air. He didn't treat her like a child, at least not to the extent that everybody else did. She felt like she could just be herself with him. She didn't have to lie or hide; she could just be Jess.

TWENTY-NINE

Charley sat in front of Quinn with her legs crossed, a magazine lying flat on her lap.

It had been nearly a week since her gran's funeral, and Charley had spent almost all of her spare time at Aiden's, avoiding her parents as much as possible.

Every time she walked into the room, she could feel their eyes on her, trying to work out what was going through her head. She couldn't stand it – the awkward silences, everyone behaving as though they'd gone completely barmy. Even Jess was acting stranger than normal; for once she actually seemed quite . . . happy. Well, happier than usual anyway, which gave Charley cause for concern. Plus, she'd started puking again, every time Jess came near her. Aiden's house definitely seemed like the safest bet.

'What's Dru like?' Charley asked Quinn, who was busy twisting Charley's hair into a long French plait.

'Dru? Pretty much the same as me. She's grumpier though, and has brighter hair. Dru gives a whole new meaning to the term redhead.'

'So what happened there?' Charley asked. 'I thought you were identical twins. Aren't you meant to be, you know . . . identical?'

Quinn laughed. 'Apparently in rare cases, identical twins can be born with different hair colours. Probably not the case with us though. I think when they say that, they mean chestnut brown and dusty blonde or something, not bone-white and pillar-box red.'

'So how'd it happen?' Charley asked.

'Something to do with the spell, I think. It can have side effects. I don't mind though,' Quinn winked. 'Makes me unique.'

'That's one word to use,' Aiden said, strolling into the living room with his arms full. 'What is this, a slumber party?' he groaned.

'We're bonding, shorty, keep your shirt on.'

Aiden walked over to Charley and bent down, kissing her gently on the cheek. 'How long are you staying for?'

'I better head home just now,' Charley sighed. 'Dad insisted we all sit down for a family meal. Wouldn't take no for an answer.' She pulled a face that showed how she felt about 'family night' in the Chambers' household.

'You never know,' Aiden shrugged, 'it might not be that bad.'

Charley raised an eyebrow. 'Easy for you to say.'

'You want me to walk you home?'

'No, I'll be fine. You should take Quinn out somewhere, it would do both of you some good.'

Aiden rolled his eyes at the suggestion.

'I'll call you.'

He smiled as she made her way down his front path. 'Later, Chambers.'

অ

Charley pulled her coat tightly around her as she walked the empty streets towards her house. It was quiet for a Saturday night, which she found quite refreshing; she hadn't had much time to herself all week, especially since Quinn had decided they ought to become bosom buddies and had barely left her side.

She liked Quinn, she really did. She'd been a bit unsure at first, especially with the dream and the stabbing and whatnot, but now she could see how genuine she really was. She cared a lot, and that meant something to Charley.

She cut through an alley and was round the back of one of the pubs when she heard a rustling noise behind her.

'I know you're there,' she said, slowing to a halt.

'Wasn't trying to hide, gorgeous.'

Marcus strolled out of the shadows, his boots scuffing the ground as he walked. He was wearing his black duffel coat, his hands buried in the pockets.

'What do you want?' Charley sighed.

'Just a chat, love.'

'Don't call me that. I'm not your love,' she said in disgust.

'You sure about that?' Marcus smiled, half his face illuminated by the street lights, the other half hidden in darkness.

'Go away, Marcus. I don't have time for games.'

'Who's playing?' he asked, a wicked glint in his eye.

Charley shook her head and began walking again, not interested in what he had to say.

'I heard you put on a little show,' he called after her.

'Yeah, what of it?'

'I saw the storm, the chaos you caused. Well, I felt it more than I saw it, but it was impressive. You're improving.'

'Could you please try and be a bit more patronising. I love being talked down to by barbaric monsters.'

Marcus laughed. 'Barbaric monsters? Is that not a bit of an exaggeration?'

'You're a demon, aren't you?'

'Doesn't automatically make me dangerous.'

'It's not written in stone, no. But you are dangerous, anyone with that kind of power is.'

He took a step closer to her. 'Yeah, you're right. That's why you're so deadly. All that strength, all that power coursing through your veins.' He ran his fingers up her arm. 'You're lethal, Charley, a time bomb waiting to go off.'

'I'm not like you,' she said, pulling away. 'My powers aren't dark like yours are.'

'Is that right?' he sneered.

'Yes, it is,' Charley said harshly. 'I wouldn't use them to hurt someone.'

'Is that why you threw a spur at Aiden then?'

'A what?'

'A spur. A bolt of mystical energy with the capability to kill someone on the spot. Hard things to generate, although you seemed to manage fine.'

'That's not what happened, it was an accident. . .' Charley faltered. 'How do you know about that?'

Marcus grinned. 'I have my ways.'

'Were you spying on me?'

'I have better things to do with my time than watch you tear apart the boathouse. Although, seeing you pummel Aiden like that would have made my day. Once you realise you can't keep secrets from me, I promise, we'll get along much better.'

'I don't have to listen to this,' she said, shaking her head. 'I am nothing like you. You're a demon and I'm not. I'm good, I'm–'

'Being a demon does not make me inhuman. Well, I guess it kind of does, but that's not the point. It doesn't mean I'm a villain, just like being a magician doesn't make you a hero. They're just words, titles. They don't define us.'

'How poetic,' Charley remarked sarcastically. 'I never said I was a hero, I just said that I'm good. What I did to Aiden was a mistake, but he's fine. It was just–'

'You're powerful, Charley.'

'I know I am. And if you don't leave me alone, the next 'spur' I whip up won't be for Aiden. And it won't be an accident, either.' She started walking again, her blood beginning to boil as Marcus egged her on, pushing her until she was just about at her limit.

'Yeah, you're strong,' Marcus yelled after her, 'but I'm stronger.'

All of a sudden, Charley was hit from behind with something heavy. She fell to the ground, her hands stinging as they hit the gritty pavement.

'What the hell was that for?' she shouted, quickly hauling herself back up.

'I lied earlier,' he smiled, sending her flying backwards into the hard brick wall. 'I do wanna play.'

Charley threw her hands up, and Marcus was catapulted into the air, moments later landing in a heap on the ground.

'Nice,' he said to her, nodding his head. 'Did you learn that in the beginner's guide to magic?' He clicked his fingers and Charley yelled out in pain as her bones began to snap one by one.

'What are . . . you . . . doing?' she stuttered, gritting her teeth as the pain got worse.

'They aren't actually breaking,' he said, getting up, 'just feels like they are. I can make it stop if you ask nicely.'

Charley groaned and, spotting a piece of glass a few feet away, reached out for it, eventually managing to grab it between two fingers. She launched it towards Marcus, the glass piercing his thigh. He screamed out as blood began to ooze from the wound, turning his jeans a dark, crimson colour. He pulled the glass from his leg and tossed it away, glaring at Charley as she slumped against the wall, the pain subsiding now that the spell was broken.

'That was sore,' he grimaced.

'And making me feel like my bones were breaking wasn't?'

'Hey, you're the one who got a big head about being so powerful. I was just bringing you down a peg. I've been doing this for a lot longer than you have.'

'Then you should know to always watch your back,' said Charley as a dustbin came crashing down on Marcus's head. As he collapsed, Charley struggled to her feet, the effects from Marcus's bone breaking spell still bothering her. It was a strange sensation; it didn't hurt anymore, but there was a tingling beneath her skin. Hot, almost burning, like someone had lit a match inside her. It wasn't sore though. She felt . . . exhilarated. She felt alive.

Leaving Marcus lying unconscious on the ground, Charley walked away. She rounded the corner, her fingers still itching with mystical energy. She could feel the magic inside her, warm and electrifying, surging through her body like a tidal wave. It was in her veins, her blood, everywhere.

She turned another corner and sighed as she saw a figure standing, leaning against an old wire fence.

'Show off,' he said, smiling at her startled expression.

'No,' Charley moaned, pressing her palms hard against her temples. 'Will you just go away?'

'Didn't know you could do levitation spells,' he said curtly, ignoring her question.

'I can set a forest on fire, knock my kid sister out without moving and go all Moses and part the water. I don't think making a dustbin float is that spectacular.'

'Maybe not, but I didn't see it coming. That's the impressive part. I see everything coming, Charley, always.'

'You didn't see the glass coming,' she said smugly, glancing back down at his leg.

'You weren't fighting fair though. That was a dirty trick.'

Charley laughed in amazement. 'You think I was the one playing dirty? You were torturing me, Marcus. It was–'

'It wasn't real.'

'You do remember I dislocated my shoulder recently?'

'Yeah, and then your golden boy fixed it for you.'

Charley didn't say anything. She didn't want to bring Aiden into the conversation, to give Marcus any more ammunition than he already had.

'You're a puzzle, Charley, that's for sure.'

'Well, go home and try to work me out then, because that's where I'm going: home, away from you.'

Marcus stepped in front of her, blocking her path as she tried to leave.

'Get out of my way, Marcus.'

'Make me,' he grinned.

'Fine.' She pressed her hand against his chest, but before she had the chance to do anything, he grabbed it and twisted, knocking her off balance so that she landed clumsily on the ground.

She jumped to her feet, dizzy from the fall and sore from the way Marcus had grabbed her.

'That hurt,' she yelled, launching enough energy his way to send him hurtling into the fence. He didn't budge. She tried again, but the same thing happened, the force merely ruffling his coat.

'Come on, you must have more than that, little witch,' he laughed. 'Maybe I was wrong about you. Maybe you aren't all that special after all.'

'I am not a witch!' Charley yelled, throwing everything she had at Marcus. Something flew towards him, something bright and sharp: a spur. It spun wildly, heading for his chest like an arrow darting towards a bullseye.

Marcus looked down. The spur was hovering in front of him, his power the only thing keeping it at bay.

'Well, would you look at that? You trying to do away with me, little witch? That isn't very nice. Saying that though, if Aiden can take a spur to the chest, I'm sure I could handle it.'

Charley wasn't sure what to do. She hadn't realised

how strong he was, how clever and cunning. All her instincts told her to run, but there was also something in her head, whispering that it was okay, that Marcus would never cause her any real harm.

Backing away slowly, she decided to go with her gut.

'You can run if you want, Charley. But you know I'll just be around the next corner, waiting for you to stumble round with that innocent look on your face, as if you can't work out how I got there. Don't play naïve, you understand how this works. Or you're beginning to, at least.'

'You want to hurt me? Fine, do it. Get it over with!' she yelled. 'Show me what you got, demon.'

Marcus took a few steps towards her, and as he did, Charley pulled back, tripping over a lump of concrete and landing on her back.

Marcus let out a deep laugh, kneeling down so that he was leaning over her.

'I don't want to hurt you, Charley. I've lost count of how many times I've told you that. Doesn't mean I won't though. I mean, come on. I can't get bested in a fight against a newbie magician who doesn't know half the power she has. That would just be embarrassing.'

He opened his hand, revealing the spur, and slowly the colour started to fade. The glow disappeared and it began changing shape, twisting into something she recognised: a nost.

'See, I could kill you right now if I wanted. Well, technically it wouldn't happen straight away. It would take a while for the effects to set in, but it wouldn't be long. By the time the nost had done its work, you'd be begging someone to kill you.'

'What's taking so long then?' she snapped, as the nost squirmed in his hand.

'I like you, Charley.'

'You've got a funny way of showing it.'

'I never said I was going to use this. I'm just showing you how easy it would be. I'm not going to kill you, Charley.' He winked at her. 'Not today, anyway.'

'How about not ever?' said a voice, coming from the end of the alley.

Before Marcus could do anything, the nost vanished into thin air and he was sent hurtling backwards, crashing through the metal fence. This time he didn't get back up, out cold from the impact.

The figure walked up to Charley, surveying her as she sat shaking on the ground. She was dressed all in black, her short hair blowing wildly in the wind. Although they'd never met, Charley recognised her immediately.

'Dru?' she said in bewilderment.

The redhead smirked. 'I see you've met my sister.'

Charley nodded nervously.

'Good. Where's Quinn?'

THIRTY

Aiden sat on the couch, waiting impatiently for Quinn to get ready. He didn't know where she was planning on taking him, nor did he care; all he really wanted to do was spend the evening with Charley. He knew seeing her family would be good for her though. At least, he hoped it would. So much was changing in her life, and not for the better, but he wasn't sure how to help her, or if he even could. He was well aware that the things they were dealing with were dark, very dark, but he also knew they would find a way to stop them. There was always a way, there had to be . . .

Quinn came strutting into the room wearing a blue-feathered coat and a sparkly pair of red high heels. Her lips were bright against her pale face and her eyes shone out like diamonds.

'What are you wearing?' Aiden asked, dumbfounded. 'You look like a cross between something from *The Wizard of Oz* and *The Snow Queen*.'

Quinn stuck her tongue out. She knew fine she was a little eccentric, but she'd always been that way.

'What can I say, shorty? You'll never find anyone like me.'

Aiden raised an eyebrow. 'Except Dru, you know? Your identical twin . . .'

'Okay, you'll never find anyone like me apart from my crabby, less talkative counterpart who has no sense of humour and dresses like some sort of leather-clad superhero wannabe. My selfish, opinionated sister who thinks it's all right to disappear off the face of the earth without a word. You know what, Dru is nothing like me. She's mean and cold and incredibly boorish and–'

'Glad to see you've missed me,' came a voice from behind her, and Quinn spun round to see Dru leaning casually on the door frame.

'Dru?' Quinn murmured, sure for a second that she was seeing things.

'The one and only,' said Dru, her face blank. 'How you been, Quinnie?'

Quinn didn't say anything for a while, she just stood there staring in disbelief. She'd imagined this moment countless times, what she would say to Dru, what she would do. But now nothing seemed enough. She didn't know whether to hug Dru or hit her.

'I don't think I ever expected to find you,' Quinn whispered.

'Technically, you didn't find me, I found you.'

'How did you know I was here?'

'Well, Newford was my next stop. Guessed you might have paid Aiden a visit.' She looked behind Quinn, cocking her head slightly and smiling. 'Long time, cousin.'

'Hello, Dru,' Aiden nodded, folding his arms. 'What took you so long?'

'This and that. Made it in the end, didn't I?'

'I thought you didn't want to be found,' Quinn said, still struggling to find the right words. 'You just left . . . no letter, no goodbye . . .'

'You know how it is, Quinn.'

'Do I? Because right now I'm finding it hard to understand. You pack up and leave without a word and I'm supposed to just accept that? The day before you left you were practically suicidal. Then suddenly you're gone and it's all meant to be okay? I'm meant to just go on with my life as normal?'

There was an awkwardness in the air.

'I wasn't going to do anything, Quinn. You know I never would.'

'Because you can't, because I'm in the way. Let's face it, if you had the choice, you wouldn't be here. You hate being stuck here. You hate this world.' Quinn paused, a tear rolling down her cheek. 'And you hate me more for keeping you in it.'

Dru straightened herself and walked towards Quinn, placing her hands on her sister's shoulders. 'I could never hate you.'

Quinn's lip trembled and Dru pulled her close, holding her as she wept. Aiden was silent, but the look he gave Dru said it all. He loved both his cousins, but he couldn't bear to see Quinn hurting.

'Are you here for good?' he eventually asked Dru, and Quinn looked up, her eyes hopeful. The thought of Dru leaving again hadn't crossed her mind until now.

'I'm not going anywhere.'

'Good,' said Aiden, his expression softening a little. 'I think we need you here.'

'Yeah, I think you do. Since when did we casually brawl with demons in the middle of the street? A little tacky, is it not?'

'What are you talking about?' Aiden frowned.

'Demon boy: brown hair, so high,' she said, holding her hand above her head. 'Bashing your little girlfriend to bits, so he was.'

'Charley . . .' Aiden said frantically. 'What happened? Is she all right?'

'She'll live,' Dru shrugged.

'Did he hurt her?'

'I think that's fair to say. She gave about as good as she got though. Not really sure what I interrupted; he was either about to kiss her or kill her.'

Aiden's eyes grew dark and before he could stop himself, the windows smashed, glass flying everywhere.

'That wasn't very clever,' Dru sighed.

'Where is he?'

'Who? Demon boy? He was still unconscious last I saw him.'

'I'll kill him.'

'No, you won't.' The three of them looked towards the door to see Charley standing there.

'Chambers,' Aiden said, rushing to her side. 'What the hell did he do to you?'

'He didn't hurt me,' she said, limping to the couch. 'Well, not much.'

'Little twit had a nost in his hand,' Dru muttered. 'Glad I got there when I did.'

'You saved Charley?' Aiden said in surprise.

Charley winced as she sat down. 'I didn't need saving.'

'You can't be serious, Chambers. Look at you.'

'I gave a fair few whacks back,' she protested. 'Marcus just seems to get up a lot easier than most do.'

'He won't be getting back up when I'm done with him.'

'Aiden, please. I don't want you getting hurt.'

Aiden's face fell. He couldn't stand the thought of Charley pitying him. 'I won't, Chambers. I've been doing this for a lot longer than you have.'

'Your girlfriend's right,' Dru said sharply. 'This Marcus kid can conjure up nosts on the spot. I've never heard of anyone who can do that. You can't compete with him.'

'I don't need to be able to summon nosts to beat him. Thanks for your opinion though.'

'Maybe not, but is rushing in there, all guns blazing really the best idea? You're smarter than that, Aiden.'

Aiden sighed and sat down, letting Charley rest her head on his shoulder. She looked exhausted.

'Take it you never made it to dinner then?' he asked, kissing her forehead.

'Nope. Guess I should thank Marcus for that one,' she smiled, but she could tell Aiden didn't share her amusement. 'He wasn't going to hurt me.'

'How can you say that?'

Charley looked down at her clothes. Her jeans were ripped and she was covered in dirt from falling on the road.

'It's only a few bumps and scrapes. I promise you, Aiden, I don't know how I know, but Marcus had no intention of using that nost. I don't think I was really in danger.'

'Do you have feelings for him?' Aiden asked suddenly, and Charley pulled back in horror.

'What? No, of course not. How can you ask me that?'

'I don't know, Chambers. I'm sorry. But he's dangerous – you know it, I know it, even bloody Dru knows it, yet you seem to think you're somehow safe with him, even after tonight. Call me crazy, but I can't wrap my head around it.'

'Do you two want a moment alone?' Quinn asked.

'We don't need time alone,' said Charley angrily. 'Aiden can say whatever he wants right here. You honestly think I feel that way about him? He's a demon!'

'A demon that apparently wouldn't hurt you.'

'It's you, Aiden.'

'What's me?' he said, his voice growing hoarse.

'Everything. It's always been you. You're the one I want. Not Marcus. It's not him I care about. It's not him I think about. It's always you.'

Dru rolled her eyes at Charley's mushy, sentimental speech, and Quinn clapped her hands like an excited child.

'How romantic!' she cooed, gently patting her sister's arm. 'Isn't it just lovely?'

'Give me strength,' Dru muttered, stalking out the room before she could hear another word.

THIRTY-ONE

The alarm clock sang out, rousing Marcus from his sleep. He hit the clock with his pillow, knocking it from the bedside table so that it landed with a bang on the floor.

'Marcus, get up,' his mother called as she passed his bedroom door.

Marcus sighed. He didn't want to get up. He didn't want to go out. He didn't particularly want to stay in bed either. He just didn't want to do anything.

Resigned, Marcus made his way to the bathroom, closing the door before switching the shower on. He turned the nozzle to high and climbed in, wincing at first as the scalding water landed on his back. It immediately turned red, the searing hot water burning his skin the way it always did, and he let out a sigh of relief.

'Marcus!' his mother called from outside. He groaned in frustration.

'What is it?'

'Door.'

'Can't it wait?' he sighed. Why did everyone insist on coming round the second he'd stepped into the shower?

'No,' came his mother's brusque reply. 'It can't wait. Door, now.'

Marcus grabbed a towel and stormed out of the bathroom.

'Be nice,' she said as he passed the kitchen, but the only response she got was a resentful glare. 'Really,' she muttered to Garth once Marcus had stomped away, 'that boy makes me want to scream sometimes.'

Garth gave her a blank look. Marcus had been making him want to scream for years.

When he finally reached the door, Marcus pulled it so hard that it felt like it might come off its hinges, leaving Jess gaping on the front step.

'You okay?' she said quietly, already regretting her decision to stop by.

'Jess, what are you doing here?' She looked towards the ground. 'I mean . . . sorry. Is something wrong?'

'No, everything's fine. Well, as fine as fine can be. I was just passing and, well, I thought I'd say hi.'

'At eight o'clock on a Sunday morning?' Marcus raised his eyebrows.

'Eh, yeah, I know it's early.'

'How did you know where I lived?'

'I . . . I didn't. Someone mentioned it in school and–'

Marcus could tell Jess was struggling to come up with a reasonable explanation. She was just like Charley in so many ways: restless, skittish, a little bit awkward – yet so different in many others. Marcus thought back to when it was Charley standing on his doorstep, babbling the same way Jess was now. He remembered the way he'd teased her, the way she'd smiled, the way her eyes had shone as she looked at him. He couldn't bear to look into Jess's eyes though.

'You wanna come in?' Marcus asked, saving her from further embarrassment. She squinted and gestured to his towel.

'Are you sure? You look a little busy.'

'You're not the first Chambers to come to the door when I'm nearly starkers,' Marcus smiled, but then frowned slightly. 'Pretend I never said that.'

'You mean Charley?'

'Well I certainly don't mean your father.' Marcus thought he was being funny, but Jess's face fell.

'Forget it,' she said, shaking her head as she took off down the path.

'Jess, wait, I was only joking.'

'Doesn't matter, Marcus. Forget I even came by.'

Marcus closed the door once she'd finally disappeared out of sight, almost banging into his mother as he turned around.

'What?' he muttered as she looked at him disapprovingly.

'You handled that well, didn't you?'

'Oh, for God's sake. Just leave it, Mum,' he said, marching towards the bathroom in the hope of finishing his shower in peace. Before he could reach the door, he was thrown back down the hall, landing at his mother's feet.

'I'm getting tired of this, Marcus.' She walked back over to the kitchen, stopping at the door. 'And don't ever speak to me like that again.'

আ

Aiden woke up as the bright autumn sun poured in his window, suggesting that it was probably later than he'd planned to get up. Charley's arm was draped across him, her head wedged perfectly between his chin and his shoulder. Aiden glanced down at her and smiled. Her mouth was open slightly and she was snoring through her nose.

'Chambers,' he whispered, nudging her gently. 'Wake up.'

'Hmm,' she mumbled, moving slightly, but she didn't open her eyes.

Aiden had wanted to get up before his parents, early enough to get Charley out the door before they realised she'd stayed over. His father would disapprove, that was certain, but his mother would be furious.

'Chambers,' he said again, pulling his arm out from under her so she had no choice but to move.

'I don't want to wake up,' she whispered, smiling as she inhaled the duvet's musky scent.

'Why?'

'Because, if I wake up, the dream will end.'

Aiden raised an eyebrow. 'And what are you dreaming about?'

'I just stayed over at my boyfriend's house for the first time. He held me all night, kissed me . . . you know the drill.'

'Sounds like a good dream,' he smiled.

'It is.'

'Not a dream, baby.'

Charley opened her eyes and grinned. 'I know. Still doesn't mean I want it to end.'

'I don't want it to either, trust me. But today's going to be interesting enough as it is, without my mother finding out you spent the night.'

Today was also the day they were going to tell Fergus and Tabitha about Dru's arrival, a revelation that none of them were keen to deliver.

'Will she be mad?' Charley asked, pulling him back in for one last hug.

'She won't be happy, let's put it that way. It might be me crashing at your house tonight.'

'I wish you could.'

Charley had sent her mum a text, apologising for missing dinner and saying that she was staying at Lucy's house, to which her mum had replied, 'Who?'

Abbie was Charley's only real friend and her mother was well aware of this, but she had no other option; she couldn't very well have said she was with Abbie, camping out at the hospital for the night.

'What time is it?' Charley asked, looking around Aiden's room for a clock.

Before he could answer, he heard the thump of footsteps, followed by his mother's shrill voice.

'Aiden, get downstairs, now. Your father and I would like a word,' – there was a short pause, and then – 'about Druanna.' They heard the sound of footsteps again and then she was gone.

'Time for the fun to begin. Buckle up, Chambers, this won't be pretty.'

'I'm coming too?' Charley asked in horror. The thought of facing Tabitha was terrifying; she'd rather be locked in a room with Marcus at full strength than have to look Tabitha in the eye after spending the night with her son.

'Unless you wanna climb out that window. Probably break both your legs though.'

'But you said–'

'I know what I said, Chambers, but we've gone and blown it now. She's going to find out you stayed.'

'Window it is,' Charley said, hauling herself out of bed. She was still fully clothed, so all she had to do was fling on her jacket and shoes and she was ready to run for the hills.

'And how will you get down?'

'Easy,' Charley smiled. 'I am a magician after all.'

'Nuh uh,' Aiden answered, shaking his head. 'Mum will know you're here the second you use magic. She'll be livid. It's better this way. At least we aren't lying.' Aiden half-smiled.

'I'm really not doing much to get into your mum's good books, am I?'

'Come on,' he said, offering her his hand. 'Let's go endure my mother's wrath together. Maybe we'll get off lightly and she'll spend most of the time yelling at Dru.'

'Not likely,' Charley mumbled as they walked out the door.

'You called?' Aiden said sarcastically as they reached the others, who were waiting in the living room.

'Yes, Aiden, I called. Please do explain why . . . wait a minute, what is Charlotte doing here?'

Charley gulped, her eyes widening, and quickly said, 'I haven't been here long. I just dropped by to pick up my purse. I left it here last night.'

'Oh, I see,' Tabitha said impassively, and Aiden raised his eyebrows in surprise, mouthing, 'Well done', to Charley when his mother wasn't looking. 'You might as well stay for this, Charley, as I'm sure you were aware of my niece's unexpected arrival before I was.'

'Charley was the first one to see her,' Quinn blabbed, and Charley sent daggers her way.

'Oh, she was, was she?'

'Yeah,' Charley said quietly, her head held low, 'Dru met me on my way home when I was, well . . .'

'Playing with fire?' Dru smirked, and Tabby frowned.

'What are you talking about?'

'Nothing, Aunt Tabitha.'

'Aiden, why did you keep this from me?'

'She only got here last night, Mum. You were still out and I was tired, so I went to bed. I told Dru to bunk with Quinn and said we'd sort it in the morning.'

'That wasn't your decision to make.'

'You weren't here,' he snapped.

'You could have called me.'

'Next time, I will. Anyway, what's the big deal? It's only Dru.'

Tabby ignored his question.

'What happened to my windows?' she asked suspiciously, looking from her son to Charley and lastly to her nieces.

Quinn and Dru had tried to fix them after Aiden had lost his temper and smashed them into a thousand pieces, but they knew Tabitha would probably still be able to tell the difference. Whether it was the finish of the glass that gave it away, the joint where ledge met window or the glazing of the frame, one way or another Tabitha was bound to notice. She always did, and this time was no different.

'Your windows are fine,' Aiden huffed, suddenly

281

grumpy as he remembered the reason why he'd smashed them in the first place.

'They are not fine,' Tabitha protested. 'What happened? Did you break them on purpose or did you just explode again?'

'Leave it, Mum. They're fixed now, aren't they?'

'Thanks to your cousins.'

'Are we done here?' he asked. 'I need to walk Chambers home.'

'I'll be all right,' Charley started to say, but Aiden nudged her to be quiet.

'Shut up,' he whispered. 'I need an excuse to get out of here.'

'I heard that,' Tabitha frowned. 'Take her home. We'll speak more about this later.'

Aiden didn't wait around, immediately elbowing Charley towards the door. Tabitha stormed up the stairs, telling Fergus that she didn't want to be disturbed, and Dru grabbed Quinn's hand, tugging her sister out the door.

Charley slowed to a halt round the corner from her house and turned to kiss Aiden goodbye.

'You'd better not come any further or my mum might start asking questions.'

'Call me later?' he said, gently stroking her cheek with the back of his hand, making it awfully hard for her to leave him.

'Of course. Good luck with, well, everything.'

'I'll be sure to fill you in,' he sighed, but then smirked as Charley wrapped her arms around his neck, giving him a final kiss.

She took off round the corner, disappearing out of sight. 'Last night was wonderful!' she shouted, and although Aiden couldn't see her, he couldn't help but smile.

'Yes it was,' he replied, turning and walking back the way they'd come.

Charley burst through the front door, her heart pounding at the risk of being found out. She hadn't planned to lie to her parents, but she didn't regret it either; sleeping in Aiden's arms all night was the best thing she'd ever done. It was the best she'd ever felt. Even being away from him now hurt, though it had only been for a minute.

'I'm home!' she yelled, kicking her shoes off and leaving them in a heap in the hall. 'Mum?'

'Charley, we're through here. Quickly!'

Charley raced through to the living room to find Jess on the floor, her face turning purple. She was writhing in pain, her mother crouched over her in floods of tears.

'I don't know what to do, Charley. I don't know what's wrong with her.'

'What happened? Where's Dad?'

'At the supermarket. He left an hour ago but I can't get him on the phone.'

'How long has she been like this? Did you call an ambulance?'

'Yes, they're on their way. It only started about ten minutes ago. She just collapsed, said she couldn't breathe. Oh, Charley, she's been clawing at her throat like . . . look! She's doing it again.'

Charley bent down beside Jess and laid a hand on her forehead. 'Jess, it's me. It's Charley. Can you hear me?'

'Get away from me!' Jess screamed, lashing out, her fingernails scratching Charley's arm. 'Don't touch me! Go, get out!'

'What's wrong with her?' Linda sobbed, her heart breaking as she watched her little girl twisting and crying in agony.

'I don't know . . .'

'Ahh!' Jess bellowed, her hands now clawing at her chest. 'Get it out of me!'

'Get what out?' Linda bawled. 'Baby, talk to me.'

'Jess, tell us what hurts.'

Three loud bangs sounded on the door, and suddenly there was someone else in the room.

'Jess?'

Charley's head whipped round, her expression one of disgust. 'What the hell are you doing here?'

'I came by to apologise. Jess came to see me earlier and I . . . I think I upset her.'

'Why would Jess visit you?' Charley snarled, but Marcus just shrugged in response.

'Your guess is as good as mine. What's wrong with her?'

'I don't know, now get out.'

He didn't listen, instead shoving Charley aside and kneeling down next to Jess.

'Listen, kiddo, it's going to be okay. I need you to breathe. I know that seems impossible, but I'm going to help you, all right? Now, take my hand and count to ten.'

Jess tried, the first few numbers coming out in a hoarse growl. By the time she got to five, her breathing was steadying, and by eight she sounded almost normal again.

'Nine, ten,' she gasped.

'That's it. Well done, trouble.'

'How did you . . .?' Jess stammered, but Marcus put a finger to her lips, which were slowly regaining their colour.

'Try to rest for a moment. I'm sure your mum can take it from here.' He got up and nodded to Linda, who was staring at Jess in disbelief.

'How did . . . what did you do?'

'Just kept her calm, Mrs Chambers, nothing more. I'll call back later to check she's okay.'

He walked from the room, closing the door as he went, but it was quickly yanked back open by Charley who came racing down the path after him.

'How did you know?' she demanded in an accusatory tone. 'How did you know what was wrong with her?'

'I didn't. I told you, I only wanted to apologise,' Marcus said, still walking.

'Bullshit. You don't apologise for anything.'

'Is there something else I should feel bad about?' he smirked, turning so Charley could see only half of his face.

'Bashing me up in an alley, you could say sorry for that. But why would you? You don't feel guilty. You don't feel anything.'

'I would say sorry for that, Charley, but I don't think you really want me to. See, I think deep down you enjoyed it.' Charley screwed her face up and Marcus spun round so he was now right in front of her. 'That's it, pull faces, make jokes. I'm not playing though, not this time. You want me to say I don't feel guilty? Easy, I don't. But do not turn round and say I don't feel anything, because that couldn't be further from the truth. I feel everything, Charley. Everything you feel. Love, longing, desire – a thirst for something I shouldn't be craving. Someone.'

'Stop it . . .'

'See, you say that. But they're just words. If you meant them, I'd be gone by now.'

'How did you heal Jess?'

'Magic.'

'Why can't I do that? Why did it have to be you who helped her?'

Marcus sighed. 'Because it's black magic. You don't want to have the powers that I have, trust me.'

Charley squinted as the sun caught her eyes.

'Tell Jess I hope she feels better soon.'

He started walking again, and this time Charley didn't stop him. She just stood, watching.

THIRTY-TWO

Ever since Quinn had been small, she'd wanted to hold a star.

'Why?' Dru had asked.

'I don't know,' she'd answered. She was a child. Children were allowed to have impractical dreams.

Her mother had scolded her. 'You mustn't wish things like that, Quinnie.'

'Why? You said that we're magical. Can't magic people do anything?'

'No, Quinn. Magicians should never use their magic for personal gain.'

She hadn't really understood what her mother was telling her; she'd only been four after all. But she'd never asked to hold a star again, although she thought about it all the time.

Today though, she had more important things on her mind: demons, curses, and the most terrifying of all, Dru.

'Are you planning on telling me where we're going?' Quinn asked, as Dru led her up a grassy hill.

'We're nearly there, I promise.'

Dru stopped when they reached the hill's summit and Quinn looked around, unimpressed.

'And you brought me here because . . .'

'Sit down.'

'Why?'

'Quinn, just sit down, please. And close your eyes.'

Quinn sighed and did as Dru asked, sitting on the grass with her eyes firmly closed. Everything was already dark, yet somehow it seemed to get darker still.

'Dru, what's going on?'

'I think that'll do. You can open your eyes now.'

Quinn did, and she gasped at what she saw before her. The sky was black, a giant sheet speckled with tiny glistening dots.

'I don't understand,' Quinn uttered. 'You made it night?'

'Yep.'

'But we can't, people will see. How will we explain–?'

'It's only night for us,' said Dru, taking a seat beside her sister.

'Dru, what's all this for?'

'To say sorry. I know I haven't been a very good sister.'

'Yes you have . . .'

'I've been awful, Quinn, let's not sugar-coat it. But I do want to try and make it up to you. I owe you that much, at least.'

'You don't owe me anything. You saved me before you were even born. How could I possibly ask for anything else?'

'You're not asking, I'm giving.'

Dru stretched her arm out in front of Quinn and slowly

uncurled her fingers, revealing a round, shiny object the size of a marble.

'Is that a . . . ?'

'Yep, Quinnie, it's a star.'

'How did you . . . ? We aren't meant to–'

'I didn't do it for me. This is for you. It's what you've always wanted, isn't it?'

'For as long as I can remember.'

'Go on then, take it.'

Quinn reached out and took the star.

'How does it feel?' Dru asked, smiling at the joy plastered across her sister's face.

'Incredible,' Quinn breathed, 'I've never felt anything like it.'

'Wait 'til you feel this then,' Dru said, and she laid her hands over the top of the star.

Immediately, Quinn felt what she was talking about. It was like a surge of energy, buzzing through her body like electricity.

'What is that?' Quinn asked, staring into Dru's eyes – a mirror of her own.

'That's us. That's who we are.'

'It's so strong . . .'

'It's power, our power. We were always meant to be a part of each other. I didn't know it until . . . well, that doesn't matter.'

Quinn frowned. 'What doesn't matter?'

'Never mind. It may have taken me a while, but I finally realise the point in all this. Apart, Quinn, we're powerful, but together we're unstoppable.'

'Where's all this coming from, Dru? You're worrying me.'

'Just something I did, or rather, didn't do. It made me look at things differently.'

Quinn gazed at her sister, the star still firmly in her grasp. 'Think we can take on a demon, then?'

Dru smiled. 'Let's find out, shall we?'

Today, the hospital smelled like body odour, Charley decided. Body odour and dirty hair. She'd spent far too much time in the building of late, what with Abbie, her gran and now Jess.

'I think I need a holiday from this place,' she said quietly as she pushed the door open.

'You need a holiday? I'll crack the jokes around here.'

Charley smiled at her friend's familiar sense of humour. She'd missed it.

'How you doing, Abbs?'

'Me? I'm splendid. The days just fly by in here. More to the point, how are you?'

'I'm getting there,' Charley smiled, giving her friend a hug and perching herself on the end of the bed. 'I'm sorry I haven't been in to see you. I was going to come down and visit last time when . . . well, you know. Everything was so sudden.'

'Charles, I'm so sorry about your gran. I couldn't believe it when I heard. I wanted to come to the funeral but–'

'Don't be silly. I just want you better. Have the doctors said anything new?'

Abbie couldn't help but smile. 'I'm going home, Charles. They're letting me out.'

'No way? That's fantastic!'

'Yep. They said I'll need to use a wheelchair for a

while, but it shouldn't be for too long. I just can't wait to get back to my own bed. My room, my things . . . I never want to see the inside of this hospital again.'

'I know the feeling,' Charley said quietly, and then looked up quickly. 'Sorry, it's just been . . . difficult.'

'Don't you dare apologise. You've no idea how much I hated not being able to support you.'

Charley smiled, although her eyes still seemed sad. Abbie took her friend's hand gently in hers.

'So, what made you come see me today? Having a day off from the supernatural detective agency?'

'Not really, no. Jess had some sort of seizure again. She's in getting checked over.'

'Oh my God, is she okay?'

'Don't know, to be honest. I've never seen anything like it. It was Marcus who ended up saving the day.'

Abbie frowned. 'Marcus? Any more info on him?'

'God, we haven't talked for a while,' Charley said, rolling her eyes.

It took her a while to fill Abbie in. She told her about the fight with Marcus, Quinn's arrival and Dru's unexpected appearance. She spoke about her gran's death and what had happened at the boathouse afterwards. She talked a lot about Jess: her mood swings, her weird behaviour, her crazy panic attacks, or whatever they were. Before she knew it the nurse was poking her head round the door, telling Charley that she would have to leave.

'I won't be much longer,' she said, her eyes pleading.

The woman nodded, deciding to give Abbie a little longer with her friend. 'Jeez, Charles, I don't know what to say. Things sound . . . hectic.'

'I know. They are a little crazy.'

'And Marcus still hasn't talked about the nost yet? He hasn't said who it's for?'

'Nope, just said it's no one I need concern myself with, whatever that means.'

'God, what a loser,' Abbie scoffed. 'I still can't believe he attacked you.'

'I took care of it,' said Charley. 'Besides, he did save Jess. Maybe he isn't–'

'Don't say it, Charley, don't you dare say he's not all bad.'

'I didn't–'

'You have a beautiful blue-eyed boy at home who loves you to pieces. Don't go ruining that for some devilishly handsome demon who beats up girls and kills people for fun.'

'Will people please stop saying that? I am not interested in Marcus, and it was you who said he was handsome, not me. I just don't know . . . maybe he had a good reason to make the nost. What if it was for someone bad, someone who deserved it?'

'Even if it was for some scumbag, do they really deserve to die? Marcus is still a murderer, or he will be, no matter what way you look at it.'

Charley sighed.

'You're always trying to see the good in people, even when there's no good to see. Whether he's all bad or not, I'm still going to smash his skull in for hurting my best friend. I swear, the minute I'm out of here–'

'You're gonna what? Roll right up to him and clobber him from your chair?'

Abbie shrugged. 'Something like that, yeah.'

আ

After leaving Abbie and visiting Jess once more, Charley left the hospital feeling slightly deflated. She wasn't sure why, she just felt flat, as if someone had stolen the good mood she'd woken with earlier.

She called Aiden, but he wasn't free to talk. Her mother had asked her not to leave the hospital, but Charley couldn't bear it; she couldn't stand seeing Jess like that: weak, feeble, frail. Jess was in such a vulnerable position and Charley, an incredibly powerful magician, felt completely helpless for the first time in ages. She had all this power, yet she couldn't even help her own sister.

Just like you couldn't save your gran.

'Quiet,' Charley growled, trying to clear her head. She didn't want to think about Jess. She didn't want to think, full stop.

She walked through the streets of Newford until she reached the outskirts, where large fields were all she could see for miles. Then she let go. She let the magic pour out of her fingertips in the form of fireworks, a sparkling storm of colour which was barely visible in the daytime sky. But the relief she felt was enormous, her muscles relaxing as her fingers flickered, sending bright flashes dancing towards the clouds.

After a moment there was a buzz from her pocket, disrupting her thoughts and spoiling the glorious show she was displaying.

'Hi,' she said warmly when she saw Aiden's name pop up on the screen. 'Did you sort things out with Mum-zilla?'

The line was quiet for a moment and then a sharp voice said, 'No, he did not sort things with Mum-zilla.'

'Tabitha,' Charley said, her eyes widening in horror, 'I never meant you were . . . I mean . . . I thought it was Aiden calling . . .'

'Clearly.' Tabitha's cold tone sent shivers down Charley's spine. 'Charlotte, I need you at the house just now, please.'

'Really? Why?'

There was no answer. The line had already gone dead, leaving Charley wondering what Tabitha's unexpected call had been about.

It took her about half an hour to walk back to Aiden's, in which time she'd imagined all of the horrible things Tabitha could possibly say to her.

Maybe she found out that I stayed.

'Oh no,' she whispered, before giving the door a quiet knock.

It opened almost immediately.

'Come in, Charlotte,' Tabitha said frostily, holding the door open as the youngster stepped into the hall.

'If this is about–'

'Take a seat,' Tabby said, gesturing towards the living room.

Aiden was perched on the arm of the sofa, his eyes lighting up as Charley walked into the room. Fergus was sitting in one of the chairs, sipping a large glass of whisky and reading his newspaper.

It must have been a rough morning. Charley glanced at the tumbler gripped firmly in Fergus's hand and then to the clock on the mantelpiece.

'Aiden, will you please get your feet off my cushions,'

Tabitha snapped. Fergus glanced over the top of his newspaper but said nothing, instead pouring another large measure of whisky into his glass.

'What's this about?' Charley said meekly, not really sure whether it was a good idea to ask that question.

'This,' – Tabby wagged her finger, pointing into the centre of the room – 'is about the little display you just put on. I'm right in saying it was fireworks, am I not? Makes a change from thunderstorms and hurricanes.'

Charley looked to the ground. 'Oh, that.'

'Have you any idea how foolish that was? In broad daylight, too. Was there something specific you were celebrating?'

'No one was around,' Charley mumbled, 'and it wasn't for long. I just wanted to blow off some steam.'

'And you thought letting fireworks flicker from your fingertips was the way to do it? Where were you putting on this spectacular show? I do hope you were at least discreet.'

'Chambers doesn't do discreet,' Aiden smirked, and both Tabitha and Charley scowled at him. 'I'm joking . . .'

'There was nobody else there, I made sure. I'm sorry, really I am. It just hasn't been a good day.'

'Why, what happened?' Aiden asked, suddenly concerned, but Charley just shook her head.

Before Aiden could say anything else, Quinn and Dru walked through the door, once again setting Tabitha off.

'And you two,' she said, pointing towards them as they came into the room, 'what on earth have you been up to?'

'Don't know what you're talking about,' Dru said,

trying not to smile. She could tell her aunt was nettled which always amused her slightly.

'You know exactly what I'm talking about, young lady. I don't know what the pair of you were up to, but whatever it was was extraordinary. How did you hide it then, hmm? A shielding spell?'

'Seriously, Aunt Tabitha, I don't know what you're on about.'

Tabitha's eyes grew wild at Dru's insolence and for once she felt like she herself might explode. She was normally so composed, but at that moment she wasn't sure if she could contain her rage.

'Do not mock me, Druanna. You are currently living under my roof. This will not be the case for much longer if you continue to insult me in such a fashion.'

'Gee, calm down. You look like an angry stick insect when you get mad.'

Quinn turned to look at Dru, a stunned expression on her face. Fergus, almost certain his wife was ready to erupt, decided to give Tabby a breather and deal with his nieces himself.

'Girls, I think it might be best for you to go elsewhere for the time being. Same goes for you, Aiden. Take Charley out somewhere, go and do what normal teenagers do. That doesn't mean you go looking for trouble though, is that clear?'

'Crystal,' Aiden said, pushing himself from the couch. 'Let's go,' he smiled, grabbing Charley's hand. Dru followed him out the door with Quinn chasing closely behind.

'What did you do that for?' Tabitha sighed as Fergus wrapped his arms around her waist. 'They need to learn,

Fergus, they need to understand that it's not all right to just use their powers so irresponsibly.'

'No harm was done,' he said gently, kissing his wife's long, slender neck.

'But what if–'

'Life is full of what-ifs, Tabby. Sometimes, you need to take a step back and let people make decisions for themselves. Keep in mind that this is all very new to Charley, she's still learning.'

'And what about your niece?' Tabitha grunted. 'Is she still learning?'

'It's just the way she is, Tabby. Dru's a free spirit, they both are, to be fair. She's only trying to do right by her sister. Give her a chance.'

Tabitha groaned, her head spinning from the afternoon's unwanted activity.

'Next time they mess up, you can deal with it. I've suffered about as much reckless teenage behaviour as I can handle.'

THIRTY-THREE

They looked an odd sight, the four teenagers, walking through the town together, each one as different as the next. Quinn was dressed in her purple hat and long orange coat, Dru beside her in her habitually sombre attire. Charley was still wearing her dusty old jeans from the night before, her hair unbrushed and her shirt creased, then Aiden, sauntering along, his hands inside the pockets of a black leather jacket.

'So,' Quinn asked, 'where are we going?'

'You tell me,' Aiden replied, more interested in what Charley had been up to. 'What happened this morning?'

'Jess,' Charley answered. 'She had another seizure, only it was worse this time. She couldn't breathe, she was clawing at her skin . . . I didn't know what to do.'

'Is she all right?'

'She's okay now. She's in Newford Royal.'

'God, Chambers, I'm sorry.'

'I don't know what's happening to her. At first I thought that maybe . . . maybe she was like me.'

'You think Jess is a magician?' Aiden sounded sceptical. 'Chambers . . .'

'I thought that maybe there was a chance, yes. I don't anymore. It's not the same . . . what's happening to Jess isn't what happened to me. I know everyone's experience is different, but Jess is too . . . too doleful, if that makes sense. It's like there's a black cloud constantly hanging over her head and she's just waiting for it to rain. I don't know what it is, but she's not one of us.'

'No, she's not.'

Aiden took one of Charley's hands, his fingers curling round hers. 'Was she still like that when you got her to the hospital?'

'No, she was fine by then. Marcus . . .' I never said Marcus was involved . . . 'Marcus showed up. He was the one who helped her.'

'And you let him in? After everything that happened last night, you still let him into your house?'

'I didn't let him in, he let himself in. He must have heard Jess crying or something. Apparently she went round to see him this morning.'

'Why?'

'I've no idea. All he said was that he thought he might have upset her and he wanted to apologise. He helped her calm down and then he left, that's it.'

'There must be more to it than that. Why was your sister visiting the demon who crippled you in an alley last night?'

'He did not cripple me,' she spat, humiliated by his tone. Aiden didn't mean to sound condescending, but that was how Charley heard it.

'You know what I mean. And how did he manage to make whatever was happening to her stop?'

'He said he used magic,' she said, but Aiden shook his head.

'It doesn't sound right.'

'Please don't say we're paying Marcus another visit,' Quinn breathed.

'Sounds like fun to me,' Dru smirked, glancing discreetly at Quinn. 'Why don't we just kill him?'

'Because he's stronger than us,' Aiden said rationally. Dru scoffed at the thought of an adolescent demon being stronger than herself and Quinn. 'All right, he may not be stronger, but his magic's darker. And he clearly knows how to use it.'

'Are we missing the most obvious reason here?' Charley asked. 'We aren't murderers. We don't go around killing people to sort out our problems.'

'Why?' Dru muttered. 'He does.'

'That's exactly why. I'd rather die right now than become like Marcus: so bitter about life. So vindictive and hateful.'

'He doesn't hate everyone,' Dru teased, and Quinn chuckled before she could help herself, clamping a hand across her mouth to stifle the laugh. Aiden didn't seem to hear.

'Is your mum home yet?'

'I don't think so,' Charley answered, 'I'm not sure. Why?'

'We're going to do a bit of snooping,' he said, and the four of them headed for Charley's house.

The door was locked when they arrived, and Charley let out a sigh of relief as she fished around for her key. Part of her was glad that her mum wasn't home, but part of her was also scared. She wasn't sure if she really wanted to find out what was wrong with Jess.

'This way,' she said quietly, and the others followed

her up to Jess's room. Everything looked as it usually did, nothing out of place.

'Where do we start?' Charley said apprehensively as Quinn began poking about in the drawers.

'She got a diary?' Dru asked.

'Probably. I don't know where she keeps it though.'

'Well, let's get looking.'

'I can't go through her diary. It's personal.'

Dru raised her eyebrows. 'Do you want to find out what's wrong with your sister?'

No!

'Yes . . .'

'Right, let's find her diary then.'

Reluctantly, Charley started searching. She looked under the bed, in the wardrobe, raked through the sock drawer until eventually she found it, hidden in Jess's school bag of all places.

'Got it.'

'Well, what you waiting for?' Dru said eagerly. 'Start reading.'

Charley didn't want to. She knew how mad she'd be if someone ever went through her diary, especially someone she trusted. It just didn't feel right. Even so, she opened it in the middle and began flicking through the pages.

Most were scribbled with normal things that teenagers write:

School sucks! If I have to sit beside that tramp, Poppy, for one more day, I'm going to rip her tongue out of her thick, useless head and feed it to a crocodile.

'Charming,' Dru smirked, reading over Charley's shoulder.

'She'll have a hard job finding a crocodile in Newford,' said Quinn, slumping back on to Jess's bed.

'How do you know what this says?' Charley asked, and Dru's head shot up towards her sister.

'Must be a twin thing,' Quinn shrugged, as if it wasn't all that important.

'You can see what I'm thinking?' Dru asked in amazement. 'You can read my thoughts? I knew we were connected but I didn't know you could do that.'

'Neither did I. It's never happened before.'

'What am I thinking now?'

'I don't know. It wasn't like that . . . I just . . . knew what you were reading, somehow.'

'Why does this surprise you?' Aiden asked impatiently. 'You've always been able to do weird stuff like that.'

'Hey, Charley, did you ever tell Dru about the vision you had of her?'

'What vision?' Dru frowned.

'It wasn't a vision,' Charley replied, before hesitantly looking at Dru. 'It was more like . . . a flashback.'

'A flashback of what?'

'Your life.'

'Why would you see my life?' Dru said, unhappy at the thought of someone poking around in her head.

'I don't know. We thought at the time you were trying to connect with us, trying to talk to Quinn somehow.'

'I wasn't doing anything,' Dru grunted. 'I didn't even know who you were.'

'So you did nothing that would cause Charley to see into your past, feel what you were feeling?' Quinn asked.

Dru was silent for a moment and then said, 'Just keep reading.'

Charley said no more on the subject. Instead, she skimmed the words on the page in front of her, sighing as she flicked to the back.

My parents are so dull I could cry. If I ever have kids, I'm going to be cool. Not a stuffy old bore who does nothing but order people around.

Charley felt a twinge of sympathy for her mum as she read Jess's harsh words. Linda wasn't nearly as bad as that.

Saw Dad tonight for all of five minutes. Whoop-de-do, that's a record.

'This is pointless. It's just her pent-up anger about how much she dislikes our family.'

'You're not done yet,' Aiden said, coming over to stand beside Dru.

Charley turned to the back few pages which appeared to be quite recent.

Charley won't leave me alone, she won't stop pestering me. I can't help feeling like we're drifting apart. I love her but at the same time I feel this hatred for her, like I don't want her to be a part of me. We're different, we always have been, but I don't feel connected to her anymore. It's as though we're from different planets. Sometimes I want to beg her not to leave me, to tell her how scared I am. Other times, I wish she'd just disappear. She's like something sour in my mouth, something I want to spit out and crush with my shoe. And then I feel bad for even thinking that . . .

I don't understand. I don't understand anything anymore.

Charley's eyes filled with tears and she looked away, unsure if she wanted to read any more. The way Jess had described her, the words she'd used: hate, sour, disappear. Is that really what Jess thought of her?

'Want me to take over?' Aiden asked, but Charley shook her head and turned the page.

It happened again. It hurts so much but I can't control it. It's like my skin's on fire. My body feels as though it's going to spontaneously combust. And the screams, they were there, too. And the voices . . .

I think I'm going mad.

It gets so loud that I . . .

Before Charley could read another word, it was her who was now screaming. She flung the diary away, vomiting on the floor.

'Chambers!' Aiden was immediately by her side, rubbing her back as she heaved again. 'Quinn, get her some water.'

'I . . . can't . . . breathe,' Charley stuttered, clutching Aiden's arm as she began to panic. There was a sharp, buzzing sound that felt like a knife being driven into her ears and her limbs felt weak, as though she would keel over if she tried to stand.

'It was that book,' Dru said, pointing to the floor, 'the diary. It did something to her.'

'Jess,' Aiden muttered. 'You only get like this around Jess . . . Chambers, reading her diary . . . somehow it's caused this.'

Charley couldn't think. Jess's bed began to shake and things began to fall, books from the bookcase, her lamp from the table, the bulb smashing as it hit the floor.

When Quinn returned with the water the chaos had stopped. Everything was still and Charley was unconscious in Aiden's arms.

'What the hell just happened?' Dru asked.

Charley suddenly opened her eyes. 'I just had another vision.'

'About Jess?'

'No . . . I don't know what it was about. There was a baby . . .'

'What baby?' Dru prompted.

'I've no idea. It was just a baby in a hospital cot.'

'Well, we can take a good guess in saying it somehow involves the kid, seeing as you were reading her diary when you went all loopy.'

Aiden picked the diary up from the floor. 'Maybe I should read the rest?'

Charley nodded, her head still spinning. While Quinn fetched a basin of water to clean up the mess, Aiden opened the diary and began reading aloud.

It gets so noisy that I all I want is to make it stop, however I have to do it.

I just want to feel normal again.

Charley has this friend called Marcus, although I don't think he's actually her friend. He came round once but then left in a hurry. I think he might have done something wrong. I met him the other day after Gran died and my hands turned black. He turned them back to normal. I like Marcus. He's different, but he's cool. I know he likes Charley, I've seen the way he looks at her. She's too blind to notice though.

'See, even Jess knows he's in to you,' Aiden quipped.

'What does she mean, her hands turned black?' Charley frowned.

'I've no idea. It just says her hands turned black and Marcus helped her.'

'Why is Marcus always helping my sister when something goes wrong?'

Nobody replied.

'Do you guys mind if I bail for a while?' Charley asked, smiling weakly at them. 'I think I need a lie down after that.'

'Okay,' Aiden said, tossing the diary on to the bed and kissing her gently on the forehead. 'You call if you need me, all right?'

'I will, I promise.'

She saw them to the door and watched them make their way down the street. Aiden turned to give her a last wave, to which she smiled and mouthed, 'Thank you.'

'Anytime,' he shouted, before disappearing round the corner.

Charley never even made it to bed after that. She walked into the living room and collapsed on the couch. She was dead to the world in seconds.

THIRTY-FOUR

While Charley slept, she dreamt about Marcus. They were back on the bridge, staring into the water, relishing each other's company. Marcus had his arm draped around Charley's neck and her head was resting on his shoulder.

'What are you thinking?' he asked, stroking her cheek with his fingertips. She giggled softly.

'Just about you.'

'What about me?' He raised one eyebrow cockily.

'About how much I love you. The way I feel when I'm with you . . . How much I want to kiss you right now.'

Her smile faded and her eyes grew wide, wanting.

'Kiss me then,' Marcus whispered in her ear and she giggled again, this time from nerves.

'I can't,' she said sadly.

'Why not?'

'I . . . I don't know.'

'Do you still miss him?' Marcus asked, a sombre expression on his face.

'Miss who?'

'Aiden.'

Charley gave him a blank look, her eyes searching his for some sort of clue.

'Who's Aiden?' she asked, frowning in confusion. 'You're teasing me again, aren't you? You know I hate it when you do that.'

Marcus's smile returned and he said, 'Of course I'm teasing you. Come on, let's jump.'

'All right, on the count of three?'

'On one condition . . . once we hit the water, you're mine, okay?'

'Deal,' she smiled, grabbing a hold of his hand. 'One . . .'

'Two . . .'

'No!' Charley yelled, waking with a start. Her mouth was dry, her palms sweaty, and it took a moment for her to realise where she was. The curtains were still open but it was dark outside, the light from the street lamps glaring in the window.

Charley got up to shut them, still shaking from her nightmare.

Why is no one home yet? she wondered, pulling away the ties that held the curtains in place.

She hated nightmares of any kind, but this had been one of the worst. Not just because it was about Marcus, but because she'd enjoyed it. She could still feel his arm around her and his breath on her cheek; she could hear the rough sound of his gritty voice, whispering tenderly in her ear; she could still see his beautiful brown eyes, looking down at her affectionately.

He's a demon, she reminded herself, trying to forget about what she was feeling – what she had felt.

Charley took a deep breath as she fetched the phone,

a knot forming in her stomach. She couldn't think of anything she wanted to do less, but she knew she had no choice.

Carefully, she dialled Marcus's number and put the phone to her ear. He knew more about Jess than he was letting on and the only way to find out was to talk to him, ask him to meet her in person.

Yeah, because that usually works, said the irritating voice in her head.

'I don't have much choice,' Charley grunted aloud.

Who says he'll even agree to meet you?

'He will.'

Marcus was unpredictable, but when it came to Charley he was completely transparent. If Charley asked, Marcus would be there.

She let the phone ring but eventually hung up when it became clear he wasn't going to answer. 'Stupid demon,' she muttered, just as the front door opened.

'Charley? Who are you talking to?' Linda came through the door, followed by a fragile-looking Jess.

'Eh, no one. Never mind. How are you feeling?' she asked her sister, who was as white as a sheet.

'She's tired,' Linda said, dropping her handbag on the couch and giving Jess a kiss on the cheek. 'Go upstairs, honey. I'll bring you some tea and a hot water bottle.'

Jess left without a word to Charley and Linda groaned in exasperation.

'You okay, Mum?'

'Oh, Charley, I'm fine. It's just been a long day.'

'Is Jess okay?'

'As far as I can gather. They don't seem to be able to find anything wrong with her. I'm not pleased, Charley.

In fact, I'm furious. People don't just stop breathing like that.' Linda was close to tears.

'Can I do anything?'

'No, honey, it's all right. Thank you for offering. In fact, there is one thing you could do, before it gets passed on. The box in the living room,' – she gestured to a tattered cardboard container – 'it's all old stuff of your gran's. Would you mind going through it to see if there's anything you'd like? It's mostly junk, the big things are all in the garage, but there might be something you want to keep.'

'Sure, I'll have a look.'

Charley wandered over to the box and began unpacking it: a pair of old brass candlesticks; a silver brooch; a pearl necklace missing half its beads. Linda was right, it was all rubbish.

At the bottom, Charley came across a small pile of photographs, held together with an elastic band. They were torn at the corners and some of them stained, the paper curling slightly around the edges. Charley took them out and began leafing through them, smiling at her gran's cheerful expression. They were old pictures, probably dating back at least forty years.

When she came to a photo halfway through, she stopped. She had to take a second look to make sure she was seeing things right.

Yes, it was definitely her. It was a picture of her gran, smiling as always, with her arms wrapped around a skinny blonde woman: Tabitha.

It can't be, Charley thought, rubbing her eyes in confusion. What the hell's going on?

And then it hit her; it wasn't Tabitha, it must be her

mother. The two were almost identical, although the woman in the photograph had a slightly squarer jaw.

But what is Gran doing with Tabitha's mother? Were they friends?

Charley suddenly became very suspicious. Why had Tabitha never mentioned the fact that her mum had been friends with Dorcas? Pretty good friends, by the looks of things.

Charley shoved the picture in her pocket and got up from the floor.

'Mum, I need to go see Aiden.'

'Charley, dinner won't be long. And you have school in the morning. Can it really not wait until tomorrow?'

'Charley!' Jess suddenly yelled from upstairs, her voice like thunder. 'What the hell have you done to my room?'

'Nope, can't wait. Gotta go.'

Linda watched bewildered as Charley ran for the door.

'Oh, I give up,' she sighed.

The breeze caught Charley off guard and she cursed as the bitter wind blew through her hair, sending a chill down the back of her neck. She started to run, determined to get to Aiden's before she turned into an icicle.

'It shouldn't be this cold yet; it's not even snowing,' she said aloud, wondering if it was just the weather itself or if somebody had been messing with the climate again.

Maybe Quinn took the whole Ice Queen thing to a new level.

'You think this is bad?' a male voice echoed around her. 'Just wait until Christmas. I hear it's meant to be a cold one.'

Charley looked about but didn't move, trying to work

out where he was. She couldn't see him and she couldn't tell where the voice had come from, but somehow she could feel his presence.

'What do you want, Marcus?' she asked warily. 'Not really a fair fight, is it, when I can't even see where you are?'

'I'm not here to fight,' he said, and she suddenly noticed him lounging against a wall up ahead.

'What are you here for then?'

'You called, didn't you?'

She took a few steps towards him. 'Yeah, but you didn't answer. I didn't expect you to show up at my house.'

'I'm not at your house. You live there,' he said, pointing down the hill. 'I'm sitting here. Not the same thing at all.'

Charley folded her arms and scowled at his sarcasm.

'So who's Red?' he asked, levering himself up so he could see her. 'She's a feisty one, isn't she?'

'Do you have to have nicknames for everyone?'

'I don't have one for you,' he said seriously.

Charley shook her head, ignoring him. 'Her name's Dru . . . Quinn's twin sister. I thought you might have got that. They are identical after all.'

'Oh, I'm sorry. I was a little busy getting blasted through a bloody fence. You never did ask how I was after that. Honestly, Charley, I'm hurt.'

'Will you drop the act, please?' she snapped. 'What did you do to my sister?'

'I didn't do anything to Jess.'

'You cured her earlier, and you helped her when her hands turned black.'

'She told you about that?' Marcus raised his eyebrows.

'Well, no. I read it in her . . . her diary. Not that it's any business of yours.'

'And what's in Jess's diary is yours? You didn't really strike me as the intrusive type.'

'I'm not. I mean . . . not usually. I want to know what's wrong with her, that's all. I just want to help.'

Marcus looked thoughtful for a second and then pushed himself up off the wall. 'She'll be all right. Probably just teenage stuff. You know what it's like.'

'People's hands don't turn black for no reason, Marcus. What happened to her? And how did you fix them? Black magic again?'

'Yep, got it in one.'

'Why would you help my little sister?'

'Because she bumped into me in the street. I noticed one of her hands was a strange colour and I made her show them to me. Wasn't very well gonna leave them like that, was I?'

Charley didn't know if he was telling the truth. She looked into his eyes but they gave away nothing; they were deep and hypnotising and . . . empty. His eyes looked empty, like they hadn't quite found what they were looking for yet.

'You're still keeping something from me.'

'I'm probably keeping lots of things from you, Charley. Why would I tell you anything? I'm just a lousy demon after all.'

'Where did you come from?' she asked, not really expecting an answer.

He gave her one anyway. 'Didn't anyone ever tell you, love? I came from hell.'

Charley crossed her arms. 'Literally . . . or metaphorically?'

'I'll let you decide that one,' he said, taking a small step towards her. She didn't back away. She couldn't seem to tear her gaze away from him, fragments of the dream flashing through her mind.

'Get out of my head,' she whispered, but Marcus only grinned.

'I can't, Charley. I'm trapped.'

She looked into his eyes again, imagining them like they were in the dream: bright, happy, playful.

'You had what you wanted.'

'What do you mean?' he asked.

'In my dream . . . your eyes weren't empty because you had what you wanted.'

'You've been dreaming about me?' he teased. 'I'm flattered.'

'Don't be.'

'It's all right,' he shrugged. 'I dream about girls I hate all the time.'

Charley didn't speak, the silence saying much more than words ever could.

And then Marcus kissed her.

THIRTY-FIVE

Charley pulled back in horror, her mouth still open as she stared at Marcus in disbelief. 'What the hell do you think you're doing?' she yelled, but Marcus just looked at her hungrily, his chestnut eyes boring into hers. 'Well?'

He laughed quietly, her reaction not really all that surprising. 'Come on, Charley, don't kid yourself. You wanted that as much as I did.'

'Are you insane? I didn't want anything of the sort. I would never do that to Aiden.'

'Is that all that's stopping you?' he asked. 'Because I can easily take care of that.'

'No!' Her hands began to shake; she was so angry. Marcus took a step closer. 'Don't! Don't come near me.'

'I'm not going to hurt you.'

'That's not what I'm worried about.'

'You can deny it all you want, but I know what I saw. You wanted me to kiss you.'

'I didn't . . .'

'Your eyes gave it away. Your scent. The tone of your voice. You waited a moment. . .' He tilted his head to look at her.

'What do you mean, I waited?'

'Before you pushed me away. You could have stopped it the minute my lips touched yours, but you didn't. You waited and you felt something and that's what scares you!' He was shouting now, his jokey exterior gone, replaced with a hard stare.

Charley looked at him blankly. 'I felt nothing,' she snarled, her furious expression matching his. 'Don't ever do that again.'

'As you wish, princess. You go on fooling yourself. But I can see right through you. There's a fire in your belly and you know he can't put it out.'

'Maybe I don't want it to go out.'

'No, you don't. You know why? You like the heat. You like the thrill. You can pussyfoot about with your boyfriend all you want, but he's never going to be enough.'

'He is enough,' Charley growled.

'Say it enough times and maybe you'll believe it.'

'I already do.'

She walked past him, but he grabbed her wrist before she could leave.

'Let go of me!'

'Just do one thing for me, and then I'll let you go.' He took a hold of her hand, linking his fingers through hers. 'Tell me you feel nothing right now. Say it and I'll go.'

Her hand was tingling, her body hot with exhilaration. She could feel the heat flowing from his fingertips, running through her veins like poison.

She let go of his hand. 'I feel nothing,' she said, and then she left.

ম

Charley banged Aiden's door repeatedly until he answered, anxious that Marcus might have followed her. The wind was bitter, yet she still felt warm, tingles creeping from her head to her toes.

'Chambers?' Aiden said as he opened the door. 'I didn't expect to see you tonight.'

'Can I come in?' she asked tentatively. His brow furrowed and he pulled her inside, kissing her softly once the door was shut.

'Like you even have to ask,' he whispered, and she smiled, nuzzling her head into his jumper. He was warm . . . familiar. She felt safe with his arms wrapped around her.

'Aiden,' she said cautiously. 'I have to talk to you about something. Actually, I need to speak to your mum.'

'My mum?' he frowned. 'What's she done now?'

'Yes, what have I done this time?' Tabitha came into the room with her arms crossed, long hair framing her face. Charley wasn't sure if she'd ever seen Tabby with her hair down. It was nice; it softened her features and she appeared a lot less forbidding.

'I found this in amongst my gran's stuff.' Charley pulled the photograph from her pocket. 'I take it that woman's related to you?'

Her tone was fierce, but she didn't care. Normally she wouldn't dare speak to Tabitha in such a manner, but enough was enough. Charley wanted answers.

Tabitha nodded. 'Yes, she is.'

'Your mother?'

'Yes.'

'Why have you never mentioned that your mother and my gran were friends? You've had every opportunity to say something. Does this have anything to do with my gran's death? Did you have something to do with it?'

'Chambers,' Aiden said in surprise. 'I know Mum can be difficult, but she'd never do anything like that.'

'How can you be sure? She knew my gran was sick before we did.'

'I knew she was sick, Charley, because Fergus passed her one day in the street. They brushed shoulders and he got a strange vibe from her, like a flash, a coldness. He said it was like the end.'

'You never told me Dad could do that,' Aiden muttered.

'It's only happened twice before, but on both occasions the person was dead within a matter of months.'

Charley turned back to Tabitha. 'How do I know that's even true? You haven't liked me from the moment I got here. You've never mentioned the fact that my gran and your mother were friends. In fact, you've never mentioned your mother at all. Somebody conjured up that nost for my gran, who says it wasn't you?'

'Magicians can't conjure up nosts,' Tabitha said quietly.

'Maybe you got someone else to do it. You're hiding something and I want to know what it is.'

The atmosphere in the room grew tense. Fergus was now standing in the doorway and Quinn had just come in with a steaming tray of chocolate chip cookies.

'Biscuit, anyone?' she grimaced. 'Or not.'

Dru came in behind her and nabbed one from the tray, taking a bite and saying, 'What's going on?'

'I'm not sure,' Aiden said, looking from Charley to his mother.

'Quinn, these are disgusting,' Dru cried, spitting the chewed-up cookie back on to the tray.

'Can everyone please be quiet?' Tabitha called, her voice trembling. 'You want to know what happened, Charley? Take a seat.'

Charley turned to Aiden for moral support and he sat down beside her. Tabitha looked at her nieces, expecting that they might give them a little privacy, but Quinn perched herself on the table and Dru lay down across the back of the couch. Fergus glanced at her in disapproval but she wasn't paying attention.

'You're right,' Tabitha sighed. 'Ingrid, my mother, was good friends with your gran. Thick as thieves, she used to tell me, practically inseparable. I can't remember where she said they'd met, just that they'd been friends for a long time. Charley, your grandmother was also a magician, as was my mother.'

'What?' Charley gasped. 'She never said anything. I asked her but . . .'

'When my mother was in her late twenties, she fell pregnant with me. My father upped and left the moment he found out but apparently Dorcas was thrilled for her. I was born and, although I don't really remember your gran, not at that age anyway, she doted on me. She was the closest thing to an aunt that I had.'

'I thought you said Grandpa died in a car crash?' Aiden frowned.

'I did. It was better than telling you the real reason.'

'You mean the truth?' he snapped.

Tabitha took a deep breath and Fergus got up, crossing the room to sit beside her.

'It's not important. When I was one, my mother got very sick. She wasn't able to look after me properly but Dorcas helped out a lot; she did just about everything for me. One day when I was playing there was an accident.'

'What kind of accident?' Charley queried.

'I was just learning to walk. My mother was meant to be watching me, but she'd fallen asleep in her chair. I managed to get out of the room and wandered over to the stairs. Mother said she heard me falling but she couldn't get out of her chair. It was Dorcas who found me at the bottom of the stairs. I wasn't conscious and barely breathing.

'My mother knew I was going to die, there was no way I could have survived the fall, so she begged Dorcas to do something. She would have done it herself, but she wasn't strong enough.'

'Strong enough to do what?' asked Aiden.

'Help me. Dorcas had to do a healing spell to save me. Apparently she refused at first, said it wasn't right, we weren't allowed to do magic like that. But my mother begged her. She pleaded with Dorcas and by the sounds of it, she more or less bullied her into it.'

'So my gran saved you?' Charley asked. 'She did the spell?'

'Yes, she did the spell. She saved my life.'

'And what happened?'

'She was stripped of her powers, as she knew she would be. Dorcas had warned my mother but she wouldn't listen. They never spoke again after that. Your mum was born two years later, Charley. She had no powers.'

'Should she have? Had powers, I mean.'

'Not necessarily, but most likely she would have been born a magician, yes. It's not written in stone but it usually passes down the line.'

'So what happened to me?' said Charley hesitantly. 'Why was I born with magic? And why wasn't Jess?'

'I don't know,' Tabby sighed, 'I guess the spell sent things a little out of kilter.'

'Is that why you've always hated me?'

'I don't hate you, Charley. I just thought it best we keep our two families apart. But I promise you, I had nothing to do with your grandmother's death. She was once like a mother to me. I will always be grateful for what she did.'

Aiden stirred, his brain running wild. 'So you're saying we can heal people? We can save people's lives? I thought–'

'No, Aiden, we can't. Not unless you want to lose your powers for good.'

'Only demons can do that,' Charley murmured.

Tabitha looked sullen. 'Do what?

'Heal people. They don't lose their powers.'

Tabby shook her head. 'Demons can't heal people.'

'But–'

'They can kill people, yes, and they're very good at it. But they cannot heal people without dire consequences.'

Charley looked at Aiden, her face full of fear.

'But . . . how did Marcus cure Jess then?'

'What are you talking about?' Tabitha asked crossly. 'I hope you're not associating with that Gillespie boy, Aiden. Of all the stupid things you could do–'

'No, Mum. I told you before, we thought Marcus might have had something to do with Dorcas dying, that's all. How did you know he was a demon anyway?' he asked, wondering why he hadn't thought of that at the time. 'You said you knew who he was . . .'

'Of course I know who he is. Marcus and his parents lived here years ago, but they moved away after their daughter was born.'

'Bud?' said Charley.

Aiden looked at her in confusion. 'Who?'

'Marcus's sister. She died a couple of years ago.'

'Apparently there was a warlock after them,' Fergus intervened, 'someone Judith had wronged in the past. After the baby was born they fled with the kids. We didn't hear another thing of them until they showed up back in town.'

'Are they demons?' Charley asked. 'His parents?'

Tabby sighed, as if this was obvious. 'Yes, they're demons.'

Dru gulped, her skin prickling with goosebumps, pins and needles in her hands and feet. Her chest began to ache and for once she felt cold, an icy feeling creeping through her. 'Are we taking about Judith Gillespie?' she asked, her voice shaking as she whispered the words.

'Yes,' Charley nodded.

'As in Judith Gillespie, the most powerful demon to ever walk the planet?'

Tabitha scowled. 'I wouldn't quite go that far.'

'Oh, she is,' Dru confirmed. 'She's here? She lives in Newford?'

'What's going on, Dru?' Aiden asked. He'd never seen her look scared before, but for once she looked petrified, like a rabbit caught in headlights.

'I . . . I haven't been completely straight with you,'

she admitted timidly. 'When I was away, Quinn,' – Dru turned to her sister – 'I was . . .' A lump caught in her throat and for a moment she couldn't seem to speak.

'Dru, what's going on?' Fergus asked.

'Well, when I left home I was . . . I wasn't feeling great. You know how I was, Quinn.'

Quinn nodded, her face falling as she thought back to her sister's depression.

'I just couldn't get a grip of this world, Uncle Fergus. I hated everything about it. So I went to look for a shaman. I needed someone who was powerful enough to perform a de-linking spell.'

Quinn looked at her in horror, the betrayal she felt cutting deep. 'A de-linking spell? So you could . . . oh my God.'

'I know, Quinnie, I'm sorry. I just couldn't stand feeling like that anymore. I was empty. There was nothing there but misery and grief. I hated the world for creating me, and I hated everyone in it for being too blind to see how I felt. I know how selfish it sounds.'

'Grief for what?' Quinn sniffed, a tear running down her cheek. 'What were you grieving?'

Dru laughed, beginning to well up herself. 'I don't even know. How stupid is that? I just felt so alone. It was like I'd lost part of myself. Even when I was surrounded with people, I felt isolated. I just wanted it to stop. I'm so sorry,' she cried, her words so quiet they were hard to hear.

Quinn got up and went to her sister, wrapping her arms around Dru's shoulders. 'It's okay. I'm here now. You don't ever have to be alone again.'

No one wanted to break up the girls' heartwarming

moment, but eventually Tabitha cleared her throat and said, 'Druanna dear, I don't mean to push you but can you tell us what happened? How does this involve the Gillespies?'

Dru wiped her cheeks with her sleeve, black pools forming under her eyes from where her mascara had run.

'It took me a while to find anyone who could help. I read about a shaman in Tokyo who was meant to be able to do that sort of thing, but it ended up just being a myth. I tried everything after that, but everyone I went to either wasn't powerful enough or refused to help me. I was almost ready to give up.'

'So what happened?'

'A witch I met, when I came back to England, told me about a demon who could do spells you couldn't imagine, things no magician could ever dream of doing.'

'Judith,' Charley said. Dru nodded.

'Turns out I didn't need to go far.'

Tabitha looked concerned. 'Druanna, when was this?'

'A few months ago. She was staying in Oakshore at the time, must have moved here shortly after. Hettie, the witch I met, told me where I could find her. I went to her house. She told me to leave but said she'd meet me later that night, alone. She stuck to her word. I told her what I wanted . . . what I needed her to do for me.'

'Well, she obviously didn't do it,' said Quinn. 'Either that or you backed out. Because as far as I can see, we're still very much a part of each other.'

Dru couldn't look at Quinn, the guilt she felt so enormous she thought it might crush her. 'She refused to do it. She said being forced to stay alive would cause me much more pain than dying, and that there was nothing she liked more than to see a magician in pain. She left after that and I never saw her again.'

'That's why she recognised me,' Quinn mumbled, 'the day we went round to see Marcus. She said I looked familiar. It wasn't me she'd met, it was you.'

'What happened after that?' Aiden asked, squeezing Charley's hand tightly.

'I moved around for a bit and then I went home. I went back for Quinn.' She looked at her sister. 'You weren't there though.'

Quinn shrugged. 'I was looking for you.'

Fergus shook his head in exasperation. 'And your father doesn't mind? That the two of you keep running off without explanation?'

'Our parents gave up worrying about us a long time ago, when they realised it did them no good,' Dru replied to her uncle, although she didn't take her eyes off Quinn. 'I'm so sorry, Quinnie. I guess I just needed some time alone, time to reflect on things. Some lame attempt at finding myself.'

'And did you?' Quinn looked expectantly at Dru, her eyes wide with anticipation. She'd never seen her sister look so terrified. Gone was the hard exterior, the front she was so used to. Dru simply looked lost.

'No, but I found you,' she smiled. 'Going to Judith may not have been wise, but it made things clearer. It made me realise that with you by my side, Quinnie, I am someone. I grew up resenting the fact that I was tied to you instead of appreciating it. I told you before, it made me look at things differently.'

Tabitha looked at Fergus. She seemed to have aged dramatically in the last half hour.

'I think we should all get some rest,' she finally said, and Fergus nodded in agreement. 'We'll discuss this further tomorrow.'

Aiden walked Charley to the door while Quinn took Dru upstairs; the pair of them had a lot to discuss.

Aiden pulled Charley close to him and she grabbed him in a vice-like grip.

'You don't need to say goodbye yet,' he smiled warmly, 'I am going to walk you home, you know.'

Charley didn't let go. 'It's not that. I don't want to be alone tonight.'

Aiden ran his hand down her back, sighing and letting his chin rest on her head. 'She'll know if you stay here, Chambers,' he said sadly.

'I know. My mum will know, too, if I don't show up home.'

Aiden was quiet for a moment, before saying, 'You got a chair in your room?' Charley nodded. 'All right, I'll come back over later. Chairs make excellent locks,' he grinned.

Charley smiled back, reaching up to kiss him.

'Come on,' he said, grabbing his jacket, 'I'll walk you home.'

THIRTY-SIX

Linda wasn't very happy when her eldest daughter arrived back. Charley apologised profusely, saying how bad she felt about rushing off but that she'd had a good reason. Of course when Linda asked what it was, Charley couldn't think of anything to say, so she ended up telling her that Abbie had called from the hospital and asked to see her. Eventually Linda had nodded, told Charley not to worry about it and headed off to bed, saying she needed an early night after the day's events.

Nick didn't say much either. He kissed his daughter on the head and smiled kindly at her, but he couldn't think of a decent conversation starter. Charley understood; her father had never been very good at those sorts of things. Instead, she went upstairs, had a shower and got ready for bed. She was just pulling on her pyjamas – or rather, her strap top and sweats – when there was a quiet tap at the window. She ran over and opened it, letting a breathless Aiden climb inside.

'Did you use magic to get up here?' she asked, kissing his cold cheek.

'Nope, just climbed up the drainpipe,' he smirked. 'Sometimes we boys like to do things the old-fashioned way.'

Charley smiled. 'I'm glad you're here.'

'Me too,' he whispered. 'Are your parents away to bed?'

'Mum is. Dad's still downstairs. Don't worry, I put the chair against the door.' She pointed over to where the chair was tilted, the back of it wedged firmly under the door handle.

'What about Jess?' he asked.

'She's in bed, too. She was already asleep when I got back, think she must have needed an early night.'

'Not surprising. And how are you doing? No more sickness?'

'No. I did feel a bit dizzy when I got out the shower. It passed.'

'I'm glad. Come on, let's get some sleep.'

They climbed into Charley's bed, Aiden pulling the lilac covers up to his chin.

'It's really my colour,' he grinned.

'Shut up, you goof. Just hug me.'

And that's what he did.

Charley woke before her alarm clock, the thought of her mum catching them at the back of her mind. She turned to face Aiden, his eyes still closed and his arm still draped over her.

'I'm not sleeping,' he murmured, before she could say anything. He opened his eyes and smiled at her. 'Morning, beautiful.'

Charley's stomach tightened. 'Morning,' she replied.

She didn't want to get up. She didn't want to leave Aiden, although she knew she'd see him again in a couple of hours. It just wasn't the same, being with him in public. She wanted him all to herself.

'You'd better go,' she said reluctantly.

'I know. What you want me to do, shimmy down the drainpipe?'

'As much as I'd love to see you, eh, shimmying down the side of my wall, you can probably use the front door.'

'Won't your parents see?'

'My dad will be away already and I just heard Mum go into the bathroom. She'll be going for a shower, so you'll have plenty of time.'

'All right,' he whispered, kissing her again before getting up and heading towards the door. Charley grabbed a cardigan and followed him.

Poking her head out into the hall, she motioned for Aiden to follow, knowing it was safe when she heard the water running in the bathroom. They tiptoed downstairs and Charley quietly opened the front door.

'See you at school?' he asked once he was outside, the sun reflecting off his sandy-blonde hair. Even when he'd just woken up, Aiden looked gorgeous.

'You're going to school? Don't you think we should be dealing with more important things? We've got so much to find out, so much to do . . .'

'And how much can we really do right now? Besides, Marcus will probably be there. We can pester him again about the nost, maybe find out a bit more about his mother. Small steps, Chambers.'

Charley froze at the mention of Marcus, his name sending shivers down her spine. She didn't want to pester him. She didn't want to see him. And she certainly didn't want Aiden anywhere near him.

'Sure,' she shrugged, 'see you at school.'

She closed the door and ran a hand through her hair. She'd gone from cloud nine to rock bottom in less than a minute.

'Does Mum know he stayed the night?' she heard a voice say, and she looked up to see Jess standing at the top of the stairs.

'He didn't stay. He just popped by to say hello.'

'At ten to seven?' Jess raised her eyebrows.

'He was out for a walk. So what if it's early, you saying you can't drop by to see someone in the morning now?'

Jess thought back to her visiting Marcus, showing up at eight o'clock on a Sunday.

'Whatever,' she grumbled. 'Like I care anyway.'

Charley's trepidation became a reality as she made her way towards the school. She could already see Marcus leaning against one of the pillars wearing a pair of jeans and his duffle coat, his schoolbag lying next to him on the ground. Charley scowled. If she tried coming to school in jeans, she'd no doubt get sent home to change.

She swallowed, her mouth dry, and continued walking, determined not to let him bother her.

So what if he'd kissed her? It's not like she'd enjoyed it. It's not like she'd felt anything apart from sheer disgust, repulsion at the ridiculous notion that she would ever feel that way for him.

'I felt nothing,' she said to herself.

Liar.

'Go away,' she snapped.

Can't. You did feel something, don't deny it.

'No I didn't.'

Tell the truth. Your heart was on fire.

'My heart was not on fire.'

Well, something was.

'Leave me alone,' she growled, just as a hand came down on her shoulder.

'Who you talking to?' Aiden asked, out of breath from running. His cheeks were a bright rosy colour after being exposed to the cold autumn wind.

'Would you believe me if I said the voices in my head?'

'I've heard stranger things than that these past few days.' He kissed her gently and took her hand as they walked towards the doors; towards Marcus.

'All right, love,' he winked as they passed, his brown hair swept messily over one eye.

Charley stopped in front of him. 'You lied to me,' she said accusingly.

He pushed himself from the pole. 'About what?'

'You said you healed Jess, used black magic to cure her.'

'Yes . . .'

'Demons can't heal people,' said Aiden.

'Sure they can.'

'Not without consequences.'

'Maybe there'll be consequences then. What do I care? My whole world came tumbling in on me last night.'

'What are you talking about?' Aiden sighed.

'Oh, nothing. Just got shot down by someone, that's all.'

'You're having girl trouble?' Aiden raised an eyebrow.

'Afraid so. It's all right though. She just hasn't worked out how she feels yet.' Marcus smiled wickedly at Charley. 'Honestly, I think she's just scared.'

'Who is it?' Aiden asked, and Charley's eyes shot open as she registered what he'd said.

Marcus smiled. 'No one you need to concern yourself with.'

Charley frowned; she'd heard him say that before.

And the nost? You gonna tell me who it was for yet?

No one you need to concern yourself with.

'Well, hopefully she'll run a million miles,' Aiden snorted, pitying any girl that ended up in the clutches of Marcus Gillespie.

'I get the feeling she won't,' he grinned. 'She'll be back.'

'Don't count on it,' Charley muttered, but Marcus only laughed.

'You saying you wouldn't go back, Charley? If you had this unbelievable connection with someone, something indescribable, wouldn't you want to explore it, find out if it was real? Isn't it better to be with the right person, even if it is a little terrifying?'

'There is no right person for you,' Aiden scoffed. 'And if there is, well, she'd need to be just as sadistic as you are.'

Charley felt that familiar knot in her stomach and, for a moment, she thought she was going to be sick.

'Can we go?' she said to Aiden, linking her arm through his. 'This conversation is making me nauseous.'

The cafeteria was filled with eager students, hurrying into queues to line up for their lunch. Charley wasn't hungry. She was sitting at one of the tables, her feet resting across Aiden's lap while he tried to finish off a pile of overdue homework.

Charley, bored and looking for something to do, began raking through her schoolbag. Something at the back of her mind was bothering her. She wasn't sure what, but it was niggling away at her, making it terribly hard to concentrate.

She leafed through her various jotters, eventually deciding that she wasn't in the mood to study. It could wait.

'Want a mint?' she asked Aiden, unzipping one of the pockets and chucking the packet to him.

Before she zipped it back up, she spotted something shiny in the corner of the pocket: the locket she'd found that day in the corridor, the day she'd heard the mysterious voice.

'What's that?' Aiden said as she pulled it from the bag, twisting it round her index finger.

'It's the necklace I found, the day you told me about my gran being sick.'

'Oh, I remember. You never did say where you found it.'

'It was lying outside the toilets. There was a woman . . . she said something, but before I could find out who it was, she was gone. The only thing left was this locket.'

'What d'you mean, a woman?'

'A woman, Aiden. As in a female . . .'

Aiden tickled her behind the knee, making her squirm in her chair.

'Very funny. You know that's not what I meant. Was it one of the other students? It is the girl's toilet after all.'

'It didn't sound like a student. She definitely sounded older . . .'

'One of the teachers?'

'Maybe. Oh, I don't know. She left in such a hurry.'

'What's it say on the front?' Aiden asked, pointing towards the locket. 'Something's written there . . .'

'I know. I tried before, but I couldn't make it out.'

Aiden took the locket from her, examining it closely. 'Looks like a three,' he said.

'A three? Why would someone have a three engraved on a locket?'

'Don't ask me,' he said, shrugging. 'What's inside?'

'Don't know, it wouldn't . . .'

Aiden pulled the clasps apart and the locket came free, leaving Charley feeling rather silly.

'. . . open. Hey, how did you do that? It wouldn't budge when I tried.'

'Maybe you're not strong enough,' Aiden winked, and Charley cocked an eyebrow at him. 'Any idea who she is?' he said, passing the locket across to her.

Charley stared at it for a moment, her heart in her mouth. 'It . . .' She frowned in bewilderment. 'It looks like me.'

Aiden took the locket back and looked at the picture more carefully. 'She does a bit,' he said, 'only younger. That kid can't be older than nine, ten at most.'

'Trust me,' she said, 'that's what I looked like when I was ten. That's me . . .'

'Why would some strange lady have a picture of you?' Aiden asked. 'You sure it's not yours?'

'I think I'd remember my own necklace,' Charley answered.

'Jess, maybe?'

'Now you're being ridiculous. Why would Jess put a picture of me inside her locket? She can't stand the sight of me most of the time.'

'Could be a front; she might secretly idolise you, just doesn't want you to know.'

'No, she used to idolise me. Now all I do is irritate her.'

'And she irritates you. It's what sisters do.'

'You know what I mean. Things aren't the way they used to be.'

Aiden closed the locket and dropped it back into Charley's palm. 'We'll find out what's wrong with her,' he said softly. 'It'll all be okay, I promise.'

'Just like it was okay with Gran? We were too late with her.'

'Yeah, but your gran died because of a nost. That's not the case with–'

'Jess . . .' Charley whispered, the colour draining from her face. Why hadn't she thought of it sooner?

'The things that were happening to her . . . the things she was saying. There was something inside her, something hurting her. She asked me to get it out . . .'

Aiden's face filled with horror. 'Oh my God,' he murmured.

Charley dropped the locket, her hands no longer able to function. 'The nost Marcus conjured . . . Aiden, it was for Jess.'

Marcus smiled to himself as he wandered home, his boots scuffing the ground as he walked. He knew he'd rattled Charley. The way she was behaving amused him no end, watching her sweat as he mocked her in front of Aiden. He also knew it wasn't completely one-sided; he'd felt the burn when their hands had touched and from the look on her face, he knew she'd felt it as well.

He turned the corner, whistling to himself as he strolled along, and then everything went black.

THIRTY-SEVEN

Marcus opened his eyes, slowly trying to find his bearings. His ears were throbbing and a dull ache stretched across the back of his head; it felt like he'd been smacked with a baseball bat. He tried to lift his hand to check for blood, but it wouldn't move, his wrist bound tightly to the arm of a chair. He checked the other – it was the same.

Marcus chuckled, his eyes finally focusing on the first person he saw: Charley.

'I knew there was a dark side to you, Charley, but I didn't realise you were such a deviant.'

'Can't we just gag him?' Dru groaned from the chair she was lying in, her legs dangling over the edge.

'Nice to see you too, Red,' Marcus said with a sneer. Dru pulled a face in return.

'No, we can't gag him,' Charley said, her voice more malevolent than any of them had ever heard it before. 'I need to hear what he has to say. Marcus has something he needs to do for me, and he isn't leaving here until it's done.'

'And what's that, love? You after a snog? Fine by me, my lips are ready and waiting . . .'

Quinn, who was balanced on the back of Dru's chair, scowled, and in disgust said, 'Like she'd ever want a kiss from you. She'd rather stick pins in her eyes.'

'Really? That's not the impression I got when I kissed her last night,' Marcus grinned, and Charley felt her stomach go, the way it does when the car drops from the top of a roller coaster. Quinn's jaw nearly hit the floor and Dru rolled her eyes, fed up with all the trivial mind games. And Aiden . . . Aiden looked ready to burst.

'He kissed you?' he yelled, not wanting to believe what Marcus had said, yet somehow knowing it was true.

'No . . . I mean, he did, but it . . . it wasn't like that. I didn't ask him to and I did not kiss him back.'

'That's debatable,' Marcus shrugged.

'Shut up!' Charley snarled.

'Why didn't you tell me?' Aiden demanded, his knuckles turning white. 'It's not like you didn't have plenty of opportunities. I was with you all night, remember?' Aiden's fist came down on the piano, the little box of chocolates bouncing off the edge.

Marcus winced, experiencing a twinge of jealousy when he heard Charley had spent the night with Aiden.

'I wanted to tell you. I thought about it, really I did. I knew you'd be upset though. I didn't want you to get mad.'

'Like I am now?' Aiden snarled.

'Yeah, pretty much.'

'You should have told me, Chambers. I would've understood. By God, I wouldn't have been happy, but I would've understood.'

'I'm sorry . . .' she whispered.

'Don't you trust me?'

Charley felt like she'd been punched in the gut. 'Of course I do! It's him I don't trust.' She gestured towards Marcus, who only smirked at her, enjoying the chaos he was creating. 'I know I should've told you. I just didn't want to risk losing you.'

'You were never going to lose me, Chambers. Not in a million years. Goddamnit, I'm in love with you, you moron.'

Everything around Charley froze, and she could have sworn her heart stopped beating. Only for a second, but it definitely skipped a beat.

'You . . . you love me?'

'Of course I do. I think I've loved you from the moment I met you.'

Dru moaned from her chair. 'Can we please not be so bloody sentimental? Haven't we got more important things to be dealing with than some demon's stupid teenage crush?'

'Hey,' Marcus grumbled, 'how come he gets to declare his undying love for her, yet all I am is some half-baked demon with a crush? Hardly sounds fair.'

'We'll play fair when you do,' Charley replied. 'Right now, you have work to do.'

'You do know I could break these ropes in a second if I tried,' Marcus boasted.

'That's what these are for.' Fergus walked through the door, a pair of metal shackles in his hand. He clamped one around Marcus's wrist, locked it shut, then did the same with the other. 'That should hold you.'

'Seriously?' Marcus scoffed. 'I can get out of these,

too. I am a demon, don't forget.' He looked at Charley wistfully. 'Not that you're likely to.'

'The restraints are bound by a spell. You can try all you like, you won't get out of them.'

And Marcus did try, although without much success. Eventually, he gave up, realising he wasn't going anywhere anytime soon.

'So what are you grilling me for this time?' he muttered.

'Oh, I don't know. How about the nost you summoned for my sister? Why don't we start there?'

Marcus's face was blank for a minute, until finally his lips curled into a sly smile. 'So you worked it out, eh? Not bad.'

'Why?' Charley barked. 'Why Jess?'

'Only Jess would do,' he said honestly.

'Do for what? What's she ever done to you?'

'You really want me to tell you?'

'Yes,' she snapped, her blood boiling.

'You sure?'

'What the hell do you want with my sister?'

'She isn't your sister, Charley. She's mine.'

Nobody in the room moved. Everybody stared from Marcus to Charley and back again. Charley didn't know what to say.

'You're lying,' she eventually said, but the words came out in a whisper.

'Wish I was, love.'

'How can she be? That doesn't make any sense.'

'Actually, it makes perfect sense. Go into my pocket. There's something you need to see.'

Charley let out an exasperated sigh and reluctantly did as he asked.

She pulled out a photograph, the one Marcus had hidden from her the day she'd accidentally emptied out the contents of his jacket. It was the girl from the locket.

'Bud was your sister,' Marcus said, 'and Jess is mine.'

'Bud...' Charley breathed, pulling the locket from her trouser pocket. 'That's who the photo's of ... not me.' She shivered, her skin now ice-cold. 'It isn't a three,' she said to Aiden, running her finger across the front of the locket. 'It's a B.'

'Aren't you a clever-clogs?' Marcus sneered, and Charley slapped him with the back of her hand.

'How?' she demanded, but Marcus ignored her.

'Why are people always hitting me?' he groaned, although he was still smiling.

'How? How is it possible?'

'Are you going to hit me again?'

'I'll do worse than hit you if you don't start talking.'

Marcus laughed. 'God, I love it when you're angry.' Charley raised her hand, ready to smack him again when Marcus said, 'All right, all right. I'll tell you.'

Charley crossed her arms, waiting impatiently for him to say something.

'Ever heard of Jensen Martinez?'

'Nope.'

'He was a warlock my mother created back when I was small.'

'What do you mean, created?' Charley asked dubiously.

'She made him. She turned a human into a warlock, wanted to use him in some war she was having with this shaman from Mongolia.'

'What exactly is a warlock?' Charley asked, turning

341

to the others. 'Is it the male equivalent of a witch or something?'

'Oh no,' Quinn shook her head. 'Warlocks and witches have zilch in common.'

'Apart from they're both incredibly powerful,' said Dru. 'And dangerous.'

'Warlocks are some of the most evil creatures you get,' Marcus said. 'They have no filter. They don't have feelings. After my mother created Jensen, before he lost himself completely, he vowed to kill her next born child. He wasn't strong enough to kill my mother himself, but a baby he could manage.'

'Why didn't he just kill you?' Aiden asked, wishing immensely that he had.

'Don't know. All he said was he'd kill her next born, whenever that was. He must have sensed it though, because a few weeks later my mum found out she was pregnant. She didn't know what to do. She knew if she ran, he'd find her eventually.'

'Why didn't she just destroy him? Surely she's powerful enough?'

'Nope. She created him, meaning he was just as strong as she was. Neither of them had the power to kill the other, but he did have the power to kill someone she cared about.'

'So what did she do?' Quinn asked, intrigued.

'She panicked. She spent months worrying about it, trying to come up with a plan. Despite being one of the most powerful demons alive, she couldn't think how to protect her unborn child. A few days before she went into labour, she decided what to do.'

'And that was . . . ?' Dru asked impatiently.

'She'd go to the hospital, have the baby as normal, then she'd leave with someone else's.'

'She took someone else's child?' Aiden exclaimed in disgust.

'Yep. She knew her baby would be safe with a regular family. Jensen would only look as far as my mother. She had it all figured out: she would take the baby, let Jensen find her, Jensen would kill it and then she'd go back for her own kid. He wouldn't come looking for her again after thinking he'd killed it.'

'And she went through with it?' Quinn murmured. 'She took–'

'Bud. She took Bud and left Jess with my mother,' Charley said, a vacant look in her eyes.

Marcus sighed. Despite his bravado, he couldn't bear to see Charley in pain.

'After the baby was born, my mum took her down to the nursery. She fried the security cameras and put a sleeping spell on the midwife. Then she searched until she found the baby most similar to her own.'

'Bud . . .' Charley said.

'Yeah. They were almost identical. She checked the family name on the cot so she could find her again when the time was right, then she took Bud and left.'

'And no one noticed the babies were swapped?' Dru asked suspiciously. 'Surely you'd notice that you had a different sprog?'

'My mum only saw Jess for a second after she was born,' – Charley paused, realising what she'd just said – 'Bud . . . she only saw Bud for a moment. She lost a lot of blood and her oxygen levels dropped – the baby was fine but Mum was rushed away for surgery. My dad wouldn't have been able to tell the difference,' she whispered sadly, looking to the floor.

'What happened with Martinez?' Fergus asked. 'Did he find your mother?'

'Not for a long time. See, when Mum took Bud, she got something she never bargained for. She didn't know Bud was a magician. Your parents were just a couple of insigs, Charley, and she didn't know about you. She knew your gran, but only as a Blightly – she didn't know who the Chambers family were.'

'What do you mean, she knew my gran? What does Gran have to do with anything?'

'Your gran was a magician. Well, that's what my mum said anyway.'

'I know she was a magician . . .'

How did she know? Charley wondered. How did she know my gran?

'What does this have to do with anything?' Dru griped, getting bored of going round in circles.

Marcus snorted. 'My mother hates magicians.'

Dru let out an amused laugh. 'Oh, I'm well aware.'

'She thought Bud was just a normal baby when she took her, she had no idea she was magic.'

Aiden sat down on the edge of the couch. 'So, what happened?'

'She did something she never thought possible, not in a thousand years. She only went and fell in love with the kid. Head over heels, like she was her own. Magician or not, my mother loved Bud, and she wasn't about to let anything happen to her. So we ran.'

Aiden frowned. 'I thought you said Jensen would find you?'

Marcus looked at the floor grimly. 'We knew he would, and eventually he did. But we had no other choice. She wasn't going to let anything separate her from Bud.

'We moved every few months, flew all over the world. Bud grew tired of it though. She just wanted a normal life. She wanted friends she wouldn't always have to say goodbye to. She wanted a home. So my mother gave in. My parents bought a house in Oakshore and that's where we stayed. The first year or so was quiet, and I think Mum actually began to feel safe again. But she was never safe, Bud was never safe. He found us a year later. Bud was playing in the garden, my mother watching her from the window. Jensen showed up. It was just before lunch . . .'

Marcus felt a twinge in his chest, a dull ache as he recalled the fateful day. Just before lunch, 11:47 . . .

'Before she could get to Bud . . .' Marcus couldn't breathe for a second. 'It was too late.'

Charley felt sick. 'Let me get this straight. The baby my mother gave birth to, my biological sister . . . is dead?' She couldn't take it all in. 'I don't understand. If Jess really is your sister, why did you conjure a nost up for her?'

'Because, Charley, despite Jess being part of my blood, she's never been a sister to me. I'd never met her, I didn't really care what happened to her. Bud, on the other hand . . .'

'So you'd kill her for no reason? Just out of what – malice? Revenge? What, Marcus? Tell me!'

'No, of course not. I'm not that immoral.' He raised one eyebrow. 'All right, maybe I am, but I wasn't without reason. Jess is the key to bringing Bud back.'

Charley gaped at him in horror. 'What are you talking about?'

'The only way to bring back Bud is to sacrifice my biological sister – a life for a life. Jess has to die at the hands of one of her relatives: her mother, her father . . . or me.'

THIRTY-EIGHT

Marcus twisted his arms until he felt the cuffs begin to loosen, the spell which was binding them not strong enough to hold him for long.

Who said I wouldn't get out of them? he thought smugly to himself.

'So why you?' Charley spat, the temptation to throttle Marcus almost too much to bear. 'Why were you the one to do it? You could have let your mum summon the nost, your dad . . .'

'My dad wouldn't have done it. He's far too noble for that.'

'He was willing to let an innocent baby die. You call that noble?'

'He had no idea my mother was planning to let Martinez kill the baby. He thought because the baby wasn't a demon, Jensen would spare her. She never told him what she was planning to do, just that once Jensen was gone, they'd swap the babies back, make out like it had never happened.'

'Yes, because no one would have noticed then,'

Charley scoffed. 'I think even my dad would have cottoned on after that amount of time.'

'She didn't care. It was just a ruse to get my dad on board, he would never have gone for it otherwise. My dad's a good guy; I told you – not all demons are barbaric.'

'Just the majority,' Aiden scowled.

'So why you? Why did you do it and not your mum?'

'It was more of a test than anything. She wanted to see if I'd go through with it. When she told me about her plan to get Bud back, I was in from the start. I couldn't believe it was actually possible. But she wasn't sure if I'd get cold feet. She knew she couldn't tell my father – he would've gone mad. But me? She knew how much I missed Bud, and she was well aware I would have tried anything to get her back.'

'So she got you to create the nost?'

'Yep. She said it would all fall into place after that. She doesn't like you though,' he winked at Charley. 'Thinks you're leading me astray.'

'How did she even know who I was?'

'You're Jess's sister, Charley. How was she not going to know who you were?'

'So she was the one who left the locket for me . . . why?'

Marcus shrugged. 'Probably just to distract you. I'm pretty sure she knows I have a thing for you, more than likely she wanted to keep you busy, keep you out the way.'

'By leaving me a locket with a picture of my own sister in it? My real sister . . .'

Marcus nodded and laughed. 'Yeah, she's twisted like that.'

'Abbie . . .' Charley said suddenly. 'It was her . . . the woman in my vision . . . it was your mum who pushed Abbie from the roof, wasn't it?'

'What? No . . .'

'Tell me the truth!' Charley shouted, diving towards Marcus and grabbing him by the collar.

'I don't know. I swear . . . I'm not lying. If she did, I had no idea . . .'

'Chambers, calm down.' Aiden put his arms around Charley's waist and pulled her off Marcus. 'It won't help.'

'Listen, I'm sorry,' Marcus said softly, his eyes not on Charley but on Aiden.

'Sorry? You're sorry?' Charley paused. 'How can you simply say sorry for something like this?'

'Oh, that's not what I'm apologising for. This is.' Marcus got up from the chair, the shackles and ropes falling to the floor as he lifted his arm up towards Aiden. A reddish glow seemed to come from Marcus's hand, and Aiden went hurtling into the wall.

'Aiden!' Charley yelled.

Fergus gasped. 'How did you . . . ?'

'You didn't really think your stupid spell was going to hold me, did you? Listen, I don't want to hurt anyone. Well, that's not exactly true,' – he gestured towards Aiden – 'that was quite fun, but if you'll just listen I–'

'No more listening,' Charley spat, and Marcus also went flying back, smacking into the opposite wall. 'Time's up.' She stormed towards him, her fingers clamping around his throat and pulling him to his feet. 'Either you call off the nost or I'll kill you myself.'

'Chambers . . .'

'No, Aiden. We don't have time.' She looked into Marcus's eyes. 'What would Bud think of you? She'd be horrified. I have defended you time and time again. I tried to give you the benefit of the doubt. When everyone else was attacking you, I was trying to see the good. And you know the funny thing? At one point I did. I saw it, Marcus, that hint of humanity. As much as you might like to make out, you aren't all bad. You do care. You care about me . . . you care about Jess. I know you do. You never actually planned on meeting her but when you did, you felt affection for her, you wanted to protect her. You couldn't bear seeing Jess in pain, pain that you'd caused. That's why you healed her, isn't it? Was the guilt of what you'd done too much?'

Marcus choked, struggling against her grasp.

'God, you're strong,' he spluttered.

'Make it stop, Marcus, please. I can't lose Jess. You know what it's like to lose a sister, how can you possibly put someone else through that? I know you loved her, I know you miss her, but Bud wouldn't want this.

'It's your choice to make, I can't force you to do anything. But I'll tell you this: you've already lost Bud. If you do this, Marcus, you'll lose Jess, too. And you'll lose me.'

Marcus opened his eyes wide, no longer struggling. 'I never had you, Charley.'

'No, but you'll lose any chance of ever having me. I will never forgive you if you do this.'

Aiden felt his chest tighten at her words. He knew it was all pretence, that Charley wouldn't look Marcus's way in a million years. He knew that. He knew . . . So why was his stomach doing somersaults?

'That was a touching speech,' Marcus groaned, 'but you needn't have wasted your breath.'

Charley's heart sank, all the hope she'd had seeping away. She'd wanted so much to believe that Marcus could be saved, that he wasn't the evil monster everyone said he was. The monster she'd once said he was.

'I was already going to call off the nost.'

Charley blinked, her grip loosening slightly. 'Wh . . . you were?'

'That's what I was trying to tell you. You're right – I never planned on meeting Jess. I knew who she was but I never had any intention of getting to know her. She was just part of something bigger, a way to be with Bud again. But when I did meet her, it was horrendous. Seeing how much pain she was in, how much I was hurting her . . . like you said, I couldn't bear it. That's why I kept healing her.'

'And you could do that, not because you're a demon but because it was your nost,' Quinn said. Now everyone finally understood how Marcus had helped Jess without grave repercussions.

Aiden shook his head. 'Who says he's even telling the truth? It wouldn't be the first time he's lied.'

Charley looked at Marcus, her eyes finding his. She looked into them for a long time, a look he returned, his gaze never wavering.

'He's telling the truth,' she said eventually, letting go of Marcus completely.

Dru sneered. 'And you can tell that because . . . ?'

'I can just tell.'

'You sure it's not a little bit more than that?' Dru raised an eyebrow sceptically.

Charley turned on her. 'No, it's nothing more than that. I just know, all right?'

'Listen,' Marcus said rubbing his neck, relieved to finally be able to breathe again. 'I don't like you lot any more than you like me . . .'

'Apart from Charley,' Quinn grunted, but Marcus ignored her.

'I don't want to hurt Jess. As much as I want Bud back, I'm not willing to put Jess through any more suffering. I'm not prepared to let her die.'

'How honourable of you,' Dru scoffed. 'Prove it then. Call off the nost.'

Marcus pulled a face at her. 'I was just getting to that.' Slowly, he stretched his hand out in front of him and began reciting something that sounded like Latin.

'What's he saying?' Quinn whispered, but Dru only shrugged her shoulders.

'It's a renouncing spell. I recognise it from one of Mum's handbooks. He was . . .' Aiden struggled to get the next part out. 'He was telling the truth.'

Something happened though. Marcus suddenly doubled over, his face contorting as he writhed in pain.

'What's happening to him?' Charley shouted, crouching down by his side.

'Quick, get him on the couch,' Fergus said, trying to lift Marcus from the floor.

Before he could get him up, Marcus went still. He opened his eyes, looking surprisingly good for what he'd just endured; a little shaken maybe, but overall he seemed fine.

'What happened?' Charley asked frantically. 'Did it work?'

Marcus looked at her. 'Eh, I think we have a problem.'

THIRTY-NINE

Judith Gillespie pottered around her house, arranging everything so it was perfect. She'd been shopping that morning, buying all of Bud's favourite foods, the lime soda she always used to drink and a huge bunch of purple dahlias; Bud had always adored dahlias.

'It won't be long now, Boudicca,' she smiled, grabbing her makeup and strutting to the mirror to fix her lipstick.

The phone rang and Judith, pouting vainly in the mirror, went to answer it. 'Hello,' she said cheerfully, gripping the phone between her shoulder and chin as she zipped up the makeup bag.

'Hello, darling,' Garth greeted her. 'You sound happy.'

'Oh, I am, dear.'

'I'm glad to hear it.' He sounded quite jolly himself. 'Listen, I finished up early today, thought we could maybe go out and grab an early dinner if you fancy? I'm sure Marcus can entertain himself for an evening.'

Judith frowned. 'What time were you thinking?'

'Whenever you're ready. I'm on my way back just now . . . say, an hour or so?'

'You're on your way home?' she asked shrilly.

'Yes, shouldn't be too long. Say, six o'clock? I can phone and book the restaurant . . .'

'Yes, dear, you do that. I really need to go for now, I've, eh . . . got something in the oven. See you soon.'

'Okay, honey, see you–'

Judith hung up the phone, her head now reeling and her stomach doing cartwheels.

'No time like the present,' she muttered, smiling down at the bundle in front of her.

Suddenly, she felt a pulling sensation in her limbs and her chest began to quake, her body trembling for a moment before relaxing again. Judith shook her head, a feeling of disappointment in her gut.

'I knew you'd let me down, Marcus,' she said darkly, turning back to the unconscious figure lying on her couch.

'Well, daughter dearest, I guess it's time.'

Jess didn't move – she wasn't aware of a thing.

'What do you mean, you can't call off the nost?' Charley shrieked as Marcus stumbled to his feet. 'Marcus, you said you would–'

'For God's sake, Charley, will you let me speak? It's not that I don't want to call it off . . . I just can't do it.'

'What does that mean? You haven't changed your mind again, have you?'

'Told you we couldn't trust him,' Aiden said, folding his arms. 'Once a–'

'Don't even say it, golden boy,' Marcus snapped, 'or I'll put you through the window next time.'

'Oh, for heaven's sake, don't do that,' Dru moaned, 'Aunt Tabby will have a fit!'

Tabitha didn't say anything, her mouth turned down at the corners. Dru wasn't sure if she'd even heard.

Marcus looked back at Charley. 'Of course I haven't changed my mind. I can't remove the nost because it isn't there anymore.'

'You mean it's over?' Charley gasped. 'Jess is going to be okay?'

'Take it easy, gorgeous, this is far from over. When I say it isn't there, I mean I can't control it anymore. Something else has taken it over, someone.'

'Who?'

'There's only one woman powerful enough . . .'

'Your mother.'

Fergus began emptying the cabinet, piling a bunch of old books on to the table. 'We're going to need to move fast,' he said. He turned to Tabitha, who hadn't said a word since the kids had started their interrogation. 'Are you all right?'

She nodded. 'Yes, I'm fine.'

'Can you handle this?'

'Of course I can, Fergus. I'll be fine.'

'What's going on?' Aiden asked, a look of worry etched on his face. 'Mum?'

'Nothing, Aiden, it's all right.'

'For the love of God, will you stop with all the lies? I can't remember the last time you two actually trusted me enough to confide in me. Don't you think this is a pretty poor time to be keeping secrets?'

Tabitha looked at Fergus, who shrugged and said, 'He has a point.'

Tabby nodded. 'All right. Aiden, your father and I fought a demon once, long before you were born.'

'What happened?'

'Your mother nearly died,' Fergus said bluntly.

'Fergus, don't exaggerate.'

'I'm not exaggerating. That thing was nearly the end of you.'

'But it wasn't,' Tabby said with a small smile. 'Really, it's nothing.'

Aiden didn't say anything, but he couldn't draw his eyes away from his mother. She'd never looked less intimidating before in her life. For once, Tabitha Cunningham actually looked frightened.

'So what's the plan?' Dru interrupted, her timing impeccable as always.

'I . . . I don't know.' Charley looked towards Marcus. 'Do you have a plan?'

'If my mother's ready to do this, the old man's right,' – he motioned to Fergus, who scowled in annoyance at being referred to as old – 'we'll need to move quickly. She'll know I tried to do the renouncing spell.'

'How?'

'Because she's linked to the nost now, she's taken over its power. She'll know I betrayed her . . .' He was silent for a few seconds, before saying, 'We need to find Jess before my mum does. Charley, where is she?'

Charley couldn't think straight. 'She's . . . she's in the house. She didn't go to school today.'

'Right, let's go.'

Marcus darted out the door, Charley close behind him, followed by Quinn and then a disgruntled-looking Dru. Aiden hung back for a second.

'Are you coming?' he asked, looking to his parents.

'Yes,' Fergus said, 'we'll meet you there. I just want to talk to your mother for a second.'

Aiden looked at Tabby, seeing her in a new light. 'You gonna be okay?' he asked, and she nodded.

'Right as rain, darling.'

Aiden sighed, his face serious. He nodded, too, and then he was out the door.

It only took him a minute to catch up with the others. Charley grabbed his hand when she saw him, relieved to have him back by her side.

'Hey,' she said, squeezing his hand. 'Everything okay?'

'Everything's fine,' he replied. 'So what happens when we find Jess?' he asked Marcus. 'What do we do then?'

'Haven't thought that far ahead. We could kill my mother, I guess that would work.'

Charley's jaw dropped. 'You can't just kill your own mother.'

'Why not? She's about to try and kill your sister.'

'But . . .'

Marcus stopped for a second. 'It's probably going to be the only way to save Jess. My mother won't remove the nost, end of story. She wants Bud back and what my mum wants, she usually gets. She has to die, Charley, I don't think there's another way.'

'Quick question,' Dru intervened. 'How?'

'How do we kill her?'

'Indeed. She's practically invincible.'

'There's always a way,' Marcus said, heading once again for Charley's house. 'We just need to work out what it is.'

'Couldn't she just create an army of nosts to kill the lot of us?' Quinn asked, suddenly feeling queasy.

'Nosts don't exactly work that way. You need to have

a good reason to summon one, it's not something you can just idly do.'

'She has a good reason to kill us,' Dru said. 'We're trying to stop her from getting her daughter back. Surely that's enough?'

'You can't conjure up more than one at a time, it takes too much out of you. She could probably pick one of you at random, but to be honest I doubt it's even crossed her mind.'

Charley thought back to the night in the alley. 'You didn't have a good reason to summon one for me.'

'Sure I did,' Marcus shrugged. 'You were in the way.'

Charley went rigid.

'You're telling me the world's strongest demon can only make one nost at a time?' Aiden said doubtfully. 'I thought she was meant to be this all powerful being.'

Marcus just shrugged. 'I guess there are some rules that can't be broken.'

'What about Chambers?' Aiden asked. 'You said your mother doesn't like her. What if she sets a nost on her?'

'Something tells me a nost wouldn't work on Charley,' Marcus smirked, but Charley only gawked at him.

'What makes you say that?' Aiden frowned.

'Just a hunch. Anyway, it doesn't really matter. Nosts don't work straight away and if we do the job right, she'll be dead pretty soon. Bang, spells broken, nosts disappear.'

'And if we don't?' said Charley. 'Do the job right, I mean. What happens then?'

'Let's cross that bridge when we come to it.'

When they finally reached Charley's house, she burst through the door, the rest of them in close pursuit.

'Jess? Mum? Hello?'

'In there,' Marcus said, pointing into the living room.

'Mum? Oh my God, what's wrong with her?'

Linda was lying on the couch, her breathing heavy and her eyes closed. Charley ran to her side and shook her vigorously, but Linda didn't stir.

'It's a sleeping spell,' Marcus said darkly.

Charley got up. Her legs felt as though they might buckle beneath her. 'But that means . . .'

'Judith,' Aiden murmured.

'Where's Jess's room?' Marcus said, his mind going into overdrive.

'This way . . .' Charley stumbled up the stairs, lurching into Jess's bedroom. 'We're too late.'

'Mum must have taken her.'

Charley fell to the floor. She couldn't breathe. Her heart was pounding so hard it felt as though it might burst from her chest.

'I was too late,' she whispered, a tear running down her cheek.

'Not necessarily,' Marcus said. 'I could try an attachment spell, although I can't guarantee it'll work. I've never done one before.'

'What does that do?' Charley asked.

'I need something that belongs to Jess, something personal. It doesn't happen straight away, but if I can connect myself to the item, I should be able to tell where she is.'

'How long does it take?'

'Honestly, I don't know. It's worth a shot.'

'Why does it have to be you?' Aiden growled. 'Why not let Chambers do it? You said yourself she's powerful enough.'

'Charley can do it if she wants,' Marcus snapped. 'You can do it for all I care, but it might work faster if I do it. I'm not trying to take your sister away from you, Charley, but Jess and I share the same blood; it might be enough to make a difference.'

Aiden crouched down beside Charley, his hand on her back. 'Chambers, you don't have to–'

'Marcus is right,' she interrupted, 'Jess is his sister. Besides, if I try I'll probably start throwing up again.'

'What are you talking about?' Marcus frowned.

'Jess,' Quinn said, taking a step into the room, 'she makes Charley sick.'

'Any idea why that is?' Aiden grunted, looking accusingly at Marcus.

'She's reacting.'

'Reacting to what?'

Marcus wandered over to the dresser and opened one of the drawers, pulling out the diary. 'Jess's demon side is surfacing. Charley's body is subconsciously trying to reject it. Let me guess, sickness, fevers, your magic going haywire?'

'Pretty much.'

'I'm guessing that's why you were so sick the day we went for that walk.' Marcus grinned at Aiden, who only glared back in contempt. 'To be honest, I'm surprised it's stayed dormant this long. Your magic must have shielded Jess from it, prevented the demon inside her from materialising.'

'Until now,' Charley murmured. Even after hearing Jess and Marcus were related, the concept of Jess being a demon hadn't occurred to her.

Marcus nodded. 'Until now.'

He looked at Aiden, waiting for him to say something hostile. He didn't.

'Can I use this?' Marcus asked, holding the diary in the air. Charley nodded.

Marcus opened the diary and laid his hand flat, his fingers stretching across the pages.

'I call on thee, to aid me now, to help me see, to show me how . . .'

'Doesn't it have to be in Latin?' Charley asked, but Aiden shook his head.

'All incantations are different,' he replied, as Marcus continued to chant.

Once he had finished, he opened his eyes, the rest of them staring in anticipation.

'Well,' Aiden grilled, 'did it work?'

Marcus shook his head. 'I don't think so. I'm sorry Charley.'

All of a sudden though, the book began to glow, a dull reddish hue, the same colour that had come from Marcus when he threw Aiden against the wall.

Marcus inhaled sharply, a huge burst of energy exploding inside him. 'It did work . . .'

Charley gasped. 'You know where she is?'

'Not yet . . . I will.'

'But we have no idea how long that'll be,' Dru complained. 'We can't just sit around and do nothing, waiting for your psychotic mother to do away with the kid.'

'Dru's right,' Charley said, pulling off her school blazer. She rushed through to her own room, grabbed a jumper and hurried back, pulling it on over her head. 'We have to do something in the meantime. We need to

361

at least try.' She looked at each of them in turn. 'We need to split up. Marcus, you and Aiden go check your house, see if your mum took Jess there. I'll go with Quinn and Dru.'

'Why do I have to go with him?' Aiden demanded crossly.

'Because it's either you go, or I do.' Charley raised her eyebrows at him.

'I'm cool with that,' Marcus smiled.

Aiden glared at him. 'In your dreams.'

'Can you two please try and get along? Marcus, the second you know where Jess is, you call me, okay?'

'Of course.'

'I don't want to leave you,' Aiden said, putting his hands on Charley's shoulders.

'Aiden, I'll be perfectly safe. I'll be with Quinn and Dru, they're probably more powerful than you and Marcus put together.'

'Where will you go?' he asked. 'You have no idea where to look.'

'I don't know . . . we have to start somewhere.'

'Check the industrial estate,' Marcus said. 'She used to go there when she was casting a spell she didn't want my dad to know about. Or the forest . . . she likes forests.'

'That's right,' Dru murmured. 'That's where she asked me to meet her, one of the forests in Oakshore.'

'What's she on about?' Marcus pointed towards Dru.

'Your mother and I have history,' she replied, her voice cold.

'There's a forest on the edge of town, we could start there,' Charley suggested, and Marcus nodded.

'Let's do it then. We'll check the house and if we

don't find anything, we'll meet you in the woods. Here, take this,' Marcus said, throwing a tiny jar of powder in Charley's direction.

'What is it?'

'It's frostbite.'

'What?'

'It's a magical dust. If you find her, throw it at her. If you manage to hit her, she'll freeze. Not for long, but it might buy you some time.'

'Why do you have this?'

Marcus winked at her. 'Always come prepared.'

'Shouldn't you take it?' Charley asked, turning the bottle around in her hand.

'I'd rather you had it.'

Charley smiled at Marcus in understanding, then she put her arms around Aiden and kissed him passionately, his hand gently cupping the back of her neck.

'By the way,' she whispered softly, pressing her nose to his, 'I love you too.'

He smiled. 'Glad to hear it.'

Marcus rolled his eyes. 'I hate to break up this little love fest, but shouldn't we be going?'

'Be careful,' Aiden said sternly.

'I will.'

He kissed her again, then began striding towards the door. 'Come on,' he said stonily to Marcus.

'Who put you in charge?' Marcus huffed, following him out the room.

'That will be interesting,' Dru chortled from the door, watching the two boys fight their way down the stairs.

'Come on,' Charley said, 'let's go find Jess.'

FORTY

Marcus and Aiden walked along the street bickering, matching scowls on their faces.

'I still don't know why I had to get stuck with you,' Marcus grumbled, shoving his hands in his pockets.

'Believe me, the feeling's mutual.'

'Guess Charley couldn't trust herself to be alone with me,' Marcus smirked. 'You never know what might've happened.'

Aiden sighed and shook his head. 'Give me a break, Marcus. Charley's with me.'

Marcus looked despondently towards the ground. He didn't give Aiden the sarcastic remark he'd been expecting. In fact, Marcus said nothing at all. Aiden turned to look at him, his eyes wrinkling as he frowned. 'You care about her, don't you?'

Marcus laughed. 'Just figured that out have you?'

'Are you in love with her?'

They weren't far from Marcus's house, and Aiden didn't have long. He needed to know.

Marcus couldn't have lied even if he'd wanted to; his eyes said it all.

He nodded. 'Yes, I'm in love with her. Just unfortunate that you got there first,' he joked. 'Might have been in with a chance if she hadn't gone and fallen for a straight-laced loser with goofy hair and no sense of humour.'

Aiden choked back a laugh. 'Yes, because trying to murder her sister is the perfect way to woo a girl. Are you completely deranged? Even if I wasn't with her, she would never look twice at you.'

Marcus smiled. 'You keep telling yourself that. Tell yourself that the kiss meant nothing.'

'It didn't.'

'Why didn't she tell you then?' Marcus beamed smugly, but Aiden didn't say anything. 'Why'd she keep it from you if it meant that little?'

'I'm done talking to you about Chambers,' Aiden yelled, losing his temper. 'I don't know why she didn't tell me and yeah, as much as I hate to admit it, I can see that there's something between you. But I also know that we have something, something you could never dream of having with her. What do you think is gonna happen? You attack Charley, try to kill her sister and she'll what, run off into the sunset with you? Doesn't work like that.'

'I didn't attack her. Charley is perfectly capable of taking care of herself, I showed her that. I showed her how much endurance she has, how much potential. Despite what she might tell you, she enjoyed that night in the alley. She was in her element.'

Aiden let out a contemptuous laugh.

'I don't expect wedding bells, Aiden. Heck, I don't expect anything. But I'll spend the rest of my life making up for what I did to Jess. I can't take it back, but I'll try to make it right.'

'And if we do save Jess, how do you think she'll feel when she finds out her brother tried to murder her? Maybe she won't be quite so forgiving.'

Marcus looked to the ground, his expression woeful. 'Charley hasn't forgiven me, nor should she. I did something inexcusable.'

'I couldn't agree more. She will though, because that's who she is. For some reason she thinks you're worth saving.'

Marcus felt a twinge in his chest, of what, he wasn't sure. Hope?

For some reason she thinks you're worth saving.

For the first time in years, Marcus felt like more than just a demon.

'No time like the present,' he said to Aiden when they reached his house.

The boys hurried inside. It was quiet, apart from the ticking of the old grandfather clock and Peewee barking, scampering around Marcus's feet.

'Scram, Peewee,' he said, shooing the dog away. She ran outside and scurried off down the street, but Marcus didn't go after her. They had more important things to take care of.

Despite the circumstances, Aiden smirked. 'Peewee?' he said, raising his eyebrows.

'Oh, shut up,' Marcus groaned. 'I didn't name her.'

They walked on quietly, Aiden staying a couple of steps behind Marcus.

'Mum?' Marcus called, pushing open the kitchen door.

'That's right,' Aiden said mockingly, 'just shout out her name, let her know we're here.'

Marcus punched him in the gut and Aiden doubled

over, gasping as he clutched his stomach. 'What'd you do that for?'

'Think I'm due a couple of hits. You nearly broke my nose that day in chemistry class; would've spoiled my handsome good looks.'

'Yeah, you're a sight for sore eyes.'

Marcus pulled a face and they walked into the kitchen to see Garth sitting at the table, sorting through files from his briefcase.

'Dad?'

'Hello, Marcus, where have you been?'

'Where's Mum?' he asked when he realised his father was alone.

'Not sure, son, why?'

'We need to find her. She's . . . she's got something we need.'

Garth ran a hand through his thick hair. 'Oh, I see. Sorry, Marcus, I'm not sure where she went.'

Suddenly a bright light flashed before Marcus's eyes, a girl and a woman appearing in front of him. They were surrounded by trees, the girl lying motionless on the ground.

Jess.

The woman – Judith – was smiling to herself, a tattered brown teddy with a spotty bow tie gripped in her hand.

Marcus quickly turned to Aiden.

'The spell . . .' he began, '. . . it worked. I was right, she took her to the forest.'

'What are we waiting for then? Let's go.'

'I'm afraid I can't let you boys do that,' Garth said, pushing himself off the stool.

'Dad, we don't have time for this,' Marcus replied, but

suddenly he was hoisted towards the ceiling as his father raised an arm into the air.

Garth smiled wickedly. 'This won't take long.'

The wind picked up as the girls walked towards the forest, each one feeling more apprehensive the closer they got. Charley was chewing anxiously on her thumb nail, the thought of coming face to face with Judith only just beginning to sink in.

'What if she's not there?' Charley asked, nodding in the direction of the woods.

'What if she is?' Quinn worried, her hands trembling. She'd had dealings with demons before, but none as powerful as Judith Gillespie.

Dru's face was blank and neither of them could tell what she was thinking.

'Dru . . .'

'Hmm?'

'What's our plan? We're not just marching in completely unprepared are we? Because–'

'Quinn, we don't even know if she's there yet. Right now, the plan's to find out exactly where they are, then we think strategies. If all else fails, we hit her with that dusty stuff. That should give us a little time at least.'

Charley frowned as she checked her pocket, finding it empty apart from her phone.

'Eh, guys, I can't find the frostbite.'

'I thought you put it in your pocket,' Dru moaned.

'I did. It's not there though. It must have dropped out. You two go on, I can run back and get it.'

'We don't have time. We'll just have to leave it.'

Quinn shook her head. 'Marcus gave us that for a

reason. Don't you think it might be important?'

'We don't have enough time, Quinn. Besides, Aiden would kill us if we let Charley go back by herself.'

'I'll go. I won't be long. You two keep going and I'll be back before you know it.'

'Quinn, you know we shouldn't split up.'

'I'll be back before you even get to the woods, I promise. I just think we should take all the help we can get right now.'

Dru sighed. 'Fine, but don't spend ages looking for it. If you can't find it, you get your arse back here pronto, understand?'

'Yes, Dru, I understand.' Quinn rolled her eyes. She gave Charley's hand a quick squeeze and said, 'Sisters, who'd have 'em?' before dashing back down the street.

'So we just keep going?' Charley asked, her stomach even more unsettled now that it was just the two of them.

'We keep going,' Dru agreed.

They carried on in silence. Every now and then, Charley would glance at her phone to see if Marcus or Aiden had called. She wondered if they'd found Judith, or if Marcus had worked out where she was yet. She also hoped that they'd managed not to kill each other in the process.

'Stay behind me when we get there,' Dru instructed. 'If we see her then I want . . .'

She stopped though as Charley suddenly fell to the ground, her head hitting the pavement and her phone shattering as it landed on the tarmac.

'Charley? Charley!'

Dru swore in frustration. Things were slowly deteriorating as the day went on. 'Well this is just spectacular.' She cradled Charley's head in her hands, frowning as she looked down at her. 'A sleeping spell?' she muttered, thinking back to Linda lying frozen on the couch. Charley looked the same.

'If she's cast a sleeping spell, that means she can't be far . . .' Dru looked towards the forest, now only a minute or two away. 'Guess it's just you and me then, Judy.'

Dru somehow managed to carry Charley into one of the nearby gardens and laid her down under a hedge. She looked rather uncomfortable but at least she was safe – well, as safe as one could be with raging demons on the loose.

'Hang in there, Charley. I'll go get your sister for you.'

And then Dru was gone, running towards the mass of trees in front of her. Alone.

Charley opened her eyes, everything around her a blur. Her skin was itchy, piping hot and tingling as though she'd been sitting in the sun for too long.

It's November, she thought to herself, desperately scratching at her arms. Something's not right.

She got up from the ground and began walking, with absolutely no idea where she was or how she'd got there. She didn't recognise the place at all.

'Lost, are you, dear?' Charley spun around to see Judith standing behind her.

'What did you . . . how did . . . where am I?' Charley stuttered, her head whirling. She didn't understand what was happening.

'You're sleeping. Don't worry, this is just a dream. By the time you wake up, it'll all be over. I'll have my Bud back. Your sister will be alive again.'

'Jess is my sister,' Charley hissed.

'Yes, well I am sorry about that, but I'm afraid it can't be helped. If I could have found another way, I wouldn't have involved Jessica. She's essential though. I can let you see her just now if you'd like? You can say goodbye.'

'How can you . . .? No, I will not say goodbye to her. She isn't going anywhere.'

'Oh, Charley, don't be stubborn. This might be the last chance you get.'

'Where is she? How can you bring her here?'

Judith put her hand on Charley's forehead. 'Why, sweetheart, all I have to do is simply manipulate your mind, make you see things that aren't really here. Show you things you want to see but can't.'

'It won't work . . . leave me alone, it's not going to work.'

'Of course it will work, Charley, I've done it before. Don't you remember that lovely visit you had from the white-haired girl? Quinn, isn't it?'

Charley's eyes widened. 'That was you? But why . . . ?'

'Just a little bit of fun. Oh, it was marvellous, hearing your screams echo through the air as your handsome young man put you back together again. And how did you repay him? Why, you nearly killed him with a spur, didn't you? How he survived that, I'll never know.'

'You were watching me . . . messing with me the whole time – that's how Marcus knew. You pushed Abbie from the roof as well, didn't you?'

Judith smirked and put her hands in the air. 'Guilty.'

'Why? What did Abbie ever do? Was it meant to be me?'

'Oh no, dear, it was always your friend I intended to push. Again, just something to amuse myself with, and to keep you out of the way. You really do like to stick your nose in where it doesn't belong, don't you?'

'You're a monster,' Charley spat.

'Yes, I've heard that a few times. I remember that was one of your gran's favourite phrases. Dear old Dorcas. Such a shame she had to go and die like that.' Judith smiled cruelly at Charley. 'Like I said, busybodies, always getting in the way. If you're not careful, you might end up like little old granny.'

'It was you . . . you summoned the nost that killed my gran.'

'And what fun it was! Did you enjoy watching her die? Writhing in pain, lungs filling up, choking, drowning in her own blood. That's pretty much how it was, isn't it? You see, I wasn't invited to the live performance. I saw the preview when I went to her house, but somehow, it wasn't quite the same.'

'Her house? When were you at her house?' Charley froze. 'The day I found her . . . you're the reason she looked so scared. She told me she'd just blacked out . . .'

'She also told you that you were telekinetic, that her mother was telekinetic. And that she had no powers. Don't you think it would have been better if she'd just told you the truth to start with?'

'I don't understand . . .' Charley shook her head. 'How did you know my gran?'

'I didn't, not personally. My mother knew her.'

Charley wanted to scream. 'Why am I just finding out that everyone's mother was friends with my gran?'

'Oh, your gran and my mother weren't friends. More

like sworn enemies. Your gran was always trying to foil her plans, put an end to her evil deeds, shall we say. Your gran murdered my mother when I was three years old, right in front of my eyes. When my father told me, when I was old enough to understand, I vowed that I would find the woman who took away my mother and put a stop to her, once and for all.'

'If my gran really did kill your mum, she wouldn't have done it without a perfectly good reason.'

'She had reasons, darling, plenty of them. That still doesn't change the fact that she left me without a mother.'

'Well you're about to leave my mother without a daughter,' Charley countered.

'Indeed.' Judith looked at Charley pensively, then her lips began to curl into a wide, toothy smile. 'Like I said, these things can't be helped. Do say hello to my son for me when you wake up, won't you? I doubt he'll speak to me again after this. Shame, I really thought I could count on that boy.'

'Marcus hates you,' Charley growled. 'You used him. You're the reason he did all those things. He thinks he's nothing because of you.'

'For someone in a healthy, happy relationship, you seem awfully concerned about my son. Aren't you angry? He did try to kill your sister, after all. Well, his sister.'

'What Marcus planned to do was appalling, but it was you who made him do it. You put ideas in his head, told him he could get Bud back. He didn't deserve to be manipulated like that.'

'No, I guess not.' Judith checked her watch. 'Well, would you look at the time? I better be going – places to be, people to kill, you know how it goes. Goodbye, Charley, I really do hope things work out for you in the future.'

Before she could reply, Judith was gone, her exit sending Charley flying backwards, depositing her hopelessly in a heap on the ground.

'No!' Charley cried once she realised she was alone. 'I need to wake up, I have to wake up!'

She began pinching herself, slapping her face until her cheeks were red and stinging. It wasn't working though. She was stuck in her dream with no way out. No escape, and no way to get to Jess.

She let her head fall as she finally realised she'd lost. She didn't know if Dru had kept going or if Quinn had returned. She wasn't even sure what had happened – the last thing she remembered was walking along the street with Dru.

Were Aiden and Marcus okay? Had they discovered where Judith was yet, where she'd taken Jess?

She felt so helpless. Jess needed her, now more than ever, and she was taking a bloody nap.

'I'm so stupid!' Charley yelled, punching the ground in anger. It didn't hurt. She didn't feel a thing.

'I wouldn't say that, darling.'

At first Charley thought she was hearing things. She shook her head, trying to make the voice disappear.

'What are you doing, Charley? Why are you still here?'

This time she knew she'd heard it, and not just in her head. She looked up.

'Gran?'

'Hello, Charlotte, dear.'

'Is . . . is it really you?'

'It's me, honey.'

'Oh, Gran.' Charley ran to her gran and hugged her, squeezing as tightly as she possibly could. She could feel everything this time. She could feel her gran's hand on the back of her neck; the fuzzy material of her itchy, grey sweater; her breath, warm on her cheek. 'What are you doing here? Is this Judith, making me see you? You're just an illusion, aren't you?'

'I am just an illusion, Charley, yes. But Judith didn't send me. I'm here because you need my help.'

'Can you get me out of here? Out of the dream?'

'You can do that yourself, Charley. That's not what I meant. I'm here to give you something.'

'What?'

'When you wake up, you're going to go straight to the woods. That's where Judith is, that's where she has Jess. You can beat her, Charley, I know you don't think you can but it is possible. You just have to believe in yourself.'

'Gran, I can't. I'm not strong enough to take on someone so powerful. I couldn't even beat Marcus and his powers are nothing compared to hers.'

'That's why I'm here. You know what I was. You know I used to be just like you. Well, when I died, when Judith . . .' Dorcas didn't say the rest. 'My magic was restored, my powers returned to me. I'm here to give them to you.'

'What? You got them back? You're . . . you're giving me your powers?'

Dorcas gave her a warm smile. 'I don't need them now, not where I am. You take them, sweetheart, and you use them. Understand? You're the only one who can end this.'

'Why did you never tell me? About being a magician . . .'

'I never thought I needed to. I was always going to be there to help you understand what you were, but I didn't feel that burrowing into my past would do any good.'

'Why'd you tell me I was telekinetic? The first time I asked, the first time I told you about my powers . . . you could have just told me straight up. Why did you lie to me?'

'I didn't want to frighten you. Not everybody accepts things the way you did. Some people try to hide from it, fight who they are. You, on the other hand, you grabbed on to it with both hands, you recognised what you were, who you were, and you embraced it. I am so proud of you, my darling.'

Dorcas put her hands on Charley's cheeks and kissed her forehead. 'Give me your hand.'

Charley did as her gran asked, stretching her arm out in front of her. Dorcas gently grasped it.

'What's happening?' Charley asked, as a strange yellow light began to travel down Dorcas's arm, into her hand and then finally to Charley.

When the light faded, Dorcas smiled and said, 'You're strong enough now, Charley. It's time to go.'

Aiden panicked as he looked at Garth, still holding Marcus in place on the ceiling. His eyes were like hollow pits, empty and dark, gaping at his son struggling before him.

Aiden raised his hand, dazing Garth who was blasted backwards, landing painfully on the table. Marcus fell to the floor, also landing with a thump.

'Cheers for being so gentle,' he griped.

'My pleasure,' Aiden smirked, but even so, he offered Marcus a hand, helping him to his feet. 'What do we do?'

'We don't have much choice. We fight him.'

'I thought you said your dad was a decent guy?'

'He is. Well, he was.' Garth was up again, sneering as he stood in front of them. 'What's going on, Dad?'

'I'm just making sure you don't do anything stupid, Marcus. Let your mother finish her work, then we can discuss this.'

'Her work? Do you realise what it is she's trying to do? She's going to kill Jess. Her daughter. Your daughter. If we don't go now, it'll be too late.'

'I know exactly what she's doing. She thinks I'm so blind that I can't see through her, work out what she's scheming. I've known for weeks, Marcus, I was just biding my time, waiting for the opportune moment. I knew she would need my help.' Garth's eyes widened. 'Your mum's not the only one who has very little faith in you, son. I knew you'd bottle it.'

'You knew what she was planning? You knew she was going to try and kill Jess and you just let it happen?'

'You're one to talk. You are the one who summoned the nost after all.'

Marcus tried to hide the guilt he was feeling, but it was written plainly on his face.

He didn't answer, so Garth continued. 'I want Bud back as much as your mother does. You have to make a few sacrifices for the things you desire.'

'Jess isn't your sacrifice to make.'

'Even so, I'm afraid I can't let you leave. Not until it's done.'

'Let's make a run for it,' Aiden whispered, deciding that it was a better idea than sticking around to let Garth obliterate them.

'Don't be a pansy, Aiden. He'll only . . .'

'Duck,' Aiden murmured.

'What? Have you . . .?'

'Get down!' Aiden threw himself towards Marcus, the pair of them plunging to the ground, just as Garth threw a ball of fire towards where they'd been standing.

'Oh, Aiden, darling, buy me a drink first, eh?' Marcus jeered, jammed between Aiden and the floor. 'I don't normally kiss on the first date, never mind–'

'No, you don't normally make it to the date part,' Aiden snapped, clambering to his feet. 'You just go after other guys' girls when they're alone and vulnerable.'

'Charley's far from vulnerable,' Marcus retorted, throwing a fireball back towards his father. 'She's as hard as nails and you know it.'

Aiden glared at him and before he could stop it, a vase was flying across the room, clouting Marcus in the face.

'What was that for, you half-wit?' Marcus groaned, stumbling as he tried to stand up.

'Sorry, it was an accident.'

'My arse it was,' Marcus snorted, as another fireball narrowly missed him.

'That's the way we're gonna play it then, Dad?'

'I guess so,' Garth smirked, readying his hand for another blazing bomb.

'Oh well, you know what they say. Fight fire with fire.'

Marcus stood stock still, his hands suddenly bursting into flames. Aiden gaped at him, the fire slowly making its way up Marcus's arms, orange wisps crawling along his sleeves. He smiled at his father before flinging his arms forward, setting the whole kitchen alight. Garth howled at the insufferable heat, his face contorting as the flames swallowed him.

'Now we can go,' Marcus said, pushing Aiden towards the door.

They ran outside, stopping to check that Garth wasn't behind them. He wasn't.

'I can do that, too, you know,' Aiden huffed.

'Do what?'

'Set things on fire.' Aiden held out his hand and a small flame appeared in his palm, flickering like a tiny candle.

Marcus threw his head back and laughed. 'You call that fire?' he said, blowing on the tiny flame which immediately trebled in size. 'I'm a demon, Aiden, we're practically made of fire. That's one fight you're not gonna win.'

Aiden shrugged his shoulders in defeat and said, 'Shall we go?'

Marcus was silent for a moment, his dark eyes seeming a million miles away, and Aiden noticed him glance back inside – back towards Garth. 'Well, I don't have a huge desire to stay and watch my house burn to the ground. Let's get out of here.'

Dru made her way through the forest, keeping a close eye out for any signs of Judith. So far, all was quiet, but that didn't mean anything. Judith was in the woods somewhere, Dru was sure of it. She just had to find her . . .

She stopped, spotting something silver and sparkly,

379

glistening between the leaves. She bent down to pick it up: a bracelet, small and stretchy with a heart dangling from its strings.

'This could easily belong to a fourteen-year-old,' she murmured, turning the bracelet over. There was a J engraved on the other side of the heart. 'Okay, that makes it simple.' She pocketed the bracelet and kept on walking, this time treading more carefully.

It would soon be dark, and she really didn't feel like trekking through the forest in the pitch black with no backup and no weapons. Well, no weapons bar her magic.

She heard a noise from up ahead, high pitched and irritating; someone was laughing.

'Thanks for the tip-off, Judy,' she smiled, climbing a large, marshy slope, ducking down behind a log when she reached the top.

Somehow – even she wasn't quite sure how – she managed to shuffle across to a large tree without drawing any attention to herself. Peeking out from behind it, she spied Judith, towering above her on a large, rocky mound. She could see Jess by Judith's side, lying flat on the ground, unconscious. Her face was stark white and all she had on was a sleeveless T-shirt and a pair of pyjama bottoms – not exactly the best apparel for November.

Poor kid must be freezing, Dru thought, but then wondered if demons ever felt the cold. Dru herself could hardly remember what it was like. She may not have been a demon, but she certainly had the body temperature of one.

She was just about to try and discreetly make her way over to Jess when a hand clamped over her mouth. Her first instinct was to scream, to lash out and strike her attacker, but their grip was strong, holding her firmly in place.

'Shh, it's me,' Fergus breathed, loosening his grasp.

'Uncle Fergus . . .'

'Dru, what the hell do you think you're doing?'

'What does it look like I'm doing? I'm trying to rescue the kid.'

'By yourself?' Fergus whispered harshly. 'Where's everyone else?'

'Aiden went with Marcus to check his house for Judith.'

'And Charley, Quinn, where are they?'

'Judith put Charley under a sleeping spell. I moved her somewhere safe, don't worry.'

'And your sister?'

'She ran back to get the frostbite . . . Charley dropped it and–'

'Where did you get frostbite?' Fergus asked.

'Marcus had it, he gave it to Charley.'

Fergus, keeping low to the ground, glanced around the tree at Judith. 'Frostbite isn't going to do much, if anything, to be honest,' he said. 'Even if we manage to hit her with it, she'll only be frozen for seconds.'

'Well we could–'

'Druanna, I can't believe how stupid you were,' he cut her off. 'Why on earth would you even contemplate coming up here alone?'

'Because there was no one else. What am I meant to tell Charley when she wakes up? Sorry, Charley, everyone else was busy so I just let Jess die. I didn't have a choice.'

'Of course you did. You do realise it's not just your

life you're currently endangering, but Quinn's as well? If anything happens to you–'

'Don't you think I know this? I'm well aware of what could happen. But it won't.'

'How can you be so sure?'

Dru looked at him, her eyes clouding over. 'Because it's Quinn. I would never let anything happen to her.'

'By God, Druanna, I hope you're right.'

They were both silent for a moment, and then Dru said, 'Where's Aunt Tabby? Is she here?'

'She's on her way. We'll wait for her here and then . . .'

There was a clap of thunder above them and the sky lit up, bolts of lightning soaring through the air.

'Uncle Fergus, we don't have time. She's ready. If we wait–'

'Dru, we have no chance against her. Not with just two of us. Our best bet is to wait and–'

'If it was Aiden, would you wait? Quinn or me?' Fergus just looked at her, his mouth hanging open. 'We do this now. It's our only chance of saving her.'

Fergus sighed, his heart battling his head. He knew that without assistance, they had very little chance of winning. He also knew Dru was right; if they waited any longer, Jess was going to die.

'What did you have in mind?' he asked reluctantly.

Dru smiled. 'You go that way, sneak round the trees and get to Jess. I'll distract Judith.'

Fergus was already shaking his head. 'No way in hell.'

'But, Unc–'

'No, Dru, I can't let you do that. You get Jess and I'll keep Judith busy.'

She let her head fall to one side. 'You know as well

as I do that that's a terrible idea. I'm stronger than you, Uncle Fergus, I can hold her off for longer.'

'You're stronger when you're with Quinn. By yourself, you're just as exposed as I am.'

Dru was secretly offended at what he'd said; even without Quinn, she was stronger than Fergus. She'd managed to knock Marcus unconscious, after all.

'I can hone into Quinn, draw out her powers. I won't be as strong as I would be if she was here, but it should be enough.'

'Dru . . .'

'Uncle Fergus, we have to try.'

Fergus looked at his niece. Dru had always been gutsy but right now, she looked about ten years old. All he wanted to do was protect her.

Eventually he nodded, putting his hand on Dru's cheek. 'You think you're in trouble, you yell, all right?'

'All right,' she agreed.

'Don't do anything rash, just try and draw her attention away from Jess, talk her down if you can. I'll try and be quick, but I don't know how easy this is going to be.'

'Okay, okay.' Fergus kissed her forehead gently.

'You be careful,' he said, and she was sure he was about to cry.

'I will be. Come on, you don't really think some moonstruck demon's going to be the end of me, do you?' Dru gave him a doubtful look. 'Let her try.'

He kissed her head again, smiling as he looked at her.

'Don't say goodbye,' she whispered, a tear running down her cheek.

Fergus nodded, wiping the tear away with his thumb. 'See you soon.'

Then he was gone, darting between the trees, on his way to Jess. Dru stood up and stepped out from behind the tree. 'It's show time.' She smiled, her eyes darkening as she looked up at Judith. 'Hey, Judy, darling, long time no see.'

Judith stopped what she was doing and focused on Dru, a smile appearing on her face. 'Well, well, would you look who it is? The feisty little redhead with a desire to die. Still not managed to top yourself yet?'

Dru laughed. She could feel her blood getting hotter. 'Nope, still here I'm afraid. Which is a–' Dru was interrupted by a bright light flying towards her, just missing her as she leapt out the way.

'I don't have time for games, Druanna. I have something important to take care of.'

'So I see. The thing is, Judith, I can't let that happen.' Dru pulled back her hand and then launched it forward, a spur tearing through the air towards Judith.

Judith laughed as it stopped just inches from her chest, the same way it had done when Charley had thrown one at Marcus.

'A spur, Dru? You really thought that was going to work?'

Dru's legs gave way, pain exploding inside them, and before she knew it, she was on the ground, blood oozing from inside her mouth.

'Oh, dear, Druanna, you do look pathetic, don't you? Maybe I should just kill you, put you out of your misery. Let you leave your sad, little life behind.'

Dru dug her fingers into the ground, trying as best as she could to drag herself to safety. Judith, about to hit Dru with another deadly blast, was momentarily distracted.

She could have sworn she heard a noise behind her: a twig breaking, leaves rustling. Judith was sure that they weren't alone.

Fascinated with the foolish being who was trying to outsmart her, Judith let her guard down, briefly forgetting about the hex which was keeping Dru subdued.

Gasping for breath, Dru rose to her feet and flung everything she had towards Judith. Judith flew backwards, the eruption of Dru's powers paralysing her, although only for a second.

'Why, Dru, dear, I think you singed my hair,' she said, her face serious. Slowly though, her hard expression diminished, and she began to laugh hysterically. 'Insolent girl!' she bawled, catapulting Dru through the air. She landed, back-first against a tree, grimacing as pain shot up her spine. Judith struck her again, and this time Dru didn't get back up. Her airwaves felt as though they were closing, her throat tight. Her eyes rolled back into her head, the lids struggling to stay open.

Can't . . . give up . . . Quinn . . .

Judith smirked, her hands ready in front of her to finish Dru off. 'I would say it's been nice catching up,' she sneered, 'but we both know that's not true. This though, this I'll enjoy.'

Dru took one last look at Judith before seeing a bright flash heading her way.

FORTY-ONE

Judith let out a long, loud cackle as the beam of light hit Dru, slowly draining her energy. Dru could no longer feel her hands, the numbness spreading up her arms to her shoulders and neck. She couldn't move, she could barely even think as Judith consumed her essence, rendering her powerless.

'Dru!' Fergus cried from halfway up the mound as he watched his niece begin to let go. Before he could help her, he was hit by a blast of Judith's power, landing painfully on the ground.

'Goodbye, little red,' Judith smirked, as she prepared to wipe Dru out. 'Sleep tigh–'

Suddenly, the light retracted, no longer touching Dru but held back by an invisible barrier that reflected the light back at Judith.

'What the . . .?' Judith stuttered as a sharp pain struck her, an icy-cold sensation worming its way through her body. She shrieked in agony as she began to spasm, a long strip of blue light boring into her chest.

Dru stared ahead in amazement, the discomfort she'd

felt quickly subsiding now that Judith was otherwise engaged. She turned her head, anxious to see where the stream of blue was coming from, and her jaw dropped in astonishment.

Quinn was standing a few feet away, her long hair blowing in the wind as magic poured from her fingers. Her eyes shone brightly as she let the power flow.

'Quinn . . .'

'Hey, Dru. Sorry I'm late.'

'Your timing couldn't be better.'

'You okay?'

'I'll live.'

Quinn smiled. 'So, how about it?' she said excitedly. 'Think we can take on a demon?'

Dru smirked. 'Let's find out, shall we?'

Dru got up, her arm extended in front of her. Just like Quinn, a bright light began to spill from her fingers, only hers was orange, the luminescent mist tearing towards Judith like a bullet from a gun.

Judith convulsed, her limbs twitching, teeth gritted as she tried to fight against the girls' power. They were stronger than she had envisaged.

'Al . . . all right, Dru . . . Druanna,' she stuttered, electric shocks exploding inside her ears. 'You . . . you came to me f . . . for a separation sp . . . spell, well here you . . . go. Ha . . . have it.'

Judith closed her eyes, clenched her fists, and all of a sudden the lights were gone, the girls collapsing to the ground.

Judith shook herself, a burning sensation searing within her, and smiled as she looked upon the helpless bodies below.

'Aren't you going to say thank you, Druanna? You got what you've always wanted. You're free to live or die as you wish.' Judith grinned. 'Well, that's not entirely true, seeing as I'm going to kill you both in a moment, but it felt like a nice thing to say.'

Dru lifted her head, her eyes frantically searching for Quinn. She wasn't far from her, although too far to reach. 'Quinn!' she yelled, trying to see if her sister was all right.

Dru spotted Fergus lying on the ground beneath Judith and Jess. He wasn't moving, his eyes closed, and she couldn't tell if he was alive or dead. 'Uncle Fergus!' she screamed.

'Dru . . .' Quinn mumbled as she too lifted her head, her hair entwined with twigs and leaves.

'Quinn, grab my hand,' Dru said, reaching out as far as she could. Quinn shuffled forward, grasping Dru's hand in her own. Their faces both fell.

'It's gone, Dru. I can't feel you anymore. I don't feel anything.'

Dru hung her head to hide the tears that spilled on to the ground. Eventually, she looked up. 'We aren't linked anymore. We're no more powerful than your average magician. And we certainly don't stand a chance against her,' she spat, glancing at Judith, her expression sour. 'What are you waiting for?' she yelled, gripping Quinn's hand in hers.

Judith laughed. 'I was just enjoying this tender, heartfelt moment. At least you get to die together.' With that, Judith shot a bolt of lightning towards the girls, a bolt fierce enough to kill a thousand magicians, never mind just two.

Dru looked at Quinn, her heart breaking. 'I'm sorry,' she whispered, before calling out, 'Retroago,' sending Quinn sliding along the ground until she was out of the lightning's path.

'No!' Quinn cried as the bolt struck Dru, the life leaving her face as it pierced her chest, before disappearing into thin air.

'Dru!' Quinn scrambled to her sister's side, desperately hoping to revive her. Her heart sank, a pain worse than she'd ever felt before coursing through it. Dru was cold.

'No, no, no . . . Dru, wake up.' Quinn's tears began to flow like rain falling from the sky as she wept over her sister's body. 'Don't leave me.'

'How touching,' Judith laughed, contemplating whether to kill Quinn as well, or to leave her alive to suffer the grief of losing her sister. 'Your turn,' she said, quickly making her decision. She was having too much fun to stop now.

'Quinn, get back!' Aiden yelled, as he and Marcus came rushing through the trees. At the same time, Tabitha came running out from behind Judith, her jaw dropping when she saw her son.

'Aiden, get out of here!' she cried.

'Can't do that, Mum. Got a girl to save and a demon to kill.'

Judith sniggered as Aiden took his turn at trying to defeat her, a wave of light coming from him the same way it had done with his cousins. The yellow beam hurled through the air, fading away as soon as it reached Judith.

Marcus cupped his hands, a ball of fire forming inside them. He hurled it at Judith, scowling as she blew it to smithereens above them, tiny embers floating back down to the ground.

'Fire, Marcus, really? That's the oldest trick in the book.'

Marcus shrugged. 'Worked with Dad.'

'What do you mean?' Judith glared at him.

'Turns out he was on your side all along. You could have made this a lot easier on yourself if you'd been brave enough to tell him your plan.'

'Where is he?' she demanded. 'Your father, Marcus. What have you done?'

Marcus took a step forward whilst Tabby and Aiden ran to Quinn, trying desperately to get her to safety. She wouldn't leave Dru's side though, so Aiden stood in front of her, acting as a shield.

Marcus grinned up at his mother. He'd always known she was selfish, bitter about what had happened to Bud. But he'd never been aware of just how evil she really was, or of the wickedness living inside her. She was rotten to the core and he could see that now.

'Dad's gone,' he declared. 'Went up in flames with the house. A fitting death, don't you think?'

Judith's face was cold, her mouth forming a firm line. She didn't say anything for a moment, tilting her chin towards her chest.

'Well, it should suit you down to the ground then, shouldn't it, Marcus? It's up to you. Do you want to die like the redhead did, a pitiful, meaningless death, or would you rather burn like you're supposed to?'

'You're doing all this to get your child back, yet you'd kill the other one to make it happen? You would sacrifice everything just to be with Bud again?'

'Yes, I would. I've never loved anyone the way I loved Boudicca. Not you, not your father. You turned against me, Marcus. For that, I can never forgive you.'

'I'm not asking for forgiveness,' he snarled, momentarily stunning her with his magic. She laughed at his effort.

'You're a poor excuse for a demon, son.'

Quinn's head shot up, for a split second thinking about something other than Dru. 'The dust,' she murmured. 'Marcus, the dust!'

'Quinn, don't!'

It was too late. Quinn pulled the frostbite from her pocket, brandishing it in the air for all to see.

Judith laughed and clicked her fingers, the bottle smashing in Quinn's hand. The powder floated down, landing on Quinn and freezing her solid.

'Foolish girl,' Judith said cruelly. Marcus gasped, and Judith's eyes travelled back to him. 'You're wasting your time, all of you. I will get what I want because I can, it's as simple as that. I will kill whoever gets in my way and leave you lot to clean up the mess. No matter how hard you try, Marcus, you can't defeat me.'

'No, but I can,' said a disembodied voice.

Suddenly a vibrant purple light shot through the trees, a whitish glow surrounding the beam as it weaved its way towards them, followed by its creator: Charley.

'Let my sister go,' she commanded, her magic holding Judith in place.

'She isn't your sister,' Judith growled, sinking to her knees.

'She's every bit my sister. Give her back.'

Charley could feel the power coursing through her,

but somehow it didn't feel like it was enough; apart from appearing to be in mild pain, Judith didn't seem all that fazed. She was still able to talk, smile, throw her head back and roar with laughter. She was able to look at each of them in turn, smirk at them, sneer at them. She was able to get back to her feet, shake her head at the lot of them and create an enormous explosion, sending Tabitha through the air, Charley into a tree, and Aiden and Marcus into the chasm she'd just created.

Quinn suddenly unfroze, her head spinning as she tried to work out what was happening.

'Quinn, watch out!' Charley yelled, but Judith reacted before she could move, Quinn's body falling limp on top of Dru's.

Charley's eyes widened as she looked upon the scene in front of her: Marcus, Aiden, a very wide, very deep gaping hole, stretching by the looks of it to the ends of the earth.

She'd seen all this before.

'Time to choose, Charley,' Judith called menacingly. 'Which one of them are you going to save? You don't have time for both.'

Charley thought back to her vision, the whole thing making sense now. That's what it had meant; in some screwed up sense, it had told her what to do, who to pick when the time came.

She got up from the ground and ran to one of the figures, clinging on desperately as his fingers began to lose their grip.

Marcus stared up at her in confusion.

'As much as I appreciate the gesture, Charley, I don't think it's me you should be saving.' He struggled, craning his neck to see Aiden at the other side of the gorge, also moments away from falling. 'Go,' Marcus said. 'Help him.'

'I'm helping you both,' she whispered, crouching down beside him.

'You what?'

'I'm going to save you both.'

'Charley, you can't . . .'

'Yes I can. Come on, Marcus, it's you who always talks about how powerful I am,' she whispered, 'and as much as he'd hate me saying this, I know you're stronger than Aiden.'

For once in his life, Marcus didn't gloat. 'All right, what's your plan?' he asked.

'Give me your hand.'

'What? Charley, I'll fall.'

'Remember the day you kissed me?'

'How could I forget?' he said, laughing softly.

'You asked me if I felt anything when you took a hold of my hand. I said I didn't but I did – I've never felt anything like it.'

'What's your point, Charley? I don't mean to rush you, but we don't exactly have time to hang around, if you'll excuse the pun.'

'My point is, I think we can beat her.'

'Who, you and me?' Marcus frowned.

'I felt the burn, Marcus. I still feel it now. I don't know what it was but when your hand touched mine I felt power like I've never felt it before. We need to close the chasm, then we'll deal with Judith. I can't do it without you.'

Marcus looked at his feet, nothing but a dark hole below them. He turned back to Charley and thrust his hand into hers, the fire igniting again as soon as their fingers met. Slowly, the chasm began to shrink, the ground rising up from beneath them.

Both Marcus and Aiden's feet made contact with it, the hole almost gone as it pushed them to the surface. Charley pulled Marcus to his feet.

'You with me?' she asked, and Marcus nodded. 'Good, let's fry the bitch.'

Judith shook with laughter as Marcus reached out and took Charley's hand. Aiden's eyebrows came together, desperately gazing at Charley for an answer. She mouthed, 'I know what I'm doing,' to him and he nodded, trusting her implicitly.

'Very clever, Charley dear,' Judith mocked. 'Does this mean you've made your choice? Have you really chosen to be with a demon? A filthy, horrid, loathsome demon with nothing to offer you but a burning flame? A flame that will disintegrate the moment you show interest in another. If that's the case, you're more of a fool than I thought.'

Charley peered at Judith from under her brows, her fingers still grasped tightly around Marcus's hand.

'People aren't defined by what they are,' she told her. 'They're defined by what they do. Marcus may have made some bad choices but he redeemed himself along the way. You, on the other hand, there's no hope for you now. You were corrupted a long time ago, Judith. There's no saving you.'

'Did I ask to be saved? I may be diabolical, Charley, but that's how I like it. That's how I want it, and that's how it shall stay. I'd rather burn in hell than become as helpless as you lot are, all impotent and weak.'

Marcus felt a vibration in his hand, something glowing between the cracks in their fingers.

'That can be arranged,' Charley said spitefully, and she thrust her hand forward, Marcus gripping on with all his might. The power that stemmed from them was incredible, the ground shaking as their magic erupted, skewering Judith like a pig on a spit.

She thrashed her arms as her skin began to crack, her chest drawing in, driving the breath out of her lungs. Judith screamed – a sharp, piercing wail which vibrated through the air, causing the birds to scatter from the tree tops. The sky darkened, the wind picking up as Charley and Marcus stood rigidly still, drawing power from everything around them.

Judith's eyes turned red and the skin which wasn't already ruptured began to melt from her face like candle wax. Her clothes caught fire, her hair turning to black ash as the flames crawled through it.

'How could you, Marcus?' she cried. 'How could y . . .'

She never got to finish that sentence. The fire consumed her and she shattered like glass, the impact knocking everyone off their feet.

Charley opened her eyes, glancing around to see Marcus on one side of her, Aiden on the other. Quinn was awake now, still lying next to Dru, her eyes wide as she gazed at the destruction around her.

Aiden looked at Charley. 'It's over.'

FORTY-TWO

Aiden helped Charley to her feet, both of them bewildered, not quite believing what had just happened.

Noticing Fergus still lying unconscious, Aiden ran to him. 'Dad? Dad!' he yelled in his ear, and Fergus stirred.

'Aiden . . .'

'Thank God you're okay,' Aiden breathed, pulling his father upright.

Charley was already at her sister's side, Marcus close behind her. The impact of the blast had tossed Jess from the mound and they'd found her face down in the leaves.

Charley put her hand underneath Jess and let out a sigh of relief when she felt a steady, thumping heartbeat.

'It's okay,' Charley whispered. 'It's all over now.'

Marcus picked Jess up, one arm under her knees, the other supporting her neck, and carried her back to the rest of the group.

Quinn was still weeping over Dru's body. 'Why'd you have to go and be so damn brave?' she sobbed. She looked up at Charley. 'Just when she decided that she actually wanted to live, Judith took her away from me.'

Charley's heart went out to Quinn; if something had

happened to Jess, Charley would never have forgiven herself.

There was a groan from nearby and they all turned to see Tabitha, lying wounded a few feet away. 'Tabby!' Fergus cried, limping to her side. His heart almost stopped when he got to her, looking down at the mess before him.

There was a hole the size of a tennis ball in Tabby's stomach, blood seeping from it at a rapid rate. Fergus gasped, his eyes widening in horror.

'No, Tabby.'

Tabitha smiled, her breathing laboured as she touched his cheek. 'It's okay, Fergus. Sometimes, it's just the way things have to be.'

'No . . . no, I can't lose you,' he whimpered, clutching her hand until his knuckles turned white.

Tabby gently shook her head. 'You won't lose me, Fergus. I'll always be with you – in here.' She put her hand to his chest and placed it over his heart.

Tabitha had arrived long before she'd actually shown herself. She'd been so frightened though, so terrified when she thought back to the first demon who'd almost killed her that she'd stayed hidden, watching from her hiding place as the chaos unfolded before her.

'I should have helped Druanna,' she whispered, but Fergus put a finger to her lips.

'Don't talk,' he said, the tears flowing freely now. 'Don't strain yourself.'

'You can,' – she was struggling to speak – 'you can still save her.'

Fergus frowned, his eyebrows coming together. 'Save who? Dru?'

Tabitha nodded.

'Dru's gone, Tabby,' he said sadly, 'there's nothing we can do for her now.'

'Li . . . link them . . . again.'

'What?' Fergus gulped. 'We can't link them, Tabby. Dru's already dead.'

'But–'

'No, we can't. Quinn could die.'

'Yes, but Dru could live.' He looked at the ground, shaking his head vigorously. 'It's not your decision to make, Fergus. It's . . . it's Quinn's.'

Tabby coughed, blood spurting from her mouth. She began to choke on it and Fergus tilted her head, trying his best to make her more comfortable.

'Take care of them, Fergie. All of them. And if need be, let them take care of you.'

Fergus sobbed, his tears landing on Tabitha's cheek as he bent down to kiss her. 'Don't leave me. Please don't leave me.'

'I never will,' she whispered. 'Tell Aiden I love . . .' But before she could finish, her eyes clouded over, her chest no longer moving. She was gone.

Fergus turned to see his son standing behind him, staring down at his mother.

'Aiden . . .'

Aiden's eyes stung as he forced back tears.

'Is she . . . ?'

'Yes,' Fergus whispered. 'I'm so sorry, son.'

A tear escaped from Aiden's eye, his chest tightening as he looked upon his mother's body.

You shouldn't have come, he thought, wiping his cheek with his sleeve. After everything, all of their quarrels and disagreements, he had finally been starting to understand his mother – why she did the things she did, why she always behaved in such an overbearing and snobbish manner. Tabitha had loved him from the bottom of her heart, and now she was lost to him.

'Is it true?' Aiden said, composing himself, although Fergus could see it was only a front. 'What she said about Dru?'

Quinn was listening now, too.

'Yes, it's true. We could try another linking spell, but it would be incredibly dangerous. You're talking about messing with life and death. If Quinn was strong enough, she might be able to withstand it long enough to bring Dru back. More than likely though, she would die trying.'

They all looked at one another, stunned by this revelation. Quinn got to her feet.

'Do it,' she said.

'Quinn, you must think about–'

'Do it, Uncle Fergus. There's nothing to think about.' Her eyes burrowed into him, down to the core, and she said it again. 'Do it.'

Fergus nodded, motioning to Aiden to sit with his mother. 'All right,' he sighed. 'I hope you know what you're asking me to do.'

Quinn bowed her head, kneeling back down beside Dru. 'She would do it for me.'

Fergus nodded, bending down and kissing Quinn's head. 'Take her hand,' he said gently, and Quinn did as he asked. Fergus waved his hand over Dru, tiny fragments falling from his fingers like glitter. He began to chant.

'Link them now and let them live, one will offer, one

will give. Let what's happened be undone, breathe not as two, exist as one.'

He could see Quinn struggling as he said the words, her face going grey as she desperately tried to fight the impending doom which was waiting for her.

She was stronger than he'd imagined she would be.

Once he was finished, Quinn lurched forward, panting, her hand coming loose from Dru's. 'Did it work?' she asked promptly, pinching herself to make sure she was still there – still alive.

Dru's eyes opened and she gasped, her eyes bulging as Quinn's essence crept through her.

Fergus breathed a sigh of relief. 'It worked.'

FORTY-THREE

Aiden handed Jess a cup of tea, her eyes vacantly staring ahead as she took it from his grasp.

'I don't understand,' she whispered, her hands turning red as she held the hot mug. She looked at Charley. 'You aren't my sister?'

Charley shook her head. 'Biologically, no, but that doesn't change how I feel about you.'

'And,' she turned to Marcus, 'you're my brother?'

'Afraid so, kiddo.'

'But you tried to kill me?'

'Well, when you put it like that . . .' Marcus stopped, hanging his head in shame. 'Yes, Jess, I did. There's nothing I can say to change that or make it right. I don't expect you to ever forgive me.'

Jess looked back at Charley. 'So if you're a magician, why are Mum and Dad just normal folk? Was . . . was she a magician, too?' she asked, referring to Bud.

'Yes,' Charley nodded. 'Gran's powers didn't pass on to Mum because she lost them before Mum was born. I don't know why they came back to . . .' Charley still felt awkward saying her name, '. . . to Bud and me, I think they must have just skipped a generation or something.'

Jess blinked. 'And I'm a demon?' She felt ridiculous saying it. 'This is ludicrous.'

'Trust me, I know. When Aiden first told me I was a magician, I laughed in his face.'

'But aren't demons bad? Does that mean I'm . . . evil?'

Marcus shook his head. 'Not all demons are wicked.'

'You're wicked. You tried to kill me.'

Marcus raised his eyebrows. 'I guess I am.'

Charley tucked a loose strand of hair behind Jess's ear. 'Marcus did the wrong thing, you're right, and it's up to you if you ever want to forgive him. He does care about you though, just know that.'

'Have you forgiven him?'

Charley smiled at Jess. At that moment she felt more like her mother than her sister. 'I'll never forgive him for what he did to you,' she said, and Marcus looked like he'd been kicked in the guts. 'I do understand why he did what he did though. Judith used him. It was all just a game to her, she wasn't bothered who got hurt along the way. Whatever you decide to do regarding Marcus, I'll support you.'

Jess looked at Marcus – her brother – and said, 'Was it really Charley and you who saved me?'

Marcus shook his head. 'Charley did most of the work. I was pretty useless to be honest.'

Charley looked at him as if to say that's not true, but said nothing.

'Can we tell Mum about this?' Jess asked.

'I don't think that's such a good idea. She might not handle it all that well.' Charley turned to Fergus, who was sitting in the olive-green arm chair, clutching Tabby's copy of *Jane Eyre*. 'Will the sleeping spell have worn off?' she asked him.

Fergus didn't answer. Instead, Marcus replied, 'More than likely.'

'She'll be worried sick. She won't be able to get a hold of us.'

'Here,' Aiden said, tossing his phone to Charley. 'Call her from that.'

Charley went to him, crouched down and lifted his chin with her finger.

'How you holding up?' she asked, trying to show her support but at the same time trying not to smother him.

'Okay,' he smiled sadly, leaning forward to kiss her cheek. 'I have you, don't I?'

'Always,' Charley whispered.

Quinn was sitting on the sofa, Dru's head resting on her lap. The pair of them had barely said a word since they'd got home, Quinn just happy to have her sister back. She wasn't sure what Dru was thinking; her face gave nothing away.

'Did I do the right thing?' Quinn said to her quietly. 'You did want to come back, didn't you?'

Dru's eyes didn't move from the spot she was gazing at, but she smiled anyway. 'Yes, Quinn, you did the right thing.'

That evening, they sat around Aiden's living room, emotions running high. Of course they felt triumphant; they'd saved Jess and thwarted Judith, but they'd also lost so much in the process. Aiden had lost one parent, Marcus, two; Fergus had lost a wife; Quinn had lost her sister, and then miraculously got her back again. No one was really sure quite what to say.

Charley had spoken to her mother, telling her that Jess was sleeping and that they wouldn't be home late. Linda had gone ballistic, yelling down the phone about how worried she'd been.

Eventually, after a lot of arguing and a lot of shouting, she'd calmed down. 'As long as Fergus drives you home,' she'd instructed. Charley had agreed, although there was no way she was going to ask Fergus to do that, not after what he'd just been through.

She'd also phoned Abbie, who'd been furious at the fact she'd missed the battle.

'Always miss the fun part, I do,' she'd whined miserably.

'I'll be sure to inform you when the next one arises,' Charley had laughed.

'Yeah,' Abbie huffed, 'make sure you do.'

They'd talked for a while, Abbie genuinely concerned about her friend. She couldn't believe everything Charley was telling her; it sounded like the ramblings of a child. But it wasn't – it was Charley's life. All of their lives.

After a while, Fergus got up from his chair and announced that he was going to bed.

'You know where I am if you need me,' he said.

'Dad . . .'

'Yes, Aiden?'

'Are you sure you're all right?'

'I will be, son. With time, I'll be okay. And so will you.' Aiden looked wistfully at his father. Fergus said, 'You've all been through a great deal. It will take some time for it to sink in. But never forget, this is the kind of thing we have to deal with. There will be more battles, not necessarily demons, but beings just as powerful and just as dangerous. There may come a time when you think you're safe, but you're not. We are never done fighting.'

They all sat staring, shivers running through each of them. Then Fergus left the room.

'Cheery fellow, your dad,' Marcus grunted, causing Charley to glare at him.

'Marcus, how could you say such a thing?'

'I'm sorry,' he grimaced. 'It's who I am, I make jokes when things get tense.'

'Well you should be ash–'

'He's all right, Chambers,' Aiden said. 'Leave him be.'

'Leave him be?'

'He didn't mean anything by it.'

Marcus looked at Aiden, Aiden returning his gaze, and nodded at him in understanding. Finally for once, and probably only this once, the boys were on the same wavelength.

Charley sat beside Aiden and put her head on his shoulder. 'I'm very proud of you,' she told him with a smile. Aiden kissed her head as she let out a yawn. 'I'm tired now,' she whispered.

'Sleep,' he answered, putting his arm around her. 'You've earned it.'

'Don't let me sleep too long.'

'I won't. Now close your eyes.'

Charley did. In moments she was sleeping, her jumbled thoughts making their way out of her head, her dreams making their way in.

She was in a bedroom, although not one she recognised. There were teddy bears on the bed and butterflies on the wall, stuck on messily with large pieces of sticky tape. There was a karaoke machine in the corner of the room and next to it, a large dresser, also covered with various stuffed animals. Charley squinted as her eyes focused on something. In front of the toys stood a small photo frame, holding a picture of Marcus and someone, someone she recognised . . .

'Bud,' Charley whispered as a little girl walked into the room.

'Hello, Charley,' Bud smiled, dimples forming on her cheeks.

'What are you . . . I mean, what am I doing here?'

'I wanted to meet you,' Bud said, 'before I go.'

'Go? Where are you going?'

'I'm leaving, Charley. I'm not needed anymore.'

'Not needed?' Charley queried. 'What do you mean?'

'I've done what I had to do. Everything's okay now. Thank you, Charley.'

'For what?'

'For stopping my mum. I don't think I could have coped if she'd brought me back.'

Charley looked at Bud, a brave little girl, still smiling after everything she'd been through. 'You're some kid,' Charley said kindly, making Bud laugh.

'That's what Marcus always used to say. Take care of him, Charley. I know what he did was wrong, but he doesn't have anyone left.'

'I will,' Charley promised.

'Tell him I won't be coming around anymore. He doesn't need me now.'

Charley didn't know what she was talking about, but she nodded anyway, saying, 'I'll tell him.'

'Well, it was nice to meet you. I always did want a sister.'

'I'm sorry I didn't get the chance to know you, Bud.'

'Me too.' Bud smiled. 'You better wake up now. They're calling for you.'

Charley got up from the bed. 'Are you going to be all right? Where will you go?'

Bud laughed, as if this was a silly question. 'Why, heaven of course.'

She put her arms around Charley's waist, squeezing her tightly. 'Goodbye, Charley.'

'See you, Bud.'

The lights began to dim and Bud slowly faded away. The room started to shake, knocking Charley back on to the bed.

'Chambers,' she heard someone call. 'It's time to get up.'

Charley opened her eyes.

'Is everything okay?' Aiden asked.

She looked up at him, and then towards Marcus.

'It is now,' she smiled.